NOT WITH SILVER

Simi Bedford

Chatto & Windus

LONDON

Published by Chatto & Windus 2007

2 4 6 8 10 9 7 5 3 1

First published in Great Britain in 2007 by
Chatto & Windus
Random House, 20 Vauxhall Bridge Road,
London SW1V 2SA

www.rbooks.co.uk

Addresses for companies within The Random House Group Limited can be found at: www.randomhouse.co.uk/offices.htm

The Random House Group Limited Reg. No. 954009

A CIP catalogue record for this book is available from the British Library

ISBN 9781856192354

The Random House Group Limited makes every effort to ensure that the papers used in its books are made from trees that have been legally sourced from well-managed and credibly certified forests. Our paper procurement policy can be found at: www.randomhouse.co.uk/paper.htm

Typeset by SX Composing DTP, Rayleigh, Essex
Printed and bound in Great Britain by
CPI Mackays, Chatham, ME5 8TD

Contents

For
Becket, Blake and Morele
And in memory of my sister Margaret

Behold, I have refined thee, but
Not with silver; I have chosen thee
In the furnace of affliction

Isaiah 48:10

BOOK ONE

Abiola, 1740–1758

I

LADY FALOYAN CUT through the crowds like a blade through sand despite being unattended and without a strong arm to clear the way for her. There was something inexorable in her bearing which prompted those in her path to step aside and let her pass even before they had noted her facial marks or priced her wrappers.

Thousands of people had descended on Oyo, first for the Shango festival and now for the annual Ifa celebrations. The city was all but impassable, its streets jammed day and night with processions. The air was acrid with the lingering smoke of torches and everywhere there was the sound of drums.

The sun was still high in the sky and the heat so oppressive that only the most urgent of errands could have induced Lady Faloyan to venture out. Beside her on the crowded thoroughfare a rope unravelled suddenly, dislodging part of a porter's mountainous load, but she was faster, adroitly vacating the spot where it crashed to the ground. Others not so fleet were caught. The bonesetters would not be short of work this day.

Lady Faloyan appeared to be pressing forward regardless, but in fact was registering everything behind discreetly lowered lids as she had been trained to do. She had for example realised immediately that the fallen load had imploded on contact, indicating a consignment of earthenware, and that it was costly, from the imprecations being hurled at the porter. She noticed, too, that the owner, an Ijebu woman of some substance judging by her dress and facial scars, elicited more sympathy from the crowd than the overburdened porter. Pots were not so easily mended and these doubtless had been traded with the white men far to the south. The skinless ones were clustered thicker than ever near the sea, insatiable, it seemed, in their desire for slaves, yet too timid to venture any distance inland.

Lady Faloyan counted, as she passed, the marks of a dozen different towns and cities on the faces of the merchants moving slowly towards the city centre. This festival in honour of the Ifa oracle, the mouthpiece of the gods, drew traders great and small from all over the empire and beyond.

Some were obliged to carry their own loads; some, like the Ijebu woman, boasted a string of half a dozen porters; others commanded caravans more than a thousand strong.

Halted momentarily at a busy crossroads, Lady Faloyan flicked a glance upwards and caught sight of a vulture, huge wings outspread, coasting in to join the others already congregating, unmolested, to pick clean the carcasses of a thousand sacrifices. It was said that these great birds harboured the spirits of the dead. Hawks hovered overhead, hanging in the wide blue sky. She pictured herself one of them, the city spread out below her, curving around the base of its protective mountain, surrounded and studded with green.

In her mind's eye she looked down upon the steep, vaulted roofs, thatched with bere grass, turned to gold in the sunlight; within the triple circuit of walls, three times the height of the tallest warrior, she saw the myriad oblongs of the open courtyards and market squares. On the roads leading into the capital slow-moving lines of traffic extended far into the distance, their progress snarled at the ten city gates where passage narrowed to a single bridge over deep ditches planted with thorn bushes. She watched the toll collectors sitting in the shade of the towering porticos, exacting their dues before allowing the caravans to pass along the wide, paved boulevards which, like the spokes of a giant parasol, led directly from the gates to the king's palace in the centre.

A mixture of overwhelming smells brought her back to earth, signalling that she had arrived at the Akésan market and was close to her destination. So dense was the crowd, however, that the rows of stalls set out beneath the shade trees were hidden from sight by a constantly shifting kaleidoscope of bright flowing robes. Lady Faloyan chose to take the longer route around the vast square instead of attempting to pass through the middle.

She was careful not to inhale as she skirted the fresh meat section, quelling her stomach by an act of will, until the sharp tang of limes and tamarind and the sweetness of mangos cleared the smell of blood from her nostrils. She closed her eyes, breathing in indigo, camwood, antimony, natron, new-tanned leather, horse liniment, iron, and the aroma of freshly woven cloth. She recalled how, as a young girl, newly arrived in the capital, one of her earliest exercises had been to negotiate the market blindfold. Her guard slipped and a smile flickered. On moonlit nights when the mats were rolled out in the courtyards, songs were still sung of how Lakoja the mighty elephant hunter of Oyo had

4

been persuaded to accept a mere girl as his pupil. He had been bewitched, they said. Lady Faloyan's smile broadened. She was that girl. The daughter, admittedly, of a famous warrior chief, but born to a junior wife with no standing in the compound. At the age of four, to her mother's deep embarrassment, she had clamoured to be among the candidates selected for training as future leaders of the army which for more than a hundred years had made Oyo supreme. Lord Lakoja had of course rebuffed her, but she'd clung to her purpose, diminutive and tenacious as a cattle egret to its host, shadowing the boys, a comic turn at first, until laughter and indulgence turned to awe. In his own way, Lakoja said, the chameleon is the equal of the elephant. At the memory, Lady Faloyan, senior wife of one of the highest nobles of Oyo and now a matron of twenty-five, could not resist a gleeful little hop.

She passed swiftly down the broad street running beside the palace walls, past the crown prince's palace, the chief eunuch's compound and the residences of the official brothers of the king until, at last, she stopped in front of a pair of tall wooden gates set into a high wall. Two gatekeepers lounging on the street verandah jumped to their feet, pulled open the heavy, elaborately carved panels, and prostrated themselves full length on the ground. Lady Faloyan inclined her head fractionally before stepping inside the imposing mansion belonging to the Princess Boladé.

'Welcome, my daughter,' the princess addressed her, as etiquette demanded, Lady Faloyan being very much her junior; indeed, young enough actually to be her daughter.

Princess Boladé's voice seduced all who heard it, and custom did not lessen its impact. Her subtle tones always had another shape or dress to put on.

Lady Faloyan recalled how that voice had spun a comforting cocoon when, bereft and far from home, she had first arrived in Oyo, where she and her sister had been betrothed at the instigation of Lord Lakoja to sons of two of the most powerful families. Intrigued that the renowned Lakoja should consider a girl worthy of training, the princess had been eager to make her acquaintance. She had been sufficiently impressed to make the young bride her protégée.

Today, the princess's words were clothed in velvet.

Lady Faloyan, ushered in by a maid she had not encountered before, sank gracefully to her knees and placed both elbows on a floor mat of exquisite quality. 'Greetings, my mother.'

5

'You have woken in health?'

'I have woken in health.'

'We give thanks.'

'We give thanks.'

Princess Boladé settled back on her couch, fine ankles crossed, dainty henna-painted feet outstretched, then beckoned her guest to join her. Lady Faloyan complied at once, her eyes fastening for an instant on the princess before being deferentially lowered again. If a person can read you he will have the advantage, your face must tell nothing; it was a cardinal rule with the princess. Yet, at this moment, Lady Faloyan thought, the princess gave the distinct impression of a cat that had recently killed. She wondered, too, what the presence of the new maid might mean.

Without warning, Princess Boladé clapped her hands together. Despite the pulse that leapt in her throat, Lady Faloyan remained perfectly still: a tribute to her training. The maid reacted not at all.

'Sadia is also mute.' Princess Boladé took a round wooden box from the stool by her couch and, removing the ornately carved lid, offered kola nuts. 'Your sister?' she enquired.

'All is well with her, my mother.' Lady Faloyan placed one half of a kola nut in her mouth, savouring the taste. White kola from the forests of the south; there was nothing to compare. Her heart resumed its usual stroke. Never waste time analysing *what*, the princess had taught her, try instead to discover *why*; it will rarely be the obvious.

'I have been misinformed then.' Princess Boladé leaned back, her head a black oval against the soft kapok cushions.

'A false alarm, no more, my mother,' Lady Faloyan replied, scrupulously deferring to the princess's seniority.

'Her time is near, is it not?'

Though the princess's voice still wore its velvet, Lady Faloyan read genuine concern beneath the casual tone. The princess, childless herself, had from the very first embraced the two new arrivals as her own.

'Any day now, my mother.'

'We must give thanks,' Princess Boladé said, 'that your sister's temperament is softer than arere wood under the axe, and that she is more fruitful even than the waters of Yemoja. If it is a daughter the god shapes for her this time, or next time, our plans can still be put into effect, unchanged. Impress upon her that no one must know for whom the child is intended.'

'Our choice, surely, is obscure enough, my mother, not to arouse suspicion? The Prince Labisi . . .'

'. . . The Prince Labisi is among those eligible to succeed to the throne. It is *my* husband who will decide, when the time comes, which princes will go forward for election. Not even the dullest of our enemies could fail to see the connection.'

Stung, Lady Faloyan replied, 'Would it not be better then, my mother, to be open from the start, thus throwing them off the scent?'

The princess, all softness gone, replied, 'It would be better, my daughter, for there to be no scent. And better still if your sister had more of *your* threads in her making.'

Though not one to dwell on the past – the futility of that had been early inculcated – Lady Faloyan could not help but recall the words that had haunted her since the Ifa oracle had spoken:

> *I am blessing two not one,*
> *This was prophesied by the sea lily*
> *Which reaches down into the mud, the origin of creation.*
> *The time of creation has come.*

At the time the high priest had delivered these words they had seemed to prophesy the thing she dared not hope for. She, who had witnessed the harvesting of the New Yams seven times between the births of her first and second child, was to have a third after only two seasons had passed. The chief priest had added that it would be a daughter. How jubilant she had been: a daughter, the consummation of all their plans. The prediction had proved correct. Except the child had died.

Lady Faloyan's sigh was soundless. When the wind comes, Lakoja said, bend with it, let it work for you. If her sister gave birth to a girl, she would make *this* child her own.

Lady Faloyan slipped from the princess's apartments, an inconspicuous shadow in the shade of the verandahs, and stepped out unseen through a narrow door at the back of the women's quarters. At the same moment the princess's maid, Sadia, left by the main entrance to meander among the crowds, drifting in and out of various compounds with the freedom of one whose imperfection made her sacred to the Maker God. At the compound of Lady Faloyan's sister, however, Sadia stayed.

~

2

LADY FALOYAN SET a pace that left her maid struggling to keep up. The one certainty in her mind was that she must reach her sister, Lady Monifa, as soon as possible, for without a doubt news of her predicament and the fact that Lady Faloyan had been sent for would have already reached the palace. If the senior wife of one of the king's councillors should die it would be a matter that touched the state.

Pulling the dark cloth that covered her head and shoulders closer about her face, Lady Faloyan gave silent thanks for the crowds that still thronged the streets even at this hour, making it more difficult for those who might try to follow her. Torches lit the sky as processions made their way across the city to the sound of the agogo bells and the mighty ipésé drum. She increased her speed, driven on by the knowledge that her sister was liable to give up without a fight. She could imagine her now, resigned to her fate, calling it the will of god. How was it possible, she thought, that two people, seed of the same father, blood and sinew of the same mother, could be so different? To that, she had no answer; all she knew was that *she* would never give up, nor would she allow her sister to do so.

Lady Faloyan's maid, Alero, was praying as she ran, for she had brought the message and messengers had been killed for less, or so she had been told. Newly recruited, young and impressionable, Alero called on her ancestors to intercede for her and promised sacrifices to all the gods if only this bad luck might fall on someone else's head.

As they turned into the wide avenue which marked the boundary of the region controlled by Lady Monifa's husband, it seemed to Alero that if her mistress moved any faster her feet would surely leave the ground. They passed unchallenged into the chief's compound, situated midway down the avenue, and went directly to the women's courtyards. Commanding her maid to wait within earshot, Lady Faloyan entered the birthing room. Moments later, the midwife emerged, peremptorily ejected. Alero heaved a deep sigh. Only God could save her now.

*

'I'm going to die.' Racked by contractions, Lady Monifa lay awkwardly on her sleeping mat in the corner of the birthing room, her back arched in pain.

Lady Faloyan slid sure hands over her sister's distended belly. Dried rivulets of sweat had left a tracery of salt on the dark shiny skin, and, despite herself, she was wrung by the sight.

'This is no time for self-pity,' she said.

'And my child will die too.'

'Your child is *destined* to live.' Lady Faloyan's fingers pressed into the groin. 'All will be well,' she said soothingly.

She had located the source of the problem. The child was curled in the right position but facing the wrong direction; she would have to be turned round. It was a manoeuvre Lady Faloyan had successfully accomplished before.

'Come,' she instructed the midwife's assistant, whom she had ordered to stay. Placing the girl's hands in the small of Lady Monifa's back, she showed her how to knead the rigid muscles and ordered her to keep rubbing.

Returning outside to the verandah she at once became brisker than ever. As the throng of women in attendance pressed round her, she set the midwife to boiling herbs and ordered a second hearth lit. While preparing certain infusions of her own at one hearth, her maid Alero beside her, she gave each of the older women some little errand to run. One was sent to fetch sweet oil to massage Lady Monifa's brow, another to prepare a restorative broth, others to bring cool water and savoury cakes from the kitchen courtyard or to burn fragrant leaves against the mosquitoes. In this way she contrived to remove their twittering anxiety from the vicinity, procuring a little peace for her sister and herself.

Alero's hand was unsteady and her voice shook as under Lady Faloyan's watchful eye she recited the simple incantation that would ensure the effectiveness of the brew of special herbs she had been given to stir. Fear had sharpened her perception and instinctively she understood that in her mistress's mind the fate of the mother and child was linked to her own.

Lady Faloyan poured the two potions into bowls and returned to the sticky closeness of the birthing room. Keeping out of sight the first bowl with its preparation of mucilaginous leaves that would make it easier to slip the foetus out should it die in the womb, she thrust the second vessel into her sister's hands. Lady Monifa drained the contents without a word.

She was used to obeying her sister. Partly because she was two seasons younger and it was not done to question your elders, but also because her appearance was against her. On the last occasion she had attempted to assert herself, her sister, wagging a small tyrannical finger, had explained, not unkindly, that hers was a face people gave orders to, not the kind they took orders from. That was the difference between them.

Lady Monifa felt the dragging pain in the small of her back lessen as her sister began to turn the child, gently pressing, smoothing, prodding with her palms and knuckles and fingertips until at last it was in the correct position to make its entry into the world.

Presently the contractions began in earnest. In the intervals between, Lady Monifa walked around the room, supported on the arm of her sister and the attendant, both crooning encouragement. And when it was time, they helped her to the centre of the room where she squatted down above a shallow indentation hollowed out of the floor. The midwife's assistant supported her shoulders and Lady Faloyan knelt in front of her. 'Push,' she commanded. 'Harder.' She cupped her hands.

The child slid into them at the precise moment that the Koso drum sounded its morning salute to the Alafin, ruler of all Oyo.

The birth attendant cried out, 'The royal drum! It is an omen.'

Lady Faloyan's eyes glittered. At last a daughter; whether hers or her sister's, it mattered not. 'This one,' she said, 'is destined for a king.' As she held up the child, she was startled by a sudden vision of her younger son. The image in her mind's eye was clear and vivid. It was said you chose the fate that accompanied you into the world at the moment of your birth. She had been given a sign, she thought, as she relinquished the baby to its mother. The destinies of the two children were linked.

Exhausted but triumphant, Lady Monifa pressed her daughter to her breast. 'You are right, this child is destined for a king. A king of priests. Last night I dreamt the oracle had marked her for its own.'

It was preposterous even to think of it, a daughter of theirs, one of the most powerful lineages in Oyo, being thrown away on a priest. In due course Lady Monifa would have to be persuaded that duty to the family must come first, but for now Lady Faloyan suppressed her anger and said lightly, 'At such times a woman's imagination conjures all manner of fantastic notions. You cannot rely on the truth of such a dream. Put it out of your mind.'

'If you say so, sister,' Lady Monifa agreed at once. Inwardly, however, she continued to believe that the truth of her dream would be confirmed when she next consulted the oracle, as she was obliged to do on behalf of her newborn child.

'I do say so.' Lady Faloyan glanced sharply at the midwife's assistant. She would have dispensed with her as well as the old midwife, but she had not dared leave her sister alone. Aware that she was being observed, the girl, who was laying out fresh cloths and a bowl of sweet oil to clean and massage the baby, looked up. Lady Faloyan examined her closely. Their enemies had ears everywhere, you could never be sure whom to trust, and the girl had heard much in here.

'Daughter, go bring Auntie, tell her she can come and attend to madam.'

The girl ran excitedly to fetch the midwife. 'Auntie! Auntie, madam is calling you. The child is born. A girl, a beautiful girl!' she cried, loud enough to be heard throughout the whole of the women's quarters.

Slopping a large basin of herbs, the midwife elbowed her way through the throng on the verandah.

Shortly afterwards, Lady Faloyan emerged, her face expressionless. Silence fell. 'All is well,' she announced, and immediately made to depart. Alero sprang into step behind her with a parting grin that flared brighter than any torch.

In the swiftly receding darkness there were now only cats for company on the streets and overhead bats swarmed home to roost in the tallest trees and hang upside down like fruit among the leaves. A little later when the two women had disappeared from view, the princess's maid, Sadia, detached herself from the throng and, unnoticed in all the excitement, drifted out of the compound gates.

❦

3

'MAMA. MAMA!'

The instant Lady Faloyan appeared in the doorway of her apartment, a small whirlwind raced across the room and gripped her by the knees.

'Greetings, little lord,' said Lady Faloyan, sweeping him up in her arms. 'You must be the only one who slept undisturbed last night.'

'Put me down,' he commanded, with all the imperiousness of a three-year-old.

'Very well.' His mother did as she was ordered, and sat down on a couch, at the same time taking a swift inventory of the room. Her maids had all dropped to the ground, elbows to the floor, as she entered, and they watched nervously from beneath lowered lids. One surreptitiously straightened the corner of a wall hanging. Lady Faloyan turned her head like a cobra about to strike, obsidian eyes unblinking. The maid, boneless suddenly, slid head down on the mat. Satisfied all was to her liking – the coverings of softest antelope hide nicely plumped, her treasured wall hangings absolutely straight and the floor mats precisely aligned – Lady Faloyan smiled at her son.

'You were not in your room,' Abiola accused her, elbows resting on her knees. 'I came and I met your absence.'

'I am here now.'

'Where have you been? And where is Nafisat?' he demanded, looking around for his nurse.

'She will come soon,' Lady Faloyan assured him. 'Have you had your bath?'

'No, Mama.' He placed his hands on his hips. 'Nafisat was not here, remember?'

'In that case we shall bathe together, and afterwards,' she announced, having made a sudden decision, 'you shall eat with your father.'

'Can I show him my mouse?' Abiola pulled a whiskered ball of grey fur from underneath his loose shirt and stroked it tenderly.

'I think not.'

He trotted back into the bedroom, throwing a scornful look at the maids, who drew back to let him pass. In a few moments he returned carrying a little round basket which he placed on his mother's lap, its lid slightly ajar.

'My lizard then.'

She gazed in silence at the creature; it peered back unperturbed, scarlet head bobbing up and down.

'Or . . .' Abiola started towards the bedroom again.

'Bring the lizard,' his mother said hastily, and rose to her feet. 'But first we must perform our morning worship. Come.' Abiola suffered his hand to be held the short distance along the verandah to the shrine.

Sunlight, seeping in through the vents in the walls, stippled the darkness inside the small, windowless room and lent a sombre sheen to the symbols of Oya the river goddess. On a low altar in the centre lay a pair of buffalo horns, arching outwards like the great blades of the double-headed axe of Shango, the goddess's husband.

Lady Faloyan placed an offering of kola nuts on the altar and poured a libation on the ground. She knelt, putting both elbows on the floor. Abiola prostrated himself full length beside her. She implored the goddess, as she did every day, to send her another child, and to ensure that no harm should come to her two sons. And no less importantly on this day she gave thanks for her sister's safe delivery.

Finally she sat back on her heels, took two more kola nuts from a raffia pouch she wore at her waist, split each in two and threw them down on the floor. They all landed face down, an unequivocal sign that no further offering was required. She stared at the pieces, unable to believe her eyes. The birth of a daughter to Lady Monifa had removed the last obstacle in their path to power. A *whole* basket of kola nuts, albeit of the finest quality, would not have been sufficient, surely, to satisfy the goddess in return for so great a favour? Princess Boladé, who was experienced in these matters, had ordered a large sack of cowries set aside for the purchase of sacrifices in preparation for just this event.

For an instant Lady Faloyan thought wildly of making another throw but Abiola, sensing her disquiet, had become restless. Collecting herself, she quickly steered him outside where a maid carrying fresh cloths and soap waited to accompany them to the wash place. Lady Faloyan's face betrayed nothing, but she felt the sweat run cold on her back.

Pushed slowly from outside, the door to the Agbakin's sleeping chamber began to open. It revealed Abiola, his brow concentrated, his shoulder against the heavy carved wood, and behind him the tall straight figure of his mother carrying a calabash in each hand. Lady Faloyan knelt and her son prostrated himself in greeting.

The Agbakin rose from his couch. Wrapped in a cloth from the waist down, he was impressive when sitting; standing, his head reached halfway to the top of the high-ceilinged room.

His son stared up at him as if searching the branches of a tall tree. He'd been full of impatience outside, waiting for his father's crier to complete the daily ritual of beating out the oriki on his drum, recalling for the benefit of the entire compound the glory of their ancestors and the exploits of their chief. Now, overcome with shyness, he remained prostrate on the floor.

Smiling, his father plucked him up and sat with him on his knee. 'Greetings, my son.'

It had been wise, Lady Faloyan thought, to bring the boy. She remained by the door. 'Good morning, my lord. May I come in?'

'You may.'

'I thank god you have woken in health, my lord.'

'Yes, I thank god.'

Lady Faloyan placed the calabashes she carried on the couch and closed the door, then with a flourish, for Abiola's benefit, simultaneously removed the covers of both, revealing water in one and a glossy white mass of porridge in the other. Curls of steam plumed upwards but the child's eyes remained fixed on the massive coral bracelet circling his father's wrist.

The Agbakin sat Abiola opposite him on the couch with the two bowls between them. He rinsed his hand in the water and, after first tasting the porridge himself, invited his son to join him. Abiola solemnly did the same and, tentative at first, was soon scooping the food to his mouth as heartily if not as tidily as his father.

Sitting utterly still on her stool by the door, Lady Faloyan watched them eat. It was the hunter's trick, acquired long ago, of remaining as if inanimate so that after a while your presence went un-remarked.

The Agbakin ate in silence and, having finished, rinsed his hand once more in the basin of water. Abiola licked the tips of his fingers one by one and, emulating his father, washed off the nonexistent residue. Lady Faloyan proffered a soft white cloth.

'Madam, your sister, she is well?' The Agbakin dried his own hand and then the small one, silently held out to him across the dishes.

'Yes, we may thank god, she has safely delivered a girl.'

'I have lost my wager then.' Her husband's face broke into a smile. 'After seven boys in a row, I did not expect such inconsistency from her. Her husband will be richer by a new robe.'

'He will be richer by a fine daughter also.'

'A man needs sons . . .'

'May you be blessed with so many that they cannot be numbered,' Lady Faloyan interposed promptly.

The Agbakin inclined his head, reached across, and sat his son on his knee again.

'. . . A man needs warriors,' he continued, scrutinising the clear round face. He brushed away a speck of white adhering to the corner of Abiola's

14

mouth. 'Your brother promises to rival us all.' His voice was full of pride.

'Ah, Olufemi,' said Lady Faloyan. 'I do believe you favour *him* above all your children.'

'He is my first born. I repeat nothing but what his teachers say. Tell me, do you not favour this one?'

Abiola looked from one to the other. His mother remained silent. She could not deny it. Seven years younger than his brother, Abiola had saved her from the disgrace of barrenness. In those intervening years her husband had fathered innumerable children by his other wives, who, as befitted a high chief of Oyo, were scarcely less numerous. As his father's first born, her elder son's position was reasonably assured, but her younger one would have to fight for his place. She would do everything in her power to help him; his brother too, if need be.

'I believe that I favour *all* my children equally.'

'Yes indeed, my lord.'

'And I expect *all* my sons to take their part equally in expanding our empire, as I did.' His expression became nostalgic, 'You know, I can still recall every detail –'

Having heard the story countless times, Lady Faloyan interjected swiftly: 'Your exploits during that glorious time, my lord, will be sung for generations to come; your name will resound for ever on the lips of young men.'

The Agbakin looked down at Abiola and bounced him on his knee. 'The young men to come will surpass those who have gone before, will they not, my son?'

At ease now, Abiola clapped his hands delightedly.

'You see?' his father laughed. Lady Faloyan allowed herself the shadow of a smile. 'And as for the present generation . . .' The Chief became suddenly serious. 'Your sister's husband could do worse for his new daughter than the Lord Gaha. He is idolised by the common people.' He spread out his hands. 'An alliance with him would be politic, would it not?'

Lady Faloyan did not reply immediately. If she were to achieve her aim, she must tread her path delicately.

'It is said,' she began, 'that if the Lord Gaha were as astute in politics as he is lion-hearted in war –'

'I know what is said,' the Chief interposed irritably. 'The Lord Gaha is not blessed with intellect. But he is a mighty warrior and he has the protection of the chief eunuch.'

'Yes, my lord.' Lady Faloyan lowered her head submissively.

Her husband glanced at her uneasily. 'So?'

'So we should be provident.'

'Provident?'

'It is likely the Lord Gaha will be elected Bashorun one day. An alliance with our family will strengthen *him* without advancing *us*.'

The Agbakin was silent for some time. At length he said, 'I follow your drift, my wife. Which of the prospective candidates to the *throne* would you propose for your sister's child?'

'The Prince Labisi.'

'My thought exactly,' the Agbakin said.

'Indeed, my lord.' Lady Faloyan kept her eyes lowered, knowing full well that her husband was wondering, *Why that prince above all the others?*

~

4

IT WAS PLEASANTLY cool inside the council chamber. Though the sun's heat was excluded by a lofty thatched roof and thick mud bricks, its light filtered through a frieze of patterned air vents set high on the walls beneath a tall domed ceiling.

The chief eunuch fanned the rolls of his neck, displacing the air around him with a long-handled raffia fan. Flicked expertly to and fro, the fan diverted attention from its owner's close scrutiny of the others in the room, who, multiplied by their reflections in the polished red surfaces of the walls, appeared more numerous than they were.

On a dais at the top of the chamber sat the Alafin, king of all Oyo, robed in silk damask, sandaled feet resting on a beaded footstool, a fly whisk of finest white horse hair looped over his wrist. Two ladies of the palace wearing identical lemon yellow wrappers stood behind his couch, one to wait on him and the other to act as his remembrancer. Pages and attendants crouched at his feet. His dark moon face wore a look of rapt attention. He was in a mood to make mischief.

Resignedly, the chief eunuch turned his gaze away from his master and directed it first at the eunuch of the right, his own neighbour, and then at the eunuch of the left, sitting opposite, both of them slender counterpoints to his own huge bulk. They evinced only bland attention but in fact were keen as hunting dogs.

Ranged on cushioned couches around three sides of the room were the seven members of the Alafin's state council, hereditary ministers of the realm, seated in order of precedence. All had their remembrancers standing beside them.

Two ministers, the Agbakin and the Asipa – second and last in rank, respectively – married to the two sisters, Lady Faloyan and Lady Monifa – claimed the chief eunuch's closest attention, for they had only recently, within a season of each other, succeeded to their titles. He scanned their faces. Hereditary titles were open to any of the men of the family and the successor was chosen by common consent. What other assets did the Agbakin possess, he wondered, besides his prowess in war and a noble expression? And what of the Asipa, whose suave cheekbones and slippery eyes promised much but conceded little? It was said that the Lord Asipa did nothing without the Lord Agbakin, who did nothing without his senior wife, the Lady Faloyan.

Reluctantly, the chief eunuch directed his attention to the Bashorun, chief minister of the council and second only to the king. He considered this Bashorun unfit for his position and an unworthy successor to his famous brother. The chief eunuch was listening with only half an ear, but he was careful that his face should not mirror his thoughts, and as he turned towards the dais, his fan continuing its measured stroke, no one would have guessed that his opinion of his royal master was of the same shade.

He had welcomed the choice of a king who was a warrior, bold as a lion on the battlefield, and a lover of art and beauty, too. But already the exercise of power had exposed the new Alafin's other qualities: rashness, vanity and greed. A man all too easily manipulated. To the chief eunuch it was a cause of bitter disappointment. His neck rolls quivered in a sigh.

The Bashorun, having reached the end of his peroration on their triumphs in the war in Dahomey, gave a sweeping glance around the council chamber. 'I think I may safely say we shall soon see the dust of a caravan at our gates, bearing the tribute owed to us . . .' He paused, relishing the sudden stir of interest. His manner remained decorous, but there was gloating in his voice. 'Yes, I think I may say this, without fear of being forced to eat my words.' He raised glistening eyes towards his sovereign.

His Majesty's eyes glistened in return. 'We are glad, my lord,' the Alafin said, 'that there is no fear of your having to swallow your words, for if by some ill chance you happened to choke upon them, our loss would be incalculable.'

In the silence that followed the chief eunuch kept his eyes on the dais and noted with approval that the faces of both the king's lady-in-waiting and his remembrancer had become unreadable masks. He noted the reaction of each of the pages and messengers and filed them in his mind before turning to the councillors. Beneath their carefully neutral expressions he read uncertainty as to whether or not the king spoke in jest.

Leaning against the cushions at his back, immaculate in robes of red and green, one of the councillors broke the silence, silkily hostile: 'How can you be so certain, my lord, that the king of Dahomey will pay his dues on this occasion?'

'Because, my lord, on this occasion, instead of withdrawing into the bush, he intends to stand and fight.' The Bashorun could not keep the triumph from his voice.

The Alapini, ranked fourth on the council, rose hastily to his feet. 'In that case my friends,' he declared, pouring oil on the waters, 'we shall be victorious. Surely you have not forgotten the words of the proverb …?' Clearing his throat, he straightened his embroidered cap and hitched the voluminous folds of his blue gown into place. His audience waited, wryly expectant; he was famous for his use of proverbs, always having an appropriate one just beyond recall. His remembrancer bent to whisper in his ear. 'Ah! I have it!' the Alapini held up his hand, ' "In the river, who can defeat the warrior who swims? In the plain, who can defeat the warrior on horseback?" There is no denying the truth of that.' He nodded sagely. 'The Dahomeans are no match for our cavalry.'

The Alapini's remembrancer, sensing he was being observed, glanced up and did not immediately look away, prompting the chief eunuch to think once again of making a serious bid for him. The young man's memory was a phenomenon even by Oyo standards and wasted on his present master. He would be better put to private use. The chief eunuch envied him his ability: being himself literate in Arabic, he committed everything to writing and as a result his memory was a feeble, ill-exercised thing. For every gain, a corresponding loss, he thought regretfully, his attention reclaimed by the Alafin, returning to the attack.

'My Lord Bashorun, the Dahomeans say of us, do they not, that when we go to war our general spreads the hide of a buffalo before the door of his tent and pitches a spear in the ground on either side, between which the soldiers march until the multitude passing over the hide have worn a hole in it? And not until then does he presume that his forces are numerous enough to take the field.' Loud guffaws forced the Alafin to pause. He held up his hand. 'The Dahomeans may possibly exaggerate . . .' the laughter redoubled, so he raised his voice: '. . . in order, I imagine, to excuse their pusillanimous behaviour. But, clearly, hitherto they have believed that our forces outnumber theirs. So how, my lord, have you disabused them of this?'

'Sire,' the Bashorun's voice slid like a serpent. 'A sudden insurrection on our northern borders has obliged us to withdraw a considerable portion of our army from their country in order to deploy them elsewhere.'

The chief eunuch's fan altered its rhythm. There was a general murmur from all but the lords Agbakin and Asipa, who had been noticeably taciturn throughout. Whether theirs was the silence of emptiness or of ambush, he had yet to discover.

Another of the councillors was heard to exclaim admiringly, 'A double feint!' And then, lest anyone think his remark had shown him to be too much an ally of the Bashorun, he added quickly, 'The appointment of the chief of staff has been brilliantly vindicated.' The chief of staff was the king's nomination.

'The idea for the double feint originated with my nephew the Lord Gaha,' the Bashorun said, his serpent voice flicking its tail in annoyance.

'The Lord Gaha!' The Alafin laughed loudly. 'The young Lord Gaha has the might of an elephant, but he has never had an idea in his life. Tell me, my lord, where will battle be joined?'

'Before the gates of Abomey, the capital itself.'

'Ogun has given us his protection,' said the Alafin.

He leaned forward on his couch. 'Even as the god of war has favoured us, it seems the oracle has favoured you, Lord Asipa. I hear your newborn daughter has been chosen to be a wife of Ifa. I congratulate you.' In the crowded chamber silence rippled outwards from the words as from a stone cast into a pool.

The Asipa bowed deep in acknowledgement, more deeply than required. Doubtless, the chief eunuch thought, in order to disguise his astonishment.

The meeting at an end, the Bashorun was first to prostrate himself at the foot of the dais, his robes spread out around him, his forehead resting on the fine matting covering the floor. Next in rank, the Agbakin, measuring his full length on the ground, made his obeisance to the king. The chief eunuch, his fan resting loosely in his hand, would have wagered a sack of cowries, even two, that the magnificent Chief, lying large as a felled tree in the centre of the room, was as surprised as anyone at the announcement that his newborn niece had been chosen to serve Ifa. Evidently his wife wished to keep it secret. And there was only one reason for that. The child must already be promised.

Lady Faloyan sat straight-backed and unmoving on the verandah outside her apartments, watching the shadows lengthen. A rain-freshened breeze rustled the leaves, and doves called peacefully among the shady branches of the umbrella trees in the centre of the courtyard. Throughout the day, fatigue had enveloped her like a robe, which, upon receiving the not-unexpected summons to her husband's bedchamber, she had mentally replaced with another: a cloak of resolve. Pulling its folds tightly round her, she had prepared as if for her wedding night.

Soon it would be dark, and it was not sleep that awaited her. Her women's faces, though, betrayed both surprise and triumph, for the Agbakin had only very recently taken another young wife. As the first stars began to appear and Lady Faloyan stalked past the lamp-lit door-ways of the women's courtyards, a drift of scented camwood in her wake, the eyes of her maids followed her proudly.

She found her husband pacing up and down. Now that it was night his room was softly lit and fragrant with herbs. The coral beads around his wrists were bright against the blue-black of his skin and the blue of the cloth which he wore wrapped round him and thrown over one shoulder. He greeted her as punctiliously as custom demanded, and it was only after he had observed every courtesy that he flung at her: 'Why didn't you tell me about your sister's dream?'

'Of what importance is it?' she countered, her voice calm. 'It is only a dream.'

'Only a dream! The entire city is agog. They say Ifa has chosen the baby.'

Lady Faloyan displayed mild amazement in place of the bitter chagrin she felt. There had been only one other person in the birthing room when her sister had relayed her dream. The decision to retain the midwife's assistant had been a costly error.

'It's women's talk, nothing more,' she remonstrated gently. 'I'm surprised it has reached your ears, my lord.'

'Women's talk, you say? This very morning after the official business of the council was completed, His Majesty, the Alafin himself, congratulated the Lord Asipa on his good fortune! And of all those present it would appear that the only people ignorant of that good fortune were the two most closely concerned. How do you account for that, madam?'

The Agbakin towered above her, the veins prominent on his forehead.

Lady Faloyan, all reasonableness, stood her ground, 'I repeat, my lord, it was only a dream,' she insisted. 'The oracle itself has not spoken. The prediction contained in my sister's dream may yet prove untrue.'

'And if it should not, what then?'

Lady Faloyan allowed a long pause, as if what she was about to say had just come to her as the result of his close questioning. 'It is not impossible to elude such a fate: there are precedents.'

He resumed his pacing of the room. 'It will bring bad luck. Very bad luck.'

'It is my opinion,' Lady Faloyan caught his eye and held it, 'that nothing has occurred which cannot be mended. With hindsight, I am sorry that I did not tell you about my sister's dream and that I advised her to keep it from her husband, the Lord Asipa, also. Our schemes may yet come to fruition.'

Placing his hands on her shoulders, her husband scoured her face with his eyes. He released her and sank down on the bed.

Silent and still, Lady Faloyan stood by. A long period elapsed. The lamp flames flickered in their niches; outside the wind gusted suddenly and rain began to fall.

At last she enquired, 'Shall I leave you now, my lord?'

Reminded of her presence, he looked up, startled. All at once he smiled.

'No, stay.' His teeth gleamed enticingly. He patted the place beside him on the bed. 'Shall we see if we too cannot produce a girl?'

What if the oracle was not to be appeased? She did not voice the thought.

She let fall her wrap. Her body was straight and tempered as a spear. Her skin glowed in the light. Her lips curved in a smile.

5

SUPERB IN MATCHING blue wrappers and a large head-tie, Lady Faloyan emerged from her room to be confronted by a bellicose Abiola.

'What's the matter?' she asked the nurse.

The nurse, Nafisat, sank to her knees, placing her elbows on the floor.

'Alafia, peace be with you, Ma. He wants to take his animals to the naming ceremony.'

'Alafia, peace be with you.' Lady Faloyan, inclined her head. She turned to her son, who became tractable at once.

'Alafia,' he said, dropping on one knee.

Grasping him by the hand, his mother set off down the verandah, closely followed by her maids. They rapidly negotiated the maze of inner courtyards and narrow connecting corridors and were soon hastening through the women's entrance of the main courtyard where a crowd was waiting outside the Agbakin's apartments. Seeing his elder brother, Abiola broke free and plunged in beside him as the drummers playfully announced the arrival of mother and small son.

Lady Faloyan waited, still as a statue. People milled about the courtyard, their robes bright in the morning sunlight. The Agbakin's brothers, easily identifiable beneath their state umbrellas, were already in position, surrounded by their retinues of wives and children and servants. She had timed her arrival well, for moments later her husband made his appearance on the verandah. As the drummers struck up a welcome he stepped down into the courtyard. Resplendent in crimson robes, and shaded by a vast umbrella, he stood head and shoulders above the crowd now lining up before him. Lady Faloyan took her place at the head of his retinue with her children and maids, as befitted the senior wife and mother of his first-born son. The guards swung back the heavy wooden gates of the compound and the procession issued on to the street, the Chief's criers and drummers leading the way.

'Make way! Make way for the Lord Agbakin. Brave as a lion. Veteran of Yansmi, and against the Igbonas! Make way! Here comes the Agbakin!

Illustrious son of an illustrious father! Guardian of the worship of Oranyan!'

Secured a swift passage through the congested morning traffic of the city, the Agbakin's train arrived in good time at the house of the Asipa.

Lady Faloyan went directly to the birthing room.

'Greetings and welcome to you, sister.' Lady Monifa knelt gracefully at the door.

Lady Faloyan knelt also and, the formalities completed, rose briskly to her feet.

'You look well.' She appraised her sister.

'If I do, we must thank God.' Lady Monifa smiled, radiant in magenta. 'Though you should take some of the credit too, for your bark tea. The old auntie,' she said, referring to the midwife, 'has driven herself nearly mad trying to reproduce the exact prescription, with no success at all.'

'My reputation is safe then.' Lady Faloyan allowed a smile.

'Your reputation, my dear sister, is a mountain no one can hope to scale.'

'How fanciful you are. And the little one?'

'She too is flourishing.' Lady Monifa turned and beckoned the nurse to bring the child forward for inspection. Lady Faloyan took the baby, who was fast asleep, and asked the young woman to fetch a cup of water from the cool jar, which would entail a long journey to the kitchen courtyard.

'That's the midwife's girl,' Lady Monifa reminded her. 'She's very good with the baby. She has kept me amused too, confined to the birthing room these past eight days. I don't know how I ever managed before. It's a tiresome custom, wouldn't you agree?'

'Most of us are glad of it.'

'You wouldn't be if you'd had as many confinements as I have . . .' Lady Monifa's voice trailed away. There was a painful pause. 'I'm sorry, I didn't intend —'

Lady Faloyan interrupted her. 'It's no matter. You were saying . . .? About the girl?'

'I have become fond of her. I'm trying to persuade Auntie to let me buy her. But she is reluctant, having invested so much already in her training. Apart from which, she tells me, the girl is blessed with good hands, something that cannot be bought. But you know that, better than I.'

'What I know is that Auntie wants to squeeze as much money as she can from you. Let the girl go. Take my maid, Alero, as a nurse for the baby instead. She was the messenger, remember, who fetched me and saved the child's life. She will bring her good luck, I feel it.'

Lady Monifa looked doubtful.

'Trust me,' said Lady Faloyan, and stroked the baby's soft cheek.

'All right, if you say so.'

Lady Faloyan glanced at her keenly. Her sister had capitulated rather too readily. 'Now, quickly, the girl will be back at any moment. Tell me!'

'What?'

'Give me patience! You know very well what!'

'Oh, the dream . . .'

'Sister, tell me at once, what did the oracle say?'

At that same moment the slightest intake of breath alerted Lady Faloyan to the presence of someone at the door and she looked up to find the midwife's assistant standing in the entrance, cup in hand.

Lady Monifa started in surprise as the girl walked into the room and, kneeling, presented the cup to Lady Faloyan.

'It's from the cool jar, madam, as you asked,' the girl said, keeping her eyes lowered. Her hands were trembling.

Lady Faloyan took the cup. Without doubt the girl had overheard her questioning her sister. And though this little spy might not understand its significance, others would. She gave back the cup.

Still on her knees the girl turned to Lady Monifa.

'Please, madam,' she said, 'the ladies are here to escort you. Everything is ready.'

'Shall we go?' Lady Monifa asked. She was fanning her cheeks, and colour had returned to her voice.

The baby continued fast asleep in Lady Faloyan's arms on the short journey from the birthing room to the small courtyard where relatives and guests were assembled. As soon as the baby appeared, her father stepped to the edge of the verandah and tossed the traditional calabash of water up to the roof. Lady Faloyan ran forward with the child and held her out under the eaves to catch the spray. The tiny infant jerked suddenly to life and yelled with astonishing power. Delighted, the audience shouted with joy and the Asipa laughed proudly at this latest evidence of his virility.

Abiola's enthusiasm for the complicated battle manoeuvres that his brother, Olufemi, had insisted on explaining to him had dissipated by the time they reached their uncle's house. Until now, he had resisted his nurse's attempts to interest him in his little cousin, but as the baby started to cry, he craned his head curiously.

'Sounds cross,' he said.

Nafisat craned too. 'I think she's afraid.'

'What is there to be frightened of?' Olufemi's tone was derisive.

'The noise, the bright light, all these people. Don't forget, she's seeing the world for the very first time.'

Abiola shook his head, 'She's not afraid, she's cross because we don't know what she's saying. My mouse squeaks very loudly when he's angry.'

'Give me patience.' Olufemi gave a snort of disgust.

'Hush, you two,' Alero broke in. 'The names are about to be given.'

Abiola stood on tiptoe. 'Who will be first? Will it be our mother?'

'Who will be second, you mean,' Alero corrected, forgetting her own demand for silence. 'No one here can be first; your cousin was born with a name already, the one she brought with her because she was born face downwards.'

Olufemi yawned. 'I just hope they will be quick about it, so the feasting can begin.'

'In an illustrious family like this one,' Nafisat chided, 'all the elders will want to claim the privilege of naming the child. You will have to eat patience instead.'

'You cannot eat patience,' Olufemi muttered under his breath, but Nafisat heard him.

'Yes you can,' she retorted, 'and it's never too late to acquire the taste, believe me.'

It was the baby's great aunt, as the officiating elder, who announced her names to the assembly. The last, given by her mother, was Oluremi, meaning 'God consoled me'.

'Her names are longer than the longest snake.' Abiola stretched his arms wide.

'So are her presents,' Olufemi observed bitterly.

The great aunt dipped a finger in the first of the seven bowls and touched it to the baby's lips: pepper so that she would be resolute; water for purity; salt for wisdom; oil for health; honey for happiness; palm wine for prosperity; and finally a taste of kola nut for good fortune.

It was the signal for the praise singers to begin their songs. Olufemi pulled Abiola into the crowd, leaving the two maids frantically calling them back.

Lady Faloyan stepped down from the verandah, her eyes searching the throng. Suddenly she pounced, grasping Olufemi by his shirttail with one hand and with the other swinging Abiola off his feet. 'Food must wait. First, come and see your cousin.'

Oluremi lay swaddled on her mother's lap, small fists curled neatly under her chin and huge eyes fixed intently on her mother's beaming smile. Her cousins arrived noisily and, having greeted their aunt punctiliously, bowing and then prostrating themselves on the ground, they jostled each other good naturedly for a place at her knee. Interposing their heads below hers they hung excitedly over the baby, critically examining her small, composed face.

Olufemi held out a finger and she curled her hand round it, drawing delighted laughter from Nafisat and Alero, who had caught up with them. Abiola, not to be outdone, offered his finger too. The baby gripped it with both hands and when he tried to pull away seemingly he could not. He tried once more, without success, provoking a renewed burst of laughter. His brother urged him on, enjoying the game. But their mother, intent as always, immediately perceived that her younger son was not playing; that, incredibly, he was unable to free himself. As he gave up trying to wrest his finger from his cousin's grip and instead stared into the baby's great dark eyes, it came to her that the two of them were in profound wordless communication with each other. She realised with absolute certainty that it was an omen for the future and confirmation of the vision she'd had in the birthing room.

As soon as the opportunity presented itself, she drew her sister into another courtyard.

'Now,' she said, 'tell me: what did the oracle say?'

Lady Monifa was perspiring copiously. She fanned her neck with a long-handled raffia fan, avoiding her sister's eyes, glancing distastefully round the small enclosed courtyard, which was used to store fodder for her husband's horses. 'My sister, do you not feel the heat? I am near expiring.' Flies buzzed and there was a strong smell of dung from the stables. Lady Monifa pulled at the top of her magenta wrapper, holding the thick material away from her and flapping it vigorously in time with her fan.

'Sister!' The sibilants hissed ominously.

'All right, all right.' With a sigh, Lady Monifa hitched her wrapper back into place. 'My dream was true. The oracle has chosen my daughter to be a "wife of Ifa".' Her chin took on a defiant slant. 'She will marry the priest. There's nothing to be done.'

Lady Faloyan considered her sister, whose fan spoke on, agitatedly. Now that it had been definitively revealed to her that their two children were linked, it was more imperative than ever to change the fate which had been predicted for Oluremi. The oracle must be appeased, enabling Oluremi to fulfil a higher destiny as wife to a king.

Aloud she said, 'I should have guessed it. From the name you gave her – "God consoled me". Very apt.'

'I thought so.'

'Yes, an excellent name. Perfect, in fact, in the circumstances.'

Lady Faloyan's voice soothed where before it had stung. It would not help to bully her sister before she'd discovered the appropriate sacrifices and what atonement should be made in order to appease the oracle. She knew from past experience that, when presented with an accomplished fact, her sister's intractability was more easily breached.

'I'm glad we agree.' The motion of Lady Monifa's fan became complacent.

'Indeed we do. And on that other matter too . . .' The fan missed a stroke. 'A nursemaid for Oluremi,' Lady Faloyan continued silkily. 'You are to take my maid, Alero, and let the midwife's girl go.'

It was late into the night but lights still burned in the chief eunuch's house. The great man lay at ease on a couch piled with skins, rum cup in hand, his expression serene. In the face opposite he saw not the young man reclining, equally at ease, before him, but the boy that used to be. It was true, he thought, that to a parent a child was always a child. In this respect, as in others, Lord Gaha, he felt, was indeed his son.

Forever in his mind's eye he would see an eight-year-old, thick-set and short for his age, backed up against a wall, outnumbered by his adversaries, five or six to one. The indomitable set of the child's head had revived buried memories of another small boy long ago; on that occasion, the opponents had been not his peers, but grown men, who had deprived him of his manhood before he was of an age to mourn its loss. Impressed by the boy's courage, the chief eunuch had stood by, ready to intervene should it be tested too far. The child's ferocity had been sufficient to rout his attackers unaided. They left him at last, bloodied and alone. It was then that the child realised he was being observed. Caught off guard, his expression had revealed a precocious intelligence, not the total lack of it implicit in the taunts and jeers of his tormentors. In that moment, the chief eunuch had realised that the boy, young as he was, understood the terrible danger he was in. The young Lord Gaha was nephew to the new Bashorun, whose instinct was to annihilate the offspring of his predecessor; hence the cloak of stupidity. The chief eunuch had taken the boy under his wing from that day.

Now, his gaze travelled from the hooked profile to the broad chest and battle-hardened limbs encased in a spotless white cotton tunic and embroidered trousers. The boy, who became the son he could never have, had matured into the man he might have been. He had been right, he thought, to transfer all his hopes to him. Lord Gaha had inherited his famous father's qualities. One day he too would be Bashorun. When that day arrived – the chief eunuch moistened his lips – together they would be manipulators of the most powerful empire in Africa.

'You have heard the news, I take it, of the priest and the Asipa's daughter?'

'Who has not?' Lord Gaha smirked. 'A bitter blow. The Asipa could have looked to a grand alliance, else.'

'It is my belief that he will still do so.' The chief eunuch hitched at his gown, which was knotted on both shoulders, revealing arms sleeved in plush dark flesh.

Lord Gaha shook his head. 'My girl was well placed to overhear.'

'No secret is ever a secret in Oyo. Your girl will need protection. Don't forget Lady Faloyan.'

'The good lady put in an offer for her but, unfortunately, the girl is no longer in Oyo.' Lord Gaha gave a snort of laughter.

The visitors knelt at the door in greeting. 'Alafia, peace be with you, Father,' they said in unison.

The high priest of Ifa knelt to welcome them. 'Alafia,' he replied in kind.

Once inside, the women threw back their head cloths. The high priest scanned their faces. He did not expect to learn anything and was not disappointed. Princess Boladé and Lady Faloyan were models of inscrutability, as was the princess's crippled maid. Lady Monifa's expression spoke only agitation. The high priest lingered on the smooth planes of her face. The princess had requested this consultation on behalf of Lady Monifa and it was not unconnected, he imagined, to the birth of her daughter.

The Asipa, her husband, had consulted the oracle three times in this same room. He wanted to be sure that it would not bring disaster if he changed the child's destiny. Three times he had received an affirmative answer. No ill luck would attach to him, provided proper atonement was made to secure the child's release from Ifa. Atonement had been made and the appropriate sacrifices performed, so what need was there for further action? At a loss as to the reason behind the visit of the women, the high priest ceased further speculation and invited his guests to take their places on his left. His eyes lingered again on Lady Monifa. He came to no conclusion.

It did not occur to him that a mother might be desperate to avoid ill luck attaching to her child, rather than to its father.

The room was brightly lit, made even brighter by the white wall hangings, symbolic of the god Orunmila, who, through the oracle, was the channel between men and gods. Anchored firmly in the corner by the door was the ornamented iron staff of Ifa that always had to be kept upright. From a line of hooks on the opposite wall hung the blue cloth bags decorated with cowries in which the instruments of divination were stored. Arrayed on two deep chests below the row of bags were divining bowls containing sets of sacred ikin nuts, and, alongside, divining bells made of wood and ivory, resembling miniature elephant tusks. All were elaborately carved.

The high priest rapped loudly with the tip of an ivory bell on the side of a circular divining tray resting on a white cloth spread on the floor mat. The bowl was placed so that the image of Eshu, the trickster god, carved on the rim of the bowl faced inwards from the east. In any transaction between men and gods, the role of the trickster must always be acknowledged. A stone post that represented him stood in every compound and was anointed daily in order to placate him.

The high priest began to invoke the messenger of the gods:

> *Orunmila Ajana!*
> *The witness to each individual's fate*
> *Deputy to Olodumare!*
> *Whom to know is to be saved . . .*

A small sob escaped Lady Monifa and Lady Faloyan's hand closed instantly round her wrist, silencing her.

Replacing the ivory bell beside the cow-tail switch on the left of the divining tray, the high priest removed the cover of the divining bowl placed at his right, and lifted out the sixteen sacred palm nuts. A

29

seventeenth, covered in white powder, lay on a ring of cowries on the white cloth beside the image of Eshu.

Eight times the high priest cast the palm nuts, each time drawing a single or double line in the white dust sprinkled on the divining tray until there were two parallel columns of four marks each.

As always, when surrounded by the assembled artefacts of Ifa, Lady Faloyan felt enclosed among mysterious presences. The sense of them intensified as, one by one, the lines appeared.

The high priest called out the name of the verse indicated by the lines drawn on the tray. Lady Faloyan exchanged a swift glance with the princess as Lady Monifa breathed out, audibly. Of the thousands of verses in the sacred Ifa canon, this was one of the most significant. Orunmila was sending an unequivocal message – but would it be good news or bad?

Two more casts would have to be made in order to discover how the message contained in the verse was to be applied in the present case, for the oracle always spoke in riddles.

The high priest wiped the tray smooth and asked Lady Monifa to stretch out both her hands. On one of her open palms he ceremoniously placed two cowries tied together, and on the other a small piece of bone.

Lady Faloyan exchanged another swift glance with the princess. It was time for Lady Monifa to put her questions to the god. She needed no instruction about what to do next. Clenching both hands, she brought first one fist and then the other close to her mouth and whispered a question to each so softly that it wasn't possible to hear what she said or even to read her lips. Still clutching the talismans, she lowered her hands and rested them on her lap.

'Ifa, you have heard the question,' the high priest intoned slowly, keeping his eyes on Lady Monifa. 'Now provide us with the answer. Is it the left hand?'

He touched the back of her hand with the palm nuts and began casting again, making a mark after each cast on the right-hand side of the divining tray until a second verse appeared.

Touching the palm nuts to Lady Monifa's other hand, he asked, 'Is it the right hand?'

He cast eight times, as before, drawing lines on the left-hand side of the tray until a third verse appeared beside the second.

The silence in the room was absolute as the high priest studied the lines. Finally, his voice rang out. 'The right hand has been chosen.'

Trembling, Lady Monifa unclenched her right hand. It held the bone. The answer was unfavourable, for the bone signified a negative response.

Again the high priest was unable to fathom the expressions of Princess Boladé and Lady Faloyan. He met only vacancy on the face of the princess's maid, Sadia; but Lady Monifa's head drooped a little, from which he deduced that she'd hoped the cowries would be chosen.

He cleared his throat and Lady Monifa raised her head, keeping her eyes properly lowered.

'My daughter, the one for whom you divined entered this world with no fixed destiny. Her fate may be chosen by others; it will be as *they* wish. That was the meaning of the first verse.' Lady Monifa nodded. 'However, the final verse decreed that, whatsoever *they* decide, the result will be as the *gods* wish.' The high priest looked down at her right hand. 'And the gods have chosen the bone. On its own, that choice would amount to an unequivocal *no* to your question, but, taken in conjunction with the first verse, it merely serves a warning that misfortune *might* result from what you decide, not that it *will*.'

Lady Monifa raised her eyes briefly; imploringly, it seemed to the high priest. He cleared his throat again, struck not for the first time by her beauty. 'It is my opinion that the oracle may yet be appeased, and that good fortune will result if the prescribed sacrifices are made.'

He led his visitors from the brightly lit room into the courtyard, where only two torches burned low. The offerings the women had brought were laid on Eshu's shrine, except for the five thousand cowries, which the high priest kept back for Ifa.

Outside in the street the princess remarked tartly to Lady Faloyan, 'It wasn't difficult for the priest to guess what our questions were. But he doesn't know that we disguised our tracks by reversing the *meaning* of the two symbols. When the news that the bone was chosen reaches the ears of our enemies, as I have no doubt it will, it will do no harm for them mistakenly to anticipate a change of course on our part.'

Lady Faloyan flicked a glance at the princess's maid, standing close as always. The princess caught the look but gave no sign.

6

'HE'S PRETTY,' SAID eight-year-old Oluremi, peering upwards, shading her eyes.

Abiola glared at her. 'No he is not: he's magnificent. There isn't another horse to touch him in the whole of the empire.'

'How do you know?' Modupé challenged. A year older than Oluremi, she was her cousin on her father's side and the two girls were inseparable.

Abiola ignored the interruption. 'Except for one other in the royal stables. And he too was a gift from the Lord Gaha. Now stop gawping and begin walking or we'll be left behind.'

They were shouting to make themselves heard above the music, and striving to keep abreast of the Bashorun, who was riding on a white horse at the head of the procession, shaded by his state umbrella.

Abiola took Oluremi by the arm.

Modupé grasped her other hand. 'We should wait for Alero.'

'She'll find you. Come on.' Abiola pushed through a gap in the press of people, pulling both girls with him so that they were right beside the groom who held the scarlet and silver bridle. The horse shook its white mane.

'Look at that neck, such a beautiful long neck!' With his free hand, Abiola described a graceful curve. 'That tells you immediately where he comes from.'

'And where's that?' Oluremi asked dutifully.

'From Borno, of course; raised in the Mandara hills. I shall have a horse like him one day.'

'You'll have to be very rich.' Modupé shouted above the noise.

'I shall be. I'll be just like the Lord Gaha.' Abiola yelled back.

'They say your senior brother is already following in his footsteps,' Oluremi put in placatingly.

'And him too.' Abiola drew himself up. 'I shall be like both of them, but bigger. Our mother says that when I am grown I shall be as tall as my father, easily.'

Releasing Oluremi's hand, Abiola turned to face the girls, walking backwards, daring them to disagree.

'You will be taller even than your father,' Oluremi assured him, giving Modupé a nudge.

'Oh, easily,' Modupé agreed.

Abiola took them both by the hand now, his eleven-year-old pride satisfied, and the three of them danced on, carried with the crowd streaming towards the city walls.

Mid-way through the Béré festival, Oyo was once again filled to overflowing. In addition to heralding the start of another year of the Alafin's reign, the festival marked the successful harvesting of the thatch used for all the houses. It was the béré grass that in the sunlight turned the soaring city roofs to gold and gave its name to the grandest and most protracted of all the annual celebrations.

The Bashorun's ceremonial firing of the fields would mark the end of the harvest. As he passed by, he was met by the men of each compound, come to the street gate to pay him homage and to present him with gifts. He in return gave gifts to the women. The whole of the morning would be taken up by his progress through the city, but the drummers, musicians and mummers ensured that the crowds lining the route and dancing behind the procession kept no count of the hours.

As Abiola had anticipated, the bottleneck at the inner city gate provided a perfect opportunity to appraise the other horses in the Bashorun's entourage. His father's grooms had informed him that Lord Gaha had arrived for the festival with a string of war stallions the like of which had never been seen in Oyo. Abiola gazed longingly as the crown prince rode by, followed by Lord Gaha and his right and left hands, sitting high on wooden saddles. Their horses passed close enough to touch, and, stroking each gleaming flank, Abiola held forth at length, for the benefit of Oluremi and Modupé, on the advantages of such height and strength and speed on the battlefield.

So intent were they that they failed to notice Alero's presence until she seized Oluremi firmly by the shoulder and began upbraiding Abiola for being so unmindful of his duty to his brother on this of all days. It would seem, Alero shouted over the din, that the Agbakin was right in assuming that Lady Faloyan's younger son wished to be a groom and not a warrior.

The enormity of what he'd neglected to do struck Abiola with full force and he fled, pushing his way through the crowd. Such was his determination that, despite the crush, he was quickly through the gate, across the bridge and out into the stretch of open ground between the two inner circuit walls. Here the road was unpaved, the air hazed with dust rising from the tamped earth that would be turned to clogging mud as soon as the early rains set in. Small clouds drifted high overhead and hawks circled, keeping a beady watch on the patchwork of green fields below. Abiola kept up his hectic progress until he neared the third and last of the towering city battlements. Well ahead of the procession now, he secreted himself in the centre of an army of slaves and servants, hauling water and firewood and sacks of beans and maize in preparation for the feast. Beneath its huge portico the wooden tollgate stood wide open and Abiola passed through, confident he would not be detected.

Behind him, the gatekeeper prostrated himself as the Bashorun and his train approached, drums beating, trumpets blaring, the horses curvetting and prancing, to be greeted with answering fanfares from the bands of his fellow state councillors, waiting on the other side. The riders dismounted and two lines of colourful state umbrellas met as the highest nobles of Oyo, led by the Agbakin, and accompanied by the visiting provincial kings and princes, their wives and retainers, made their obeisances.

Abiola raced towards his father's section of the encampment that had sprung up outside the city walls among the fields of the home farms. As he slipped into the enclosure, his brother, Lord Olufemi, was addressing a semicircle of eager faces.

Olufemi broke off as heads turned. 'You honour us at last, little brother. The leader of the small boys will give you your instructions later.'

'Yes, sir.'

Abiola, who was to have been leader, joined the semicircle on the mats spread on the ground. If the small boys acquitted themselves well today, their leader would retain his position until it was time to join the youths. A fact not lost on all of those present. By his absence, Lord Olufemi's brother had forfeited the opportunity to make his mark and to take the first step on the path of a successful warrior. Their mother would be humbled.

Abiola sat stone still, his face burning, his shame compounded by the knowledge that he'd brought the disgrace upon himself.

Olufemi rose to his feet. 'As long as anyone can remember, the house of the Agbakin has been unbeaten in the hunt, for which we give thanks. We give thanks also that the elephant hunter Lakoja, the greatest of all, was born into our compound, and taught us his skills.'

Olufemi beckoned Abiola, who had prostrated himself on the ground with the others, to follow him. His manner was reminiscent of their mother's.

'Little brother, only a fool risks losing more than he stands to gain. The hunter Lakoja told our mother on your naming day that you were destined for greatness. It seems he was mistaken.'

The hunters of the Agbakin's compound had chosen a piece of land on the Chief's home farm, not far from the edge of the thick belt of forest surrounding the city. It had been left fallow for several seasons, and for days the farm slaves and servants had been weeding and keeping clear a large strip around it to act as a firebreak. A bird's-eye view of the plain would have shown a series of concentric circles among the farm plots, with tall weeds, bush and scrub trees in the centre, and short-cropped grass on the outside.

Abiola had to content himself with being the leader's right hand, and after appointing his own right and left hands, he left them to appoint their own aides and to assign tasks to those who had taken part before while he attended to the younger ones who were joining in the hunt for the first time. He took them through their duties, and made them repeat his words back to him before sending them off in high spirits to gather the green leaves they would use to put out any unplanned conflagrations.

The boys did not participate in the sacrificial feasts, instincts being more alert on empty stomachs. At the beginning of the hottest part of the day when the sun was directly overhead they took up their prescribed positions. The professional hunters and young warriors blocked the single exit that would be left when the fields were fired. The youths, who would be responsible for starting and controlling the fires, spread out around the circle, armed with cudgels. Behind them, the small boys spaced at short intervals on the firebreak were ready with palm branches, thick stems of green leaves and strategically placed water jars.

The drums began softly and the Bashorun, with stately measured steps, danced to the edge of his chosen field accompanied by three priestesses from the palace carrying calabashes of palm wine and corn beer covered with white cloths. He poured a libation on the ground to placate the trickster god. Next he invoked the blessings of the god of farming, thus ensuring the fertility of the home farms in the coming year.

The Ifa priests came forward to cast the kola nuts, and the drums rose to a crescendo when it was shown that the sacrifice had been accepted.

The Bashorun put the first torch to the grass. One after another the chiefs set their fields alight and in all directions the flames leapt high.

Banging their cudgels together, the young men and boys set up an uproar, dancing round the red rings of fire, stamping, singing, clapping. Sparks flew and kites swooped low above billowing clouds of smoke. Terrified animals, flushed from their burrows and dens, could be heard above the roar and crackle of the flames as the fires spread inwards. An impenetrable barrier blocked all escape routes but one. Maddened, the beasts dashed towards it.

Many of the smaller creatures, unable to move fast enough, were burnt alive, tainting the air with the smell of singed flesh, but most escaped: snakes, grass cutters, bush rats, cane rats, porcupines, duikers, emerged in a rush from the burning scrub to be met by the youths, the first line of hunters, who began clubbing and hacking them to death. Deer and antelope, bounding out of the flames, and hogs, running for the safety of the home forest, were cut down by the arrows and javelins of the second line of hunters: the professionals and warriors. As the carcasses piled up, the vultures came in to land.

Abiola noted with pride that his brother, who had only this season become a warrior in the vanguard, never missed his target, firing with speed and a seemingly effortless technique. One day, one day, he thought, as he ran to make an inspection of the far end of his section.

All was in order. The small boys remained vigilant, dashing about excitedly, chasing every errant spark and flailing into extinction any that fell on the ground.

Moments after returning to his post, Abiola saw the hunters lower their bows and he too stared in disbelief: a leopard and her cubs confronted them. Hunger at the end of a long dry season must have driven her to raid the farms, and now she was flushed out by the flames. She crouched for an instant, tail flicking; then, fast as a sling bolt, she shot through a break in the lines towards the trees, the two cubs at her heels. The hunters let her go, for the leopard, like the red monkey, was sacred to their King, the Alafin, and each one of them hoped to be the one to present her to him alive. Confident that they would be able to track her down in the forest, they lost no time in deciding who should make up the hunting party and set off swiftly in pursuit, shooting their arrows upwards to prevent the kites from preying on the defenceless cubs.

If he could only secure one of those cubs, Abiola thought, he would redeem himself in the eyes of his mother and brother. On the pretext of inspecting another part of the firebreak, he left his right hand in charge. By running in one direction and doubling back, he was able to sneak into the forest, undetected, in the wake of the hunters. On the open plain, Lakoja taught, the hunter is a rock in the waving grass; among the trees of the forest, a leaf, drifting down the hidden pathways. Abiola turned himself into a leaf, and settled to watch.

The hunting party, having set off on the spur of the moment and without a plan, had failed to separate the leopard from her cubs. It would be impossible now that she had reached the safety of her den to take her alive. Eager to seize the initiative from the men of Lord Agbakin's compound, one of the hunters stepped from the protection of the trees, scooped up two handfuls of leaves and piled them in front of the entrance to the cave preparatory to smoking her out. Fire stick in hand, he bent to kindle the leaves but was stopped by a warning shout and he leapt aside as the leopard launched herself out of the dense shadow above the entrance.

Instantly an arrow pierced her jugular and she fell with a roar that sent the monkeys shrieking high into the treetops. While some of the men searched for the cubs, others quickly selected a thick branch of wood and tied the dead leopard to it by her feet, using sturdy roots as ropes. Eventually, having given up hope of finding the cubs, the hunting party emerged from the forest carrying their trophy in procession, jubilant at their success. Even her pelt would transmit mystical power to the Alafin.

It was not the first time Abiola had witnessed a hunter narrowly miss death, but he was shaken all the same. The man had been badly trained, he told himself. He closed his mind to what Lakoja would say about his own adventure and, slipping out of his hiding place, began searching for the cubs.

He found them less than a slingshot distant from the den, hidden in a snug cranny well above the ground. He reached in and lifted them out. They did not come willingly. Snarling and hissing, they flailed at him with their paws; ears flattened, claws out, baring their baby teeth ferociously, scoring his arms and chest with bites until he had them safely stowed in a sling he made from his tunic. He was so elated at having found the cubs, and the glory to come when he delivered them, that Lakoja's strictures were driven from his head; he didn't see the viper's sand-coloured coils, dappled like the forest floor, unwinding towards him. He stepped backwards, tripping over a root and, in his attempt to protect the cubs, fell badly, hitting his head against a stone.

As he lay unconscious, around two small punctures on his ankle the flesh began to swell.

'Auntie! Auntie!' Oluremi came running into the enclosure where Lady Faloyan was directing her maids in clearing away the remains of the feast.

'Abiola's in trouble in the forest,' Oluremi cried, and Nafisat, working beside her mistress, gave a small scream.

Lady Faloyan sank down on her haunches so that her face was level with Oluremi's. Taking the girl gently by the shoulders, she looked into her eyes. 'Abiola cannot be in the forest. He is responsible for a section of the firebreak. He knows how important that is, he wouldn't leave his post.'

Oluremi's eyes were staring and she was trembling, in the grip, apparently, of a very real terror. 'I have *seen* him.'

Lady Faloyan held her close. The child's second sight was no secret.

In a crisis, Lakoja taught, *think only of the present.*

'Where is Abiola?' Lady Faloyan quietly asked Oluremi, whose face was pressed hard into her shoulder. 'Is he in the forest? Can you tell Lord Olufemi where to look?'

'Where they killed the leopard.'

'Has he fallen? Is he injured?'

Oluremi would only shake her head.

Lakoja's teaching notwithstanding, Lady Faloyan sent silent prayers to Oya the river goddess to spare the life of her son.

Olufemi and his two lieutenants found Abiola on his back, both arms clasped across his chest. Olufemi's face lost its sheen as he dropped down beside his brother. Wasting no time, he used a leather thong to make a tourniquet above the swelling on the boy's ankle. Then Olufemi put his mouth to the wound and began sucking out the venom.

He spat hard and wiped his mouth, then felt Abiola's brow. 'He'll live,' he said. 'But for how long, I wouldn't care to bet, not after our mother has finished with him.'

Abiola attempted to sit up.

'They'll suffocate,' he whispered.

His rescuers looked at each other bemused.

Olufemi pushed him down again. 'Stay still,' he ordered. 'Lakoja boasts that you are his ablest pupil. I pity you. Shango's thunderbolts will be nothing compared to his wrath.'

Abiola unfolded his arms, and the sling he'd been hugging to his chest began to heave.

'So that's the reason!' Olufemi exclaimed. He eased the makeshift pouch from Abiola's shoulder, lifted out the two squirming bundles of black-and-gold fur and held them in the air. His lieutenants whistled appreciatively and flicked their fingers loudly. The cubs bared their fangs, provoking admiring laughter.

'For His Majesty,' Abiola said.

Lady Faloyan put a fresh poultice on Abiola's ankle, and, strapping it securely into place, pictured him once again, stretched out on his back, lifeless. She gave thanks to the goddess.

Modupé said, 'Our brother has covered his family in glory. The mother's pelt is nothing in comparison to her two live cubs.'

Silence fell, only the palm fronds moved. Lady Faloyan did not have a high opinion of this niece. Modupé flinched in anticipation of the reprimand, but her aunt contented herself with the words of a well-known proverb: "'The death that will claim you does not call you by name,'" Lady Faloyan said, affecting not to notice the astonishment on every face except those of Abiola, who was Lakoja's pupil, and Oluremi, who was hers.

Her eyes lingered for an instant on Oluremi. The high priest had been right, she thought: changing the girl's fate had not resulted in misfortune after all.

A sudden commotion at the entrance set the women aflutter once more. A drum heralded the presence of the Agbakin, arrived to see his son. The Bashorun himself accompanied him, attended by three of his most celebrated war chiefs. Lady Faloyan and Lady Monifa knelt with the rest, placing their elbows on the ground.

Abiola was the hero of the afternoon, and the Bashorun made a declaration: while there were many, including the men of his own compound, who could claim a share in the honour of presenting the leopardess to the king, the gift of the cubs was an accolade that belonged to the house of the Agbakin alone.

Beneath her lowered lids, Lady Faloyan studied the trio of young war chiefs listening attentively to their elders. To see one was always to see the other two. Such close bonding was perhaps to be expected in young men who had been comrades in arms continuously for eight seasons, the Alafin having made war a way of life again for the young men of Oyo. But ever since their campaign against the Dahomeans, it was noticeable that Lord Gaha and his right and left hands had been thicker than sons born to the same mother. Why? she wondered.

'We give thanks,' Lord Gaha now said, 'that it was a viper and not a green mamba that the Lord Agbakin's son encountered in the forest. This day has shown that the boy possesses that most important of all attributes: good fortune. Opprobrium is always overturned by success.' Lord Gaha smiled pleasantly, having contrived to draw attention to Abiola's disgrace in forfeiting the leadership of the small boys and quitting his post during the hunt.

Lady Faloyan caught the look that passed between Lord Gaha's two lieutenants and suddenly she knew the answer. These three young men were bound not by events of the past but by plans for the future. It struck her that Lord Gaha's right and left hands were both potential candidates for election to the state council. Gaha had long since thrown off the cloak of the dullard and shown himself a master strategist, a brilliant tactician and an inspired commander in the field. Personally, she'd never been deceived by his pretence of being small-brained. As the Princess Boladé had early pointed out, if Lord Gaha had been truly stupid, why would the chief eunuch have taken him under his wing?

Outside, the hunters celebrating the success of the day's killing joined in praise of the most cunning of their kind:

> *Gentle hunter, they sang,*
> *his tail plays on the ground*
> *while he crushes the skull.*
> *Beautiful death*
> *who puts on a spotted robe*
> *when he goes to his victim.*
> *Playful killer*
> *whose loving embrace*
> *splits the antelope's heart.*

Smiling, Lord Gaha bent down and stroked Abiola's skull. Again, Lady Faloyan felt herself close to the abyss. To quell her fear, she imagined herself looking into the eye of the leopard – an old trick of Lakoja's: Picture yourself in a situation so terrible it makes the one you are in seem as nothing in comparison. She was then able to follow once more the movement of Lord Gaha's hand, apparently caressing her son's small head. She had, she thought, stepping back from the rim, underestimated him.

Lady Faloyan's two sons waited with apparent equanimity for the reckoning that must follow in the wake of their near-fatal lapses of judgement. It was a tribute to the very training of which they had been in breach. Their mother noted it, but allowed no quarter, exercising to the full the power of her silence. They were Lakoja's pupils; he should deal with them. She confined herself to tending Abiola's leg and ensuring that he would be well by the time his teacher returned to Oyo. While his mother applied balm to his body, it was his cousin Oluremi, visiting every day, who applied balm to his wounded spirit.

Lakoja allowed Olufemi, who was old enough, to draw his own lessons from the events of the day of the hunt. He told the proud young warrior that the hardest master should always be yourself. Olufemi left his teacher's presence pierced to the heart.

Abiola's punishment was to practise the hunter's trick of standing stock still, from dawn through the searing heat of the day until sundown, without food or water. And while he was doing so, he was to meditate on the words Lakoja gave him: *Glory on its own will not protect you from an unmarked grave.*

~

7

A CROWD OF five thousand or more was gathered in the outer court of the palace. Loquacious and colourful in their festive best, they had come to witness the climax of the month-long celebrations. Caps were knocked awry and elaborate head-ties came to grief as the tightly packed throng combined a sly jockeying for position with the movements of the dance. Keeping perfect time with the music, they craned for a glimpse of their sovereign, whom they saw only during the three great festivals.

The earthly representative of the god Shango sat enthroned on velvet in an open-sided pavilion decked with scarlet hangings; at his feet were spread the finest mats; above his head, a pointed gable, supported on wrought brass pillars tied with purple and shining bright as new-minted gold. His face, on which it would have been sacrilege to gaze, was veiled by the fringe of a tall beaded crown, and over layered silken robes he wore a necklace of coral reaching to the knee. In his right hand he held a beaded sceptre and in his left a cow-tail whisk of spotless white.

His favourite wives formed a screen round him, and the most favoured of all held a small silk parasol above his head. Three hundred of the royal bodyguard stood at the entrance to the pavilion. Grouped opposite them, the court musicians, two hundred strong, provided a fitting accompaniment to the closing ceremonies.

A wide avenue had been cleared in the centre of the courtyard, shaded on either side by four rows of state umbrellas. Seated on the right, on long wooden benches, were the crown prince and members of the royal family, the principal eunuchs and other senior officials of the palace. And on the left sat the junior eunuchs, the king's sheriffs and members of the nobility. All eyes were on the seven state councillors in the centre of the avenue as they performed the elaborate steps of a traditional dance with precision and practised grace prior to paying homage to the king.

Feigning faintness, Princess Boladé left her place beneath the umbrellas and, signing to her maid, Sadia, to follow her, she slipped quietly away. She was soon settled on a couch in her private chamber, having exchanged her elaborate wrappers for a simple cloth, and refreshed her face and neck and henna-painted hands and feet with cool, scented water.

Sadia reached under the couch and drew out a small talking drum and drumstick.

Where shall I begin, madam? She beat the words softly on the drum.

'From the beginning.' Princess Boladé lay back and closed her eyes, remembering how the Hausa merchant, in trying to draw her attention to his more expensive merchandise, had achieved the opposite. Princess, he'd insisted, you should not take that one. The child, dumb since birth, was a lyre without a string, he'd said, fit only for firewood.

Within weeks, her new purchase had begun to speak, tapping out simple sentences, having been taught that the Oyo language could be rendered as precisely on the talking drum as by the spoken word. Recognising that the child possessed a considerable intelligence, the princess had at once apprenticed her to a master drummer a good distance from Oyo. The Hausa merchant had lied, of course. Sadia's

42

condition was the result of a childhood illness; now the sounds she had once heard long ago came to her as vibrations, passing through her body like the wind through leaves. She had soon learned to interpret them. She was not totally deaf. She was truly dumb, though, trapped in silence, and might have continued so for ever had she not become drummer as well as drum. It was a secret shared only with her mistress and her teacher. Her disability made her sacred to Obatala, the maker god, allowing her to come and go throughout the city as she pleased. And as her mistress pleased also.

As Sadia continued beating the drum, the princess began to concentrate minutely, constantly interrupting the flow to check or clarify some detail. At the narration's end, she nodded, satisfied. Then, changing into another set of magnificent wrappers, the princess headed swiftly out again.

Idling through the market, Lady Faloyan paused in front of a stall offering bean cakes simmering in smoking palm oil, roasted corncobs and long skewers of suya, a peppered beef delicacy from the north, grilling on a charcoal brazier, before passing on as if unable to decide. The stall keeper merely shrugged and rolled her eyes; there was no lack of custom during the festival.

In the centre of the market where the crowds were thickest, as if by accident, Lady Faloyan came upon Princess Boladé and her maid, both ostensibly examining bolts of cloth, pinching the material of first one and then another between thumb and forefinger. The princess indicated by a slight movement of her hand that a cursory acknowledgement would suffice and so Lady Faloyan merely dipped a knee in greeting. They attracted little notice, although ordinarily the princess's facial scars and the broad ribbon marks of royalty along the length of her arms would have secured immediate and fawning attention.

'Greetings, my daughter. I trust your son is none the worse for his adventure?' the princess enquired, her voice all tenderness.

Lady Faloyan replied in the same high Oyo of the court, impenetrable to the people around them.

'Life can leave the body of a sick child quicker than an arrow from a bow, but if that child survives, he mends faster and comes back stronger than weeds on the farm. I thank you, my mother.'

'What reason will your other son give for refusing the offer of a household of his own in the Lord Gaha's new fief town? When the Lord

Gaha succeeds his uncle, as he surely will, and becomes Bashorun, the overlordship would then be the Lord Olufemi's for the taking, and, who knows, the town might one day merit a king.'

Lady Faloyan glanced at the princess's maid. The girl gave one of her idiot smiles in response. Reassured, Lady Faloyan said, 'The new fief town would almost certainly merit a king, my mother. It stands at the head of the caravan trail to the coast and if the trade with the skinless ones continues to expand at its current rate . . .' she gestured eloquently with her hands. 'But, king or not, the overlord of the town would still be the lackey of Oyo . . .'

'I understand the position as well as you, my daughter.' Princess Boladé's voice was a knife drawn across the skin.

Lady Faloyan became still.

The princess resumed. 'A son of the Agbakin, however talented, cannot aspire to control of the empire unless, of course, he is prepared to become a eunuch and enter the service of the Alafin. But he *can* aspire to his father's title, and the Lord Gaha's offer would put Lord Olufemi's feet firmly on the way to realising that ambition. In addition to his other attributes, he would have men and means, making him even more likely to be chosen as his father's successor when the time comes. How then will he explain his refusal?'

'He will say that he has already accepted just such an offer, and, having given his word, cannot now withdraw.'

'Is this true?' the princess asked.

'It will be, as of this afternoon, my mother.' Lady Faloyan kept her lids decorously lowered.

The princess's slanted eyes studied her. At length she said, 'It will suffice. But you would do well to keep always in the forefront of your mind that, however early you go to the forest, you will find the trees already there.'

Lady Faloyan looked up involuntarily. The princess's expression was unreadable.

The celebrations continued throughout the night and at cock-crow groups of rowdy young warriors, reluctant to bring the festivities to an end, were still carousing in the streets. A young man appeared unannounced at the gate of the chief eunuch's compound, evidently drunk. Following a noisy altercation and an undignified scuffle, the guards succeeded with some difficulty in restraining him while word of his arrival was sent and permission to admit him granted. A quarrelsome journey across the outer courtyards and winding maze of corridors brought him at last into the master's presence.

'Water! Before anything else, water.' Lord Gaha stumbled into the room, laughing, both hands held to his head.

The room was sumptuously furnished with exquisite wall hangings and mats and carved stools and couches strewn with soft skins. Large as an elephant, the chief eunuch, draped in a simple toga, one voluminous shoulder bare, dismissed the three slaves needed to escort his visitor. With a wave of his long-handled fan, he commanded the servant standing beside him to pour some water and, after first prostrating himself on the ground, the young man moved towards the water jar.

Part of the chief eunuch's vast bulk rippled over the edge of the low couch as he peered at the new arrival.

'So?' he observed.

Lord Gaha bowed and pulled up a stool, glancing pointedly at the servant.

'Ah, my new remembrancer.' The chief eunuch tapped the servant lightly with his fan. 'Purchased for an inordinate sum and after much persuasion. There is not another like him in the whole of the empire, believe me. He has over two thousand proverbs in his repertoire. His former master felt his loss so keenly, he immediately offered to buy him back, but sadly the price was no longer within his reach.'

'Now I remember – it was said that he had been sold at the coast, and was no longer in Oyo.' Lord Gaha snapped his fingers as he absorbed the implications.

'Quite so.' The chief eunuch's neck rolls quivered in silent mirth. 'You may continue; he is privy to all.'

Lord Gaha searched the face of the remembrancer, who remained impassive under his scrutiny. Then, dropping all pretence of drunkenness, the young warrior turned to the chief eunuch.

'The crown prince will be remembered for this night, and not with love. He and his followers have laid waste to half the city. The high court will be in permanent session for the next few weeks, dealing with claims for compensation. Not a few lives were lost in the brawls.'

'Unfortunate.' The chief eunuch studied a manicured fingernail. 'We must hope that on this occasion the king will enforce his authority. The citizens of Oyo are becoming increasingly intolerant of the excesses of the crown prince, for which they blame the father.' He shook his head in mock sorrow, 'They have begun to ask how a king who cannot govern his son can govern his people. In addition, the king has roused the ire of the Shango priests by experimenting with the electrical properties of the sun leaf. They say that, instead of appeasing the gods, he appears to be challenging their power, which will result in disaster. The way is being paved, it seems, for the rejection of both father and son.' It was the custom in Oyo that if the king were rejected by the people he must die, and the crown prince with him.

Lord Gaha laughed aloud. 'When the time comes, they will fall from the tree as easily as ripe fruit.'

'So far so good.' The chief eunuch signed to his remembrancer to refill his cup, and invited Lord Gaha to join him. Lord Gaha declined. 'When do you leave?' the chief eunuch asked.

'Before midday. After I have called upon the crown prince and perhaps on the Princess Boladé.'

'Princess Boladé?' The chief eunuch pursed plump lips in surprise.

'I have a mind to make an offer for her maid.'

'You *are* prodigal. First you make an offer to the Agbakin's son, then another to the Asipa for his daughter.' The chief eunuch sipped his palm wine.

'On the contrary,' Lord Gaha replied. 'I have twice been refused. A sojourn in a forgotten outpost of the empire is not, I imagine, what the Lady Faloyan had in mind for her first-born son. And, in declining my proposal, the Asipa has been forced to reveal that his daughter is promised to the Prince Labisi. At no expense to ourselves, we have our enemies on the run.'

'And the maid?'

Belatedly, Lord Gaha realised he was being teased. Dryly he said, 'What is more appealing than a woman who cannot speak?'

'So that is the reason you have been summoning her at every opportunity to carry presents to the princess.'

Lord Gaha flushed. 'The girl is beautiful, I admit, but I did not *summon* her. She is always there, charmingly, like a flower growing unexpectedly by the wayside.'

'On the beauty of women, I am not qualified to give an opinion.' The chief eunuch eyed with distaste an errant fly that had landed on his couch. 'But the suitability of princes is another matter entirely.' He swatted the fly. 'If the high priest is to be believed,' he said, as Lord Gaha rose to leave, 'the message from the gods was not entirely favourable. It may be that the naming of Prince Labisi is no more than a handful of sand thrown in our eyes.'

~

8

MODUPÉ CHARGED ACROSS the sunlit courtyards of the women's quarters, calling Oluremi's name at the top of her voice and arriving somewhat breathless on the verandah outside Lady Monifa's apartments.

'You are calling in vain. She's not here.' Alero sat cross-legged on a mat at the entrance, almost invisible in the shade of the overhanging roof.

Modupé took a startled step backwards, her eyes adjusting to the darkness after the brilliance outside. 'I did not see you, Auntie. Please, where is she? Has she gone far?'

The maid shrugged, enjoying her distress. Modupé rarely let it pass that Alero was in pawn and unlikely to be redeemed.

'She promised, she promised.' Modupé's wailing had drawn a small audience, who looked on, amused. It was no secret that Oluremi was helping her prepare for her bridal outing and time was running short.

'Eh.' Alero clicked her tongue. 'Life is not fair.'

Modupé buried her face in the loose end of her wrapper, bemoaning her fate louder than ever.

'Modupé! Why so much noise?' Lady Monifa rounded the corner, followed by Oluremi.

Alero and Modupé scrambled to their knees, elbows on the ground.

'Has someone died?' Lady Monifa demanded, looking around.

Embarrassed now that she saw Oluremi, Modupé did not reply.

'Answer me.' Lady Monifa turned her palms over, exasperated.

'I could not find Oluremi,' mumbled Modupé, dabbing at her eyes.

'Before you started your shouting, you could have asked Auntie here and then you would have discovered that your cousin, who is not one to break her promises, had not gone far. Is that not so, Auntie?'

Auntie maintained a judicious silence.

'I did ask, my mother,' protested the girl, glaring accusingly at Alero. Modupé was not popular but it had always to be remembered that her

47

father was brother to Lord Asipa and next in seniority in the compound.

'Madam,' Alero said, 'you know I have these holes in my head and sometimes things fall out.'

Alero was not to blame, Lady Monifa, declared, dismissing the crowd amid laughter. Auntie might not be clever, but she was smart.

Anticipating the onset of another of her headaches, Lady Monifa waved the two girls away and bid Alero stay and massage her temples.

'Where were you?' Modupé demanded.

Oluremi smiled placatingly, 'Your mother wanted mine to come and admire your bridal finery and also to advise. My mother insisted I accompany her because she knew yours would break down and cry otherwise.'

Modupé dabbed at her eyes again. 'I have cried rivers already, and I shall cry many more before I'm finished.'

Oluremi put an arm round her waist. 'It won't be so bad.'

'Yes, it will.' Modupé's voice rose to a wail. 'What could be worse than to leave your home, your family and all your friends to go and live among strangers? To be junior to everyone else, at the beck and call of people who will certainly hate you, and to be forced to treat even the smallest boys with respect? There is no unhappier plight in the whole world than that of a new bride.'

'Hush,' Oluremi admonished her. 'Imagine, you could be like Auntie Alero, with no husband and no children.'

Modupé brightened. 'That's my one comfort: I shall not be falling over *her* everywhere I go. Come.' She grasped Oluremi's hand and, eschewing the coolness of the verandahs, the two of them made off quickly in the direction Modupé had come. All was tranquil once more in the afternoon heat and even the laughing doves sheltering in the thick shade of the almond trees were silent. Modupé kept a tight grip on Oluremi's hand and did not release her until they had reached the herb garden, its wild green profusion in riotous contrast to the neat swept sand of the other courtyards. They settled themselves in the furthest corner behind a screen of bushes. Everyone knew that Oluremi was helping her cousin rehearse her bridal chant, but they were not aware that Modupé was also being coached by an old auntie from Lady Faloyan's compound whose praise songs could put even the professionals to shame.

Modupé sighed. 'I can't think why they call it the bride's enjoyment. Bride's ordeal would be nearer the mark.'

Oluremi nodded in commiseration. The bride's lament as she was paraded around town was as much a part of the display as the magnificence of her wrappers and the quality and quantity of her jewels. Long and complex passages of the bride's family history – both her father's and her maternal grandparents' exploits and accomplishments – would show diligence; copious reflections on marriage and the expression of a proper filial gratitude would show maturity; a becoming reluctance to enter the married state, combined with a modest pride in the bride's impending fulfilment as a woman, would show presence of mind.

It was no wonder, Oluremi thought, that Modupé was nervous. No doubt she would be too when she reached fifteen and her turn came.

'Come here,' she smiled. Modupé laid her head on her shoulder and Oluremi patted her encouragingly. They had shared the same sleeping mat every night since they were eight and nine years old. Oluremi, probably because of her training, had always felt like the older one. Might as well try to train a moth away from a flame, Lady Faloyan had replied caustically, when Oluremi suggested that perhaps her cousin might join in her lessons. It was certainly true that Modupé hated to apply herself, which was no doubt the reason the auntie had decided that the chorus should play a large role.

'Imagine,' Oluremi said, 'you'll be the centre of attention. How often does that happen? This is your one opportunity to show who you really are.'

Modupé sat up. 'I shall remind you of that in a year's time.'

Oluremi's face clouded. Next year when she married Prince Labisi she would be exiled not only from her home compound but from her home city.

The old auntie arrived just as the afternoon heat was subsiding. She was leaning on the arm of Princess Boladé's maid.

'Alafia, Ma.' The girls knelt in greeting, exchanging surprised glances.

'Peace be with you, my daughters,' the old woman responded in a voice like the pealing of a silver bell. 'My legs were giving me trouble today and I mislaid my stick, but I could not call on anybody for help because I did not want them to know where I was going. So it was a lucky thing I found this one to lean on instead.' She patted Sadia's arm affectionately with her fan. 'She cannot be of much use to her mistress, deaf as she is, and wandering off everywhere as she does, but to the rest of us, I must say, it is frequently a blessing to find her underfoot. Princess

49

Boladé is a charitable woman to keep such a one, admirable.' Auntie waved her fan imperiously, 'Now, help me down, all of you.'

They spread a wrapper and gently lowered her to the ground with her back resting against a low wall. She closed her eyes and gave the signal to start. Sadia knelt nearby and, under her serene gaze, tentatively at first, Modupé began her chant. Her small voice was enhanced by Oluremi's accompaniment like a jewel presented on velvet. The old lady ordered a second recitation and when it was finished took her time. They waited in silence for her verdict. At last she opened her eyes.

'We will have no cause for shame.'

Modupé squealed with relief.

Oluremi, trained by Lady Faloyan, let her breath out soundlessly.

Departing as she had come, on Sadia's arm, Auntie threw over her shoulder casually that the crown prince was to be in the audience. She smiled at Modupé. 'You are greatly honoured.'

Too much so, Oluremi thought.

> *'I took my calabash and went to Oyo town*
> *The prince of Oyo took the calabash from my head.*
> *I said, Sir, why did you do that?*
> *He said it's because I am a slender beauty*
> *I have a neck worthy to wear blue Segi beads*
> *May good luck attend me today.'*

Modupé looked magnificent and she knew it: decked in shimmering foreign silks with ribbons of gold and coral wound round her head and neck, falling in bright loops to her waist. None of the other half-dozen bridal processions making their tours of the city had attracted anything like the same following. In front of her a distinguished audience, come to honour a relative of Princess Boladé, looked on from the deep-shaded comfort of the verandah by the main entrance to the compound. Her performance had been near faultless and she paused triumphantly to acknowledge their applause before turning to the spectators crowded into the adjoining market square, most of whom had followed her from the gates of her father's house to the heart of the royal quarter. Younger and less discerning, they were considerably more vociferous in their enthusiasm.

She resumed her song with no trace of nervousness:

'I am going to my new home now
I am going to my new home to have wealth
I am going to my new home now
I am going to my home to bear children
If you say your good luck will escort me
It will escort me to my room
May good luck attend me today.'

Oluremi's voice soared, leading the chorus:

'On this day, do not forget us
My dear playmate
My dear playmate, do not forget us
May good luck attend me today.'

Modupé turned towards her friends; she was leaving her girlhood behind her; she wished the afternoon would go on for ever.

'How could I forget you?
What you and I said to each other
Was not said to be forgotten
My companion, how could I forget you?
May good luck attend me today.'

Oluremi stretched out her hands.

'We call the spirits of the dead, the spirits of the dead do not listen
We call the gods, the gods pay no attention,
When we call you
My playmate, you do not respond.
May good luck attend me today.'

Under cover of renewed applause, Princess Boladé leaned towards Lady Faloyan. 'I had grave doubts about the child, but she has acquitted herself well. I am grateful to you, my daughter, for your intervention.'

'It seemed a sensible precaution, my mother,' Lady Faloyan replied. It would not surprise her to discover one day that even the geckos reported back to the princess. She shifted her position as if to obtain a better view of the performers, for she had caught a glimpse of her younger son who, according to the messenger, should still have been on the road.

Abiola was eighteen and a leader in the vanguard. He had spent much of the preceding rainy season as part of his brother's household at Ogodo, attending to the family's business interests. Lord Olufemi, under whose direction Abiola had found himself, had proved no less exacting than their mother or the hunter Lakoja. It had been a testing period, and he was glad to leave it behind and to be back in Oyo once more with his two lieutenants at his side.

He was jubilant, too, on account of the magnificent string of horses he had brought back with him. This purchase would refute once and for all his brother's opinion that he had not one entrepreneurial bone in his body. He had been obliged to take personal delivery of his new acquisitions, the reason ostensibly for his arrival in Oyo earlier than planned. He laughed aloud, thinking of his mother, who was bound to have seen him. The Lady Faloyan would have spotted the one ant lacking a feeler among a host of a thousand, and he was as conspicuous as an araba tree towering above all the others in the forest.

Finding the real cause of his early homecoming standing next to his cousin in the midst of the chorus, looking at him out of the corner of her eyes, Abiola quickly ceased laughing and took to sighing to show how much he had missed her these many months.

His left hand, almost as tall as Abiola, and not to be outdone, sighed even more exaggeratedly. 'Modupé is beautiful. I had not realised it until now.'

His right hand, short in comparison, and sensitive on the point, pushed in front of them. 'Modupé is enhanced by her setting. The prize, my brother, is your little cousin. Prince Labisi is the luckiest man alive.' He made a soulful face at Abiola.

'I agree, my cousin's well enough,' Abiola laughed. 'But she is like a sister to me. My choice would be the one standing just beside her.'

'Ah well, as we cannot choose whom we marry, the trick, surely, is to find beauty in them all. Like that, we avoid disappointment and yearning for what cannot be.'

'A man without disappointment is a man without dreams.' Abiola wagged a finger in mock sorrow at his lieutenant, 'I pity you.'

'And I shall feel sorry for you later.'

' "The eyes will not see a beautiful woman without saluting her." ' A new voice, immediately behind them, quoted softly, cutting short their laughter. 'But experience teaches us,' it continued, mournfully, 'that, once the eyes become accustomed, she becomes like any other. Incidentally,' the tone became conversational, 'I expect you all at the practice ground tomorrow, ready to begin at first light.' The voice belonged to Lord Olufemi, who, it was supposed, was two days' march away from Oyo.

Abiola reacted not at all, but his lieutenants jerked round in surprise and, failing to locate the speaker, turned back again, clearly doubting the evidence of their ears.

'As well search for a single mite in the roof thatch,' Abiola remarked. It was typical of his brother, he thought, to inform him in this way of his succession to a junior captaincy in the cavalry.

Inspired by her audience and the occasion, Modupé sang beyond herself, leaping the barriers of her small talent.

> *A certain river, a certain river*
> *In the middle of the forest,*

She turned to the audience seated on the verandah.

> *People at the front must not go there*

She turned to those in the square.

> *People at the back must not go there*

And to them all.

> *But I went there and splashed my face*
> *My face became the face of lovely youth*
> *My waist became a waist adorned with beads*
> *Beads which if you count them and they're not complete*
> *I say you should strip me and take my clothes away.*

She was beautiful; she was a virgin; they should bear witness to this moment of perfection that would soon be lost for ever.

The chorus joined their voices with hers:

> *May good luck attend me today.*

Flushed with success and plied with gifts of precious cloths and beads and sumptuously decorated calabashes, Modupé and her bridal chorus departed, laughing and giggling, to make a triumphal return to her father's compound. A large group of faithful admirers accompanied them, clapping and dancing through the crowded streets as the sky reddened and the evening darkness approached.

Lord Gaha, in the train of the crown prince, knelt in parting before Lady Faloyan. Her niece Oluremi, he said, was a gift fit for a king.

Kneeling in response, Lady Faloyan kept her eyes correctly lowered. 'Her father, the Lord Asipa, made a promise long ago to the father of her betrothed . . .' Lady Faloyan paused eloquently. 'A deathbed promise is not to be broken.' (It was true, at least, that the Asipa and the father of Prince Labisi had been warriors together when they were young.)

'Nor is a fate lightly altered,' Lord Gaha returned agreeably. As always, his words were not without a certain menace. 'You are to be congratulated also, I believe, on the Lord Olufemi's elevation to a captaincy in the cavalry. An Esho title is the aspiration of every young man in the empire, and so few succeed. The house of the Agbakin will have much to celebrate when he and his brother arrive in Oyo.'

Lady Faloyan, who had seen the exchange between her two sons in the crowd of spectators, continued impassive. 'I pray for their safe arrival,' she said.

'Alafia, my sister.'

'Peace be with you, my brother.'

They bowed to each other under the watchful gaze of Princess Boladé.

❧

9

A DUST CLOUD and the thunder of hooves swept across the open plain towards the river where, on the soft ground at the water's edge, noise and dust evaporated to reveal a group of horsemen bent low, racing each other along the winding course of the river beneath the trees.

Abiola resigned himself to being outrun. With the possible exception of Lord Gaha there was none to equal him as a horseman. But in a race, his height and weight put him at a disadvantage. As he dug his heels into the flanks of the raw-boned black, he thought with envy of its sire, seventeen hand-spans at the shoulder, imported from Iberia, the land of the white men, beyond the northern deserts and the sea.

He remembered the story with which his manservant Juma had frightened him as a child. It was said that, in the time of the Alafin Obalokun, eight hundred messengers were sent with presents to the king of the white men's country. They never returned. But afterwards the sound of bells ringing in the skies was plainly heard in the Akésan market. It was the voices of the unfortunates speaking to them from the other world to tell of their fate. Abiola smiled in recollection of his childish self. He hadn't wanted to leave the security of his nursemaid's care for that of a male Nupé slave. Lakoja had insisted upon it. At the time, Abiola had taken it as further punishment for deserting his post to chase after the leopard cubs. He was glad of it now though, for there was no denying that his superior horsemanship and skill with a sword were the result of Juma's strict tutoring; the old man could still outdo him on occasion. And without a doubt, Juma had been yet another shield against the enemies of the house of the Agbakin. He was grateful for that too.

An arrow whistled past and knocked off his cap, erasing the smile from his face, and, with it, all thought. The bellbird's danger signal issued piercingly from his throat as he raked his horse on to its hind legs, stopping it in mid-gallop. He leapt to the ground and backed up swiftly against a tree, gentling the frightened animal with his voice and positioning it as a shield in front of him. The horse stilled; he waited, reins firmly in one hand, his throwing spears in the other.

His companions had wheeled instantly in response to his call, each one turning on a leaf. They needed no direction. Arrows were raining on them now, as they galloped back, slung on the sides of their saddles, clinging to the pommels, feet braced against the stirrups, out of sight. It was as it had always been, whether as small boys in the hunt, or in this past season on the battlefield. They formed a circle, backs to the tree, horses in front of them, lances at the ready.

The arrows ceased. Were the horses the targets, not the riders?

'An appropriate proverb does not immediately spring to mind, though I don't doubt there is one,' Abiola's right hand joked.

'Save your tongue,' Abiola hissed, furious with himself at their predicament, which might yet cost them their lives. They had left their swords behind. Impossible to calculate who their assailants were or how many. Who could have known where . . . ? A sudden intuition made him look up. In the same moment, armed men dropped like fruit from the branches of the tree, cynically mimicking the frenzied chatter of frightened monkeys. Some of their face markings, Abiola realised, were identical to his own. Landing astride the ring of horses, they severed the reins in one continuous movement and raced away. Olufemi!

Abiola dashed his spear into the ground and dragged it out again, on the run. The others followed in silence, goaded by the mocking calls of the bellbird as the horsemen jeered their warnings of danger. Rage lent the runners speed and the firm ground was in their favour as the riders, hampered by shortened reins, veered away from the river towards the open plain, making for home. Then the runners saw a second company of horsemen ride down upon the first, swords flashing in the sunlight. This was no game. Two of Lord Olufemi's followers soon lay writhing on the ground. Abiola was within throwing distance. Drawing back his arm, he hurled his spear. He shook out his whip, snaked it round the saddle pommel of a riderless horse and, hauling himself up, managed to vault into the saddle. His lieutenants followed his example: they plunged into the thick of the fight, brandishing swords retrieved from the fallen. The rest of Abiola's troupe circled at a distance, hurling their javelins until they too had procured themselves horses and could launch into the fray.

Hacking his way towards Olufemi, who was fighting for his life in the centre of a ring of attackers, Abiola stabbed upwards with the handle of his whip, snapping the neck of one of the assailants. His right and left hands felled two more. But yet more men pressed in on Olufemi; clearly he was the one they wanted to kill.

Venting the anger they felt at their recent humiliation, Abiola and his men fought with the ferocity and persistence of a pack of hyenas and would have pursued and killed every last one of the attackers had not his brother called halt.

'Let them go,' he commanded, staunching a cut above his eye. 'Hired assassins; in due course they will lead us to their paymaster.'

'Who is he?' Abiola asked, and immediately felt foolish. Even if he knew the identity of the enemy, his brother was unlikely to tell him in front of witnesses, however loyal.

'I thank you all for your aid in routing the horse thieves,' said Lord Olufemi, wiping his sword. They digested his words in silence. He smiled dryly. 'On our return, I shall make a sacrifice to Ogun and I invite you all to join me in a feast tonight.'

'Horse thieves, eh?' the chief eunuch tittered, raising himself on one dimpled elbow, his dark perfumed flesh overflowing the sides of his couch. Lord Gaha, seated on a low stool at his side, did not answer. He remained with his head thrown back in seemingly rapt appreciation of the star-studded blackness above the little courtyard that was his host's innermost sanctum.

The chief eunuch's fan chopped back and forth, mirroring his annoyance. He was in no mood to admire the beauty of the night.

Lord Gaha removed his gaze from the sky. 'It was a ruse merely to distract attention.'

'A wasted opportunity, in my opinion. It is said that the Lord Abiola, the hunter Lakoja's most valued pupil, is able to search out the Dahomeans in the fastnesses of their home forests as easily as a boy raiding nests for eggs. In consequence, his brother, the Lord Olufemi, the most junior captain of the cavalry, has become the commander with the highest tally of war captives. Any move against those two, now that they have made a name for themselves, will not be interpreted as accidental.' The chief eunuch's neck rolls glistened. He held out his cup, and his remembrancer, stepping out of the shadows behind his master, quickly filled it. The servant looked enquiringly at Lord Gaha, who shook his head.

Brushing an imaginary speck from his embroidered robe, Lord Gaha glanced sideways at the chief eunuch. 'I believe the crown prince has on several occasions now brought the Lord Asipa's daughter, Oluremi, to his father's attention.'

'Did the Alafin like what he saw?

'Oh indeed. And heard. She would put a lark to shame.' Lord Gaha fixed his gaze on the sky once more. There was an air of triumph about him.

The chief eunuch, his mind working, waited attentively. He sipped his rum, rolling the liquid round his mouth, patience incarnate. The silence lengthened.

At last he said, 'The Alafin interests himself in everything save government. Art, music, experiments with magic, they all take precedence over the business of the state, which he will neither tackle nor relinquish. The result – stagnation.'

'What is more important than art and music and magic?' asked Lord Gaha. 'The Alafin's interests attract the very best talents to Oyo. Our poets and musicians, wood carvers, weavers, leather workers, silver-smiths, brass casters are second to none. Is the Sekéré drum not vastly improved by the Iyun, Okun, Erinla and Segi beads now ornamenting it? And what other king can boast of seven silver doors to the seven entrances of his sleeping apartment? Such things make Oyo the wonder of the world, do they not?'

'You jest, my son. The Alafin may be blind, but there are others with eyes to see. We have built a great empire and now it must be maintained. Without an effective system of administration, the entire edifice will tumble about our ears. A greater portion of the wealth and revenues accruing from our conquests should be channelled towards creating and sustaining that system. The solution is simple enough. Instead of being sold, war captives must be incorporated into the service of the Alafin, their loyalty secured by a bigger share in the distribution of luxury goods coming into the city.'

Lord Gaha cracked his fingers, 'My uncle, the Lord Bashorun, and the others on the state council will see any expansion of the palace staff as an increase in the centralisation of power on the part of the Alafin and they will resist it . . .'

'Ah, but consider, my lord, when *you* are Bashorun . . .'

'Furthermore,' Lord Gaha continued, 'the state council controls the army.'

'But you, as Bashorun, will be commander in chief of that army. There have been times in the history of Oyo,' the chief eunuch continued softly, 'when the political and the military were so closely connected as to be synonymous, and the Bashorun more powerful than the Alafin himself – as in the time of your illustrious father.'

Their eyes locked, each trying to read the other.

Lord Gaha was the first to look away. He reached for the cup at his side and proffered it to the remembrancer to be filled. 'I will drink now.' He drained the contents at a gulp and held out his cup again.

The chief eunuch observed him, lips pursed. 'The rum is excellent, is it not? Carried from the coast two days ago.'

'The skinless ones,' said Lord Gaha, wiping his smooth shaved head with a spotless white cloth, 'possess certain refinements despite their uncouth behaviour. Riding escort with the slave caravans, I have had ample occasion to witness this first-hand.'

'It has not been my fate to encounter any one of them. They are not well made, by all accounts.'

'All the workings of their bodies may be seen clearly as through water, and the majority are black toothed and hairy as monkeys. They –'

'No more, I beg!' The chief eunuch, a mountain of smooth silken flesh, shuddered fastidiously.

Laughing, Lord Gaha knelt to take his leave. The chief eunuch inclined his head, but his smile did not reach his eyes. He murmured, 'So, what now?'

'I believe you know that, sir, as well as I.' Still laughing, Lord Gaha quit the courtyard.

Upon receiving the request from the Alafin for his daughter, her father, Lord Asipa, had hurried to the Agbakin's compound. The latter, with equal haste, had summoned his wife.

'Oluremi's betrothal to the Prince Labisi must be set aside. There is no help for it. We have been outmanoeuvred,' he told her, pacing his sleeping chamber as was his habit when agitated.

Lady Faloyan, already apprised of the situation by a messenger from the Princess Boladé, did not betray her prior knowledge nor did she remind her husband of her repeated warnings. This had all the marks of Lord Gaha. *Your niece Oluremi is a gift fit for a king*, he'd told her. She saw it clearly now: they had been guarding the wrong gate.

Remaining calm, she said, 'All is not lost. By his own actions, and those of the crown prince, the Alafin is paving the way to his rejection by the people, whose patience, as we all know, is very nearly at an end. In due time this Alafin will go, and the Prince Labisi will be elected to the throne. He will inherit Oluremi as one of his wives and our plans will be once again on course.'

Reassured, Lord Agbakin departed to congratulate Lord Asipa publicly on his good fortune.

Lady Faloyan did not have the same success with her sister. Lady Monifa was inconsolable at the prospect of parting with her only daughter to a king who was rapidly losing the support of his own people. As the day approached – so much sooner than she had expected – she ceased crying at intervals and took to sobbing continuously, causing her sister to observe that it was a pity this had been a year of plentiful rain otherwise she could have been put to use watering the fields, along with her maid Alero. The end of Alero's wrapper was permanently damp from mopping her eyes. You would have thought that she was the one about to be married. It was true she was torn: glad to be going with her young mistress, broken hearted not to be staying in the family courtyard. But mostly Alero was afraid. It was said that the palace was a city within the city, but from what she had heard it was another country entirely, full of mystery, betrayals and dark doings. Many who entered did not come out alive.

Oluremi was frightened, too, but years of training ensured there was no crying on her part. She was aware that she was simply a counter being moved in a murderous game that had begun before she was even born. A dangerous precedent had been set in the time of Bashorun Yamba, who had usurped all power to himself and shown that the sovereign was not invincible. Although resentful, the royal families and noble houses had been powerless to do anything about it. After his death normality was resumed, but the damage had been done. Henceforth the noble houses were forever seeking to position themselves at the centre of power, and the plot hatched by Princess Boladé and the hunter Lakoja was just such a strategy. All the same, Oluremi thought, they hadn't reckoned with the emergence of Yamba's son. Now she would have to be her own pathfinder inside the palace, but she had been preparing all her life and the game was far from lost.

Dry-eyed, her head held high, Oluremi entered the main courtyard decked in her bridal clothes, perfumed with camwood, hands and feet painted with henna, attended by her train of women. Oil lights burned at intervals on the surrounding verandahs, casting a glow on the familiar faces of her family and assembled household. In the silence that greeted her arrival, she walked resolutely forward to be met by Abiola and the three other male cousins who would be among her escort to the palace. They stood beside her as she knelt in front of her father. Lord Asipa placed both hands on her bowed head and in a voice that all could hear gave her his blessing.

'May God go with you, my daughter; may God bless your household. No evil will happen to your husband; you will bear both sons and daughters, and will live to give your daughters in marriage and see your sons married.'

Oluremi knelt next before her mother, who repeated falteringly the words just uttered by her husband. Lady Faloyan, seated immediately behind her sister, signed to Abiola with her eyes. Placing a steadying hand beneath his cousin's elbow, he helped her to her feet while attendants positioned her white veil so that it covered her face. At his signal, the drummers struck up. Singing, clapping and dancing, the bridal party swept through the big wooden gates of the compound.

'Abiola, don't you wish sometimes you were a simple farmer?' Oluremi asked, free for the moment to speak openly as even the most adroit of eavesdroppers would have been defeated by the din of her father's drummers as their procession wound its way through the crowded city streets.

'No,' he replied. 'That's your fear talking. Don't try to run away from it. Lakoja the hunter teaches us that fear opens our eyes more fully to danger. If fear is our familiar, it cannot be our master. Do you remember the game we used to play? Picturing yourself in a situation so terrible it made the one you were in seem nothing by comparison?' Oluremi nodded. 'Imagine that you are looking into the eye of a leopard.'

'It won't be a leopard's eye I conjure up,' she said, laughing, 'but another, equally effective.'

'More so,' Abiola agreed, picturing his mother as their laughter died. He searched for more words to offer the comfort that Oluremi had given him in his loneliness and isolation following his disgrace on the day of the hunt. It had been the start of their own closeness, quite separate from the ties of family: a closeness which in the seven intervening years had increased year by year. She was the first person he'd told when he was made a leader of the youths and again when he was promoted to leader of the van. And it was to him alone that she had confided how much she missed her cousin Modupé, married into another compound and lost to her. And now on her own marriage she would be stepping into danger as great as any he had so far faced in war, and with the same uncertain outcome. He was afraid for her.

At last he said, 'We are linked, you and I. It seems that at the moment of our birth we chose the same fate. So this parting of the ways is not for ever but only for a while.' Words he hoped would help her through the darkness.

Oluremi pressed his hand, and he knew that he'd succeeded. He sent a fervent prayer to Ogun, god of war and god of iron, who opens up the way.

Abiola held her hand until they reached the palace gates where the bridal procession was welcomed by the eunuch of the left at the head of a small delegation of titled ladies and junior wives. The formalities of greeting completed, they followed his back, narrow as a whip, across the vastness of the public courtyard to the entrance of the visitors' courtyard.

Here they were greeted by a second delegation accompanied by slaves carrying bowls of scented water for the ceremonial washing of the bride's feet before she could be carried over the threshold of her new home. Inside the well-lit courtyard they found the familiar figure of Princess Boladé's husband, chief of the official fathers of the king, waiting to receive them in the presence of the sovereign's official mother. Oluremi knelt with the other women, placing her elbows on the floor, and Abiola prostrated himself with the rest of the male escort before delivering the traditional message from the bride's father.

Lord Asipa sent his compliments and his heartfelt prayer that his daughter might be delivered of nine, nay ten, children and that she might not suffer the loss of her children nor the loss of her husband. She should not be allowed to suffer hunger and nor should she be given the freedom to go where and when she pleased. She was an inexperienced and not always tractable person, and she was not a person on whom the use of the whip was forbidden if she offended.

'Remember,' Abiola whispered in her ear as he took his leave, 'the eye of the leopard.'

The Alafin made no secret of his delight in this latest addition to his harem. The eunuch of the left was despatched in state to her father's compound accompanied by drummers and attendants and a messenger whose name signified His Majesty's pleasure carrying aloft a white calabash decorated by the hand of a master.

The king was not to be parted from his new songbird and it was noted that his enforced seclusion had never sat as lightly on him as it did now. It was no surprise. Those who had witnessed Lady Oluremi's bridal chant felt they had witnessed the sublime. Copper-skinned, long-limbed and graceful; the beauty of her voice, the exquisite sensibility of the words, moved even the most hardened observers to declare she was indeed a bride fit for a king. But they soon whispered in the palace that the sovereign was bewitched and, once ignited, the rumours ran like trails of burning oil through all the courtyards of the city.

'It will not do,' Princess Boladé said, her face an unreadable mask as usual, but Lady Faloyan thought that she detected a minute crease marring the silken surface of the voice. Such agitation on the princess's part was evidence of the extreme gravity of the situation. 'It is said,' the princess continued, 'that the Alafin has no interest in anyone except your niece. If this continues, the child will be poisoned for sure.'

Lady Faloyan's eyes flickered for an instant in the direction of the princess's beautiful deaf mute, Sadia. It was said that the princess had refused a king's ransom for her from the Lord Gaha.

'Oluremi's maid tastes every morsel first,' she said.

'And what of her mind? That too can be poisoned.'

'She is well trained.'

'Then they will try some other way. But what?' Princess Boladé brought the red tips of her fingers together.

They laid their plans throughout the afternoon, and the light had faded and lamps were burning on the night market stalls as Lady Faloyan made her way home. She found Alero waiting for her. The king's official favourite was dead. Lady Oluremi had been appointed in her place.

'What now?' Lord Agbakin demanded. 'Tell me, what now!' The calabashes containing his morning porridge and water for his hands remained untouched as he paced the length of his sleeping room. At a stroke, the trickster god Eshu had undone them.

'We will begin again.' Lady Faloyan sat unmoving on her stool by the door.

'And Oluremi?'

She did not answer him. She could not.

Lady Monifa's prayers for a long life for the Alafin went unanswered. Before the season was out, the royal palace was struck by lightning during a storm. The Alafin suffered a direct hit, leaving him paralysed on one side of his body. The Ifa priests pronounced the strike to have been caused by Shango worshippers. Under royal patronage, they had persisted in experimenting with the sun-leaf plant, which was known to have electrical properties. It was said that by ignoring the message delivered through the oracle advising them to desist, the devotees had provoked the wrath of the god. A king who was crippled could no longer carry out his duties. Here, finally was the pretext needed for his rejection. Under the constitution, there was but one course of action.

On the appointed day, the chiefs of Oyo assembled at the gates of the palace, their arrival announced by the dundun drummer stationed in the public courtyard. Headed by the Bashorun and the other six members of the state council, they passed in procession across the main courtyard to the morning courtyard, where ordinarily they came each day to pay their respects to the king. The Alafin awaited them, robed in red, his face veiled by the fringe of his tall beaded crown. As he slouched awkwardly on his throne, it was evident he had no movement on his left side. In attendance were the chief eunuch, the eunuchs of the right and left, and the other titled eunuchs to the sixth degree. The titled ladies of the palace formed a semi-circle on either side of the throne, among them Lady Oluremi, holding a red silken parasol above the sovereign's head. Two hundred senior messengers sat at His Majesty's feet.

The chiefs prostrated themselves before the throne and the Bashorun stepped forward. 'You have challenged Shango to single combat and you have been worsted. The gods reject you. The earth rejects you. We reject you.'

In his right hand, the Alafin raised the white cow-tail whisk he wore looped over his wrist and, masking his mouth, which was now pulled at the left, addressed the eunuch of the left, who relayed his master's words in a loud voice so that all should hear.

'I accept the judgement of the gods. I accept the judgement of the earth and of the people.'

After his rejection by the people, it was the custom in Oyo that by sundown on the following day the king must have taken the poisoned cup and begun his journey to join the ancestors in the next world.

It was also the custom that the lives of the Alafin's closest attendants were dependent on their master's life, for this had proved an effective measure against the risk of poisoning or the dagger of the assassin.

The Asipa's eyes were fixed on Lady Oluremi, who returned her father's look without flinching.

❧

IO

DEEP INTO THE night the Koso drum announced that the king had begun his journey to the next world. He was the Alafin, lord of the world, and companion of the gods. Custom decreed that he should not journey to the next life unattended; so, on this bright morning, preparations for those who were to accompany him had already begun.

To the beat of the leader drum, the palace gates, carved with images of the king's protective deities, swept majestically open, revealing by degrees an ordered tableau of trancelike stillness within the vast courtyard. Gradually the stillness imposed itself on the mob outside: the vicarious thrill of watching others confront mortality was usurped by a real terror as each one in the crowd involuntarily contemplated his own death.

The colossal boom of the wooden gate panels, coming to rest against the palace walls, reverberated around the square and people shoved forward, making use of their elbows, intent on securing a good position. Other drums, pounding in unison, joined their voices to the leader drum and the first of the processions surged through the gates and out into the square.

The crown prince led the four royal princes, heads angled proudly, robes swirling, dressed in purple, viridian, scarlet and gold. They swung down the main boulevard from the palace. Their relatives and friends flocked round them, eager as birds at harvest time, preceded by praise singers and drummers beating loud funeral dirges. One hundred and twenty yards wide and lined with people, the paved avenue easily accommodated all four princes and their retinues walking abreast beneath magnificent umbrellas.

Behind them strode the king's horse master and the eunuch of the left, the king's personal bodyguard. Surrounded by their entourages, their drummers and criers running ahead, they looked neither left nor right. Wrapped in their death cloths, they carried themselves as proudly as each of the royal princes. Next came the women's processions in order of precedence: the two queen mothers; the high priestesses of Ifa and Shango, three lesser priestesses of the palace and, in the last procession of all, Lady Oluremi, the king's official favourite.

As she passed, many in the crowd were visibly affected by the poignancy of her youth. Lest she should falter, they yelled encouragement above the clamour. Her fate was an honourable one, they reminded her, and the death cloth around her shoulders a coveted symbol of office, carrying with it the certainty of the same privileges in the life to come.

Oluremi's mind was elsewhere. Between waking and sleeping she had experienced another of her sightings, and her overriding concern was to recount it to Abiola.

Abiola lay sprawled on his bed in the Agbakin's compound. He had passed a sleepless night thinking of his cousin and, not used to reflection, he was now in the grip of powerful emotions which, had he been asked, he could not have named. He lay in the darkened room, shaded against the sun, with his eyelids tightly closed and his face pressed into the covers. Stopping his ears with his fingers failed to shut out the noise of the drums, and in his mind's eye was the image of a boy and girl clutching hands, round-eyed at all the pomp of other processions long passed by. He turned abruptly on to his back and stared fixedly at the ceiling. Imprinted there was the face of the small round-eyed girl, grown tall and beautiful, whose bridal train he had escorted only a short while ago. Pressing his hands over his eyes, he flung himself violently face down again only to leap up in an instant, reaching at the same time for his sword.

His body servant, Juma, who had entered as silently as a gecko, threw himself down in feigned alarm touching his forehead to the floor.

'We are not under attack,' Juma commented with the licence permitted an old slave who had known his master in his swaddling cloths. Sheepishly, Abiola put away his sword. 'Your revered mother,' Juma said, 'requests your presence as a matter of some urgency, at the house of your cousin, the late king's favourite. Your august father and your brother also wait your arrival there.'

Although unmarked by drummers, Abiola made his way effortlessly through the crowds. The opulence of his clothes, combined with his height and the width of his shoulders, was sufficient to clear him an immediate pathway. He was wearing a superb giriké, the most lavish of masculine attire: an enormous robe of iridescent peacock blue. Hitched back over his shoulders and much embroidered at the neck and breast, the strident yards of material swirled and billowed around him, revealing a white tunic over loose, embroidered trousers.

He gave the appearance of a big blue wave rolling down the boulevard, causing the superstitious to avert their eyes and finger their charms as they hurriedly removed themselves from his path, unwilling, even metaphorically, to transgress the fetish which forbade the people of Oyo to gaze upon the sea. Connoisseurs, though, remarked that the silk, from its colour, was obviously imported, before noisily directing attention to the pointed ends of his cap, turned up to display the decorative lining, and the fine-tooled sandals on his feet. Censure, appreciation and salutations alike went unrewarded. He was conscious only that the unaccustomed weight of his ceremonial dress matched the heaviness of his mind.

His progress was halted at the gates of his uncle's house by the sheer press of bodies. All who could boast of even the most tenuous connection to the favourite herself or to any member of her family had come to pay homage and show respect. There were yet others with no connection but who believed that a show of support on this occasion might secure favour in the future. The ones with no hope of entering inside were naturally the most persistent. Many had been waiting since sun-up and they stood their ground, unwilling to yield one jot of space.

Abiola was forced to ram his way into the main courtyard of Lord Asipa's compound. It was scarcely less noisy or crowded than the street outside. He pushed through to the front and his eye was immediately drawn to the pavilion jutting out into the courtyard on the opposite side. Beneath a high gable resting on four carved wooden posts, Lord Asipa was prominently displayed. In crimson robes, a gold embroidered cap on his head and a black cow-tail whisk in his hands, he sat expressionless, presiding over the ceremonies. In front of him, whirling up the dust in the unshaded centre of the courtyard drummers and singers spun the verses of their oriki-like hoops into the air, praising his lineage, its history and the valour of its chief. His uncle, Abiola thought grimly, mirrored the colours of the sun; not as it appeared now, approaching its mid-point in the sky, but as it would be at sundown.

Straightening his cap, knocked awry in his ruthless passage into the compound, Abiola rearranged the folds of his robe. He stood still for a moment while he took stock of the others on the dais. Lord Asipa's brothers were seated on his right hand, his sons behind him; their silks shimmered less brightly, but their faces were equally free of expression. Oluremi sat on her father's left hand, beautiful as ever, her head smooth shaven and uncovered in the manner of the wives of the Alafin. She had exchanged the silk damask death cloth in which she had left the palace for an indigo under-wrapper and another of foreign yellow velvet tied around her waist. It was the first of many costume changes she would make before the day was ended. Clustered round her were the women of the family, easily identified by their indigo wrappers and yellow turbans.

Lady Monifa's eyes were fastened on her daughter, as if wishing to imprint the image for ever. Quickly glancing away, Abiola inadvertently caught his mother's eye already upon him. Pointless to speculate how in that dense crowd she had gauged the exact spot at which he would materialise. It required all his soldier's training to withstand her gaze as it bored into him. Lady Faloyan contrived simultaneously, and without the flicker of an eyelash, to communicate to him her anger at his late appearance, her imperviousness to any mitigation he might offer, and the strength of the retribution to follow.

He needed no prompting to begin pushing his way towards the pavilion. Easing round the back of the verandah, he slipped into place on Oluremi's distaff side.

'Careless little brother, your absence has been well noted and doubtless construed as a weakness in you and, therefore, in us.'

Silently cursing, Abiola suppressed any outward reaction.

'Knowing that the reverse is true,' the voice continued, overturning his expectations again, 'we shall use that apparent weakness to our advantage against our enemies.'

Olufemi was trickier than a chameleon. A question formed itself.

His brother answered it: 'You have looked into the eye of the leopard.'

Surely, Abiola thought, he had done quite the opposite. He leant against one of the many verandah posts supporting the thatched roof. It would tax even the powers of an Ifa priest to divine the meaning behind some of his brother's utterances. He arranged himself as comfortably as he could, grateful for the relative coolness in the shade and for the thickness of his robe, which cushioned him against the sharp protuberances of the elaborate carving at his back. He surrendered himself to the spectacle of grief unfolding in the brightness of the courtyard.

An old auntie lifted her arms to the sky while her feet traced an ancient pattern in the sand as she sang:

> *'She who sat under the iroko tree told it of her sadness*
> *The leaves of that tree fell like tears*
> *And joined in her sorrow.'*

Lady Monifa's principal apartment had been turned into a robing room for the day. It was cool inside, the high vaulted ceiling and thick walls protecting the occupants from the fierce afternoon heat. Prettily patterned air vents filtered the light and the drumming, continuing in the outer courtyards, was softened here to a heartbeat in the background. The room was teeming with women come to help Oluremi prepare for the feast, and filled with the sound of their laughter. All the tears of the morning were wiped away. Oluremi herself had set the mood, telling them that the time for lamentation was over.

'I wish it was the Lord Gaha who was making the journey to the next world. He is the cause of all this,' cried a child, burying her face in the long wrapper she had been given to hold.

Everyone ignored her outburst except Modupé, who was holding the adjacent portion. She hurriedly tweaked the material from the eight-year-old's grasp and pulled it straight again. 'The simplicity of the child!' she declared, 'I would have him staked out in the sun and soldier ants eating him alive, particle by particle.'

Her companions glanced involuntarily over their shoulders. There was a horrified silence. Modupé raised her chin defiantly. 'We are among friends, are we not? Or do you imagine the Lord Gaha has his spies hidden behind the wall hangings?' There was a burst of nervous laughter and sheepishly the women shook out the wrapper and held it taut again.

Crossing the room, Oluremi knelt and put her arms round the child, who hung her head. She lifted the little girl's chin and, looking into her eyes, spoke softly but in such a way that her words carried the length of the room. 'Reeds driven by the wind cannot but sing; it is not given to them to choose whether it is wise to do so or not. You are not a reed, little sister, you must not follow their example. Do you hear me?' The child nodded and Modupé, knowing full well for whom the rebuke was really intended, sharply recalled everyone's attention to the task in hand.

Oluremi was passed from group to group to be bathed, massaged with shea oil, her hands and feet painted with henna and perfumed with camwood as if it were a festival day. She glanced at intervals at the still figure sitting on a couch against the wall. Lady Faloyan's eyes never wavered from her and she drew strength from them like water from a well.

When at last Oluremi, laughing, reached her mother, Lady Monifa was obliged to ask her to sit still because she was making it difficult to put the final touch of antimony on her eyes. The child who had spoken out of turn earlier, finding her temporarily captive, crept on to her knee.

'I shall be sad when you are not here, Auntie Oluremi.'

Lady Monifa's hand did not falter, though she drew in her breath sharply as she finished the line she was drawing. For the second time there was silence in the crowded apartment. The child leant back, her fingers tracing the henna pattern on Oluremi's hands.

Oluremi said, 'Do you feel sad when you see a butterfly?'

The little girl shook her head.

'A butterfly is here only for a moment and then it is gone, but its passing makes you happy. Think of me every time you see a butterfly hovering over the river or flitting in and out among the tall grass, and you will be glad.'

Lady Monifa, keeping her voice steady and smiling into her daughter's eyes, took her hands and raised her up.

'Come, it is time.'

Lady Faloyan, watching them both, felt the bile rise in her throat.

Dressed in a short white petticoat tied at her waist, Oluremi pirouetted in the centre of the long room so that her audience, which had begun to clap and sing in praise of her beauty, could better admire their handi-work. She turned a full circle and then stood still, facing her mother.

Carrying one end of the silk wrapper from which every crease had been removed, Lady Monifa danced slowly towards her daughter at the head of a procession of the senior wives of the compound, each carrying a portion of material. The women spaced themselves out, forming a line, and spun Oluremi, her hands high above her head, round and round from one to the other down the length of the room so that by the time she reached the last person the cloth was wound neatly around her body. Finally they beckoned the child, who reached up on tiptoe, and the clapping reached a crescendo as she tucked the loose end into place.

Taking up the length of cloth lying across her lap, Lady Faloyan tied another layer of stiff silk in a wide band around Oluremi's narrow waist. The love she felt flowed through her fingers, making the same wordless connection as when she had turned her in the womb and received her, soft as unfired clay, in the cradle of her palms.

'I have something to tell you,' Oluremi whispered.

'There will be time.' Lady Faloyan moved back and Lady Monifa stepped forward to reclaim her daughter.

The feast continued throughout the sun-drenched hours of the afternoon. Servants and slaves silently passed on bare feet among the guests, presenting enormous platters of beef, bush meat, poultry and fish, replacing them before they were empty. There would be no wastage, however. The house was supposedly closed to all except Lord Asipa's closest followers, but many more had managed to squeeze into the public courtyard and outer courtyards, where the second and third ranks were being feasted.

Abiola tried to appear intent on the practised courtesies of his neighbour, with whom he was sharing a calabash, politely accepting the portion of guinea fowl offered him. He dipped desultorily into the dish in front of him, careful to use only the first three fingers and thumb without immersing them beyond the first joint as etiquette dictated. And, as the servants filled and refilled the drinking calabashes from flagons brimming with beer and fresh palm wine, he wished that he too could escape from the unbearable tension by a swift progression into unconsciousness. A servant bent to replenish his cup and he caught the watchful eye of his brother, but he needed no reminder to keep his wits about him. He was in fact abnormally sensitised. The sound of raised voices around him and the clatter of cups and dishes were all grotesquely magnified; he was aware of the grain in the wood at his back and the infinitesimal movement of air against his skin.

In the centre of the courtyard Oluremi danced for the last time, flame bright in homespun crimson silk and garlands of coral. Circling around her, the women raised their voices, echoing the drums.

Abiola could not look until he remembered his words to Oluremi on her wedding day and his brother's to him earlier. He must stare the leopard in the eye. He raised his eyes, dreading what he might see, only too conscious of the blood clamouring for life in his veins; saw immediately that she was not afraid; and in an instant understood how near was the boundary of the world beyond and how easily crossed.

Oluremi was waiting for him in Lord Asipa's visitors' room with Alero in attendance.

'This is not the end,' she said.

Abiola searched her face.

He sighed, 'You're right. We'll meet again in the next world.'

'I don't mean in the next life. I mean in this one.'

Abiola took both her hands in his. Like everyone else, he knew that death was not the end, but as a soldier he had no great faith in dreams, nor did he believe that he would ever see her again on this earth.

It was Oluremi's turn to sigh. 'You don't believe me!'

He made no reply.

She pulled her hands away, and reached inside her wrapper. Round his neck she placed a narrow thong from which hung two small charms encased in leather. He squinted down at the two dark crescent moons among the rich blue embroidery of his robe.

'I'm sure you have many other charms, but wear these when next you go to war.'

'I shall wear them wherever I am.'

'Our fates are intertwined. When the time comes, you and I will travel together again, here, on *earth*. I have seen it.'

Abiola enveloped her in his arms. Pity must move you to action, not to tears, the hunter Lakoja taught. So it was Alero who cried for them both.

Lady Monifa, supported by Lady Faloyan, was waiting in the apartment of Lord Asipa's second wife, who, tears glistening on her cheeks, whispered, 'The words of the proverb are true: only a person buried by his child can truly be said to have one. And not to have a child . . . There is no agony which matches that.' She glanced at Lady Faloyan, who remained dry-eyed and silent.

Oluremi had thought that she would need all her training if her mother broke down, but Lady Monifa had been well trained, too. Nor did Oluremi have need of any formula with which to console. She found that her mother had fashioned herself into a rock in whose shelter she could safely rest. In the time that was left they were able to recapture the unconditional sweetness of Oluremi's childhood. Lady Monifa and her daughter communicated directly and simply, something they had been prevented from doing while she lived at the palace.

The rock held strong until Oluremi, accompanied by Lady Faloyan, stepped over the threshold into Lady Monifa's own apartments.

A tiny oil lamp was burning in the wall niche by the door and Alero, entering first, took one of the grass tapers lying beside it and quickly lit the other lamps. While the maid busied herself in the sleeping alcove, Lady Faloyan beckoned Oluremi to sit beside her. There was very little time. She had, for her sister's sake, waited until the last possible moment. The sun was sinking fast and before it disappeared over the horizon Oluremi must have begun her journey.

Oluremi said urgently, 'Part of me will always remain with Abiola and part of him will travel with me.'

'For ever,' Lady Faloyan replied.

She grasped the girl's hand and glanced at the figures depicted on the wall hangings, which seemed to take on a life of their own in the soft flickering of the lamps.

'We weave our pattern,' she began softly, 'and we think it is the whole. Then we discover another pattern and beyond that, perhaps another. And we are only aware, it seems, because sometimes the colours run, bleeding from one into another, as in your dream . . .' Lady Faloyan paused, gently stroking the hand she held in hers. She looked into Oluremi's eyes. 'It would appear, child, that you and Abiola, who are woven into our pattern here, are colours from another, possibly larger, pattern, in which there will be a little of us.'

'All is ready, Ma.' Alero held the alcove curtain to one side.

'Come.' Lady Faloyan placed an arm round Oluremi's shoulders.

The curtain dropped behind them.

Oluremi died cradled in Lady Faloyan's arms and was buried in the customary manner. Her grave was dug six feet deep beneath the floor of her mother's room. Alero, who had asked to drink from the same poisoned cup, was buried with her so that she could serve her mistress in the next life as she had served her in this. Placed around them were Oluremi's treasured possessions and the magnificent wrappers and cloths presented by her relatives and friends. The favourite would be a fit companion for her king in the world beyond.

Her family mourned her with pride.

On the seventeenth day, Oluremi's friends walked in procession to a place outside the city where two roads met. They said farewell to her spirit as it began on its journey to the next life.

Abiola called out her name three times as required. He knew that death was always near, but what he hadn't known was how deep the pain of loss could be.

The sound of one of Oluremi's songs drifting on the air he dismissed as a trick of his imagination.

Lady Faloyan sat alone in her room, a single lamp burning, recalling the occasion of Lady Monifa's consultation with the high priest shortly after the birth of her daughter. Earlier at the feast marking the fortieth day and the final departure of Oluremi's spirit from this world to the next, her mother had cried out in her grief that the gods could not be cheated.

Lady Faloyan stared unseeingly at the lamp flame. She had had her suspicions at the time, and in truth there had been indications of her sister's defection before this. Distrustful of the high priest, Princess Boladé had suggested that they reverse the usual meaning of the symbols so that a seemingly negative answer would in fact be positive for their purposes.

The gods cannot be cheated! The words echoed in Lady Faloyan's mind.

Lady Monifa had clearly *not* reversed the meaning as she'd been instructed. The gods had *not* been appeased and they had taken back what was rightfully theirs.

In everything is its opposite, Lakoja said. Lady Faloyan extinguished the lamp flame. Let the Lord Gaha savour his victory, for the day would come when he would see the ruin of all his clan. And she would be the cause.

II

THE STATE COUNCIL were divided equally between the two candidates put forward for election to the throne, so it was left to the Bashorun to give the casting vote. His health had been a matter of concern for some time and now he was fading fast, but nearness to death had brought with it clarity of vision, enabling him to grasp the full extent of his nephew's ambition. He saw that Lord Gaha, who was certain to succeed him as Bashorun, would never be content with the office of chief minister: it would not take him long to usurp the power of the Alafinate after his puppet was elected. He also saw clearly that his nephew, to whom a populace tired of the tyranny of successive kings now looked for protection, would prove no less a tyrant than former rulers.

Knowingly, against Lord Gaha's declared wish, the old man gave his vote to Prince Labisi.

'My uncle was a fool,' Lord Gaha sneered in private audience with the chief eunuch.

'A fool is recognised by his words as well as his actions. It is unwise to speak ill of the dead.'

The elaborate ceremonials following the death and the burial of the former Bashorun and the installation of Lord Gaha as his successor had not disguised the fact that battle lines had been drawn between Lord Gaha and Lord Agbakin; their cavalry leaders and retainers thronged the city, each side facing the other across a dangerous vacuum at the heart of the kingdom.

'I shall have my way,' Lord Gaha said, his voice laced with menace as always.

'I don't doubt it.'

Captains loyal to Lord Gaha were stationed in key provinces throughout the empire and the general populace chanted for him daily in the streets. The chief eunuch examined Lord Gaha's closed countenance, seeing in it, even now, the boy who had taken the place of a son. That was why he had failed to realise until too late that he himself was merely a tool. He said, 'At least we know now why the Asipa promised his daughter to Prince Labisi.'

'My enemies will feel my anger in due course.' Lord Gaha held the chief eunuch's gaze. He was seeking to recruit him anew.

'Your enemies have the ear of the Alafin-elect.'

'As do you.'

'I shall not oppose you,' said the chief eunuch, signalling to his remembrancer, who knelt to offer Lord Gaha a bowl filled with kola nuts.

'Fit for a king,' the chief eunuch said, his face free of expression.

'The dundun player does not lead songs,' Lord Gaha replied, equally dry. The proverb enjoined those who were too forward to remember their place.

He rose to leave and the chief eunuch, who had himself rubbed the leaves into his protégé's head at his installation, lowered his bulk to the ground with surprising lightness, prostrating himself, as he must, to the new Bashorun.

Lord Gaha had barely departed before the chief eunuch bowed his head again, lowering a portion of himself over the side of his couch so that it touched the ground, as, preceded by her maid, Princess Boladé was ushered into his inner courtyard. That *she* had come to *him* was an unprecedented concession, proof of his measure.

'I am honoured, Princess.'

'A mountain in motion is not easily disguised,' the princess replied, banishing his complacency.

She settled herself comfortably on a couch opposite. A warm breeze stirred the leaves of the tamarind tree and a drift of sandalwood perfumed the air. In the soft light of the lamps, age, it seemed, had taken no toll and her voice still seduced. He beckoned to his remembrancer, who presented, on his knees, a bowl of kola nuts. The princess took one and placed it, red as her painted fingers, delicately into her mouth.

'I have a plan.' She crossed her pretty feet.

She had been a worthy adversary and she was going to be equally testing, clearly, as an ally.

Very slightly, the chief eunuch rippled forward. 'I am listening.'

There was no sound, merely the slightest displacement of air beside the bed. Abiola's hand shot out and, encountering his servant Juma's fat neck, closed around it. Juma calmly uncovered the light he held hidden in his hands. The slight flame in its minute saucer of oil did little to disperse the dark, but it was sufficient to disclose his eyes bulging out of his head, the result of his master's throttling fingers on his throat. Abiola released him instantly and the old man, already on his knees, touched his forehead to the floor and sat back on his heels without spilling the lamp.

'I could have killed you,' Abiola hissed.

'My compliments, my lord,' Juma whispered back. 'You rival your brother.'

'Some think I surpass my brother.'

'Yes, my lord.'

'Well?'

'The Lord Olufemi requests your presence.'

'Why didn't you say so before?' Abiola leapt up from the bed and hurriedly pulled on trousers and tunic. He slipped a dagger into his waist cord, a spiked bracelet on to his wrist, snatched up his cutlass and raced barefoot for the door. A sigh which might have been a lizard slipping along the floor caused him to turn. Juma, still on his knees beside the bed, silently proffered the black robe he had brought for him to wear. Abiola snatched it up, shrugged it over his head and whirled again towards the door.

'The lamp, sir. I omitted to pass it to you, sir.'

Abiola felt rather than heard the words, breathed into the small of his back, but it might as easily have been a knife. Lose your head, lose your life, Lakoja said. Sweat started on his forehead at the recollection of his earlier boasting. He still had much to learn.

'I beg you to forgive me, my lord,' Juma thrust home. 'I fear my faculties have become dulled with age.'

Abiola took the lamp. 'The roar of a lion cub frightens no one,' he said.

'But should the cub live, it will one day be a lion.' Juma touched his forehead to the ground once more.

Abiola slid into the heat of the night, gliding noiselessly along the verandahs. On his home territory he had no need of light and the aniline folds of his robe blended with the darkness. He slipped with such stealth through the open courtyards and covered walkways of his father's compound that his passing went unremarked by people and animals alike. Outside on the streets, the lamp concealed in his palms enabled him when necessary to see without being seen, the tiny flickering dismissed as the random flitting of a firefly. He hoped that the call was to avenge Oluremi. Action would bring a welcome freedom from his thoughts. Her death had changed him. For the first time he imagined how it would be to occupy another's place. Reflection was the food of old age, Lakoja said; young men do, while old men reckon. Well, he had begun to reckon.

'What took you so long, little brother?' Lord Olufemi's right hand enquired. Abiola had in fact made remarkable time. They both knelt.

'Some of us have far to travel.' Abiola removed his black gown and placed it with his sword and lamp on top of a carved chest by the door.

'So you do, so you do.' His companion laughed loudly and slapped him on the shoulder.

'My heart rejoices to find you all in such good spirits.' Lord Olufemi entered unannounced. They knelt again. 'While you joke, our enemies gain ground. If I had wanted entertainment, I would have waited for the masquerades.' He commanded them to sit. 'The caravan from Busa should arrive in Oyo the day after tomorrow. When it leaves again for the coast, we shall be riding escort.'

Surely, Abiola thought, this was not the time to leave Oyo. With the city up in arms, now was the moment to strike. But, trained to obey, he merely asked, 'When do we leave?'

His brother answered his unspoken question first. 'Our new Bashorun will be anticipating a move from us for he intends to strike against the Prince Labisi. He will also expect that the Agbakin's sons, hot to avenge the death of the late king's favourite, will provide him with a legitimate opportunity for their permanent removal. He will be disappointed . . .' Lord Olufemi paused, 'We leave six days from now.'

Feeling foolish, Abiola glanced at his sword by the door and fingered the spiked bracelet on his wrist. He did not ask who would stay behind to defend Prince Labisi.

On a fine morning seventeen days after his nomination to the throne, Prince Labisi found his way barred as he tried to enter the outer court of the palace. In front of the closed gates stood the ranks of the palace slaves with a senior Esho captain, loyal to Lord Gaha, accompanied by four hundred men on horseback armed for combat. Of Prince Labisi's followers there was no sign.

Bereft of support, the prince was unable to resist the demand for his suicide when the new Bashorun, arbitrarily exercising the prerogative of the state council, rejected him.

Before sunset that same day Prince Labisi took the poisoned cup from the hand of Princess Boladé.

The state council was again divided equally between the two princes now put forward for election, and again it was the casting vote of the Bashorun that decided which of them should succeed.

By then, however, the caravan from Busa was many days' march from Oyo with a guard of two hundred mounted soldiers and a dozen marching on foot between each line of captives. They were joined by a mass of ordinary travellers and merchants, availing themselves of military protection for the journey as they headed for the southern markets, bringing with them their strings of horses, grooms, hired porters and carrier slaves. Two thousand strong – men, women and children, on horseback, on donkeys, on foot, carrying heavy loads, driving cattle, sheep, goats – they flowed across the mountains and down the other side. Lord Olufemi's captains, Abiola among them, melted in and out amongst the inhabitants of the valleys and villages, unobtrusively questioning, talking, listening, gathering information which remembrancers carried to Oyo, speeding back and forth, effortlessly mingling, departing and rejoining.

It was at Asunora, where the plains were scattered with shea-oil palms and covered with long grass, that a royal messenger brought news of the death of Prince Labisi. Privately, he delivered a second message to Lord Olufemi, lodged near the main gate of the high-walled town, advising him of the route taken by the chief eunuch's remembrancer, who had two days' start.

'Is there trouble?' Abiola asked hopefully when his brother took him aside. Escorting slaves to market was no substitute for wreaking vengeance on one's enemies.

Olufemi explained that the sacrifice of the Prince Labisi had been unfortunate but necessary. The chief eunuch had been powerless to save him; and now a protégé of Lord Gaha was in line for the Alafinate. On

Abiola's face much was written. 'However,' Olufemi continued, his own face unreadable, 'we are well prepared. Princess Boladé is of the opinion that once Lord Gaha's nominee learns of the chief eunuch's new allegiance, he too may change sides. The chief eunuch's remembrancer has been charged with delivering a message to the prince who is to become the new Alafin. But we would all rest easier if there were a reliable witness to the exchange. Is that trouble enough for you?'

The moon rose bright and full. In the market squares and compound courtyards of Asunora, the storytellers rolled out their mats and gathered their audiences around them to while away the long moonlit hours with tales of ghosts and spirits. Abiola and his two lieutenants slipped separately through the gates. Mimicking the chirring of the nightjars, they kept track of one another until, at a safe distance from the city, they converged. Anyone they chanced to meet would have taken them for hunters, unshod and armed only with light spears, leather pouches slung over their tunics.

In jacket pockets they carried subtly altered cowrie shells, of great significance to the prince but, should they happen to be ambushed, meaningless to anyone else. Laughing aloud, they raced each other across the long grass of the open plain, turned silver in the moonlight, overjoyed at the opportunity to stretch their legs after weeks in the saddle, confident that they who as children had followed antelope on foot could easily catch their prey.

The real race, Abiola thought, was against the official messengers from Oyo who would soon be on their way, on horseback, to inform this latest candidate of his election to the throne. The reasons for choosing him were no doubt the same as those governing the choice of his predecessor: that he would be clay in the hands of his supporters. As he tried to recall what he knew of the prince, Abiola settled into the steady lope of the hunting hyena which, with scant rest, could be maintained indefinitely.

They caught their quarry with more than a day to spare as he bent to drink on the banks of a broad river. He too might have been taken for a hunter, but they recognised his face markings.

Abiola displayed his cowrie shell in the palm of his hand and the chief eunuch's remembrancer homed swiftly in on the virtually invisible marker. If he was surprised, he gave no sign of it.

'In a city full of strangers,' Abiola said, 'we depend on you to be our guide.'

It was dusk and the drums were sounding as Abiola and his companions entered Ifonyin, mingling with the last of the travellers, devotees of the god, Shango, whose yearly festival ushered in the dry season. As they carried no loads they were soon through the gates, but they kept their heads down, for the tollkeeper, a member of the Oyo palace staff, would have recognised their face markings.

As in Oyo, each of the town gates opened on to a broad boulevard which led straight to the king's palace in the centre. On this festival night inhabitants jostled for space with visitors in the market square in front of the palace, where moths wheeled in the light of hundreds of torches. The devotees of Shango danced in a great circle while the bata drums beat out the sacred rhythms. The remembrancer pushed to the front of the crowd; Abiola and his lieutenants followed.

'Which one is the prince?'

'My lord, he is seated immediately on His Majesty's right.' The reply came in the same court language.

The king, in beaded crown and flowing robes, sat enthroned among his chiefs, one of whom wore the face markings of a prince of Oyo. A bundle of smouldering grass was handed to the father of the ceremonies, who, still dancing, blew into the bundle, fanning the grass into flame. A tongue of fire shot high in the air and a violent trembling ran through his body, his eyes widened and he began to reel. At these signs that the god was beginning to take possession, his fellow worshippers rushed to support him. Twirling faster and faster, he danced out of the square, reappearing moments later in a new robe sewn all over with cowries, which whirled round him as he continued turning in the midst of the circle of dancers.

Suddenly, speaking with the voice of Shango, he produced a long knife, the blade glinting in the light of the torches. He held it aloft for all to see, then drove the point through the flesh of his bare arms again and again without flinching, and not one drop of blood spilled. Awed by this manifestation of the god, the spectators pressed forward for a better view, but with the slightest movement of his head the remembrancer signalled it was time to depart. Hastily collecting themselves, Abiola and his two companions began edging round the back of the crowd and out of the square.

His right hand grumbled: 'The best was still to come. I hope you have good reason for pulling us away from the show, because if not . . .'

'If we were observed before, we are not now,' Abiola silenced him.

They pressed on into a small lane behind the main square and came to a halt in front of an ancient wooden door, the only interruption in the smoothness of the high compound wall running alongside. In response to their knock, the door opened narrowly revealing two beady eyes in the light of a lamp. The remembrancer held an amulet to the light, the door opened wider, and the others followed him inside through a series of courtyards, deserted and in darkness but for the gatekeeper's glimmering light. The old man conducted them into a small apartment, lit the lamp and, knowing little of Oyo facial marks, merely knelt before departing.

The remembrancer stood patiently while Abiola's lieutenants prowled the room, looking behind the wall hangings and up into the roof space. Abiola peered into the darkness beyond the entrance. There had been black clouds swirling overhead ever since they had arrived and rain falling during the Shango festival ceremonies was a bad omen, notwithstanding the fact that thunderstorms characterised the start of the dry season. Ill luck now would be disastrous. Lightning tore the sky, illuminating the courtyard and the gatekeeper returning to collect them, cowered on the ground, terrified lest the wrath of Shango fall on his head. They waited anxiously. No drops fell.

The gatekeeper scurried into the room.

'The prince awaits you.' He addressed the remembrancer, who looked enquiringly at Abiola.

'We will go together.'

The gatekeeper led them across several other unlit courtyards eventually relinquishing them to a servant who ushered them into a small apartment where the prince was seated on a leather cushion, his gown hitched back exposing the broad ribbon marks of royalty along his arms. All four of his visitors prostrated themselves on the ground.

'I expected to see one, instead there is an abundance – a sign of the season, no doubt.' The prince addressed them in the language of the court, his eyes lingering on Abiola's facial scars. He turned to the remembrancer.

'You, I know. Speak.'

'Your Royal Highness also knows the one who sent me.'

The prince inclined his head affirmatively.

'I was charged to give you this,' the chief eunuch's remembrancer handed him two cowrie shells strung together face to face; their meaning, *I will see you.*

The prince's eyes rested on Abiola. 'And since when did the lion and the leopard share the same sleeping mat?'

'They do not.' Abiola reached into a pocket of his hunting jacket, and proffered another cowrie.

The prince's searching fingers found confirmation in the minute irregularity on one of the shell's serrated edges, proof that the chief eunuch had changed allegiance and no longer supported Lord Gaha. The silence lengthened as the prince digested the implications. The working of his mind, thought Abiola, was as clear as a trail of prints on wet sand. He should have been prepared. If you can see the way ahead, Lakoja said, you know where to tread. Aware of the remembrancer's eyes on him, Abiola shifted his attention. The remembrancer's face gave away nothing. There was the possibility, of course, that the prince would remain loyal to Lord Gaha; but the desire for power would be stronger.

The prince returned the two cowries to the remembrancer. 'Take these back to the one who sent you and make sure you deliver them safely into his hands.'

Abiola thought he caught something in the remembrancer's eyes as he prostrated himself to the prince, and it occurred to him that they still couldn't be certain that the chief eunuch was not playing a double game.

Lord Olufemi noted his brother's return, but it was not until the caravan reached its final destination on the banks of the Yewa River, and their captives were safely delivered to the middlemen who would sell them on, that they spoke to each other directly.

'I wanted obscurity, little brother.' Lord Olufemi reined in alongside. They had arranged to meet at daybreak outside the city, where they could mingle with the crowds on their way to market. 'But with you on such a horse, we might as well have brought a hundred attendants. I hope for your sake word of his quality does not reach the ears of the king here. He is a chief like any other and would certainly demand your stallion as a present. And in his place, so would I.'

Grinning, Abiola said, 'He has been well hidden until now and I have arranged to keep him quartered outside the town. I shall be returning on foot.'

'Why bring him in the first place?' Lord Olufemi leaned across and patted the horse's neck admiringly.

'I wanted to test him in preparation for the campaign season. He has stood up well; he has spirit and stamina, in fact, all the makings of a war horse.'

'Provided he does not first succumb to the sickness. Horses sicken faster in the south.'

'Conditions are better where the plain reaches right down to the sea. They fare worst, it seems, in the forest regions.'

'You're certainly knowledgeable on the subject of horse-flesh. Perhaps I should quarter mine with yours.'

'With age comes wisdom.' Abiola grinned again. 'So Lakoja taught.'

'And due deference also,' Lord Olufemi retorted. 'Where are you quartering your horse?'

Laughing, Abiola gave him the name. They nudged into the thick of the crowds that stretched as far as the eye could see along the riverbank.

'What kind of man is this prince?' Lord Olufemi asked at last.

'Ideal for our purposes.' Abiola became serious again. 'He is one who bends with the prevailing wind but does not consider what will happen when the wind stops. He is intelligent enough to appreciate what we are offering him, but he has neither the wit nor the foresight to penetrate what lies behind.'

'Those same qualities no doubt endeared him to the Lord Gaha.'

'I fear,' Abiola said, 'that he might meet with the same fate as the Prince Labisi.'

'Lord Gaha may eliminate as many Alafin as he likes. Removing them will not destroy the organisation on which royal power is based. The chief eunuch has made sure of that.' Lord Olufemi urged his horse forward into a canter without looking back.

Abiola veered in the opposite direction towards the river, seizing the opportunity to inspect at close quarters the boats moored in their hundreds among the thick reeds at the water's edge. His horse trod lightly to avoid the swarms of errant children, goats, sheep, chickens and baskets of produce, which would have been at risk beneath his polished unshod hooves.

'Stop them! Stop them!'

Two children ran out in front of the horse, fleeing from a merchant seated under a nearby awning. 'Well? Run after them!' the merchant shouted, jabbing an irate finger at two of his servants, who set off in pursuit. The children though had a good start. The merchant flung out his arms in appeal and, catching sight of his Oyo face markings, Abiola turned his horse round and overtook the servants.

Hearing the drumming of hooves behind him, the boy stumbled but was quickly pulled back on to his feet by the girl, who shouted at him to run. When he hesitated, she put both hands in the small of his back, screaming, 'Go!'

He dashed blindly on and she threw herself directly in the horse's path. Abiola had to use all his horsemanship to avoid trampling her. She doubled back the way she'd come, darting in and out among the crowd, but Abiola plunged after her, people hurriedly scrambling out of the way. He leant down from the saddle, scooped her up under his arm, cantered back and set her down beside her owner. The boy, retrieved by the servants, lay there already, whimpering.

The merchant, aware now of Abiola's rank, prostrated himself on the ground, all gratitude, 'My lord, I thank you. Your kindness shall not be forgotten.'

A bolt of fine cloth might not come amiss, Abiola thought.

'Peace be with you, uncle,' he said.

The girl blurted something suddenly in the Tapa language.

'What was that?' Abiola stared at her in astonishment. She backed away without answering. He turned to the merchant. 'Did I hear correctly?'

The merchant gave a snort of derision, 'Yes, my lord. But not in this world, eh?' He prostrated himself once more. 'Go in health, my lord.'

'Go in health.' Abiola bowed briefly.

The girl's words had been spoken as a curse.

Troubled, he glanced over his shoulder. Her eyes caught his and he reached instinctively for the amulets at his neck. Words had power even from a child. Turning away, he noted with irritation that the sun was higher than he'd thought and he would not after all have sufficient time to inspect the canoes. Applying his heels with more force than usual, he urged his horse into a gallop and the stallion charged off along the riverbank past the lines of captives chained together in the sun.

∽

12

THE NEW ALAFIN was crowned at the third appearance of the new moon following the death of his predecessor. Before it had made a fourth appearance, he too had been laid to rest in the Bara, the royal burial ground, beside Prince Labisi. An announcement from the palace proclaimed that, having wielded the royal sceptre for just one hundred and thirty days, His Majesty had succumbed to a sudden and fatal illness.

Princess Boladé, in swift consultation with the chief eunuch to whose inner courtyard she was now a frequent visitor, accepted a kola nut from the hands of her own maid, Sadia.

'It is said,' the princess smoothed a crease from her yellow silk wrapper, 'that the late Alafin met his fate because of some trivial matter of protocol, so touchy and tyrannical has our Bashorun become. I trust that the palace rumours are correct, and it was not because the Lord Gaha had been apprised of the new Alafin's true affiliation?'

'Impossible,' the chief eunuch replied, his fan underlining the word vigorously. 'There is only one who might have . . .' Briefly, the chief eunuch pictured his remembrancer. 'And, if he had, he would not be walking the earth; he would be treading the grass of the afterworld.'

'Are you certain?'

'Unless he began his journey to the next world after *you* arrived here, Princess?'

The princess's voice lost its honey. 'You jest, my lord; I have marked it. Perhaps now you will answer my question.'

'I am as certain as I am that the sun will rise tomorrow,' the chief eunuch assured her. He was already devising a trap.

'I could perhaps be of assistance,' the princess offered, reading his mind, her voice all sweetness now.

They should do nothing for the moment, Princess Boladé said after her meeting with the chief eunuch.

Lady Faloyan immediately relayed the message to her husband. Sitting straight-backed as usual, observing his morning pacing of the bedchamber from her seat by the door, she put it in such a way that the Agbakin imagined the decision to be his own.

Summoning Lady Faloyan's two sons, he ordered them to abide by the wisdom of Lakoja the hunter. If your prey suspects your presence, you should remain perfectly still, downwind, until his suspicion is allayed.

Lord Gaha's next candidate for the throne received unanimous endorsement from all the members of the state council and once again the crowds flocked to witness the coronation. However, unlike his predecessor, this Alafin submitted with good grace to the humiliating demands of his Bashorun. He had been well briefed. For it was Princess Boladé's husband who, as chief of the official fathers of the king, was responsible for conducting the Alafin-elect through all the preliminary ceremonies. Morning and evening, accompanied by the other six members of his state council, the new Alafin presented himself at the Bashorun's palace to pay homage to Lord Gaha, whom no one now outwardly opposed.

This Alafin remained in good health. Meanwhile, two of the Asipa's sons, together with two of the Agbakin's – the lords Olufemi and Abiola – were promoted to senior and junior captaincies in the cavalry.

'I'm confused,' Abiola's left hand declared, 'because I ask myself, why should the Lord Gaha reward his enemies? I'm honoured, of course. But perplexed.'

'That is because you are in direct contravention of your training, which is specifically designed to avoid that state of mind by conditioning you to accept *without question* any proposal handed down by your elders.' Abiola shook his head in mock sorrow. In the company of his lieutenants he was on his way to the practice butts. The heat was lessening and the light still good.

His right hand said seriously, 'It avoids confusion, I grant you, but it avoids enlightenment too.'

'Our training has served us perfectly well until now,' Abiola's left hand protested, looking from one to the other.

'But it may not continue to do so,' his right hand insisted. 'If we are to take advantage of opportunities arising from the presence of the skinless ones at the coast, we will need new answers. And how will we arrive at them when our elders are so determined to retain their power that they refuse to share their knowledge, and the young are not permitted to put forward ideas?'

'I agree.' Abiola nodded emphatically, recalling the recent meeting with his father. 'If the next generation was allowed to stand on the shoulders of the one that went before, we would all stand taller and see further.'

'Exactly!' his right hand declared. 'We need to advance.'

'We have advanced, my brother,' – his left hand shrugged exasperatedly – 'very far from the point. And yet I am no further forward. So, once again, why would the Lord Gaha reward his enemies?'

'There is no problem, my brother,' Abiola said, clapping him on the shoulder, 'once you recognise the Lord Gaha's generosity as a *tactical* move.'

'I have it!' Abiola's left hand cried. 'Your promotion was to gain your father's compliance.'

Lord Gaha favoured, of necessity, a policy of military expansion in order to secure the loyalty of his followers. Grown rich on the spoils of conflict, his war chiefs, whose support had enabled him to seize power, looked to him to continue to provide them with the means to sustain their own followers. War captives brought high profits at the coast. Under the constitution, however, only the Alafin was empowered to give the order for a military expedition, and the present incumbent preferred a policy of consolidation, as privately recommended by the chief eunuch.

A necessary pre-condition also was the invocation of the god Oranyan, founder of the royal dynasty of Oyo, who alone could guarantee success in battle. The custodian of the temple and keeper of the cult being none other than the Agbakin, it transpired that, instead of continuing along the path of territorial aggrandisement, Lord Gaha must content himself with keeping the boundaries of the empire intact and inviolate.

But after three seasons of unprecedented peace there were many besides Lord Gaha who resented the fact that in its pursuit they had been forced to forgo the spoils of war. It was time, the chief eunuch advised the Alafin, to ease the rope.

The chief eunuch made his customary check of the faces reflected in the polished red surfaces of the walls. The council chamber was crowded for the morning session. Besides the Alafin and his remembrancers on the dais and the messengers spilling from it at his feet, all seven of the state councillors were present, together with the eunuchs of the right and left, each with their remembrancers standing by. The Alafin betrayed his nervousness, one foot tapping on a beaded footstool, fingers playing with the handle of the white fly whisk roped over his wrist.

Bashorun Gaha rose to his feet. 'Majesty, the vassal king of the Popos has showed scant respect for our dominion.' At the recent Bébé festival, the robes of the proverbially rich sovereign of the Popo region had all but outrivaled the Alafin's in opulence. Honour was saved on the last day only by the ingenuity of the royal robe-makers. They had sewed the Alafin's gown with floss from the silk cotton tree which took on a dazzling silver sheen in the sunlight, the silken flosses lifting in the breeze like a flock of white birds hovering round him as he danced a stately measure to the music of the ogidigbo drum, played only for the king.

The Alafin defended his friend. 'During the Bébé festival everyone is allowed by custom to dress in his best. How much more should a king do so?'

'He came not to honour but to disgrace Your Majesty, to flaunt his wealth to your disadvantage,' Lord Gaha replied, striking his palm with his fist. 'Those who mock the power of Oyo must be punished.'

It had been agreed in advance, even among his enemies, that Bashorun Gaha should have his war. The Agbakin spoke in his support, as did the Asipa.

Bashorun Gaha and the Agbakin, magnificent in their robes, were foremost among the spectators who came to see the army ride out. In the sacred grove, the Agbakin had invoked the god, calling upon him to grant them success against the enemy. A sword had flashed in the sunlight, severing in one clean stroke the head of the sacrificial victim whose blood, hastily collected, spilled like precious coral across the altar. Oranyan had heard their prayer and accepted their sacrifice. The commander had led his captains from the grove. Drums beating, column upon column, they had marched through the streets to the Bashorun's gate. Carrying aloft the newly anointed war standard, they pitched it in front of the commander's tent outside the inner circuit walls where the army was mustering. The sun glinted on a thousand spears and the citizens of Oyo danced and cheered to the thunderous accompaniment of the drums as the gates in the outer circuit were thrown open for the first of the foot soldiers to pass through.

Lady Faloyan was among the spectators, her attention fixed on her younger son riding between his right and left hands in the first column of cavalry. Both her sons were seasoned campaigners and many times she had watched them head off to battle, but her present unease went far beyond the usual anxiety a mother would feel on such an occasion, for she'd had a premonition during the preparation of Abiola's war cloth. After the padded jacket had been soaked in special herbs and all the necessary incantations completed, she'd had a vision. Secluded in her room, sewing on the charms and amulets away from prying eyes, she had suddenly pictured the face of her dead niece Oluremi. The image was as vivid as the one of Abiola that had arisen in her mind's eye at the moment of his cousin's birth. Lady Faloyan's sense of foreboding that it was a sign

88

her son was about to join his cousin in the next world had grown with each passing day. Now, without realising, she gave voice to her fear.

'No, my daughter.' The caution came from Lord Lakoja, who stood beside her in the crowd. 'No,' he repeated. The elephant hunter was still formidable at seventy, and though his hair, no longer shaved, frothed white as river foam around the edges of his embroidered cap, he stood tall and straight, and his shoulders appeared as broad as a pair of compound gates.

'I have had a premonition: I fear for my son Abiola,' Lady Faloyan persisted.

'The death that will claim you,' Lakoja reminded her, 'does not call you by name. Your son is a warrior who has fought many times before; the death that stalks the battlefields knows his name. Ogun will continue to protect him; it is not in war that he will die. Calm your heart.'

Lady Faloyan nodded but could not do as he said. She fixed her eyes once more on Abiola as his horse tossed its head and he reached forward and ran his hand along the curve of its neck. She saw that, while he was careful to appear dispassionate, inwardly he was elated to be once again on his way to war with his trusted lieutenants. Before them was the prospect of glory and rich spoils. Lord Lakoja might be proved right, but she wished now that she had embraced her son when he'd come to take his leave.

Abiola was conscious of his mother's eyes on him and wondered briefly why she had been so insistent that he should anoint his sword in the sacrificial blood. His life was in far less danger as a captain in the cavalry than as a leader of the young warriors in the vanguard.

His right hand caught his eye and smiled. 'All the omens are good.'

Abiola fingered the new amulets his mother had attached to his padded war jacket. 'Never better,' he replied.

Despite having sworn to avenge his cousin, he had seen now the other face of power and discovered in himself a taste for it.

Lord Olufemi summoned his brother after they had been a week on the road. Abiola strolled through the encampment, which was hidden behind the brow of a hill. The messenger had not stated any urgency. Darkness had fallen. Glimmering with lights, a colony of palm-branch booths the size of a small town stretched from the foot of the slope to the bank of a nearby river. The Alafin's master of the horse and the war elders had been busy supervising a second army of servants and sutlers, who scurried now between the huts, hauling wood for fires and carrying food and water for both men and horses.

'My brother, I have another mission for you,' Lord Olufemi said as, ducking under the awning, Abiola sank down beside him on a mat. 'As you know, the Alafin only gave his consent to this expedition because he was promised that the king of the Popos would be warned in time to escape. He has no wish to see his friend's head brought in triumph to him at Oyo. We have since learnt that the Lord Gaha intends to ambush the king. He must be warned.'

'Won't I be missed?' Abiola asked.

'You should be able to complete your mission and be back with us before the main body of the army reaches the enemy capital, Ifonyin. You have travelled the route before and you are familiar with the town.'

'See you at Ifonyin then.'

Abiola knelt to take his leave, his mind running ahead. He would take his right hand only and leave in command his left hand to whom, in truth, he preferred to entrust his precious horses.

Abiola and his right hand spared neither themselves nor their mounts. The sound of their hooves as they swallowed up the ground in the dark put deer and buffalo to flight, sent the wild pigs and bush rats burrowing for shelter in the undergrowth. The first faint streaks of light each morning found them travelling across open countryside beneath tall spreading trees and round stands of bamboo, over streams, and ditches full of flowers, past lakes of sweet water and fields thick with yams, maize, beans; cotton, indigo and sugar cane. But they saw and stopped for nothing.

'I doubt our speed could have been bettered even by Lord Olufemi,' his right hand said with satisfaction as they rode through the city gates.

Abiola patted both horses. 'These two outran the wind.'

'In the matter of horse-flesh, sir, you have no equal.'

'It is said I am no mean judge of people, either.'

'You only chose me because I am a light load to carry.'

'That too, of course.' Abiola grinned down at him.

Before entering the town they had rested their horses and changed into over-gowns befitting moneyed sons of a noble house. Arriving at the gate of the compound to which they had been directed, they gained immediate entry on the production of their marked cowrie shells. Straight away they were ushered into the presence of the master of the house, who received them in his private apartment. He dismissed the servant and, as soon as the three of them were alone, enquired of Abiola, 'What business do you have with us?'

'We have come to deliver a message.'

'For whose ears?'

'For yours, sir. It is said that our friend, the king of the Popos, would be wise to change his route. An ambush awaits him along the path he has chosen.'

'Your words will not go unheard.' Their host clapped his hands and the same servant entered. 'Food awaits you and my house is at your disposal for as long as you please.'

'We thank you, my lord, for your hospitality, but we will not trouble you beyond this one night.'

Abiola and his right hand both prostrated themselves and then followed the servant who led them back across the courtyards to a guest apartment near the main gate of the compound. Lamplight and the smell of food met them inside. Abiola's right hand sank down immediately in front of a low wooden chest on which several calabashes were set out.

'I could eat an elephant,' he declared.

Rinsing his hands, Abiola joined him at table and they ate in silence which they maintained until the servant had cleared the dishes and departed.

'So far so smooth,' his right hand said. 'Providing our horses perform as well on the journey back, we might even arrive in time to join the first attack.'

'Ever the optimist. Come, a game of ayo while we digest our food.' Abiola brought out his miniature board from inside the deep pocket in the front of his robe. 'What shall we bet on?'

'On our joining that first attack on Infonyin!'

Abiola shook his head and centred the board. 'You begin.'

They played three games before retiring for the night, the right hand insisting on a second having lost the first, and on a third having won the second. Abiola remained adamant against a fourth.

Abiola woke, instantly aware of body heat. He lay as if still asleep, mentally reviewing the room's disposition while trying to gauge how many visitors they were entertaining. There were enough to effect a change in the density of the darkness, so six at least, he calculated, perhaps eight. The intention then was to take them alive. He ceased further speculation remembering Lakoja's teaching: successful action requires you to be fully present in each moment without thought of the one before or the one after. He felt one of the intruders move and, gripping his dagger in one hand, he brought both arms straight up and struck out left and right. He leapt from the bed and moved, arms flailing rapidly, until his back was against a wall. He continued punching in all directions.

A lamp, hastily lit, revealed his attackers and his right hand's empty couch.

Holding the lamp was the chief eunuch's remembrancer, who told him, 'My instructions were to kill you. If you continue to resist, I may have to do so, my lord.'

Killing was not the chief eunuch's style.

Abiola dropped his arms to his sides. He said with careful emphasis, '*The Lord Gaha* is an unforgiving master. You would be wise to follow instructions.'

The remembrancer's eyes rested for a moment on the empty couch. 'Yes, my lord, your guess is correct. I changed my allegiance at the same time as my former master, the chief eunuch, changed his. The Lord Gaha made me an offer, and power to the powerless is irresistible. However,' sweat started on his forehead, 'I was foolish enough to fall into a trap set for me by the chief eunuch. Unwisely, I met with the Lord Gaha in the presence of the Princess Boladé's crippled maid. She, it transpires, understands everything and, dumb though she is, in some mysterious way she is able to relay all to her royal mistress.'

Deliberately, Abiola allowed a flicker of disbelief to cross his expression.

'Oh, yes, my lord,' the remembrancer said, 'I know it to be true, for the chief eunuch repeated to me word for word what had passed at that meeting. It was in his interest to keep me alive in order not to alert the Lord Gaha who, in ignorance, entrusted me with my present mission. He wishes you dead because he knows how dear you are to your mother.'

If the remembrancer expected another reaction, Abiola gave him none.

'I shall not be returning to Bashorun Gaha's service. If I did so, I would certainly be killed. Now that I have been discovered by both sides, I'm of no use to either. The price you fetch will be more than enough to buy me a new start, out of reach of Oyo.' His glance swept over the men standing in a semi-circle around Abiola, all heavily armed. 'The sale of your horse will pay off these.'

The man was a fool, Abiola thought, there would be no horse, his right hand would have taken both of them. 'And if I resist?' he said.

'No man chooses death,' the remembrancer said. He gave a slight nod and an iron chain swung with force struck Abiola's head.

It was daylight when Abiola regained consciousness. He was naked but for his trousers, and his war charms had also been stripped from him. There was an iron collar around his neck, his left wrist was chained to the collar and he was fettered at the ankles. His limbs were cramped in the small space and he had a raging thirst. He prayed that Ogun would continue to protect him.

The chief eunuch's remembrancer entered carrying a bowl of water and a bowl of porridge, which he placed on the floor in front of Abiola.

'The lord your right hand took both horses with him.' His tone was accusatory. It provoked no reaction from his prisoner. 'Those brigands were obliged to accept your robes and war charms in lieu. I barely escaped with my skin.'

Abiola rinsed his fingers with a little of the water poured from the bowl and, despite his thirst, ate first from the bowl of porridge. The remembrancer examined the lump on the side of his head.

'A little harder,' Abiola said, 'and that blow might have lost you all your profit.'

'It was necessary.'

Abiola looked him in the eye. 'Fear is an unwise counsellor. You said yourself, any fate is preferable to death.' He continued eating. When he'd finished the porridge, he drank nearly all the water left in the bowl and rinsed his hands again.

The remembrancer gathered up the dishes. 'Take your rest. We shall be travelling by night.'

Put yourself in the mind of your enemy Lakoja said. His right hand, Abiola knew, would have done exactly that. He must have quit the room to relieve himself and hidden in the courtyard when the strangers entered. Noting how many there were, he would have come to the obvious conclusion: that the assailants were intent on kidnap and ransom, not murder. He would have judged, rightly, that he alone could not rescue Abiola, and that his best cause was to gallop for help.

The remembrancer, Abiola reasoned, would not try to ransom him himself. He could expect only death from whoever came to redeem his captive. So it would not be here at Ifonyin that Olufemi would find

Abiola but somewhere along the route. In the slave markets of the south, the remembrancer would be able drive a hard bargain, for any canny merchant would recognise that he could expect a large ransom for a captive with the markings of a noble house of Oyo. He shifted position in an attempt to ease his limbs, the iron collar around his neck and the fetters on his ankles already chafing the skin. With two horses his right hand would make fast time back to the camp. Abiola had every confidence that he would be redeemed, but he dreaded the confrontation with his brother once the ransom had been paid.

Lord Olufemi, senior Esho captain and pupil of Lakoja, abandoned his command. Riding with all haste, he was accompanied by Abiola's right hand and five war captives to be given as ransom for his brother. They made first for Ipomu in Ifé territory where they found and lost the trail. At Ijebu Odé they knew they were close, so they sped to Oworu on the coast but could discover no trace. And from there they followed the Lagos River to Badagry, arriving as dawn was breaking.

A slave ship had been riding at anchor on the waves, they were told, its captain needing only ten more captives, after a wait of many moons, to give him the complement he required. That very night a trader had arrived with a small string of captives and, most unusually, among them there had been one with Oyo markings whom it had taken four men to overpower when they emptied the slave pen.

Heedless of the fetish that forbade the Oyo people to look upon the sea, Lord Olufemi gazed after the brother whom, until now, he had not known he loved. It is the thing you imagine cannot happen that undoes you, Lakoja said. The ship, a small speck on the horizon, had set sail the night before.

BOOK TWO
Cornelius, 1758–1783

I

'WHAT AM I bid? What am I bid for this prime Negro?' the auctioneer shouted above the hubbub.

Abiola loomed over the crowd, his feet set wide on the auction block, naked but for a loincloth, and as still as a figure carved on an ancient frieze.

On this late October day mild weather coupled with the chance of a bargain had persuaded from their homes many who might not otherwise have come. Small farmers, arrived from inland by boat, tavern keepers and tradesmen travelling in mule wagons from Jamestown and Williamsburg, added the clatter of their wooden-soled boots to the clang of iron cartwheels and the noise of loaded barrels being rolled across the cobbles towards the line of boats tied up alongside the busy planters' wharf.

Observing the proceedings from the back of the throng, the owner of the wharf and the magnificent James River plantation on which it stood, permitted himself an austere smile from the dignity of his high-backed chair. The sale was under his aegis, and he could now be certain not only of recouping his expenses but also of a handsome profit. Though it was late in the season, the advertisement for the disposal of the cargo just arrived from Guinea had attracted many more prospective buyers than he had anticipated.

Standing beside the planter's chair, the ship's captain loosed his necktie, his smile broad with relief; he too could be sure of a substantial gain for himself and his English shareholders once their costs had been met. He silently thanked God for the improvement in his fortune. His brig had very nearly been destroyed by the severest squalls he could recall in all his fifteen years navigating the Middle Passage, resulting in the loss of more than a third of the cargo. Competition for the remainder had been unusually keen, however, and the bidding brisk. It would be brisker yet, he hoped, for the final lot now on the block; a magnificent specimen still, despite the depredations of the voyage. He congratulated himself on having bought well, and tried not to dwell on the profit the lost one hundred might have fetched.

'Come, gentlemen – your bids!'

Abiola continued utterly still. He was practising the hunter's trick of remaining motionless in repose, little short of miraculous after many weeks adjusting to the rolling of the sea. That he could do so was a manifestation of his will and a measure of his anger. He understood nothing of the words being shouted. The harsh cries of the gulls overhead were scarcely less intelligible than the babble of the men surrounding him. Though he could not yet distinguish gradations of tone or shades of expression in the flat cadences and pale inchoate faces of the skinless ones, there was no mistaking the signals. These people stared up at him out of their strange blue-blind eyes with the same cupidity as the horse dealers in the markets of Bornu, as if he were indeed prime horseflesh. The realisation still shocked him; the shame of it was seared on his consciousness as indelibly as the mark on his breast. He turned his eyes away from the wharf and the pink, excited faces craning up at him. He looked instead at the broad stretch of river – two bow shots wide, by his reckoning – where the ship that had transported him to Virginia rode at anchor on the water. How innocent it seemed, here in its home surroundings, a great bird floating on the smooth blue surface, white wings furled. But he had seen it in its hunting grounds. He knew the food on which it thrived.

There rose in his mind's eye the image of another quayside, bordered by dense green mangrove trees trailing long roots in the water between mats of purple sea-hyacinth. And all at once the fresh salt tang in his nostrils was replaced by the smell of smoke and burning flesh. His ears resounded with the screams of women and children as the hot iron bit through their skin. He tasted once again the bitter humiliation of being tethered to the ground, then examined and branded like an animal.

The signs even then were unmistakable, but he had clung to the teachings of Lakoja the hunter: the successful man was one who remained unaffected by good fortune or ill. His fate might have been worse had he been taken in war. As a war captive he could have been a sacrificial victim, facing certain death. But he had been taken by treachery, and delivered into the hands of dealers. Life in this world, even as a slave, was preferable to the next. Slavery could be overcome. He had seen proof enough in the number of men who had arrived in Oyo in chains and subsequently succeeded to high office. Why should he not follow their example? Even as he was stowed with his fellow captives in the huge belly of the white men's boat, he had persisted in believing that, although everything would be different, everything would also be the same.

At first he had marvelled at their death-dealing guns and their boats as big as temples, half-fish and half-bird, moving across the water with the aid, it seemed, of supernatural powers. Now, he marvelled at his former ignorance, at the depth of his unknowing. Their captors had kept them chained below, laid head to head in long rows like so many sacks of grain, layered one above the other, on wooden planks with precious little light and without the means to relieve themselves decently. The living lay side by side with the dead, shackled to each other at wrist and ankle, two by two, in the fouled spaces between the planks. The healthy, steeped in the secretions of the sick and dying, could only be impotent witnesses to their last agonies, while the stench overpowered strong and weak alike, a living, poisonous presence, ingested with every breath. A people who valued courtliness and cleanliness were reduced to a stinking mass, visited daily by the god of suffering and disease.

Abiola could hear their voices still. A people who valued life above all had called for death to come and take them. They were soon punished for this betrayal of everything they had been brought up to believe. Shango had unleashed his thunderbolts, blasting the ship, making it dance wildly on the water, as if in time to the beat of his drums. As spears of lightning pierced the narrow gratings along the deck and the captives cowered before the wrath of their god, the covers were swiftly bolted down above their heads, cutting off all light and air. Unable to secure themselves on their wooden bunks, they were flung helplessly from one side to the other, buffeted at every pitch and turn of the ship by the iron chains coupling them together, abrading their skin and wrenching limbs from their sockets. Splintered bones punctured flesh as they were slammed against the bunk posts or on to the floor. Each one tried to save himself. The storm's end, Abiola recalled, had found him pinned beneath a bloodied heap of bodies. He was bruised and badly cut, but alive. He had given thanks to Ogun that he had survived. Astonishingly, so had many of the others. It seemed the gods, though angered, had not abandoned them altogether. They had prayed then not for death but for deliverance. In that moment of euphoria, Abiola saw the small figure of a child half spilled from the mouth of an overturned soil barrel into which, unnoticed, it had fallen and drowned.

Now, at the moment of his auction, he tried to block the images, but they persisted. He could control his body it seemed, but not his mind. He saw again the Nupé warrior, one among the many who had perished during the tempest and to whom he was chained. He had carried his corpse with him, into the sunlit calm after the storm, for a count to be taken. They were strangers, divided by race with no words in each other's language, yet fate had joined them so that they had become as sons of the same mother. When the warrior's body, uncoupled from his, was thrown into the sea with the rest of the dead, Abiola had made ready to accompany this new brother to the next world. Slavery with the hope of freedom he could endure. A life in which he would be less than human he could not. Death was preferable to such dishonour.

But he had not made the leap that would have taken him to join the ancestors. For the notes of a song drifting on the breeze had suddenly scattered his strength like a broken string of beads and made him drop to his knees on the deck where, offering no resistance, he had been swiftly pinioned to another survivor. He was listening to a melody, persistent as the scent of camwood, carrying him back to the shaded courtyards and soaring roofs of Oyo, turned to gold in the sun. He heard his cousin Oluremi's voice in his ear: 'Choose life, Abiola. You must live so that we may be avenged. Remember, you have a special destiny to fulfil. Abiola, our journey has just begun.'

'Come, gentlemen, your bids!' The auctioneer had the crowd's attention now. Men pressed forward.

Abiola observed them dispassionately, no longer dazzled by the shimmer of their magic. He had chosen life, he thought grimly, among a people who had no respect for life. He recognised some of the men in the semi-circle below him. They had visited the ship to view the merchandise prior to the sale. Their fingers had prised open his mouth and examined his teeth, probed his ears, his nose, his anus; hefted his genitals. The same fingers had pawed the women and girls, groped their breasts, squeezed their buttocks, delved between their legs.

'Twenty pounds, thank you. Twenty pounds I am bid. Do I hear twenty-five? Twenty-five! Thank you, sir. Who will give me thirty? Thirty for this colossus here! Look at him, gentlemen. A truly magnificent specimen! Able to do the work of four.'

'Fifty pounds.' A voice rang out from the back. Heads turned and the crowd parted to let the bidder through.

Abiola observed him closely, but without so much as the flicker of an eyelid. This face resembled any other skinless one. Transparent. He could see the blood pulsing. There was the same protruding nose and thin line of mouth. The pale eyes of a blind dog. The man was dressed according to their usual manner in a close-fitting coat of foreign velvet, a bright red in colour, and tight knee-length trousers of yellow silk, which matched his richly embroidered under-tunic. Silver ornaments adorned his black leather shoes, and the long strings of his hair, covered in white powder, were tied behind his ears. He was not long past his first youth, for his skin was as yet unmarked by the lines which creased the faces even of those not very advanced in age among these people. The quality of his clothes denoted a noble; his manner, arrogance. Arrogance, Lakoja taught, was the first defence of the timid. If this man was to be his new master, Abiola thought, he must take care not to frighten him.

'Fifty pound, eh?' There was derision in the planter's voice. 'I did not take you for a gambler, Gilbert.'

'You are correct, sir – I am not.' Gilbert de Fromont walked unhurriedly to the front amid sniggers from the crowd. Obedient to his mother's dictate, Gilbert kept always in the centre of his mind the fact that the blood of kings ran in his veins. He gazed around, an expression of studied amusement in his eyes. He was aware that as a Frenchman, whose country was currently at war with England and her colonies, he was the object of nearly as much speculation as the figure looming so large on the auction block. Let them speculate; he was on nobody's side but his own. 'I know my Negro, I believe. We have a long acquaintance with him in the French colonies.' Longer, the implication was clear, than in Virginia.

His profit already secured, the planter replied with increased derision, 'But to bid so high for an unskilled, unseasoned slave direct from Guinea? It is too late to put him to work on the tobacco crop, he will have to be unprofitably fed until the spring.'

Gilbert raised his voice for all to hear. 'If I were a gambler, sir, I would wager another fifty that no one here will exceed my offer.'

The planter spoke the truth: Guinea slaves were cheaper than home-born ones, and this far advanced in the season prices generally fell steeply. Gilbert flicked the lace of his immaculate cuff. The creature on the stand was a bargain at any price, exactly what these small farmers, innkeepers, horse traders and speculators would have hoped to find. He had called their bluff; he would see now if they would call his. He would go to seventy-five pounds if need be.

Removing a scented handkerchief from his sleeve and putting it to his nose, Gilbert moved to stand beside the auction block. It was said that you could smell a slave ship from five miles away, and no wonder. The Negro stank horribly, but he was newly shaved and looked healthy enough, although the sheen on the skin was certainly oil, a common ruse of the ships' captains. He was well muscled, there was power in every line of him, a quite repellent physicality, but strength was the principal requirement. Gilbert pressed the folds of his spotless handkerchief firmly against his nostrils and drew closer still. There were raw, raised welts around the wrists and ankles, but no whip scars on the back and shoulders, which would have marked him out as recalcitrant or ungovernable. He appeared uncannily still; petrified with fear, no doubt.

Gilbert scrutinised the pattern of cuts on the dark face, a set of four horizontal lines half an inch long on either cheek. He had never seen that precise configuration before, neither in the French Caribbean islands of St Domingue, Martinique or Guadaloupe, nor in Carolina. He skimmed the notice of sale posted on the wall behind: *To Be Sold . . . A Cargo of . . . Negroes . . . Just Arrived . . . in the Brigantine Bemba . . . From the Bight of Benin.'* Gilbert would have preferred a Negro from Senegambia, for they generally possessed a higher intellect. This leviathan appeared to have none; there was no discernible glimmer of intelligence in the downcast eyes. But there was something . . . Gilbert took an involuntary step backwards. He wished suddenly that he had availed himself of the opportunity of an examination on board ship. If the creature proved vicious, there could be no appeal to reason; there would be one recourse only: to put him down.

'Do I hear any advance on fifty pounds? Any advance on fifty pounds?' There was no response.

Gilbert, affecting indifference, sauntered back the way he had come. He understood now the cause of their reticence and cursed his stupidity. He had been a fool. He could have secured this pig in a poke for half the price.

'Fifty pounds. Once. Twice. Very well, fifty pounds it is. To the gentleman on my right here.'

'I congratulate you on your *bargain*, Gilbert.' The planter slapped the arm of his chair. A burst of laughter greeted his words.

'Thank you.' Bowing exaggeratedly low, Gilbert made an ironic flourish with his handkerchief. 'He will suit my purpose.'

The planter's smile broadened. 'If only all our purchasers were so astute. I trust you will honour us with your presence again before too long,' he said, eliciting mirth on all sides.

'You flatter me.' Gilbert bowed again, his face flushed red. 'And now, if you will excuse me . . .' He sauntered away towards the stand to take possession of his new purchase.

'*We* have some acquaintance with Negroes in Virginia *too*,' a wag shouted after him.

Gilbert ignored the shaft. How he despised these colonists. They were ruffians and even the richest among them had no lineage. The planter, for all he was the owner of numerous plantations, had a candle-maker for a grandfather.

Gilbert addressed the auctioneer. 'Behold me!'

'Eh?'

'I am here,' Gilbert said testily, venting his anger at last, 'to collect.'

The auctioneer gestured to his assistants. A rifle butt in the ribs on one side and a blow from a cudgel on the other, accompanied by a yelled command, propelled Abiola down from the auction block. His complete lack of reaction to the blows made Gilbert's chest contract. So intent was he on weighing up his acquisition, he had failed to notice the violent commotion breaking out behind him. At the last moment he swung round to discover a bolting horse practically upon him, a broken cart shaft dragging along the ground behind and a half-dozen of the planter's Negroes in yelling pursuit. The crowd, visitors and workers alike, scattered in panic sending bales, boxes, and barrels in all directions.

'Move! Move! *Imbécile!*' Gilbert shouted at his new purchase, who stood directly in the path of the flailing hooves.

Cursing, Gilbert kissed adieu to his fifty pounds and leapt for cover.

Abiola reached out and instinctively caught the horse's bridle in both hands. He hauled down hard. The frightened animal continued on its headlong dash, dragging him the length of the wharf until it seemed that the two of them must end in the river. But eventually the weight of Abiola's chains and his gentling voice brought the runaway to a lathered halt just short of the water's edge.

As a servant hastened to right his upturned chair, the planter readjusted the white stock he wore at his neck, shook out the capacious folds of his black velvet frock coat and, sitting down once again, addressed the Frenchman with new respect. 'Gilbert,' he said, 'your Hercules will need to be broken. Allow me, if you will, to buy him back from you.'

Gilbert stared at his new possession, who, could he but have known, was berating himself for forgetting one of the principal rules of his training and throwing the game away before it had even begun. If your enemy believes you to be foolish, Lakoja taught, you have the advantage. Gilbert continued to stare. Abiola hung his head submissively. The Frenchman tilted his chin triumphantly. The blood of kings. He turned back to the planter. 'I thank you, but no. I shall be David to his Goliath.'

'Virginians have a preference for the virtues of Rome.'

'I have no dispute with that.' Gilbert flourished his handkerchief with an insolence that could not but be noted yet was insufficient for a quarrel. The planter inclined his head. 'Nor indeed with Virginians.' Gilbert turned, looked at Abiola again and, smiling, he said, 'In his lines he is reminiscent, is he not, of a figure painted on an urn? I shall name him Cornelius.'

2

CORNELIUS LAY BETWEEN sleeping and waking, listening to the birdsong beginning outside, in transition from his night- to his day-time self. In his dreams he was Abiola communing with Oluremi, secure in the knowledge that his ancestors were watching over him, certain that they would intercede on his behalf with Olodumaré, the supreme being, to grant him the strength to fulfil his destiny and restore the honour of his line. Each night he was reminded that, although the web which held all together had unravelled, the thread had not broken. And each night it was as if he were reborn, as if he were once again choosing his ori, reaffirming the fate he had selected at birth to accompany his spirit into the world. As morning approached, Abiola heard the sound of his father's drum beating out the family oriki, summoning him from his bed, and Cornelius awoke with the verses on his lips, knowing that, one day, he would return home.

He slid his narrow pallet and thin blanket out of sight beneath his master's high bed. A board squeaked and he paused, but the snores continued behind the heavy embroidered curtains tight closed like the window drapes against the chill of early fall. Shoes and stockings in hand, he slipped noiselessly from the room, down the uncarpeted stairs and out of the house, across the yard to the pump. There was frost on the ground but he was as inured now to the cold as he was to heat. He welcomed the privacy of darkness during the one brief period of the day that was his own. Invisible in the dark, he sank to the ground beneath the branches of an old fruit tree and leaned his back against its lichen-covered trunk to review his plans. He had been plotting his escape since the day of his purchase three years before and perhaps even before that when he'd noted the presence of African crew members on board the slaver. Now at last the way was prepared. The trick, Lakoja taught, is not to counter your enemy's moves but to choose them. You are ready when it is his broom that is clearing the path. Cornelius smiled to himself in the darkness. It would be his master who would unwittingly aid his escape.

Carrying Lakoja's teachings always in his mind, thoughts of Lady Faloyan, his mother, were never far behind; she who had had the foresight to have him trained by the great hunter, and who would no doubt be disappointed to see him return to Oyo as a messenger and not as a king or conqueror. But his destiny might yet prove greater than even she had imagined, for if he succeeded in his mission he would be instrumental in saving their people from destruction. Thinking of his mother and how she had fared these past three years, he imagined her wounded and unforgiving, rendered infinitely more dangerous by the pain of his loss – and he pitied her enemies.

He permitted himself no further travel in his thoughts, preferring instead to hone his anger on a precise recollection of what it was to be a slave in the world of white men. He understood his purpose now: it was to bear witness. And within the week he would take the first step. He rose to his feet and, still protected by the darkness, removed his shirt and breeches and hung them on a branch of the apple tree under which he had been sitting. Standing in the open courtyard with only the eye of the morning star as witness, he washed himself thoroughly, drenching his body in icy pump water. Under his breath, he recited the lines of his oriki, girding himself with the verses, fashioning a war cloth to wear next his skin. 'And help me,' he finished, 'not to strangle that pinprick, my master.'

'Good morning, my brother.' Zobeide, the cook, greeted Cornelius over her shoulder. She was already at work, seated on a low stool in front of the fire tending a dozen or more pots on the open hearth that ran the length of the chimney wall.

Closing the kitchen door softly behind him, Cornelius returned her smile with genuine warmth. He owed her more than he could ever repay. In those first days in Williamsburg when Gilbert had kept him tethered on a chain in the courtyard beside the necessary house, Zobeide had eased his injured spirit by the elaborate courtesy with which she served him his food each day.

'Good morning, my sister.' Cornelius bowed. He stowed his scrap of soap and chewing stick wrapped in a cloth behind the oak dresser against the opposite wall and joined the cook in front of the fire. 'It will be a fine day,' he said, warming his hands at the blaze.

'Better for some than for others,' she replied, her voice heavy, ladling stew from a black iron pot into a bowl.

Cornelius took the bowl in both hands and with a sudden flourish brought it close to his face, burying his nose in the steam and inhaling deeply. 'Excellent,' he proclaimed, kissing his fingers in a perfect parody of Gilbert. Then, shooting his cuffs, he shook out the folds of an imaginary frock coat before sinking gracefully on to a nearby stool, one foot placed just so in front of the other.

'*Idiot!*' Laughing, Zobeide busied herself with her pans. 'But you will go to heaven.'

'I hope not. From what you describe, it is all playing and singing, a place fit only for children.' Helping himself to bread, Cornelius began spooning the stew from his bowl.

There was an easy silence while Zobeide attended to the individual fires burning briskly under the pots on the hearth, using a long-handled shovel to shift the hot embers about as needed. Words were always sparse between them. At first it had been because Cornelius had none except in his own tongue. Zobeide began giving him a few words of French, but Gilbert, over-hearing them in the kitchen, quickly took it upon himself to do the teaching. So now, though valet and cook spoke the same language, in doing so each muddied the pool for the other, she with the barefoot Creole of her native Guadaloupe, Cornelius with the well-heeled syllables of a royal courtier. But theirs was a deeper intimacy. They shared the secrets of each other's lives. She had seen him chained like a dog. And since he slept at the foot of their master's bed, he was witness to her violation.

'The master's water is ready,' Zobeide said, the meaning of these words plain enough; they were the signal for Cornelius to begin his morning tasks. By the time the fire in the master's bedroom had been lit, his clothes laid out and his shaving things prepared, the water would be at exactly the required temperature. He jumped up from his seat, but Zobeide waved at him to finish his food. She removed a large cauldron from the fire, set it down on the hearth and replaced it with another. Juggling six or seven pans suspended from sturdy pothooks at various heights above the flames, she busied herself with the elaborate preparation demanded by Gilbert's exacting taste.

Cornelius wiped his bowl clean with the last of his bread. He was tempted to confide, but erased the idea as soon as it occurred. It would be a poor return to add the burden of betrayal to the punishment she would inevitably receive.

'Thank you.' Tenderly he touched her face, the gesture conveying all he could not say.

When Cornelius pulled back the curtains surrounding his master's four-poster bed, Gilbert de Fromont squinted up at him from the deep comfort of a feather mattress and thick coverlets, a milky hand shading his eyes against the light entering dimly through the leaded window-panes. A white worm blinking in its burrow, Cornelius thought, intercepting his master's sneaking sideways glance at the place beside him on the bed. It was empty, as usual, the cook's departure having followed immediately upon Cornelius's exit to the yard.

'Good day, master.' Cornelius forced a smile and, for one fantastical moment, gazing down at the blue-veined face pillowed on finest white holland, he imagined Oyo words issuing from that scant mouth. His yearning for the music of his own tongue was sharpest at the start of the day, when its echoes resonated in his head, lingering remnants of his dreams.

Blind to the poignancy of that smile, Gilbert swung his legs out of the bed. He did not deign to return the greeting. Cornelius knelt to guide his master's feet into a pair of velvet slippers precisely positioned on the floor, before helping him into a silk robe slipped over his nightshirt for the short journey to the bathtub drawn up by the fire. He had long since adjusted to the discovery that, in matters of etiquette, the skinless ones were as coarse and unrefined as in their personal habits. Gilbert, though, had acquired the habit of taking a daily bath in the Caribbean islands and in this small respect Cornelius had come to realise that he should consider himself fortunate. He had not thought so in the beginning, needing the whole of his resolve to overcome his revulsion. Now he could smile at the irony of using his warrior training to carry out women's work. He had become adept at bathing his master; his stomach no longer turning as he meticulously worked down from the top of Gilbert's shaven head to the tips of his pink soled feet, rinsing the dirt from the soft, white-furred trunk and limbs, careful that no soap should enter and sting those colourless eyes.

Gilbert did not speak until he was comfortably settled in the chair that had replaced the bathtub in front of the fire. He proffered his chin. Cornelius wrapped it in a hot towel.

'How does the day look, Cornelius?'

'The day promises well, master,' Cornelius replied, in the same beautiful French. 'The air is crisp and clear. I foresee no rain.' He removed the towel.

Gilbert's face brightened. 'You cannot imagine what pleasure it gives me to hear my native tongue. The ache is sharpest, I find, at the start of the day.'

'Yes, master,' Cornelius said evenly.

'So. I shall indulge myself. Recite something for me. One of the Greek stories, I think. I prefer the Greeks, whatever I may say outside. They were superior to the Romans in precisely the same way as the French are to the English.'

'And the Virginians,' Cornelius said, soaping Gilbert's face.

'Indeed.' Gilbert shut his eyes in anticipation. 'Tell me the story of Prometheus,' he commanded, choosing at random from the store he himself had furnished.

'Prometheus,' Cornelius began obediently, 'was the fire god of the Greeks, a son of the Titan Iapetus and the nymph Clymene.' He stropped the razor on a leather strap, tested its edge on his thumb. 'Some say his was the gift of life itself, that he modelled mankind out of clay . . .' The blade stroked Gilbert's soft cheek, downward from the ear. 'When Zeus, chief of all the gods, angered at receiving less than his due share of sacrifices, deprived mankind of fire, Prometheus stole a flame from the workshop of Hephaistos and gave it to them. In retaliation, Zeus chained him to a rock and sent an eagle every day to feed on his liver, which was restored each succeeding night.'

Gilbert, listening with his eyes shut, gave a little shiver of delight; then, opening them again, experienced another frisson at the sight of

Cornelius's big black hand on the razor which, instead of removing the hair from his upper lip, might just as easily have slit his throat. 'Who would have believed it?' Gilbert said, as if he himself could not bring himself to. 'Your intonation is perfect, your accent so refined. To think when you first came into my possession three short years ago you had no language at all.'

Cornelius smiled. Those three short years of Gilbert's had been the longest of his own life. At first he had retreated into silence, until the cook succeeded in conveying to him that this maddened Gilbert, who took it as a sign he was being ignored. A vocal response, she advised, would avoid the kicks and blows. So Cornelius had produced a kind of gibberish, loath to use the Oyo tongue in such degrading circumstances.

Gilbert gazed up at him nostalgically. 'People said it could not be done, and I confess I was not without qualms in teaching a slave to read and write. After all, you have only to lift your heel a fraction for any creature trapped beneath to try and make good its escape.' Gilbert's eyes lingered pointedly on the marks scored across Cornelius's cheeks. 'But in truth, the risk was small. Your appearance is, shall I say, a little too arresting for you to pass as a freed man hereabouts and, allied to exquisite French but precious little English, you would get . . .' Gilbert shrugged his silk-clad shoulders, 'How far would you get, Cornelius?'

Cornelius gave him a big open smile and threw up his hands. 'No further than the door.'

Gilbert grinned back. This was a game he liked to play, safe in the knowledge that what he said was true.

Except, in one respect, Cornelius thought, enveloping Gilbert's face in a hot towel. His English was rather better than Gilbert's, for he had applied himself assiduously to learning it, and, equally assiduously to hiding it. Gilbert imagined, and he encouraged him in it, that his slave spent his time sleeping whenever required to wait for his master to emerge from the theatre, a ball, or a long evening in the tavern. English had not come as readily to Cornelius as French – to which his ear, used to the cadences of Oyo, seemed more attuned – but eventually he had mastered it.

Cornelius removed the towel from Gilbert's face. Able to see once more, Gilbert burrowed deeper into his chair and stretched slippered feet towards the fire. He shut his eyes again and commanded, 'Tell me, Cornelius, who rescued Prometheus from the mountain?'

'Heracles, son of Alcmena and Zeus, who was driven mad by Zeus's jealous wife, Hera. In his madness, Heracles slew his own family, and in expiation undertook the twelve labours.' Cornelius continued to remove all traces of beard from Gilbert's face. 'After slaying Iphitos, Heracles was sold as a slave to Omphale, queen of Lydia, and set to women's work. He died as the result of poison from one of his own arrows.'

Gilbert's lashes fluttered open. Slyly he glanced up. 'The ironies are delicious, are they not?'

Cornelius gazed back, his eyes uncomprehending.

'Never mind. It seems I need not have worried,' Gilbert said. 'Although I suppose I did hope that you would possess something more than the usual capacity common to Negroes.' He patted Cornelius's arm. 'Don't look so crestfallen. You are far more amusing than a parrot, and a near faultless servant besides. I could not wish for a more accomplished valet, serving man or groom. There! You have exceeded my ambitions. Base metal can't be turned to gold, but I have come as close as it's possible to do. I have transformed you, Cornelius, into a servant worth his weight in gold.'

'That is indisputable, master.' Cornelius's teeth flashed. Schooling himself to servitude had been the hardest won of all his attainments.

Gilbert glanced at him sharply, but Cornelius's grin was guileless.

'I shall not part with you, Cornelius. When I establish myself in Carolina, you'll come with me. I shall put you in charge of ordering my household. And Zobeide, too, though she will be confined to the kitchen once I am master not of two but two hundred slaves.'

Gilbert's frequently declared intention of purchasing a plantation was dismissed about the town as an empty boast. Usually he was in his cups.

'You will be a great lord,' Cornelius assured him. He knew, as others could not, how very near Gilbert was to achieving his ambition. In truth, he was Gilbert's closest confidant, which was not, he imagined, what his master had envisaged when he bought his African slave.

Plucking a phial from the crowded dressing stand, Cornelius admired for a moment the colour of the liquid inside as it turned deep amber in the glow of the firelight and winter candles. Gilbert had hit upon a certainty to relieve the newly rich tobacco planters of Virginia of their surplus. Knowing how the owners of the big plantations aspired to the refinements of Europe, and above all to the accomplishments of music and dancing, Gilbert had become a purveyor of the finest musical instruments Europe could provide. Cornelius accompanied him, driving the wagon, and loading and unloading the harpsichords, claviers, harps, violins and violoncellos at each distinguished destination.

He removed the stopper from the bottle, poured a few drops on to his palms, and began massaging the lemon-scented oil into Gilbert's close-shaved scalp.

Gilbert, he had soon come to understand, had not acted out of cruelty in keeping him on a chain but out of fear for his own safety, there being no one else in his household beside himself and Zobeide. And it was loneliness, Cornelius realised, that had led him to educate his new slave in the ways of a nobleman of his native country. Gilbert's vanity forbade him entry to the highest circles in Williamsburg, and that same vanity held him aloof from the dancing masters, the musicians, actors and journeymen of the town. Gilbert had fashioned in Cornelius a fit companion, in whose company he might imagine he was home again in his beloved France.

How well Cornelius understood Gilbert's longing for home! He too would have conjured an age-mate from Oyo if he could. He poured more scent from the bottle and began working downwards from Gilbert's forehead to his cheeks and chin. In the art of sword fighting, he had soon overtaken his teacher, who had neither the co-ordination of hand and eye, nor the supreme horsemanship required of the Oyo cavalry. Gilbert, he reflected, would have benefited from a warrior's training. An Oyo warrior, for his part, would have benefited from mastering the art of study instead of disdaining literacy as an attribute of slaves. He applied a final dab of scent to Gilbert's chin. It was no accident, he thought, that their lives had been entwined these past three years. It was part of the fate each had chosen at birth.

Gilbert sighed noisily. 'I am soul-weary of this continuous huckstering from county to county, this undignified importuning from one plantation to the next.'

Cornelius handed him a looking-glass. Gilbert subjected his reflection to close scrutiny, angling his head this way and that before announcing himself satisfied. Cornelius stepped forward and for a moment the two of them were within the frame, admiring their handiwork. Gilbert addressed Cornelius's image: 'There were those who said you could not be tamed. I believe I have more than proved my mastery.'

Gilbert returned the looking-glass. Cornelius received it with a respect-ful bow. Power, Lakoja said, came in many guises and its successful exercise lay in recognising them.

*

Fallen leaves gleamed like fresh-minted coins in the play of sunlight on the green in front of the governor's palace and along the verges of the roads. It was, as Cornelius had predicted, a bright, clear day and Gilbert, in polished boots and a curled brown wig with two long ringlets secured at the neck by a black ribbon, cut a well-dressed swathe through the traffic, doffing his hat to acquaintances on all sides as he cantered by on his gleaming chestnut mount. Cornelius was hard pressed to keep up. He was driving a heavily loaded cart, which was testing even for the two powerful black dray horses pulling valiantly between the shafts.

As they turned on to the Richmond Road, heading out of town, Gilbert's mood lightened; he began to whistle and fell back to ride beside the cart. It was remarkable, Cornelius thought, that a man could make such large profits from the sale of musical instruments despite having no ear, nor any feeling for music. He was grateful, though, for Gilbert's considerable intelligence; as a result of listening to the Frenchman's discourses he, too, had profited from these journeys. He would not be shamed now beside the best of the Oyo remembrancers. He looked up in anticipation as Gilbert reined in beside him.

'Know a man's weaknesses and you have the man,' Gilbert said.

And he might have added, Cornelius thought, that it was the reason so few had possession of themselves.

'Is that so, master?'

'Robert Farrer, Esquire, whom we have the honour of visiting, is a true Virginian aristocrat.' Cornelius noted the thin ribbon of contempt threading the words. 'To which, Cornelius, you might respond, "What does that signify?"'

'What does it signify, master?' Cornelius asked, this being a game *he* liked to play.

'It signifies' – Gilbert pulled the ribbon tight – 'that his genealogy will not bear scrutiny, that he will be haughty and overbearing, eager to impress his social inferiors with the trappings of his wealth and power. He will detest being reminded that, despite all his expenditures he remains a *parvenu*. Terrified of appearing provincial, he will spend too heavily, gamble too much, and be over protective of his dignity.'

'A fat capon easily plucked,' Cornelius said.

Gilbert gave a shout of laughter.

*

'Elegant.' Gilbert pursed his lips in admiration. 'And prettier still, I dare say, on the river side.' Gesturing to Cornelius to follow him, he turned off the main road and cantered down a broad avenue lined with majestic beeches through which, a distance away, could be glimpsed the severe façade of a brick two-storey mansion.

Cornelius turned in skilfully behind him, driving the wagon at a smart pace beneath wide overhanging branches, glancing from side to side at the neat fields and scattered woodlands stretching to the horizon. They were met halfway from the house by a horde of slave children, racing alongside on a carpet of yellow leaves, dangerously close to the heavy wheels and horses' hooves, forming a noisy, chattering escort to the entrance.

Before Gilbert could dismount, the door of the house was thrown wide by a liveried footman, bowing from the waist. Relinquishing his horse to a groom, Gilbert straightened his coat, shook out his snowy shirt ruffles and swept inside, abandoning Cornelius to the children and the curious stares of the servants.

The groom waved a hand at a young man hovering at a distance, summoning him to hold the heads of the two wagon horses. He shouted over his shoulder. 'Auntie! Auntie! Come! These children are worse than a swarm of bees. Call them off before the gentleman here gets stung to death.' He smiled at Cornelius. Cornelius returned the smile and climbed down from the wagon. He swung two of the smallest infants high into the air and sat them astride the horses, encouraging the rest to clamour louder than before. In a moment a gleeful half-dozen were riding high while the others, yelling, arms up in the air, were pitching to join them. An old woman hustled round the corner of the house, her switch expeditiously applied to the bare legs of the nearest children, strewing them like chaff. Cornelius greeted her with a deferential bow. She returned his greeting with a nod, her look of surprise replaced by one of enlightenment as she registered his face markings.

'My daddy was from Africa,' she informed him. 'They know how to train up children in that place all right. Not like here, where they grow up with no behaviour.' She kissed her teeth at the head groom and his assistant. Cornelius lifted down the remaining children, who dashed off, nimble as grasshoppers, with the old lady in pursuit.

The laughter of the grooms as they turned to Cornelius was abruptly halted by Gilbert's reappearance in the open doorway, admonishing his slave to make haste to unload the wagon.

The two grooms stared at Cornelius.

'What kind of lingo was that?' asked one in astonishment.

'Don't you recognise a Frenchman when you see one?' the other replied.

'Of course I do, but *he*'s not one, is he?' said the first, pointing his chin at Cornelius.

His companion addressed Cornelius directly. 'Do you speak English?' he demanded.

'Small.' Cornelius demonstrated just how little with his thumb and forefinger.

'No chance of this rabbit running, eh?' The footman cast a sly look round, provoking a ripple of laughter from the servants sweeping leaves from the drive.

Cornelius stared innocently about him.

A voice called to him from the doorstep. 'You're wanted. Look sharp, or you'll be spoken to in a language we all understand.' Framed in the doorway beneath its handsome fanlight, the speaker hovered for a moment and was gone. In his place, he left a subtle silence, which spoke loudly, Cornelius thought, of one who was favoured above his peers.

The groom shivered. 'That was Cato,' he said.

Gilbert paused theatrically beside the baize-covered 'mystery' in the centre of the music room. Sunlight pouring through the many tall windows sparkled on his coat buttons, jewelled the portraits pinned high on the fine wood panelling, gilded the expectant faces below. The Frenchman's eyes rested tantalisingly on each in turn: the master of the house, his lady, two round-eyed children, and the servants ranged along the walls. He signed to Cornelius, who stepped forward and with one flick of his arm removed the green cloth covering.

'Madame,' Gilbert addressed the mistress of the house, 'what do you see before you?'

'A harpsichord, and a very plain one at that.' The corners of Celia Farrer's rosebud mouth curved downwards.

'*Non, non, non!*' Gilbert waved a reproachful finger. 'I promised you something absolutely extraordinary, and I am a man of my word.' His eyes toured the room once more. 'What you see before you is a piano forte. Even the king of England does not have one. This is from the workshop of Herr Gottfried Silberman, manufacturer of these wonderful new instruments to none other than Frederick the Great of Prussia. I assure, you they will soon be all the rage.'

'Piano forte?'

'Exactly, madame. As the name implies, it plays both soft and loud.'

He sat down on a stool that had been pushed forward in anticipation by Cornelius, and on the keyboard struck some phrases that he had learned by rote.

'You hear?' Gilbert cocked his head, affecting a finely tuned ear. 'Here, you have all the resonance, the magnificence, the glitter of the harpsichord's sound' – he played some more – 'combined with the gentleness, the expressive delicacy of the little clavier.' He rose from his seat and, hand on breast, fixed his fine eyes on the lady of the house. 'This beautiful instrument, in common with the human voice, is able, with its rise and fall in volume, to match the ebb and flow of the emotions of the human heart.'

Celia gasped and clasped her hands together.

Cornelius gave thanks to Ogun. The sale was assured. Within a week he and Gilbert would be in Carolina and he could put his plans into action. He relaxed his guard and could not prevent his eyes from straying towards the servant girl, sixteen or seventeen, he thought, standing behind her mistress's chair. They made a pretty picture, maid and mistress, one dark, the other pale. One small child peeped out from her nurse's skirts and the other leant an elbow on her mother's knee.

'Will you not try it for yourself, madame?' Gilbert invited.

'Oh, yes.' Celia Farrer jumped up, stopped, glanced at her husband and, advancing rather more sedately, plucked up a sheet of music and placed it in front of her at the piano forte. She arranged her wide paniered skirts over the music stool and began to play, singing to her own accompaniment in a pure, sweet voice. Gilbert stood by, gallantly turning the pages at her nods. At the end, Celia, her cheeks flushed with elation, took a curtsey to enthusiastic applause.

'Robert, we must have it. I insist.' She looked up at her husband through her lashes, 'Can we?'

'Of course, my dear. And the other.'

'The other?'

Robert Farrer gestured languidly towards Cornelius. 'His man here.' He turned to Gilbert. 'What is his name, monsieur?'

Two of the young servant girls tittered. Celia glanced instinctively at Cato, her husband's valet, stationed behind his master's chair. Like the footmen standing against the walls, Cato stared intently at the floor in the now silent room.

'He is not for sale, sir,' Gilbert said haughtily, taking an unconscious step towards Cornelius, who had become as inanimate as the wood panelling behind him. Cornelius breathed a little easier. Gilbert was so close to achieving his ambition of owning his own plantation, he could afford a heroic gesture.

'Both or none.'

'His worth is quite esoteric.' Gilbert waved his handkerchief. 'He is valuable only to me.'

'Your boast earlier over a glass of wine, sir, was somewhat different. Even if we discount the unique entertainment to be gained from his speaking French like a viscount, he is an excellent valet, you said, and a waiting man, coachman and groom –'

Gilbert broke in: 'The fact remains, sir, I could not in fairness ask a sum that would adequately reflect his particular worth to me.'

'Name your price.'

Farrer no doubt imagined that Gilbert's reluctance was a ploy to drive up the offer. He was mistaken. Gilbert had had no intention of selling.

Making a pad of his handkerchief, Gilbert dabbed at the sweat stippling his upper lip, and paced about the room. Would Farrer pay enough to deliver his dream at one stroke? Minutes passed, punctuated only by the squeak of his silver-buckled shoes and the click of his heels on the wooden floorboards. 'Very well,' he conceded finally, with a perfunctory bow to his host. He named a huge sum. To his surprise, agreement followed in a single curt 'Yes.'

'Perhaps now you will oblige me with his name,' Robert Farrer added dryly.

'He is known as Cornelius.'

Former master and slave exchanged a deep look.

Gilbert felt badly used by fate, which would not permit him to have his cake and eat it. The pity of it brought tears to his eyes.

Cornelius, on the other hand, sought refuge once more in the hunter's trick, but it had deserted him and he leaned against the wall for support. On the rice coast of the Carolinas new fortunes were being made. There, Gilbert would take the Farrer money and seek his future. Cornelius might have accompanied him. Among the thousands of slaves newly imported from Africa, one more might not have attracted attention. One who had striven and saved money and laid his plans might have slipped away and been safely smuggled aboard a boat bound for one of the French islands or Barbados. From there he might have worked his passage home. *It is the thing you imagine cannot happen that undoes you*, Lakoja had said.

∾

3

ROBERT FARRER WAS soon as much in thrall to his new toy as his wife was to hers. Neglecting the stillroom and kitchen, Celia spent hours in the music room practising on her forte piano, as she had learnt to call the instrument in the English manner, while Robert remained closeted with his slave in the library when he might have been better occupied at this time of year in his curing sheds where the tobacco crop, hung up to dry, needed constant attention. His was the more serious dereliction, for want of care at this stage might well result in the loss of the year's profit. Proper curing, they said, represented the planter's most serious challenge; too much moisture and the leaves would rot, too little would render them dry and brittle enough to disintegrate before reaching England. But he was deaf to everyone except Cornelius.

As a young man, at the end of his grand tour of Europe, Robert had spent several years in Paris and he still considered the French court the epicentre of the civilised world. He took endless delight, therefore, in speaking the language again, immersing himself in the culture and revisiting that glorious time of his youth. He gave Cornelius old and new works from his library to study, afterwards testing him and encouraging questions. Cornelius was careful to reveal a sufficient intelligence to be interesting but not enough to be threatening, or endangering to himself. And if Robert's complacency was shaken at times, it was restored by the knowledge that Cornelius was making precious little progress in English. His new slave, it appeared, was a marvellous talking manikin and moreover one who, deputised to shadow Cato, had quickly picked up the ways his new master liked things done.

The familiar sight of Robert going about the plantation accompanied by his right hand, the slave Cato, had been supplanted by the sight of the master with a left hand as well as a right hand.

There was novelty for Robert, too, in Cornelius's being an African rather than a home-born slave. Not since Robert's grandfather's time had the Farrers purchased outlandish slaves for the home plantation. In fact, they had only infrequently purchased slaves at all, their field hands as well as the house servants being almost without exception descendants of those first Africans.

'Tell me about your home, Cornelius,' Robert asked, as he was preparing for the day in his dressing room. 'As I recall, my father used to say that, if the Africans were to be believed, they were all princes in their own country. Is that true of you?' Robert threw an ironic glance at Cato, who was holding up a patterned waistcoat for him to wear over silk breeches and ruffled linen shirt.

'No, master, not prince.' Cornelius too glanced at Cato. He knew Cato resented his sessions with Robert in the library, and the times when the three of them were together and Robert insisted on conversing entirely in French, excluding Cato.

'I thought not.' Robert considered another waistcoat. 'My father also used to say that those who had been princes among their own people were haughty and ungovernable.' Cornelius did not reply. 'Well? I await enlightenment. Just what is the condition of life among the savages? You may tell me in English.' Smiling, Robert slipped his arms into the waistcoat Cato proffered. He held Cato's eye, now prepared for some sport at Cornelius's expense.

'Master . . .' Cornelius spoke haltingly in English, 'life there . . . same as here . . . on plantation.'

'You amaze me. Continue.' Robert stood still as Cato fastened the long row of silver buttons.

'In city of Oyo, where born, king rule. But his chiefs, masters in own compounds. Some also master of small towns ruled by junior chiefs. Like you, master. You master of home plantation and also quarters upriver ruled by overseers. Chief, like you, is father to all. Servants and slaves all his children. In him all power and all benefit come.'

It was Robert who now glanced covertly at Cato, as his valet shrugged him into a burgundy frock coat, smoothing the velvet across the shoulders, adjusting the high collar, aligning the frogged edges, which fell away so that the embroidered waistcoat could be seen underneath. Robert shook out his cuffs and studied his reflection full length in the looking-glass. 'The similarities must appear striking to someone with a naïve understanding of our system. But morality divides us utterly. You are strangers to Christianity and its values, your culture is demonstrably debased and without refinement of any sort. I shall probe no further. It was foolish of me to imagine that something might be gained.'

'Yes, master,' Cornelius replied, making an effort to appear crestfallen.

They were interrupted by a small boy scratching at the door. Cornelius was sent for. The mistress required his presence in the weaving house: his clothes were ready to be fitted.

'You may go.' Robert dismissed Cornelius with a wave and, when the door had closed behind them, lowered himself on to a chair. 'At last,' he said, 'I can present my new wonder to the public. But how best to do it, eh, Cato?'

Cato came to kneel by his chair. 'I have an idea . . .'

Cornelius ruffled the curls of the young boy trotting at his side and smiled down into the big trustful eyes. The child was handsome and could have been taken for a brother of Cato. They were both of the same light brown complexion, indicative of a skinless one as a father. Cornelius was disappointed that Cato was holding to the promise of that first glittering smile of hatred towards him. He had not expected him to be an ally – the nature of their situation precluded that – but he had hoped to prevent him from becoming an enemy. Even a fool could see Cato would be a dangerous adversary. Cornelius resolved to ensure that Robert, whose reaction had been entirely predictable, did not begin to suspect that his new slave was more than he appeared. He would have to guard himself more closely than ever; any slip would prove costly. His master, he knew, would have banished him to his furthest quarters had he told him exactly how similar Fairlawns Plantation was to a chief's compound in Oyo. It had not taken him long to discover, for example, that the beautiful Delilah, the mistress's personal maid, was Robert's junior wife and, as in any chief's house, there were rival factions around Celia and her servant. There was a crucial difference, though: Delilah would be for ever a slave and her children also. Cornelius had thought he was beyond being shocked by this society until at Fairlawns he saw with his own eyes how the skinless ones were so perverted in their beliefs that they condemned even their own offspring to slavery. He was more than ever resolved to return home to Oyo and open the eyes of his people to the fate to which they were sending the captives they sold across the sea.

In his dreams, Oluremi had not deserted him; he felt her presence a dozen times a day, strengthening his determination and reassuring him that Ogun would show him the way to fulfil his destiny. He looked down at the child prattling happily at his side and, for an instant, saw him grown like Cato, his anger a poisoned arrow in his gut. Ruffling the boy's curls again, Cornelius vowed that, whatever happened and however long he lived, he would never father a child while he remained a slave.

'Cornelius,' Celia said as soon as he entered the weaving house, 'put on your livery so that we can see if it needs any alteration.'

'Here, mistress?' Cornelius glanced around the room, which was full of female servants.

'Yes, here.'

Cornelius glanced around again and all except Celia averted their gaze. Her eyes remained unblinkingly upon him as he shed the coachman's rig in which he'd arrived, dropping everything on the floor in his haste to cover himself again. It was not until he was arrayed in the green plush coat and breeches and red waistcoat all lavishly edged with livery lace which was the uniform of the male house servants at the Fairlawns Plantation that the other slaves joined their mistress in appraising the fit of the suit, which like every garment in the house, had been ordered, irrespective of expense, from London. The suit did in fact fit remarkably well and the women's eyes travelled from Cornelius's sharply defined cheekbones to his broad shoulders and down to his shapely calves, exposed now in white knitted stockings.

'Turn round,' Celia commanded. Cornelius did as he was bid.

'Tabitha' – Celia gestured to the young woman beside her – 'bring me the stool.' Tabitha steadied her mistress as she stepped up. 'Delilah, come.' Celia beckoned her forward, so that all three stood directly behind Cornelius, whose back was now turned towards them. 'Look, the coat is not quite wide enough. Lift your arms, Cornelius. See, it pulls.' Celia reached up at full stretch, pinching the material between finger and thumb on both sides. 'The material will tear at the slightest exertion. See for yourself.' She stepped down and Delilah, much taller than her mistress, stepped forward and ran her hands from armpit to waist. Cornelius stood with his arms uplifted as if turned to stone, sweat trickling down the inside of his shirt. He flushed from the top of his head to his boots, thankful that his face was turned to the wall. He felt something of the humiliation he had experienced on the auction block. Celia's unflinching gaze while he had shed his garments and this exposure in front of the women slaves brought home to him once again that neither they nor he were considered as men and women.

'You can turn back now,' Celia said as Delilah stepped away from him.

Cornelius turned and, avoiding the women, caught the eye of Johnson, the plantation shoemaker and the only other man present, who winked at him.

Cornelius found himself smiling back as he submitted to the scrutiny of the women.

'What do you think, Delilah?' Celia asked. In matters sartorial, Delilah was unsurpassed. She had a perfect eye, counselling a tuck there, a nip here, and her magic touch could transform an ordinary frock into a thing of wonder. Her mistress, as a result, was the envy of all her friends.

'It's simple. A day should do it,' Delilah said.

'You can show Tabitha what to do. Cornelius, take off your coat and give it to Tabitha. And, Tabitha, be quick, the master's chafing already at the delay.'

Celia waited impatiently, tapping her foot while Delilah conferred briefly with Tabitha. When they were done, she admonished Cornelius to try on his shoes, then swept out, followed by Delilah and the other women, leaving Tabitha alone with the two men.

'Don't worry about your coat,' Johnson assured Cornelius, waving him on to the stool and slipping the first shoe over Cornelius's new white stockings. 'Tabitha is the finest seamstress this side of the York River.'

'That's not so, Johnson,' Tabitha said. 'I can cut and sew well enough, but Delilah far surpasses me in both.'

'But not at weaving or spinning or knitting. Just look at these stockings, eh, Cornelius?'

'Very fine.' Cornelius nodded.

'You are making me blush, Johnson.' Tabitha slapped him on the shoulder. 'Get on with the shoe-fitting. You heard what the mistress said – the master's wanting to show off his new wonder.' She smiled sideways at Cornelius, who returned her smile politely. He was recording the details of the weaving shed, his eyes travelling over the timbered walls and ceiling, the loom in the corner, the two spinning wheels and the bale of cloth on the trestle table running along one side.

'That must be why the master asked me to put buckles on these shoes.' Johnson eased Cornelius's foot into the other shoe and sank back on his haunches to admire his handiwork.

'Very fine,' Cornelius said again.

'Walk in them first before you make up your mind.'

Cornelius made a circuit of the room. He cut a comic figure walking gingerly, the shoes creaking with every step.

Johnson laughed out loud. 'They're bound to rub at first and they need greasing, but they won't break. How do you like them?'

'Very fine.' Cornelius sat down again, glancing at Tabitha who was trying to stifle her laughter.

'Do you hear that, Tabitha? Very fine. The stockings are very fine. The shoes are very fine.'

'I go now.' Cornelius started to remove his shoes, umbrage in his voice.

Johnson took hold of his foot. 'Did I mention that Tabitha's a great cook? I happen to know she's cooking something special tonight and wants to invite you along.'

No longer hiding her laughter, Tabitha said, 'You are supplying the meat, Johnson, so I suppose it's only fair you should do the asking too.' She said to Cornelius, 'You're very welcome to share with us tonight.'

Forgetting he had only one shoe on, Cornelius jumped up. 'It is honour,' he said, and caught sight of his feet. Johnson burst into fresh laughter and Tabitha too. Afterwards, Cornelius remembered it was the first time he had laughed since coming to America.

Robert Farrer was away from home and had taken Cato with him to act as his waiting man. Celia retired early to bed and so, having served at table, Cornelius was left to his own devices instead of being on call, as he would have been if his master had been at home. The night air was crisp as he stepped outside, the sky moonless and full of stars, but he did not need light to guide him. In three months he had made himself as familiar with the lie of the land at Fairlawns as he'd once been in his father's compound. If an enemy can surprise you on your own territory, you are lost before you begin, Lakoja had taught him. Robert had unwittingly helped, delighting in despatching his new slave from his office in the counting house with notes for his wife, so that Cornelius was soon used to finding his way inside the house as well, traipsing after Celia on her rounds from music room to dining room or to the bedrooms on the upper level.

Now he slipped out of the big house by the back door that led from the main hall to the gardens on the riverside, pausing for a moment to glance behind him at the two rows of long windows. Not only did they let in the light, they were also eyes through which you could see and be seen. Privacy, as in an Oyo courtyard, was hard to come by. Satisfied that he was unobserved, he continued on his way, keeping close to the clipped hedges and trellises of the formal gardens until he reached the wrought-iron gates set into the brick wall enclosing the square of the big house. Opening them a fraction, he passed swiftly through and took the path along the orchard to where the house servants' quarters were clustered. Stooping through a low doorway Cornelius emerged into the circle of light provided by the fire in Tabitha's small room adjoining the weaving shed.

'Come sit by me, brother.' Johnson made a space on the rough bench inside the door.

Cornelius greeted both Johnson and Tabitha haltingly in English but elaborately in the manner of Oyo. He hoped they had woken in health. He bowed. They had, they said, exchanging giggling glances and uncertainly returning his bow. 'I give thanks.' Cornelius bowed lower. They stared at him blankly. He waited. At last, enlightened, Johnson replied, 'Oh aye, we do too.' He nudged Tabitha, who nodded. Cornelius bowed lower still and, keeping a straight face with difficulty, made ready to speak again. Johnson flung up a hand. 'I beg you, sit down. You have honoured us enough.'

Cornelius did as he was told. He maintained an innocent expression as he produced a cloth-wrapped parcel from inside his jacket and passed it to Tabitha. She unwrapped the package carefully, revealing a loaf of wheat bread, which she and Johnson stared at reverently before breaking into joyful laughter. There was no need to ask where it came from.

'I have friend in kitchen,' Cornelius said.

'And two more here.' Johnson's laugh continued to rumble. 'I can speak for both of us, eh, Tabitha?'

'I can do my own talking.' Tabitha smiled at Cornelius. 'Yes,' she said.

'And a sweetheart too?' Johnson asked.

'I can do my own courting.'

'I meant, does *he* have a sweetheart in the kitchen,' Johnson said to Tabitha, who now suddenly busied herself with the pot she was stirring over the fire.

'No,' Cornelius replied.

There was a silence. Johnson broke it. 'So you *do* understand English. Rumour has it to the contrary.' Johnson looked sideways at him.

Cornelius's expression was inscrutable. 'If speak plain,' he said.

'Cato speak plain enough for you?'

'Yes,' Cornelius said, giving nothing away.

'Lucky for us that both he and the master are away from home tonight so you could come visiting.'

Cornelius nodded. He had been correct in supposing that it was not by chance that he had been invited on this particular night. He was to be probed.

Tabitha shared out the bread, giving Johnson and Cornelius bigger portions than herself. She filled three wooden bowls with stew from the pot on the fire, and from a jar standing on the hearth she produced three gourd spoons. Cornelius inhaled deeply before dipping his spoon into the stew. After the first mouthful he looked up and smiled appreciatively.

'You like it?' Tabitha had been watching for his reaction.

'Very fine,' Cornelius said.

'There he goes again. It's damn, bloody fine,' Johnson spluttered with his mouth full. 'That opossum gave up its life for you, he deserves more than that.'

'Remind me of home,' Cornelius said quietly.

There was silence again and this time Johnson did not break it.

'Do not even think of saying no to some more,' Tabitha said when they had emptied their bowls. 'For tomorrow, who knows?'

Cornelius had emptied his bowl a second time and Tabitha had just poured him a cup of her persimmon brandy when he heard a noise.

'Wretched chickens,' exclaimed Tabitha loudly. 'Sometimes their scratching keeps me awake all night.'

'Sounds like rats to my mind,' Johnson said.

The scratching could be heard again, accompanied by a low moan. It seemed to come from the cellar.

Johnson tensed. There was silence. Cornelius sipped his drink.

A loud groan, unmistakably from below, broke the silence.

Tabitha opened her mouth to speak.

'Rat for sure,' Cornelius said.

Johnson audibly exhaled. 'I must take a look.' He rose to his feet.

'It's late, I go.' Cornelius rose too and thanked Tabitha for supper.

Johnson opened the door for him and he slipped out into the darkness.

He had no reason to return to the big house for several hours so, instead of retracing his steps through the orchards, he cut out across the fields towards a favourite spot in the woods where the trees grew thickly to the very edge of the riverbank. There was no denying that he missed the excitement and variety of the life he had known in Williamsburg, but the loneliness and isolation he had felt since arriving at the plantation had been compensated for by moments like this when he was able to recapture aspects of life in Oyo. The trees were different from those that grew at home and he did not know their names, but in spirit he felt they were the same. The animals and birds were different too, but he recognised them all by sight now. The skills he had acquired in his childhood continued to serve him well. On the plain, Lakoja said, you must be as a stone in the waving grass, in the forest a leaf drifting among the trees.

Cornelius sat silent and still, nestled in the roots of a giant cypress listening to the activity going on all around. It would be good to experience once again the thrill, the exhilaration and companionship of the chase. He wondered what it would be like to hunt with Johnson, to hunt with a gun. Gilbert had taught him how to use a gun for their protection on the road, confident enough that the weapon would not be turned on him unless, as he said, Cornelius had become tired of his own life. With his conspicuous tribal marks, his lack of English and his lack of friends, he would have been caught within the day and summarily executed. Well, Cornelius thought, he had friends at last, although he had yet to master the English idiom of the quarters. That was his next task and it should be easier now that he would be able to prove he was not reporting back to the master. Thus far he had been treated with circumspection by everyone.

He pictured the scene again with Johnson in Tabitha's firelit room. Fate had conspired to bind him to them. The scratching he had heard had come from someone hiding in the space beneath the cabin. Someone almost certainly on the run. He thought of the day Gilbert had sold him to Robert Farrer, thereby destroying all his hopes and plans. Perhaps he was being shown the first faint indication of a new trail, one that might lead him home to Oyo.

Robert shut his ledger with a satisfied snap, sending dust motes dancing in the light pouring in through the windows of his counting house. He was pleased with life. His tobacco crop was ready for shipment, and later in the day he would see the last of it loaded on to the ship docked at his landing stage. There promised to be a boom this year after a run of low prices. Two of his overseers had sent tolerably encouraging reports from his more distant plantations, but he suspected them of telling him what he wanted to hear; soon he would have to make a tour of inspection of his various holdings.

In the meantime, he was pleased that his wish to display his new wonder had been granted and in a manner that had exceeded all his expectations. It had been Cato's suggestion that Cornelius might provide entertainment for the party of French aristocrats currently travelling through the colony. Luxuriantly, Robert recalled the scene in the dining room: candle flames glimmering like iridescent flowers in the wall sconces, their light reflected in the polished surfaces of the sideboards and tables, gleaming with silver and glass and crystal all emblazoned with the family crest. In the vast fireplace, the brightness of Siena marble had echoed the colour of the flames leaping up the chimney and the brass firedogs sparkled in the light. Magnificent in emerald velvet laced with gold, he had sat at the head of the long mahogany dining table with his guests ranged on either side and his wife at the foot, elegant in a sprigged dress, a white fichu resting on her breast, snow on snow.

The visitors must certainly have been in settings of greater magnificence, accustomed as they were to the palaces of Europe, and even in Virginia there were great houses to rival Fairlawns. But where else could they have heard the cadences of Homer's *Odysseus* exquisitely declaimed in their native tongue? The words had fallen upon their ears like a shower of gold from the mouth of a coal-black African, his face scored with the barbaric markings of his tribe. He seemed to have the whole of it by memory, for he was able to recite passages picked at random by his excited audience. It would be no exaggeration, Robert laughed aloud at the recollection, to say that those sophisticated recipients of all the best the civilised world had to offer had been transfixed with amazement. And so had he. That same night he had decided that such talent must be put to use.

Robert swung his chair away from the window to face the room where Cornelius and Cato awaited his pleasure. He beckoned them forward. It was possible, he thought, that he had misread his new slave's intelligence, but, if Cornelius proved as capable as Cato, he could be groomed as the right-hand man for the overseer on another plantation.

Digging into his pocket, he produced two coins and held them out in the palm of his hand. 'You both deserve a reward. I was very pleased with the entertainment two evenings ago. You, Cato, are to be congratulated for devising the plan, and you, Cornelius, for executing it.' To each of them he handed a coin, which they received with deep bows. 'I did not think, Cornelius, when I selected the passage for you to consign to memory that you would be able to accomplish it in so short a time. But you did, and moreover recited the lines with such expression, such meaning, as if you were Homer himself.'

'Thank you, master.' Cornelius bowed again. The meaning and expression had come despite himself. His heart, overturning his head, had spoken the words for him. In the brightly lit room glittering with gold and silver and polished wood, he had remembered a bright courtyard with everything turned to silver in the moonlight and a storyteller seated on a mat weaving a story in harmony with a drum.

Robert said, 'Monsieur de Fromont taught you well.'

'Yes, master.'

'As for you, Cato, there is no need to ask where your ingenuity comes from.' Robert smiled broadly at them, looking from one to the other. Cato's smile glittered. It was no secret that his father was the master's uncle. Addressing Cato, Robert went on, 'We must teach him English, Cato. I –' He was interrupted by his daughters pushing open the door and running in, followed by Delilah. He frowned, remembering how one of the guests at his entertainment had slyly marvelled as much at her perfection as at Cornelius's performance, imagining, no doubt, that he would be flattered. But it was not pride of possession he felt when he looked at Delilah. What he felt was inadmissible and, he would have claimed, entirely against his will. He had once told her the story of Tristan and Iseult. How Tristan was sent to escort Iseult to her wedding and how by accident they had drunk the love potion that the bride's mother had provided for the bride and her groom. Delilah's only response had been to point out that in the legend not one but both the lovers had swallowed the potion.

'Yes?' Robert embraced his daughters, his mood darker than before.

Delilah dropped a curtsey and, eyes downcast, delivered her message. The mistress wished to make a visit and desired Cornelius to drive the carriage. Robert laughed sardonically. Celia was anxious to discover news of her triumph and to show off Cornelius to her neighbours at the same time.

Unobserved, Cato took in the scene. His smile was no longer false; he had thought of a way to bring Cornelius down.

Delilah looked up at Cornelius. Tall though she was, she was dwarfed by his height. 'Congratulations, Cornelius. You were a great success.' She spoke across the two little girls trotting, hands linked, between them.

'You no have French,' Cornelius laughed, 'so how you know?'

'I could judge by those French people's reactions. Besides, I know a good storyteller when I see one. If you could do the same in English, you could be a preacher. Preachers have power. Only conjurers have more.' Delilah gave him a velvet, sidelong smile. 'But you have power already, breaking hearts in the quarters, I hear.'

The children turned from one to the other, ears pinned.

'Not everything you hear is true.' Cornelius's expression was inscrutable.

Delilah shot him another smile, steel inside the velvet, 'Very little gets past me.'

Cornelius forced himself to remain impassive.

'It would be unwise to make an enemy of me,' she said.

Celia was waiting in the deep window seat in her bedroom, her skirts spread out around her, tranquilly looking out across the formal gardens to the wide river beyond. She addressed Delilah without taking her eyes from the scene. 'I wonder if we should have gone by boat. But I think we will be cosier in the chariot. Are the children ready?' She looked round. 'Delilah, what's the matter? You look as if you had lost a shilling and found sixpence. I was watching you with Cornelius just now. Are you as smitten as the rest of them?'

'Me? With that African?' Delilah snorted.

'He has taken a vow of celibacy – Cato told me. Tabitha's broken-hearted. Nothing can tempt him, apparently.' Delilah's eyes glinted. 'No, not even you Delilah.' Celia laughed. 'I wager you cannot.' Delilah's eyes said the contrary. Celia looked suddenly sly, 'My blue dimity dress says you cannot.'

'Watch me,' Delilah said.

❧

4

DELILAH LOOKED HER best. There was no one to touch her, no beauty to compare, though they had gathered from miles around. A Christmas party at the quarters of the Fairlawns Plantation was not to be missed, but Delilah was the reason the young men flocked there, a fact of which she was not unaware. Her red-and-white striped petticoat was a gift from the master. Shameless, the older women muttered, and the younger ones had envy in their hearts. They noted her stays, a present no doubt from the mistress, which, gallingly, bestowed on her the posture of a lady while accentuating the smallness of her waist. Beneath the hem of her full skirt there was a glimpse of ankles in white knitted stockings, and below them high arched feet in dainty-heeled shoes laced with red ribbons. Delilah held her head high, her mass of shirred silk hair piled on top, and round her neck she wore a red ribbon which emphasised its hand-span slenderness and set off to perfection the dark smoothness of her skin.

'You look pretty as a picture.' Cato materialised beside her. 'But why, I ask myself, is the lady casting her pearls before swine?' His arm made a wide gesture at the black faces all around them.

'I need your help,' Delilah said, ignoring the compliment.

'I am always ready to help *you*, Delilah.' He bowed.

'It concerns Cornelius . . .'

'In that case, it depends . . .'

'I intend to make him break that stupid vow of his.'

'Not you, too, Delilah.' Cato clasped his hands theatrically against his breast. 'Pity your admirers. With the master, we can continue to think that your heart is still free and that there is hope. But if you bestow it on the African, all hope is gone. I would not like to answer for his safety after that.'

'As if you did not know. As if it was not your idea.'

'You overestimate me, my pigeon.'

'I'm not your pigeon. It was you who put the ruse into the mistress's head, playing on her as skilfully as she does that precious instrument of hers.'

'If I help you, dear Delilah, what advantage do I gain?'

'Two pull stronger than one.'

'If they are striving in the same direction. And I do not have to be a conjurer to know there is only one direction in which you pull.'

'As do you,' Delilah said sweetly. 'Look –' Heads swivelled as Cornelius entered the door. '– there he is at last.'

'Shall we dance?' Cato swept her into the middle of the floor, causing heads to swivel again.

Cornelius stood by the door, his eyes, like everyone else's, drawn to Delilah. Her beauty, he thought, was as seductive as the first greening of the trees in spring, as the perfect blue of a fall sky.

The floor cleared. Delilah and Cato stood facing each other, holding hands at arm's length, his head high, hers tilted back, smiling up at him. The music pulsed from two French horns, a fiddle and a drum, and they swung into the dance, bending toward each other from the waist and up again. They circled to the left and then to the right, bodies swaying to the melody, feet stamping on the ground, echoing the beat of the drum. Compelled by the music, another couple joined them. Heads up, backs straight, they held the pose for a moment or two and then swung into the dance, kicking high and bringing their feet down hard. They were followed by another two, and another, and another, until very soon the space in the middle of the room was packed with couples.

Cornelius caught sight of Johnson, as conspicuously tall as himself, standing against the opposite wall. He started towards him, working his way round the edge of the floor, threading gingerly between the dancers. The cabin, the largest on the plantation and ordinarily a dormitory for twenty-four men, was filled to capacity and vibrating with such force to the sound of the music that Cornelius fancied it might lift into the air were it not for the dancers hammering out the complicated rhythms of the dances and securing it to the ground.

'You were missed,' Johnson yelled when Cornelius had arrived by his side. He pointed with his chin towards Tabitha, who was kicking her heels and stamping her feet in the thick of the dancing, her petticoat twirling, her skin glowing in the rush-light. Cornelius returned her wave. Tabitha had taught Cornelius the dance, called 'Setting the Floor', inspired apparently by the tamping down of the earth in a new cabin. There was nothing like it for stamping out your anger and frustration. Tabitha had of course demanded more dances from him in return for her teaching, and he had yet to confess that in Oyo they would have been astonished to see a woman dancing to warrior chants.

Johnson nudged him. 'All this beauty on display. A man might think he had died and gone to heaven. Not that it's of any concern to you, Cornelius. You have broken Tabitha's heart, you know. And Venus's and Juno's . . .' Johnson waved to the girls on the dance floor, both craning in Cornelius's direction. 'Not to mention every other female under sixty years of age. And now that they've heard all about your vow, they're more eager than ever.' Johnson shook his head. 'Who said Africans were dumb? Look at me standing here while Delilah dances with every other man in the shoes I made for her. A fine move, that vow of yours, Cornelius, very fine. I am going to announce my own tonight . . .' Johnson broke off, realising that Cornelius had ceased to listen to him.

Cornelius was gazing across the room. He felt his blood jump as the object of his attention smiled. Johnson followed his gaze. The girl was lovely, her teeth were very white, her face flat-featured and delicate, her cheekbones high and wide. Still smiling, she made her way towards them, a black poppy moving in the wind.

Johnson looked at Cornelius in disbelief. 'You're using charms! There's no other explanation.'

Having reached them, the girl greeted them both and they bowed, but her eyes were on Cornelius.

Johnson muttered to his friend, 'I want to buy some of this magic, whatever it costs.'

The girl addressed Cornelius, 'You don't recognise me, do you?'

Cornelius shook his head. His heart was pounding.

'Think back,' she said, grave now. 'You were riding a beautiful horse. It was easy for you to overtake a small girl and her brother running for their lives. You caught them and returned them to the slave dealer in the market near Ipokia. Do you remember?'

Johnson looked at Cornelius in consternation: the sheen on his skin had dulled to grey, like dust settling on a polished surface.

The girl said, 'I told you, then, we would meet again.'

Cornelius was incapable of speech. He saw once again the market, the crowds stretching as far as the eye could see along the low banks of the Yewa River, the boats plying up and down and moored in their hundreds among the thick reeds at the water's edge. He remembered his horse treading lightly under his direction. The two children running in front of the polished hooves. The girl throwing herself directly in his path in order to save her brother. The curse.

'I remember,' he said, passing a shaking hand across his eyes.

'You and I were lucky,' she said. 'My brother did not survive. He perished on the slave ship that brought us to America. I did not discover his death until our journey's end. Men and women were kept separately on board, as you must know.' He knew. He knew, too, all she had not said. He saw once again among the bodies of the rats strewn on the floor the corpse of a small boy who had fallen unnoticed into the soil bucket and drowned.

'Our mother weeps for us still. As does yours.'

*

131

'Oblivion,' Johnson said, taking Cornelius by the shoulder and steering him forward. 'That's what you need, and I have just the thing.'

Head bent and slightly unsteady on his feet, Cornelius allowed himself to be led through the crowd, provoking the knowing looks bestowed on one who has had too much to drink. Tabitha left off dancing abruptly and pushed her way through to Johnson's side, but Johnson shook his head.

Emerging into the cold air outside it was indeed as if Cornelius were drunk. He staggered and would have fallen had Johnson not supported him all the way to the cabin. He fell back on to the bed as Johnson filled a small gourd from a jar hidden under the mattress. Having forced him to drain the contents, Johnson refilled it and made him drink a second time. 'This liquor,' he said, 'has the kick of a mule and is twice as effective. It will knock you out and keep you out for days. You just have to keep at it. I shall leave the jar here beside you, see, and the moment you feel yourself coming back, take another slug.'

Johnson returned to the party and did not notice Cato as he passed him in the darkness.

'Are you sure? Shouldn't I go to Cornelius?' Tabitha asked yet again, having heard the story. 'He needs comforting.'

'Sister,' Johnson put a restraining hand on her arm, 'the lash of the whip must be borne alone, you know that. Tomorrow or the next day we can begin to salt the wounds.' And with that she had to be content. 'Come –' he slipped an arm around her waist. '– let's dance.' Together they began to stamp and kick. 'We are young, we are beautiful, and tomorrow, who knows?'

Inside Johnson's cabin, Cornelius was in torment, the jar by the bed untouched since Johnson's departure. All his will, all his resolution and training could not prevent memories from rushing in, piercing his mind like the arrows Lakoja the hunter had taught him to fashion so long ago, the pain seeping through him as deadly as the poison in which they had been tipped. All that he had not allowed himself to feel, he felt now. The wounds inflicted by his capture and enslavement, by the violence he had experienced, by the humiliation visited daily upon him, and the knowledge of the countless others he had condemned to the same fate, were re-opened. He cried at last for all that he had lost. Shaken and afraid, he felt totally abandoned.

'Oluremi,' he called aloud. 'Oluremi.'

'Here I am,' a voice responded softly and a hand was laid gently on his brow.

'Oluremi?'

'Hush.' Soft arms slid around his neck. A warm and fragrant body pressed insistently against him. A voice whispered in his ear, gentling his heart, and where it led he followed throughout the night.

Delilah slipped out unseen and when, sometime later, Johnson looked in, Cornelius, too ashamed to face him, feigned unconsciousness.

'The master will wonder where he is,' Tabitha said. 'He has duties in the big house, Christmas or no.'

'The master will be inclined to overlook small sins at this time, and Cato will be only too glad to cover for him. As well as the devil's own luck, Cornelius has an impeccable sense of timing. If this had happened at any other time he would have received a whipping. Tabitha, you look fit to eat. Come on, let's go.' Johnson held the door open for her and they set off across the white-frosted fields to go visiting.

Cato walked back with Delilah from the landing by the riverside. Their master and mistress and their two daughters had set off by boat to visit a neighbouring estate where they were to dine. It was a journey that would have taken several hours by road but was a mere half-hour by water.

Delilah stretched luxuriously. 'Why can't it be Christmas every day?' Her steps were light; her duties were over until the evening.

'Let me guess – this has something to do with the African?'

'It has not.'

'You were with him half the night. You accomplished your mission, I assume?'

Delilah's lips curved upwards and she gave him a sidelong look.

'Wasted on me, my pigeon.' Cato laughed. 'I am at your feet already.'

Delilah walked towards Johnson's cabin. She entered quietly and approached the bed where Cornelius lay, apparently asleep. She could not have said why, but she wished to prove that her success had not been entirely due to Cornelius being drunk. She reached towards him and Cornelius's hand shot out and gripped her arm. 'No,' he said.

'Cornelius, your vow is broken and, see, the sky has not fallen in. African superstition has no power here.'

Cornelius released her and sat up. Delilah rubbed her arm; his grip had marked the skin.

'I made that vow because I *never* want to give child of mine to slavery.'

Delilah twined her arms around his neck. 'You are safe with me; I am barren. A stillbirth at thirteen that nearly cost me my life made certain of that.'

Cornelius removed her hands.

She slid her arms back around his neck. 'It's no use locking the stable door, Cornelius, after the horse has bolted.'

'Last night, I was thinking not of you, Delilah.'

Delilah withdrew her arms. 'It would be dangerous for you if the real reason for your vow should reach the master's ears. Such talk is rebellious,' she said, the sweetness in her voice shot with menace now.

Cornelius held her gaze. 'If you throw words to the wind, you cannot say where the wind will take them.'

Delilah had never encountered a man who neither coveted her beauty nor was afraid of her. 'You're a fool, Cornelius,' she snapped, slamming the door behind her.

Cornelius found himself banished from waiting on his master. It was no hardship to be relieved from emptying dirty chamber pots and being on call throughout the night, but it was a sign that Mr Farrer did not like Cornelius to be around him as much as before.

The master's wife had lost no time in relating to her husband the story of the blue dress and her wager with her maid, and no secret either that the master had been climbing the private staircase to his wife's bedroom every night since.

Cornelius waited until a good meal and a succession of fine wines might have softened Robert's anger, but his request for a pass was curtly refused. With newly acquired insight, he realised that Robert Farrer was a man injured not in his pride but in his heart. He bowed respectfully and retreated. He had already determined that he would go and seek out the African girl about whom he knew everything and nothing – not even her name.

5

'THERE'S A RUMOUR that the master has refused your application for a pass,' Johnson said. He spoke under cover of the hiss of steam from the cooling horseshoe that was clouding the cold January air. Only Cornelius, standing at the head of the master's horse, which had thrown a shoe the previous day, could hear him.

'The chances are high, it seems to me, that you will go anyway.' Johnson extracted the shoe from its bath of water and set it down on the bench. 'And, I imagine, others will have reached the same conclusion.' He measured the shoe against the horse's hoof. 'As you are new here, you'll not be familiar with certain little tracks known to those of us who have lived here all our lives.' Dissatisfied, Johnson brought the shoe to the fire again, heated it and re-commenced hammering. 'I shall be your guide.'

'Why would you help me?' Cornelius's voice was all but drowned as Johnson dipped the molten iron once more into the water.

'I'd be returning a favour,' Johnson said, referring to that first evening in Tabitha's cabin when Cornelius had not betrayed the presence of a runaway.

'I accept,' Cornelius said, observing closely as Johnson fitted the shoe on the horse's right forefoot. With his powerful forearms and massive shoulders, stripped to the waist in his buckskin breeches and set against a background of fire and smoke and billowing steam, Johnson could have been the god Ogun incarnate, or Hephaistos the iron god of the ancient Greeks, called Vulcan by the Romans. Cornelius laughed. In response to Johnson's look of enquiry, he said aloud, 'Among my people, Ogun the god of iron is the one who shows the way.' The gods, it seemed, had not deserted him.

Cornelius chose a night when the master was away from home and had taken Cato to wait on him. Johnson had designated a meeting spot in the woods familiar to them both, the trysting place for their nocturnal hunting expeditions. With no moon, the darkness was absolute; another propitious sign Cornelius thought, as he slipped soundlessly and invisibly between the trees to the meeting place. He was glad that Johnson was to accompany him. There was, he knew, a network of secret paths, as yet unfamiliar to him, that was used by the slaves when they were without a pass or on the run. These were trails unknown to the patrollers, who policed the roads day and night, constantly on the lookout for runaways.

Johnson materialised at his side and, as he had been taught long ago, Cornelius instantly emptied his mind of all thoughts, the better to concentrate entirely on the present. If caught, a slave would be subject to a whipping on the spot before being dragged home in chains to be punished again, or, in the last resort, shot.

They travelled in silence, Johnson leading. Using all his senses, Cornelius mapped the route, memorising infinitesimal gradations in the density of the darkness – where trees grew thickly, where they were sparse, minute changes in the air around him, in the ground beneath his feet – recording every sound, every smell, so that each or all of his senses could lead him this way again. They maintained their silence until they had crossed the boundary on to the Redhill plantation. Johnson, who often travelled with the master and was familiar with plantations for fifty miles around, knew where to find the African girl. He was able to lead Cornelius straight to the slave quarters.

The dozen or so wooden cabins were clustered randomly under some trees near the bank of a small stream. The wooden shutters were closed, but the light from the fires inside could be seen through the gaps between the planks. Children running around barefoot greeted them politely and stared after them for a few moments before resuming their play. There was a fire burning outside one of the cabins and some people gathered round it. Johnson approached and greeted them respectfully; Cornelius too. They both removed their hats.

'We are looking for Betsey,' Johnson said. 'And would be much obliged if you could tell us her whereabouts.' Surprised, Cornelius shot him an accusing look. Johnson gave a smug grin in reply. 'I thought you'd prefer to hear her name from her own lips. That's why I didn't tell you.'

'Who is it wants to know?' said an old lady sitting by the fire.

They were both from the Fairlawns Plantation, Johnson told her. He gestured at Cornelius. 'Auntie, my brother here is from Betsey's home country and wants to speak with her.'

'She is not here.' The old lady replaced the pipe she had taken from her mouth and fell silent.

'She is sold,' another voice said quietly. 'To settle a debt.'

'Do you know where she has gone?'

'Down south. We don't expect to see her again. Nothing to bring her back. She was straight from Africa. She had no kin here.'

'Much obliged,' Johnson said, replacing his hat. Cornelius silently followed suit.

'You will stay and have some beer and a scrap to eat,' the old lady spoke again. It was a command. 'Fairlawns is a thirsty walk away. And while you are here, you can give us your news.'

They stayed for two hours, during which time the old lady casually, seemingly, extracted every piece of information in Johnson's head on each and every one of the inhabitants of the Fairlawns slave quarters. Cornelius listened attentively, his ear increasingly attuned to the dialect of the quarters. She knew who was kin to whom down four generations and she elicited the information so skilfully that Cornelius was reminded of his mother. Lady Faloyan herself could not have bettered it he thought, no longer surprised that Johnson had managed to discover the girl's name. At length, charged with messages to deliver, the visitors departed, sped on their way by a chorus of good wishes. But the good wishes did little to raise Cornelius's spirits or lessen his disappointment. He would not now be able to beg forgiveness.

As they approached the boundary of Fairlawns, Johnson clapped Cornelius on the shoulder. 'Well, your vow is safe.'

Cornelius twisted away from him and hung back.

When Johnson emerged from the thick undergrowth, lights came towards him. Men on horseback were shouting, dogs barking.

'A trap,' Johnson spat, 'set for you. This is Cato's work. Stay back.' And when Cornelius would have protested, Johnson waved him off and ran forward to meet the patrollers.

Cornelius slithered like a snake in the undergrowth towards the stream, which would cover his scent. Behind him he heard the tenor of the shouting and the barking alter as the hounds were set loose.

Robert agreed that Johnson should be made an example, ostensibly because a slave – even one as valuable as Johnson who could shoe a horse, steel an axe and lay a plough, who was an excellent carpenter and sawyer and shoe maker – could not be allowed to flout the master's authority. And it must be seen that he could not. He was to receive a public flogging. The true reason, unacknowledged even to himself but guessed at by everyone else, was the anger Robert felt at being cuckolded by a slave, even though that slave was not Johnson. There was also the underlying fear, never far from Robert's mind, that perhaps some conspiracy was afoot. Ordinarily, Johnson, who knew his worth, would simply have requested a pass and it would have been given; even if he had been refused by the overseer, he could have appealed directly to the master. So why had he not done so?

Johnson had been tethered all night in the smokehouse alongside the bell that called the slaves to work each morning. Its ringing assembled them now. House servants and field hands stood in small groups in a loose semi-circle. On a wooden bench in front of them sat the master and mistress and their two small children. Immediately behind them stood Cato and Delilah with the other house servants. Cornelius was there too, tidy and clean in his livery. All eyes were on Johnson, his back towards them, stripped to the waist and tied by his wrists to a beam with his feet a few inches above the ground.

The overseer cracked his whip to test it and walked slowly around, gauging his aim, for Johnson's back was heavily scarred from previous beatings and bloodied as a result of his thrashing the night before at the hands of the patrollers. Placing one foot firmly in front of the other and tightening his grip on the bullwhip in his hand, the overseer swept his arm back in a wide arc and brought it down, following through with such force that he was almost thrown off balance. The smack of the whip reverberated through the still air and it drew a dark stripe on Johnson's skin.

The overseer took aim again and drew an identical stripe below the first, then repeated the action until there were six slanting weals marking the skin from shoulder to hip. He moved now to stand on the opposite side of his victim, passing in front of him in order to look into his face and assess his condition. Satisfied, he cracked his whip once more and, pulling back his arm again brought the whip down with his whole strength until there were another six stripes crossing the first set diagonally from left to right. Then he stood back and nodded to a young boy, who stepped forward with a bucket full of brine and splashed its contents over the lacerated flesh.

The whip crossed and re-crossed Johnson's back as the overseer methodically followed his customary procedure, striking first on one side and then on the other, until all thirty-nine lashes had been administered. By the time he had finished, his hair dripped and his linen shirt stuck to his skin. Wiping the sweat from his brow, he stepped back and made a small bow to Robert, who sat impassively on the bench beside his wife. Their daughters clung to her whimpering. From the watching slaves there was only silence.

Robert inclined his head in acknowledgement to the overseer, rose from his seat and, signalling to Delilah, Cato and Cornelius to follow, he strode off with his family in his wake. Cornelius, after exchanging a swift glance with Tabitha, huddled with two women from the weaving shed, reluctantly made his way towards the house.

Tabitha answered Cornelius's knock on the door of Johnson's cabin. She was sitting on the edge of the bed where Johnson lay, spreadeagled.

'All this my fault,' he said.

Johnson turned his head towards him. 'You'll pay for it, have no fear.' He winced as Tabitha rubbed grease into his back.

'How?'

'You can join us.' A spasm of pain creased Johnson's face and he closed his eyes. 'Tabitha, you tell him.'

'We have a plan,' Tabitha said, 'to go south. Johnson and me could pass for free in Charleston, hire ourselves out and make a good living. We've been working on the scheme for three years now and we are all prepared and ready to go.'

'So why do you need me? I would be a hindrance,' Cornelius said. 'My tribal scars would attract too much attention.'

'If we were heading for Williamsburg or Richmond – which is where they'll look for us first, because they are places we could pass – then you would stand out. But we aim to hide in the woods to begin with and then, when the trail has cooled, we can make our way into North Carolina and on down to Charleston, where even Africans can pass. Or' – Tabitha looked at him sideways '– they can get on a boat and go home, especially if they speak French. Since you and Johnson started hunting together, he's seen how handy you are out there and . . .'

Johnson's eyelids fluttered open. 'You'd think those woods were your natural birthplace, Cornelius. I noticed even the other night that you could have come back by yourself. I don't know how, but on the return journey, having travelled it once, you were more sure of the route than me, who had been that way countless times.'

'What made you think I would be willing to go with you?'

Tabitha smiled. 'You gave yourself away that first night in my cabin.

When you didn't betray the presence of the runaway, we began watching you more carefully.'

Cornelius remained silent and Johnson opened his eyes again. 'The master's not pleased with you right now. The beating I took, the first for a long time, was really meant for you. Ordinarily, I would only have been grounded or transferred to another quarter for a month or two. I reckon he is planning to transfer you – and not just for a month or two, either. And Cato will not be idle, having caught the wrong rabbit in his trap.'

'If it *was* Cato.' Tabitha applied the last of the ointment to Johnson's back.

'Who else?' Johnson asked.

Tabitha folded her lips, but the name Delilah hung in the air.

Tabitha moved across to the hearth and filled a wooden bowl with broth from an iron pot on the fire. Kneeling by the bed, she cajoled Johnson to lift his head and started little by little to spoon the contents into his mouth. Cornelius thought, watching them, that there was sense in what they offered. He had hoped to find the possible beginning of a trail – and here the trail was, laid out entire before him. He had thought it would take him years to prepare a new plan of escape, and here was one already prepared. They had shown they trusted him by revealing their intentions thus far. Should he in turn trust them? To do so would be to abandon one of the principal tenets of his training: trust no one unless they are children of the same mother. But perhaps this was Ogun showing him the way, showing him that fate had made the three of them as children of the same mother. Cornelius looked at Tabitha and Johnson in turn.

'I'll sleep on it,' he said.

Robert's distaste for Cornelius had become palpable since the flogging. It was as if he could not bear to have his erstwhile favourite near him. Celia, on the other hand, appeared to have developed a corresponding fondness for Cornelius and required him always by her side. Now it was the mistress he shadowed on her rounds from the kitchen to the stillroom and the kitchen garden, where he surprised and delighted her with his knowledge of herbs, learnt from his mother in Oyo. Cornelius was the one who invariably drove her chariot or rowed the boat when she visited her friends or attended church, and who, in addition to maintaining the instruments in the music room, turned the pages for her as she played for hours on the guitar or harpsichord and her beloved forte piano.

Certain that Celia's new-found fondness for Cornelius was motivated by revenge, Robert was determined to transfer him to one of his remote quarters upriver and put him to work in the fields. Cato gloatingly confirmed Cornelius's suspicions. Cornelius was careful to appear cast down, though inwardly he was unmoved, for he would be gone. Celia, however, defeated Robert by announcing she was pregnant. Surely, she asked, he was not prepared to jeopardise the health of what might prove to be the longed-for son? Cornelius made certain that the delight with which he received the news was transparent.

He was surprised when Delilah knocked on the door of the cabin that he shared with three of the footmen and two grooms. She had ignored him since he had rejected her. Despite being thrown together constantly in their mistress's company, she acted as if he did not exist, except when it was absolutely necessary to acknowledge his presence.

'Walk with me,' she said.

He complied, wondering what it was she wanted; there was always a purpose with Delilah. In silence they strolled through the house servants' quarters, past the weaving shed, stables, carpenter's and blacksmith's shops, making their way by a roundabout route down to the river to sit hidden from view with their backs against a tree trunk. In front of them flowed the wide sweep of water. There was a breeze and the wave ripples were silvered by the moonlight.

At length Delilah said, 'I am going to have a child.'

'Why are you telling me?' Cornelius asked stupidly.

'Because you're the father.'

Cornelius's mind reeled. 'But you said –'

'I know what I said . . . I am as surprised as you.'

'How do you know it's mine?' he asked.

'You'll see soon enough when it's born. Believe me, it will have a black face just like yours.'

Cornelius had prayed that the gods would not desert him and here, he thought dryly, was the proof that they had not. Eshu the trickster god had been at work.

'It will be at the end of the summer, at the same time as the mistress's.' Cornelius groaned and covered his face with his hands. Delilah observed him dispassionately, 'And I imagined you'd be pleased.' Her sarcasm brought his head back up sharply.

'I told you I did not want to give a child of mine to slavery.'

'I'm not thrilled,' Delilah said bleakly, her eyes on the river. 'I nearly died the last time. Perhaps this one will die too, and me as well.'

Cornelius put his arm around her. 'No,' he said with sudden certainty, 'the gods have willed it otherwise.'

Johnson and Tabitha were persuaded to postpone their departure. When the child was born, Cornelius argued, Delilah would agree to the escape; once she had held it in her arms, she too would want it to be free.

Time had never passed so slowly. The days crawled by, marked on the home plantation by the stages of the tobacco crop. The winter was mild so the seeds had been sown twelve days after Christmas in specially prepared beds well fertilised with wood ash. The seedbeds, covered in branches in case of a sudden frost, dotted the winter landscape, for every planter sowed far more than were needed, against destruction by cold, disease or pests. By the end of May, the seedlings had all been transplanted to the main fields. As the tobacco ripened in the fields, the tension generated by the anxious wait for the cutting of the crop was heightened in the big house by the wait for the imminent births to mistress and maid, both of whom were burgeoning visibly in the warmth of the summer sun.

In mid-August Celia was delivered of a girl after a long and difficult labour, attended by the mistress of the neighbouring plantation and assisted by Tabitha and two housemaids. Robert was disappointed, but the child, named Maria, was healthy and his wife was young and strong. There would be time enough. A few days later, Delilah too gave birth to a girl after an unexpectedly easy labour, attended by Tabitha. The baby's face, as Delilah had predicted, left no room for doubt. 'Look, Cornelius,' she held the bundle out and Cornelius took it. Celia had given him permission to visit. 'Is she not beautiful?'

Cornelius gazed down at the child in his arms. She was wrapped in a soft white cloth, a present from Tabitha. 'Yes,' he said. The baby's eyes opened and, looking into them, he recognised his cousin Oluremi, reborn as his daughter. This, he realised was to be Oluremi's true life. He understood now the link between their two fates. This was what she had meant in Oyo when she had told him they would be travelling to the same destination but by different routes. As she had accompanied him to America, so he would journey back home with her to complete their destiny. He kissed the child tenderly on the forehead and, looking up, said, 'Let us name her Oluremi.'

'Whatever you like.' Delilah put her arms out. 'But I shall ask the mistress to let me call her Epiphany.'

Cornelius replaced his daughter in her mother's arms. He felt his heart open as he stroked the baby's cheek. *We shall go back to Oyo together*, he promised her. Aloud he said, 'Epiphany. That is fine, very fine.' He knew from Gilbert's teaching that Epiphany, like Oluremi, signified a consolation from God.

Cornelius was so certain that the gods had manifested themselves through this child that on his second visit to Delilah he broached the subject of escape.

'No,' Delilah said, holding Epiphany tight. 'If we were caught, I would lose everything, including my baby. We would be sold separately for sure. The mistress loves me and so does the master. They wouldn't do anything to harm me. I can protect Epiphany. She will never have to work in the fields. I shall make certain that she learns skills. She can be a lady's maid and seamstress like me, a spinner and weaver like Tabitha, or a cook perhaps. She can have a good life. There are worse fates.'

'You can *protect* her?' Cornelius kept his voice low but he could not disguise his fury. 'You can *protect* her, Delilah? Like this ant?' He stamped his foot on the ground and, lifting it up again, pointed at the crushed trail of ants on the floor by the bed. 'That is what your precious master and mistress will do to you, to me, to her, should the need arise, or simply if it pleases them. That is the reality.'

'It needn't be like that. Look at me, look at you.'

'Even if she escapes the worst, what of her spirit? It can only be a half-formed, crippled thing. What of that? This is the best opportunity we may ever have. Don't throw it away.'

'No, no. I won't risk it. You go.'

'We can't go without you. You know we can't.'

'Why not?'

'Can we trust you not to betray us, Delilah?' Cornelius held her gaze. 'Under the lash?'

Delilah looked away.

'Well, I can't trust *you*,' she said. Cornelius forced up her chin with his finger so that she was looking into his eyes. 'That is . . . I can't trust you to bring us through safely.'

'Is that your final word?' He let her go of her chin.

'Yes,' she said.

Once again Cornelius forced himself to walk away from the wreckage of his hopes. This hurt bit deeper, knowing that because of him the others would have to sacrifice their plans. He was humbled by the grace with which Johnson and Tabitha did so. The three of them were indeed as children of the same mother, and it struck him that perhaps the same could be said of all of them enslaved in America. They were all children of the same mother.

Delilah was back at her duties within the week, acting as wet nurse to her mistress's baby.

Celia, slow to recover, lay in bed observing her daughter at Delilah's breast. 'She will be just like us,' she said.

Delilah looked up. Celia was referring, she knew, to Epiphany, left in the care of the cook in the kitchen. Epiphany would not be fed until the mistress's child was safely settled.

'As soon as she is old enough, I shall give Epiphany to Maria as a present, as you were given to me on my eighth birthday. You cried and cried. Do you remember?'

Delilah's heart shrank. 'Yes,' she said, remembering how she had been separated from her mother. She heard Cornelius's words again. *Even if Epiphany escapes the worst, what of her spirit?* What if he was right? She pictured the ants crushed under his boot. Maybe she should reconsider.

Celia clasped her hands together. 'You and I were inseparable, weren't we? And so innocent. A child's innocence lasts for so short a time.' She sighed.

Delilah crossed the room, blood beating in her ears, and placed the now sleeping Maria in the cot beside her mother's bed, tucking in the soft blankets carefully. 'Shorter for some than for others,' she said, adding, before she could stop herself, 'Your father made me a woman at eleven.'

Celia's eyes flashed angrily; and then she saw the tears pouring down Delilah's cheeks. 'I know,' she said. Delilah's legs gave way and she sank down on the edge of the bed. Celia took Delilah's hands in both of hers. 'And you have made me pay. Robert married me, but it's you he loves. Poor Robert. He owns you, but you don't belong to him. He doesn't own me, but I belong to him body and soul.'

'That's because you are yourself to give.' Delilah's voice for once was free of artifice. 'I am a stolen thing.'

'The truth is,' Celia said, tears in her eyes too, 'we both want what we can never have. What use is my freedom to me or Robert's heart to you?'

6

'. . . *IN AS MUCH as the Rebels have adopted the practice of enrolling Negroes among their troops I, General Sir Henry Clinton, Commander in Chief of His Majesty's Forces in the Colonies, command that whenever captured by the British, Negro soldiers or auxiliaries be purchased for the public service . . .*'

Old Mattie read out the words haltingly, holding the paper close to his nose. He was seated on a log surrounded by twenty or more of the Fairlawns slaves, one of several groups lingering in the clearing deep in the woods. They had gathered early for an open-air church service conducted by one of their own, an itinerant slave preacher spreading the word of the Baptists.

'Speak up,' a voice called out. 'We can't hear you back here.'

'Come nearer then,' another admonished, glancing over his shoulder. 'Do you want the whole world to hear?'

'Continue, Mattie –'

'Not yet,' Rosie, the cook at the big house broke in. 'What does it mean, *purchased for the public service*?'

'It means, if they catch you, they put you to work in the lead mines.' There was a ripple of grim laughter.

'Huh.' Rosie sniffed. 'Negroes should stay out of the war, if they know what's good for them.'

'Read on, Mattie,' Rosie's neighbour urged. 'No disrespect to you, sister,' he bowed.

Mattie continued slowly: '*And from henceforward I forbid any person from selling or claiming any enemy-owned slave who takes refuge in the British Lines.*'

'Does that include themselves?' The question was greeted with merriment.

'Hush now, let him finish.'

Mattie waited for the laughter to die down. '*. . . I hereby promise, to every Negroe who deserts from an enemy master full security to follow any occupation he* *wishes while in the British Lines.*' Silence ensued as Mattie smoothed and folded the paper, the crumpled leaves rustling loudly. It was a week-old copy of *Rivington's Royal Gazette*, which had carried General Clinton's proclamation in every issue for two months now. Mattie's audience looked at one another as they digested the words.

Rosie straightened her Sunday-best starched cap. 'No one need tell me what this means. I know what it means, it –'

'May I?' Cato strolled in a leisurely manner through the men, who immediately became guarded at his appearance in their midst. As usual, he had arrived without being noticed. Taking the paper from Mattie, he sat down on the log beside him and read the page again, all eyes following his silently moving lips. Cato lowered the paper. 'The devil you know is better than the one you don't.'

'The British are offering us freedom,' Rosie persisted.

'And you believe them?'

Cornelius, listening unobtrusively at the back, would have liked to have read the paper himself, but he was not prepared to give Cato the satisfaction of asking him for it. It certainly seemed, though, that Rosie was right and this time the British were truly offering freedom. Britain and America had been at war for four years now following the first confrontations in Massachusetts. The war had aroused hopes that the colonists, suing for liberty themselves, would have been sympathetic to those same aspirations in their slaves. But it was the British, Cornelius reflected dryly, who had seized upon the obvious recruiting tactic of offering freedom in return for bearing arms. The first offer had been made by order of Lord Dunmore, governor of Virginia and commander in chief of the army. Issued in a broadside from on board his man-o'-war in Norfolk harbour, the proclamation had caused great excitement in all the plantation quarters. Cornelius had the words by heart:

> *. . . And I do hereby further declare all indented servants, Negroes, or others, (appertaining to Rebels) free that are able and willing to bear Arms, they joining His Majesty's troops, as soon as may be, for the more speedily reducing this Colony to a proper Sense of their Duty, to His Majesty's Crown and Dignity.*

Newspapers had lost no time in publishing the proclamation in full, as information, but also as a warning to the whites. Local patrols had been doubled, all the highways were under strict surveillance, and owners of small craft were ordered to exercise vigilance.

Even so, many hundreds had defected to the British. Cornelius himself had been sorely tempted, but the offer was open only to those 'able and willing to bear arms' and he could not bring himself to leave his daughter Epiphany, nor Johnson to abandon Tabitha. Besides, freedom, they had soon learned, was not so easily come by. Cornelius recalled a visit to a nearby plantation where he'd accompanied his master. He'd been out in the yard behind the kitchen, helping the owner's valet with his work. It was a fine day, and the magnificent collection of silver they were cleaning was spread around them. It was a task that left leisure to talk and he had enquired after the head groom and coachman, an inspired horse doctor, whose advice he often sought.

His companion had lowered his voice. 'Caught fighting alongside the British.'

'What happened to him?' Cornelius had asked, leaning close.

'Sold to the French sugar islands. He was one of the first to join Lord Dunmore's Ethiopian Regiment.' Sorrow had been uppermost, but there had been pride also. There wasn't a slave in America who'd not heard of the governor's black regiment, marching off to war with *Liberty to Slaves* emblazoned across their breasts. The head groom, it transpired, had fought at Kemp's Landing and in the battle of Great Bridge and been captured during a raid on the Eastern Shore.

'They say that if the British win the war they will set all the slaves in America free.' The excited voice brought Cornelius back to the present.

'They say,' Cato retorted, 'that if the colonists are defeated the British will sell their slaves to the sugar plantations in Jamaica and Barbados. The proclamation doesn't offer freedom to the slaves of owners who remain loyal to the king, only to slaves who defect from Rebel masters. The British aren't on a mission to liberate slaves.'

True, Cornelius conceded, but under the terms of this new proclamation, aimed at *all* the Negroes, there did seem to be a chance of freedom for those prepared to take the risk with the British, whereas it was clear as day that the Virginia Bill of Rights and the Declaration of Independence did not apply to blacks. He continued to listen intently as the arguments went back and forth, just in case there was a rumour among all the rumours that he had not yet heard.

'They say the British are not waiting for people to join them, they're raiding the plantations and carrying away Negroes whether they will or not. They seized over five hundred in Norfolk County alone, and I heard that when General Edwards left to join General Clinton in New York he took the same number of men, women and children with him.'

'But they say hundreds more are deserting to the British of their own accord.'

'That must be true, otherwise why are they stepping up the patrols?'

'Some of the masters are moving their slaves further inland. I heard that's what the master's planning to do with us.' The speaker turned to Cato. 'Is that why they're packing at the big house?'

'Not as far as I know,' Cato replied. 'The mistress is making an inventory, that's all. But I do know that the master is relying on *his* people to stay loyal. As I'm sure you all know,' Cato continued conversationally, 'the punishment for attempting to escape to the British is death.' He strolled away.

Cornelius watched him go, elegant as usual in buff breeches and faded strawberry-coloured waistcoat, cast-offs from his master which he wore, Cornelius thought, with even more aplomb than their original owner. Cato mingled with ease among the groups of slaves scattered around the clearing. It was high summer and the grass underfoot was a carpet of white clover. The scent of the flowering dogwoods filled the air. Strolling unregarded among the butterfly colours of the women in their striped skirts and red jackets, Cato was gathering information for later use. It saddened Cornelius to see the way Cato had given in to despair; he was a man without hope, freed thereby to work evil.

Keeping hope alive, Cornelius had come to realise, was the only possibility for a slave in America, the one sure path to survival, giving significance and meaning to an existence that would otherwise appear worthless. This conviction underpinned all that he was passing on to his daughter, Epiphany. According to Tabitha, the Baptists preached the exact same message and it was transforming peoples' lives. Christianity kept hope alive, she said, and it was to see and hear for himself that Cornelius had attended the church meeting today. Tabitha had spoken the truth. He'd been surprised to discover the similarities to the beliefs of the Oyo people and to learn that the Christians too thought death was the doorway to life in the next world.

The group that had gathered to hear Mattie read out the proclamation had dispersed, but the old man remained seated on the fallen log, reverently caressing the paper folded on his knee.

Cornelius approached and asked respectfully, 'Uncle, may I read the words for myself?'

'God has different purposes for each of us,' Mattie said. 'For some, it is to stay alive; for others, to be free. And I dare say freedom will not be any easier for those to come than slavery was for those who have gone.' He gave him the paper.

'True, Uncle.' Cornelius sat down beside him to read the words and, having done so, returned the paper. He rose to leave. Mattie beckoned him closer and Cornelius bent down.

'We have carried the torch this far, go steady with it now.'

'We will, Uncle.'

'I'll be with the ancestors and we'll be watching.'

The old man's words made Cornelius think of his daughter. Epiphany was twelve years old, and the years had worked as many changes in her as they had in the landscape around. Back when she'd been born, the fields he was now walking through had been clothed in the rich green leaves of ripening tobacco, but in the intervening years the master had switched to wheat and so now they were dressed in green in the spring and in gold in August. Cornelius sighed deeply: his love for his daughter and his ambitions for her were the chains that bound him in place. He had taught her, as his mother had taught him, to be the complete mistress of herself. She'd proved an apt pupil, her strength of character allied to an equally firm will. She lacked the physical perfection of her mother Delilah, but she combined the straight-backed carriage of her grand-mother, Lady Faloyan, with the grace of her cousin, Oluremi, whose presence was revealed in the same high cheekbones and great dark eyes.

Epiphany had Oluremi's gift of 'sight' too. At eight years of age, when Cornelius was debating how much he should reveal of his history, she told him she had 'seen' the ships – 'sea coffins', she called them. The people buried in the darkness were still living, she said, and she could hear their cries. And strung out behind were captives chained together in a line that stretched back across the ocean all the way to Africa.

Delilah regarded their daughter's gift as an unwelcome reminder of her Africanness, which would do her no good in America. And, at the beginning, it seemed as if Delilah might be right. Reporting for her first day of work at the big house, Epiphany had refused to enter, declaring she 'saw' flames. The fright this gave the mistress, and the uproar caused among the house servants, had prompted the child's immediate banish-ment to the fields. And there she might have languished had a chimney not caught fire in the quarters the week after. Three slave cabins were destroyed and a sick field-hand and her baby burnt alive.

As they were both now employed in the big house, Cornelius saw Epiphany each day. From an early age she had accompanied him on his nightly forays and he'd taken her out hunting with Johnson; now she was as much at home in the woods as he was. She could stalk and lay traps as well as any boy. He had imparted his knowledge of herbs, and taught her to read and write and cipher. In these ways he had been able to distract her from reality.

As he approached the quarters, Cornelius saw Epiphany dashing past on some errand of her own on this bright summer Sunday. His spirit joined her in a stride and he called out to her and waved. She dropped him a curtsy, her face bright and full of laughter, and continued on. But he was only too aware of how heavily her condition had begun to weigh on her. Her young mistress, Maria, hitherto her closest companion, now spent her days in the schoolroom and the gulf that separated the slave from the white child yawned ever wider. To be with his daughter now was pain and pleasure in equal measure, for he knew that she was starting to understand the full implications of her situation, and that of her father and mother too.

'Johnson has news,' Tabitha said as she closed the door behind Cornelius and Delilah.

Johnson sat by the fireplace, wolfing stew. Cornelius and Delilah declined Tabitha's offer of food for themselves, but Delilah had brought a gift: peaches filched from the kitchen. Cornelius looked expectantly at Johnson. He had been on the road continuously since the day before, travelling forty miles to the coast and back. Untying his bandana, he mopped his face then laboriously folded the frayed piece of cloth and tied it round his neck.

'Well?' Delilah could contain herself no longer.

'The day after tomorrow.' Johnson grinned. 'Before dawn.'

'How many?' Cornelius asked.

'A big party,' Johnson replied, serious again. 'A hundred or more, and they are coming here first.'

'Are you certain?'

'I got it from the horse's mouth,' Johnson assured him. 'From Pompey, who used to work at the Coles' place as a boatman. The British use the slaves for foraging because they know all the waterways.

Which plantations are run-down and which are worth plundering for livestock, horses, grain, slaves – anything they can lay their hands on . . . They took five hundred slaves from Norfolk County alone, and General Edwards –'

'– carried away the same number. We heard that, after the church meeting this morning.'

'But did you hear about the proclamation?'

'That too. Uncle Mattie read it out of the paper.'

'We have no reason now to tarry.' Johnson looked meaningfully in Delilah's direction.

Delilah said nothing.

There was an awkward silence.

'A toast,' Tabitha interjected hurriedly. She filled cups for them all. 'To freedom!' They raised their cups.

Delilah was incorrigible, Cornelius thought; it was pure mischief on her part now not to set Johnson's and Tabitha's minds at rest. He was tempted to tell them the secret she had kept well hidden these past twelve years, but he doubted they would believe it from his lips. 'The ancestors are watching over us,' he said with conviction, and poured some drops of brandy on to the floor before drinking.

Johnson poured some too. 'The more the merrier.'

'Now,' Cornelius said briskly, 'let us go over everything again. Johnson, you begin.'

The forthcoming raid on the plantation, only a rumour before but confirmed now by Johnson, was a lucky stroke. Contrary to what Cato had said after the church meeting, the master was indeed preparing to move his slaves from the home plantation further inland, but the knowledge was confined to a few trusted house slaves. Cornelius and Johnson had decided to make a break under cover of darkness during the transfer of the household from Fairlawns Plantation to Sands, thirty miles away on the Appomattox River. Now, though, the time of their escape could be moved forward to take advantage of the disturbance the raid would cause. They still intended, as they had before the birth of Epiphany, to make their way to Charleston. Then, the journey would have been less perilous, but the outcome – to pass as free Negroes or to take passage back to Africa – more so. Now, the situation was reversed: the British policy of recruiting slaves meant that the Rebels were more vigilant in their efforts to deter runaways, making the journey more dangerous, but the outcome less so, for once they were behind British lines their freedom was guaranteed.

Johnson told them everything he had gleaned on his journey. He ran through the new arrangements he had made, and those he had reaffirmed. The new were incorporated into the old; each member of the group recited his or her part in the operation, reiterating every detail. Cornelius felt a surge of excitement. He thought of his mother and father, of his brother and the campaigns they had planned and fought together, of his former companions and comrades in arms. At last, at last, he was on the road that would lead him back to Oyo.

Delilah was distant and preoccupied next morning as she and Celia sorted and packed the household things to be taken with them or to be put away until their return. In a temper, Celia decided that Delilah was so sulky she would be best on her own: she ordered her to cut the sugar in preparation for the journey. Sugar being such a precious commodity, it was a task reserved for herself and only rarely relinquished to Delilah. Celia escorted her maid in silence along the covered walkway, scented with mint and thyme and marjoram wafting from the kitchen garden, to the storehouse in order to unlock and then lock the door afterwards. Banished to the dining room, Delilah lifted the giant loaf of sugar, weighing more than nine pounds, from its blue wrapping and set it down on a silver tray under which she had placed a cloth to protect the polished tabletop. She folded the wrapping paper into a small square and slid it into her petticoat pocket: carefully soaked, it would produce a blue dye with a purple tint that was prettier than indigo and would colour enough wool to make a skirt or bodice. She stood for a moment with the sugar-shears in her hand, idly opening and shutting the blades, gazing at the blue river beyond the lush green framed in the windows of the dining room.

Her dilemma was not whether she should join in the escape, but whether she should warn her mistress of the impending attack on the plantation. She felt very differently, now, from the time twelve years ago when she had categorically refused to run away. That was before motherhood had taken hold of her. Her daughter had made her ready to sacrifice everything. It had surprised her, and Cornelius too when he discovered the change. But, as the transformation was only in relation to Epiphany, it had required no great effort on Delilah's part to convince the world that it would be futile to attempt to injure her through her child. A sound behind her recalled Delilah to the task in hand and she glanced over her shoulder to see Cato's head round the door. He grinned and disappeared. Delilah sliced off the top of the sugar cone and put it to one side, then commenced cutting the piece she had removed into equal-sized lumps. The process was tedious and exacting but left her mind free. When Cato smiled, she thought, it was more a baring of the teeth, like a guard dog on the leash. Robert should have a care. In other circumstances, Cato's father being the elder son, Cato would have been master of Fairlawns. She picked up a lump of sugar from the tray and admired it against the light, it was crystalline, enticing, and she popped it into her mouth, savouring the sweetness. She sliced another round from the cone, divided the piece into oblongs and, using the scissor-sharp edges at the base of the shears, cut the strips into squares.

Thinking of Cato and Robert led her to thinking again of herself and Celia and her current dilemma. Celia had been eight when her father had made her a present of the pretty little four-year-old Delilah. The two girls, Celia motherless and Delilah deprived of her mother, grew up together on Celia's father's plantation beside the York River. Although Celia had often arbitrarily and hurtfully exercised the power even children had over slaves, she had protected Delilah and helped her navigate the treacherous currents forever swirling in the big house until she was able to swim on her own. The favourite of daughter and father both, Delilah had never felt the lash nor been subjected to the routine punishments and humiliations visited on other lady's maids. She had led a charmed life, until the father's partiality turned to rape. At the time, Celia was away at school in the north. The two girls never spoke of it, but everything had changed. Paradoxically Delilah had become not fearful but fearless; from that point on, if you challenged her, you had to be prepared to kill her. And no one was. The ravished child grew into a ravishing woman, an exotic rose with poisonous thorns.

Delilah laid down her shears and flexed numb fingers; she had transformed half the sugar loaf into a sparkling mound of uniform squares. She leaned her elbows on the table, her mind still on the past.

When Robert Farrer's eyes had fastened on her instead of Celia, whom he had come to court, Delilah had sensed that his was not the usual lusting after a pretty servant. Celia must have felt it too, for on the eve of her wedding she had remarked, only half in jest, that she doubted Robert would have married her had Delilah not been part of the dowry.

Except in so far as it might be useful, Robert's attachment to her was a matter of supreme indifference to Delilah. But mindful of Celia's earlier kindness, she had tried to minimise the hurt it caused her mistress and had helped her establish her authority over the servants at Fairlawns, steering Celia through the currents in the new house just as once she had come to her aid in their childhood home.

Having cut the entire loaf, Delilah selected one of the wooden boxes from the array on the table and began filling it with the daintily cut sugar. She let one or two of the lumps melt slowly on her tongue, and stashed a few more in her pocket. Celia, she reflected, had been the only family she had had. But was that reason enough to risk Epiphany's chance to be free? Now, Delilah had a family of her own, a daughter. But, still, she could not decide.

Celia summoned Delilah to her bedroom, her former ill humour forgotten. Giggling excitedly, she ordered her to shut her eyes. Delilah did as she was asked.

Celia drew her inside the room. 'Now look.'

Delilah stared blankly for an instant, then, 'Of course!' she exclaimed, recovering swiftly.

Laid out across the quilt on the curtained four-poster bed was the pink silk gown, flowered bodice and underskirt that Celia had worn when Robert proposed to her.

'And this is the very day! It's a good omen, don't you think, that I should come across it now?' Delilah nodded agreement, although she thought the gown was sure to have been discovered in any case; every clothes press in the house had been turned out in preparation for the removal of the household. Reverently, Celia removed the bodice from on top of the bed and measured it against herself in front of the full-length looking-glass. 'My waist is still the same?' She frowned enquiringly at Delilah, who had crossed to stand with one hand on the heavy mahogany frame to steady it.

'You are as slender as a girl,' Delilah said. That much was true. The light slanting in through the window at Celia's back was not unkind. In Delilah's eyes, she had the look of a newly pressed flower: no longer vivid, but the bloom not entirely gone.

Celia turned away from her reflection and replaced the bodice on the bed. 'I have a mind to wear the gown to dinner,' she said. 'I doubt there'll be visitors. Nowadays the few people who are left in the neighbourhood we see only at church, and in a short time we too will have flown.' She sighed wistfully. 'I'm afraid Robert finds it dull with only me for company. It might amuse him to see me in my betrothal gown and to talk of happier times. It will be novel, at least.' She stretched out a hand to Delilah. 'Will you help me to look my best?'

'Trust me,' Delilah said. But she thought: *Can she trust me?*

At the dinner bell, Celia descended the stairs in pink silk, her blonde hair dressed high with ringlets framing her face on either side beneath a gauze and lace cap trimmed with white ribbon and an ivory silk rose. Quitting his study at the same time, Robert met her in the hall. He had changed for dinner into a green brocade coat and white embroidered waistcoat and his hair was powdered. He offered Celia his arm and escorted her into the dining room. Cato and Delilah hastened to pull out their chairs and as soon as the master and mistress were seated at opposite ends of the long table the waiting boys entered, somewhat out of breath, having carried the platters at a smart pace from the kitchen fifty yards distant. Puddings, dishes of fruit and cheese were already laid on a side table together with the wine and porter, cider, rum and brandy toddy.

As he prepared to say grace, Robert surveyed the table with satisfaction; there was ham, beef, greens, boiled fish and pickled crab. If a large party had suddenly and unexpectedly arrived, there would have been more than enough to feed them all. For the same reason dinner had been postponed until later than usual. Celia sat toying with her food, stealing glances at Robert and exchanging covert looks with Delilah. Robert conducted himself as befitted the master of the house when presiding over the dinner table; he omitted none of the necessary ceremonial even though only he and his wife were present. He carved the meat, drank her health, enquired if she would rather he helped her or if she wished to help herself to her preferred dishes, passing an hour in polite conversation until it was time for the toasts which always concluded the meal.

Celia, her restraint at an end, interrupted him before he could raise his glass. 'Stop! Robert, don't you know what day this is?'

Robert looked at her in surprise, twisting his wine glass by the stem. He smiled, 'It's a Tuesday. I don't see any particular significance in that.'

'Fifteen years ago today, you asked me to be your wife. See, I'm wearing the same dress I wore that day.'

'Ah . . .' Robert nodded his head. 'I remember now, I recollect it well.'

Celia shot a triumphant glance at Delilah. Smiling, she asked Robert, 'Where were we? Tell me, refresh my memory.'

'At your father's house?'

Celia rolled her eyes. 'Where in my father's house?'

Robert glanced surreptitiously at the flower in her hair. 'In the rose garden.'

'No, the peach walk.'

'What time of day?'

'The doves were calling, it was evening.'

'You remember nothing of it at all!' Celia appeared near to tears.

Robert said cajolingly, 'My dear, you are wrong. The joy caused by your acceptance put all else out of my head, even now. Come –' he raised his glass for the first of the toasts, and after the last had been drunk, he raised his glass once more. 'My wife!'

Celia was not entirely convinced, but she was smiling again as Robert held the door for her. She walked with a light step into the hall. Delilah followed them, one pace behind.

Robert glanced over his shoulder. 'It has come back to me. Delilah wore blue.'

Celia waited until Robert's study door closed before rushing up the stairs to her bedroom. She slammed the door, forbidding Delilah to enter.

Delilah left her alone until it was nearly dark and she felt it safe to approach again. She had come to a decision and, treading softly, she entered the music room, knowing that she would find Celia there, seeking solace as always among her beloved instruments.

Celia sat in one of the deep cushioned window seats looking out into the dusk where the last birds were roosting in the treetops. Her son, her precious last-born after a succession of daughters, rested his elbows on her knee.

'Ah, Delilah,' Celia said, without turning round.

Delilah stared out of the window too, taking in the wide sweep of the lawns, the boxed hedges and yews surrounding the formal gardens and, beyond, the orchards and rolling fields, the old tobacco barns, the hillock crowned with trees, the granaries on the wharf beside the river, becoming indistinct in the slowly deepening dark. It was the place she thought of as home, where her child had been born. 'I have something to tell you,' she said.

'Yes?' Celia's face was swollen from crying. They looked at each other in silence, a weight of unspoken anger and sadness between them.

Delilah threw a glance over her shoulder, and was disconcerted to see Cato.

Celia looked round and acknowledged Cato with a nod. 'Delilah, you had something to tell me?'

Delilah glanced nervously at Cato who began to light the candles near the window.

'What was it, Delilah?' Celia ruffled her son's curls.

'There's a rumour in the quarters,' Delilah spoke quietly, 'that there is to be a raid on the plantation. By the British.'

'I know that,' Celia said coldly, and raised her voice. 'There have been rumours for weeks, have there not, Cato?'

'Yes, mistress.' Cato hovered, candle-lighter in hand, like an owl that has spotted something moving on the ground. 'Do you know something more, Delilah?'

'No.' Delilah avoided his eyes. 'Only . . . it's a feeling, a portent. I had a dream of impending doom, sooner perhaps than we imagine.'

'*We?*' Celia rose to her feet, clutching her son close to her side. She drew herself up. 'The master,' she said, very much the mistress speaking to her slave, 'has everything well in hand. You may be sure that he's taken every precaution to prevent his *property* from falling to the enemy.'

Cato lit the last of the candles, bringing the room and its complement of musical instruments into bright focus.

Celia continued, 'It's time for the children to be put to bed. See to it, Delilah.' She released her son to the care of his nurse and started towards the door. Cato hastened to hold it open.

'A dream, eh?' he said as Delilah passed. 'Fancy that!'

∽

7

THE GREAT HOUSE was astir long before sun-up, as it had been for the past two weeks. Upstairs the mistress was folding linen, assisted by Delilah and two other servant girls. The drapes were drawn across the windows and, careful not to wake the children, the women kept their voices low, tiptoeing across the polished boards with their arms full of clothes as they methodically emptied the contents of the tall ornate cupboards into cedarwood chests lying open on the floor. The scent of lavender from the cupboards mingled with the fragrance of the wood.

Downstairs in the library the master directed the packing of his books. He was perched at the top of some wooden steps, selecting volumes from the higher shelves and passing them to Cornelius who in turn handed them to Cato, who was placing them in neat piles on some green baize spread out on the floor. Here, the window drapes were open and the room brightly lit. Suddenly the darkness outside was illumined with red and Robert, craning from his perch, shouted, 'The granaries!' and jumped to the ground. He raced to the door and into the hall, followed by Cornelius and Cato.

His wife, hearing the commotion and at that very moment crossing the gallery, called out from the top of the stairs.

'Keep calm,' Robert yelled. 'There's a fire.'

'Fire,' she shrieked. 'My God, the children! Rouse the children!'

'No, no, I beg you, keep calm. The fire is not here in the house but at the granaries, and shall be put out directly. Go back to your work.'

Celia's servants drew her into her chamber where they immediately opened the drapes and saw the sky lit by the flames. Delilah led her mistress gently away from the window and entreated her to lie down for a short while on the bed; she would fetch a reviving drink from the kitchen. She sped out of the room.

'Cato, you stay here,' Robert said, pulling on his boots. 'Cornelius, go to the stable, saddle up three horses and bring them to me at the overseer's house.' He dashed out, followed by Cornelius. The overseer was already outside with a troop of half a dozen militiamen ostensibly drafted into the plantation in case of an attack, but whose real purpose was to guard the slaves on the journey inland the next day. After hurriedly conferring with them, Robert kept the overseer and one other by his side, despatched two to guard the big house and sent the other three to the slave quarters to rally a team to fight the fire.

Cornelius, arriving with the horses, was ordered to rejoin Cato at the big house and continue with the work in the library. Robert and the two he'd deputed to ride with him galloped away down the main driveway towards the glow in the sky.

With a snap Cato put the book he was dusting down on the library table. Cornelius had not returned. Cato crossed the room, noiselessly pulled the door open and looked out into the great hall. It was deserted but for the two militiamen posted on either side of the main entrance.

He heard his mistress's voice calling for Delilah, and in a sudden flash he pictured again the scene in the music room. Cursing himself for a fool, he stole soundlessly out of the house by a side door, unnoticed by the two men resolutely guarding the river entrance.

He made his way through the predawn blackness to the stables and in moments was away over the fields on one of the master's best horses. He felt the blood racing through his veins. He had disobeyed the master's orders and taken one of his finest horses – a hanging offence, but not, he laughed aloud, if it led to the recovery of some of the plantation's most valuable slaves. Cato bent low over the horse's neck and, digging in his heels, galloped towards the river. There were only three places the runaways could be.

Cornelius watched the torches growing smaller in the distance, as Robert galloped away followed by the overseer and a militiaman. All was pandemonium now in the slave quarters, with the dogs barking, men shouting, children bawling and women running to and fro as the news spread and a fire-fighting team hurriedly assembled.

Cornelius melted into the dark, moving in the direction of the big house. He kept on the grass beside the drive as the two militiamen guarding the house dashed along the middle of the avenue, underneath the beeches, crunching up the ground in their heavy boots and clattering their rifles, unaware of the silent presence keeping pace with them. When they drew level with the orchard, near enough to be seen in the light falling from the windows of the big house, Cornelius ducked away from the road, weaving in and out among the trees until he reached the formal gardens.

He slid over the wall, keeping low until he reached the edge of one of the vast stretches of lawn fronting the river. He dropped to the ground and, winding smooth as a snake through the grass, skirted around the side, making for the river bank where, bordering the lawn, a thick strand of cypresses grew right down to the water's edge. It was here he had sat with Delilah on a moonlit night twelve years before and she had told him she was to have his child.

Luckily, on this occasion there was no moon. He rose to his feet, soaked in dew, and moved swiftly through the trees and across the park, slipping like a shadow among the deer as he had done so many times before. Although they marked his passing, the animals barely stirred. At the edge of the park he dropped to the ground again and slithered through the grass towards a dense screen of trees fringing the swamp.

He inched forward, probing the darkness, making for a particular tree, halting when he was within a few yards of it. In a deep pit below the giant cypress, requisites for a long and arduous journey had been steadily accumulated. Satisfied that the earth around the base of the tree had not been disturbed and that he was the first to arrive, he placed two stones in position to signal his presence and continued on through the trees to the edge of the swamp. He tested the ground with his foot and, as he had feared, sank in nearly to the top of his boot.

The last few days had been hot and dry, but clearly not sufficiently so to counteract the rain of the preceding week. He had hoped to walk through the swamp and then paddle across the Back Creek, which at this point was normally shallow enough to do so. It would be too dangerous to attempt that now. Countless runaways had sunk unmarked into the quicksands bordering the narrow safe-ways, known only to a few. Johnson had shown him the paths through the swamps over and over until he too could walk them blindfold.

At night the air was filled with the presence of the spirits of the departed whispering warnings. Instinctively Cornelius offered thanks for their guidance. He retraced his steps to the shelter of the foliage and was immediately aware that he was no longer alone. A few paces from the tree he detected a deeper shadow between two of the roots.

He dropped to the ground and moved forward until he too was in the shadow of the tree. He held out his hand and Epiphany's small cold one was put into his. He gave thanks silently and some of the tension left him. She was the one he had been most anxious about. Slipping away amidst all the commotion would have been easy for her, but then she'd had to make her way alone. She had learnt her lessons well.

He gripped her hand tightly and felt her smile in the darkness. Moments later Johnson materialised and shortly after, equally stealthily, Tabitha. They waited, hidden amongst the roots, for Delilah. Finally she arrived, making as much noise, Cornelius thought exasperatedly, as a wounded elephant. He waited for the turmoil surrounding her arrival to abate before he spoke.

'It is just as I feared,' he said, 'the stream is too high here for us to ford.'

He had no need to explain further; they knew what they must do. Working methodically, swiftly and in silence, they dug out the baggage hidden under the tree, dispersing it about their persons so that they looked as if they carried nothing at all, and then set off at intervals, one by one.

Arriving at the stream and finding his quarry gone, Cato dashed on. On horseback he had the advantage; he was almost certain to have caught up with them by the time they reached the next crossing point at the creek. And if not there, then for sure at the edge of the swamp where the narrowest of paths led through the marshes to a ford across the river. Exultantly, he lifted his fist in the air; they would not be able to escape him.

Racing ahead of his overseer and the militiaman, Robert halted briefly at the top of a small hill and surveyed with mounting anger the blaze in the distance. His entire wheat crop would be destroyed. Increasing his pace down the other side, he dashed across the fields with his two companions, torches streaming, past the chaos of the slave quarters in the direction of the granaries.

As they approached they were able to see that it was not the granaries on fire but the hayricks close by which had been set alight. The three of them leapt from their horses and ran into the nearest granary, returning with long-handled flails. Robert and the overseer began beating the fire while the militiaman unhooked a couple of buckets kept handily nearby and rushed to the creek to fetch water. A team of fire-fighters from the slave quarters quickly joined them and formed a chain, passing the leather water-buckets from hand to hand.

The fire had been started deliberately, Robert thought, but he could not immediately decide by whom. He cast his eye down the line of fire-fighters. Was it one of his own slaves in retaliation for revoking all passes until the household was safely removed to his Sands plantation? That would be his first guess, as it was only the hayricks that had been set alight. On the other hand the blaze might be a ruse, merely, to divert attention. It was a common tactic of the British; but he was as certain as he could be that news of the impending removal to his furthest quarter upriver had not reached their ears. Only two of his most trusted servants knew exactly when the move was to take place. He would find out soon enough, he promised himself.

'Master! Master!' someone shouted. Robert stopped beating the flames and spun round as a servant came racing towards him. 'It's the

British – soldiers, a hundred or more, and there's runaways with them. Up at the big house' – the man clutched his side, breathless – 'and down the quarters. Swarming all over. From the looks of them, they aiming to leave the place empty.'

From the direction of the big house a burst of musket fire sounded loudly in corroboration.

'I have been tricked,' Robert shouted. He dashed towards his horse. His feet were already in the stirrups when he was halted again, this time by the sound of a horse's hooves.

Cato galloped into the clearing. Seeing Robert he wrenched his mount to a standstill and slid from its back.

'You.' Robert pointed at him, 'You.'

'No, master. *No!*'

Cato, grasping the situation in an instant, dropped to his knees.

'Seize him,' Robert ordered.

The overseer lunged forward and delivered a blow with his rifle butt, sending Cato face down on the ground.

'This is how you repay me! By betraying me to the British?' Cato lifted his head to protest and received another blow on the back of his neck.

'Raise him up,' Robert said. 'He'll keep.'

Robert gestured to the militiaman to train his gun on the fire-fighters, who resumed their work.

Hauling Cato to his feet, the overseer dragged him to the edge of the clearing and steadied him against a tree. He retrieved a nail from the pocket of his breeches and, using the end of his rifle, hammered the nail through Cato's ear, pinning him to the trunk of the tree. He then winded him with a final blow to the stomach.

Leaving the militiaman to guard the slaves, Robert and the overseer mounted their horses and galloped towards the house, leading Cato's horse by the bridle.

The musket fire became louder and louder as they breasted the hill once more, to see the mansion in flames. Robert's thoughts flew to his wife and children trapped within, his life and work entirely destroyed. He swung his horse around and galloped back down the hill and into the clearing. He took aim and shot Cato full in the face.

'Listen,' Tabitha whispered. They were travelling together now, in single file, moving towards the boat Johnson had hidden by the creek. They had all heard the noise issuing from beyond the screen of trees fringing the clearing, deserted now that the team of fire-fighters had been marched away. Smoke was still rising from the blackened haystacks; in the distance the glow from the burning house lit the sky. All four adults turned to look at Epiphany, recalling how on her first day of work at the big house she'd 'seen' it consumed by fire.

Tabitha drew the child close.

The noise came again from beyond the trees: a high-pitched whimpering ending in a long-drawn rattling gurgle.

'Rat. Caught in a trap,' Johnson said.

'Credit me with a little more sense than that. I'm no hunter, but that inhuman noise is coming from a human.' Tabitha released Epiphany and darted swiftly through the trees. She was as quickly back. 'It's Cato, but I could recognise him only by his livery. Half his head is shot away, but he's not dead. He's talking, talking, talking.'

'Stay here.' Cornelius put an arm around her briefly. Tabitha was shaking. 'And you too,' he told Delilah and Epiphany. 'Come, Johnson.'

The two men stood for a moment, motionless at the sight of Cato's mangled face from which words were issuing in an incomprehensible stream, and then moved as one towards him.

Cornelius slit the gurgling throat with a sweep of his knife.

Johnson freed Cato's ear.

They laid Cato gently on the ground and Cornelius cut the arteries at wrist and ankle before carrying the body back to where the others were sheltering in the trees.

'We have no time to bury him,' Cornelius said. 'But we can lend some dignity to his death. We can wrap him in the best cloth we have. Delilah, give me your shawl.'

'I will not. Why do you think he was here? He was looking for us to betray us.' Recalling her last encounter with Cato in the music room, Delilah clung on to her shawl.

Cornelius began easing the fine material from her shoulders.

'Cornelius, why are you doing this?'

'Because fate has made us children of the same mother.'

8

DELILAH STOOD BY the open door glancing with satisfaction round the small neat yard. A delicious smell wafted in from the kitchen. A deep voice sang an out-of-tune accompaniment to the clucking of the chickens as they pecked at the grains of corn scattered beneath the glossy green branches of the magnolia tree.

It was certainly the best-kept yard in the district and possibly in the whole of Charleston, Delilah thought. As was the house, in spite of its modest location on the edge of a warren of dark alleyways running down to the wharves beside the Cooper River. But house and yard were a vast improvement on how things had been when they had first arrived over two years ago.

Delilah shuddered. The wonder was that any of them had survived. Arriving behind British lines half-starved and ill from fatigue after weeks of hiding by day and journeying down difficult and dangerous paths by night, they had been welcomed by the British with a lack of consideration that matched the attitude of their former masters.

Instead of being given guns and put to fighting, they were set to digging trenches, building fortifications, washing, cooking, cleaning. Escaped slaves were last in line for everything – food, shelter, medicines. Whatever their differences, white people were always of the same mind, apparently, when dealing with black people. More fool the British, Cornelius said, as it was the blacks who had a real stomach for this war, for they were not after killing white people, they were after their freedom. A good many of the blacks, Delilah thought, were after both.

Those first months had been grinding. Delilah rubbed at the calluses on her palms. Most of the runaway slaves were not field hands, used to hard labour; they were skilled artisans and house servants, but they had willingly put their backs into the work because the whole of their future lay in the balance. During the siege of Charleston they had drained ditches, constructed breastworks and built redoubts alongside the regular troops, as the British army under General Clinton dug closer and closer to the city. And when the Rebels had clogged the Cooper River with

164

scuttled ships, it was a gang of blacks, Cornelius and Johnson among them, who dragged the rowboats overland to bypass the blockage.

Cornelius's luck turned when a British officer, intrigued by his face markings, discovered while questioning him that he spoke French and straight away had him in front of the commander. Before you could whistle, Cornelius and Johnson found themselves acting as scouts, guiding couriers or carrying messages along the secret tracks known only to wolves, bears and runaway slaves. They were away for weeks at a time.

Before departing on his first mission, Cornelius had commended Delilah, Epiphany and Tabitha, in his absence, to the care of the same British officer. In turn Lord Fitzalan commended the women to the quartermaster, who had melted like butter in the sun the instant he caught sight of Delilah. From that moment the fortunes of their little group, which by then included two new members, had been made.

Never having wielded a hoe or a pick or a shovel before, Delilah, Tabitha and Epiphany would have been hard pushed to qualify for the two shillings paid each day to the common labourers had it not been for Carver and Big Mo. Drawn by Delilah's siren smile, they had attached themselves to her on the very first shift. Big Mo lived up to her name; at fifteen she was taller than most men, and Carver, two or three years older, was as big as a tree. Motherless and biddable, each could do the work of three. Delilah had gathered both giant fledglings under her wing.

A voice called crisply for her to come back inside the house and Delilah smiled to herself, recalling her first meeting with Auntie Sam, and how, shortly afterwards, the 'family' had increased again.

Following the surrender of Charleston to the British, she and Tabitha had been put in charge of running the soup kitchen, assisting the quartermaster to feed and clothe the huge number of Negroes flooding into the city. The refugees were *all* needy; many arrived naked, and many more sick and dying of the smallpox. In the midst of such a crowd, the saffron-skinned woman, exquisitely dressed and carrying a dainty parasol, seemed an apparition from another world as she passed by morning and evening, scouring the faces of the people queuing for food. Intrigued, Delilah had approached her and been amused to learn that Auntie Sam was not, as Tabitha had speculated, searching for a long-lost relative. She was on the lookout for likely girls for the establishment she'd set-up above her tavern on the quayside. A day or two later, Auntie Sam and Delilah were in partnership, and Delilah, Epiphany, Carver and Big Mo were all ensconced in Auntie Sam's house. Cornelius and Johnson had objected at first, and Tabitha elected to continue making her home a pallet in the corner of the storehouse, but, gradually, even they had accepted Auntie Sam as a part of the group.

Delilah turned to go inside. To her mind the balance was exactly right: two for Cornelius and *three* for her. Except that now the balance might be about to shift. Cornelius had met the African girl again, the one he'd gone looking for years before only to find that she had been sold. Abetted by the quartermaster, Tabitha had taken to doctoring the runaways as well as feeding them in a ramshackle lean-to that served as a hospice. She discovered Betsey – or Tamari, as she was now known – while treating her sick husband. The husband had soon died of the smallpox, leaving his wife a widow and his daughter fatherless. Her plight brought out the gallant in Cornelius, and he seemed smitten all over again. What if he decided to include her in the group? Delilah put the thought aside; she had other, more pressing problems. For her part, she would have been happy for the hostilities to continue for ever but the British were beginning to lose the war, putting her hard-won prosperity in jeopardy.

'Hurry up, Big Mo,' Delilah called, re-entering the house. She winked at Carver and Auntie Sam seated at a small table.

Big Mo, the owner of the less than tuneful singing voice that had been wafting into the courtyard, emerged from the kitchen carrying a small platter, which she placed on the table, inviting each of the others to taste one of her little cakes.

Carver disposed of his in one mouthful. Delilah gazed at him fondly. If it were not for Carver, Cornelius always said, they would never have succeeded in hauling those rowboats overland. Carver had been the natural choice to make sure everyone kept in line at the soup kitchen. Auntie Sam shook back the frills of her stylish morning gown and bit delicately into a dainty, round, white cake. They were gathered on the ground floor of her narrow three-storey house in the little tavern room that was a natural extension of her establishment upstairs.

'Delilah, you try one.' Big Mo pushed the plate towards her. Delilah meekly obeyed. She had rescued Big Mo from grave-digging, thinking to use her to do the heavy work, only to discover the girl was a conjurer in the kitchen. Her mother, who had collapsed and died within hours of their arriving behind British lines, had been a cook on a plantation in Georgia. She had passed on her gifts to her daughter, but the mistress had found the great hulk of a girl too frightening a presence in the big house and had exiled her to the fields. Big Mo's cooking, coupled with Delilah's laundering skills, had swiftly turned Auntie Sam's into the favourite haunt of the senior ranks of the British army. Who else in Charleston had money to spend? Cornelius, Johnson and Tabitha still objected to the nature of the business, but if the British lost the war, reasoned Delilah as she smoothed the lace on her bodice, her friends would not quibble at using her money to buy their passage out.

Big Mo crossed corded forearms across her chest. 'Take another,' she urged Delilah and Auntie Sam, 'before Carver finishes them all.' Carver's huge hand reaching out for more was swiftly withdrawn. He looked down at the table.

'It's all right, Carver.' Delilah pushed the plate towards him. He took one of the cakes and this time bit into it delicately. The other three burst out laughing.

'Where did you learn to eat like that Carver?' Auntie Sam mimicked him, holding her cake gingerly between finger and thumb. 'I reckon you could teach a bear a thing or two.'

'I'm practising for the ball,' Carver said.

'We must be thankful you won't be dancing.' Auntie Sam patted her brow in mock relief.

Carver reached for the plate again.

Delilah helped herself too. 'Are you going to tell us what these are, Big Mo?'

'They're my own recipe. Rice cakes with a touch of rum. I'm practising for the ball too.'

Delilah blew Big Mo a kiss. 'Those British officers will think they are in paradise.' Big Mo's grin stretched wide as the bay outside.

'This ball is going to cause big trouble,' Carver said. 'It's going to offend everyone. The Negroes will not be happy about it, and the white people won't like it either, whichever side they are on, Loyalists or Rebels. Whoever heard of an Ethiopian Ball?' He swallowed the last of the cakes.

Auntie Sam stretched peachy arms above her head and her eyes glinted. 'The British will like it, Carver, never you fear. Why just the thought of it – His Majesty's officers dancing all night with Negro women – will cause more fatalities behind Rebel lines than all the British cannon put together.'

'And *we* will like it,' Delilah said. 'We stand to make a good profit. If the British are forced to leave, we might as well take their money before they go.'

'If they lose the war, what will happen to us?' Big Mo asked anxiously.

'Whatever happens,' Delilah reassured her, 'we are *free*. They can't take that away from us. Don't worry, Big Mo. I'll take care of you. We'll all go to the north and open up another place. Go back to the kitchen now, there's a good girl, and carry on the fine work.' Delilah put the empty plate into Big Mo's hands and shooed her out.

'She can certainly cook, and so elegantly,' Auntie Sam said as soon as Big Mo was out of hearing. 'You wouldn't think it to look at her though. She's like you, Carver, big as a mountain and twice as ugly.'

'She's beautiful on the inside, that's what counts,' Carver said.

'Is that so?' asked Auntie Sam mockingly.

'The Reverend George says so. All God's children have a soul and it is the prettiness of that we should worry about, because the Lord Jesus Christ can see clear through to the centre.'

Delilah sighed, 'It's the Baptists. The people are flocking to them, exchanging one master for another. I can't think why white people's religion would do anything for us.'

'God is on *our* side,' Carver said. 'He is on the side of the slaves.'

'We aren't slaves any more,' Delilah reminded him. She sighed again. She had imagined Carver of all people would be safe from the Reverend George and his preaching. In a fight, you'd have more chance against a loaded gun than against Carver. That was why she had chosen him.

'It's the poor people who get to go to heaven,' Carver continued doggedly.

'Do the poor whites go there too? They're just as bad as the rich ones,' Auntie Sam said, and kissed her teeth loudly. 'If white people go to heaven, then I certainly don't want to end up there.'

'Me neither,' Delilah said. 'Unless they're there to wait on us.'

The two of them leant against each other, laughing.

'Christianity's serious business,' Carver said reproachfully. 'The first thing I'm going to do when I become a proper Christian is forgive the white people.'

'Forgive them!' Delilah spluttered. Auntie Sam slapped her on the back.

Tabitha entered the room with her quick step and, seeing them speechless with laughter, asked to share the joke.

Delilah's expression soured momentarily at the sight of Epiphany's beaming face at Tabitha's shoulder. Wherever Tabitha went nowadays, Epiphany went too, accompanied by her own faithful shadow, Quality, who curtsied a greeting. Delilah acknowledged her with a smile. Quality was a bold child despite her mother, for if Cornelius was to be believed, Tamari rivalled Tabitha in piousness.

Smiling, Delilah said, 'Carver's talking himself out of a job. If word gets out he's full of Christian forgiveness he won't be any use to us. We need people to think that if they so much as move he'll kill them, which until now was the truth.'

'Whatever you do, Carver,' said Auntie Sam, dabbing her eyes with a spotless handkerchief, 'don't get baptised before the ball.'

Mention of the ball made Epiphany and Quality shiver with excitement. 'When can we see our dresses, Ma?' Epiphany demanded.

'All in good time,' Delilah replied repressively, and Tabitha's smile vanished.

'They shouldn't be going to the ball. Apart from all the other considerations, they're much too young.'

'Nonsense.' Auntie Sam pinched Epiphany's satin cheek. 'They're perfect, just coming to ripeness. They'll break hearts, the two of them.'

'You've turned their heads,' Tabitha replied, flushing, 'with all your promises of silks and satins and ribbons. They're still children.'

'But not *your* children,' Delilah said nastily. Really, Tabitha could be so tiresome, persistent as a summer fly, buzz, buzz, buzz; that was how the old maid had harassed them into letting her use the tavern as a schoolroom during the day. Buzz, buzz, buzz; and into giving the leftovers, which they could easily have sold, to the destitutes overrunning the city. Well, she was not going to get her way this time.

'Tabitha why don't *you* come to the ball?' Delilah put an arm around her waist.

'You're a beautiful woman,' Auntie Sam cajoled. 'As well as being an ornament, you could chaperone the girls.'

Tabitha moved away. 'The church forbids dancing.'

'No dancing?' Auntie Sam swivelled her hips. 'The Christian God is definitely a white man.'

'You know the thing I like about freedom?' Delilah executed a neat two-step. 'No one can forbid me any more.'

Often on a Sunday now Cornelius was to be found dressed in his best: a blue livery coat supplied by Lord Fitzalan, somewhat incongruous with buckskin breeches and boots. An interesting combination, Johnson remarked, on seeing him, but no more so he supposed than Cornelius's sudden thirst for Christianity. Cornelius had passed by Johnson's place to discuss the final arrangements for their departure the following day. They were to act as guides for a courier carrying letters to Lord Cornwallis's army stationed at Yorktown, Virginia.

The service had already begun by the time Cornelius reached the cornfield outside the city where the Reverend George regularly held his Sunday-morning meeting. As usual, Cornelius was astonished at the huge number of people present and as always he was swept up by the sheer joyfulness of the singing, the clapping, the dancing. Although, as Tabitha insisted, it was not *actually* dancing, because they did not cross their feet. Catching his breath, Cornelius glanced at the austere cut of Tabitha's profile, brushed an imaginary speck from his sleeve, eased a finger around the inside of his high collar and was about to surrender to an insuperable urge to look behind him at Tamari when he discovered Tabitha's eye upon him. Reverend George had begun his sermon. Cornelius scrutinised him instead. The preacher was unprepossessing in appearance, but there was no mistaking the energy and inner strength contained in his thin frame. He was clearly a man of powerful magic, of deeds as well as words. As ever though, listening to him, Cornelius could not rid his mind of the suspicion that this Christianity was yet another weapon in the white man's armoury, tailored for slaves.

'Let us pray.' Head back, eyes shut, Reverend George lifted up his arms to heaven. Prompted by a nudge from Tabitha, Cornelius bowed his head and clasped his hands together as the Reverend George commended two erstwhile members of his congregation to the mercy of the Almighty. They had been snatched in broad daylight on the street and returned to slavery. Rumours of a British withdrawal had drawn a plague of bounty hunters who, confident of rich rewards from slave owners eager to retrieve their property, had begun prowling the city, seizing black people with impunity. While Reverend George asked his God to grant the abducted brother and sister the strength to bear the burden of their bondage, Cornelius prayed to Ogun for a way to escape should the same fate befall anyone in his group. He could not imagine how they could find the power to endure, having tasted freedom, however briefly. His *amen* was as heartfelt as any. A long moment passed in silence as all of those present confronted the unthinkable.

'So?' Tabitha enquired when the service was over.

'I would certainly like to learn more.' Cornelius smiled at Tamari, who'd arrived within earshot. Tabitha drew her nearer.

'It's good to see so many new faces,' Tamari said. 'People are coming to Jesus like plants seeking water.'

'Is that what it is?' Tabitha's tone was dry.

'With the Lord, nothing is impossible,' Tamari said.

'Quite so,' Tabitha agreed. 'Well, I must be getting on, I have plenty to do at the hospital. Sickness is no respecter of Sundays.'

'Let me walk with you,' Tamari linked an arm through hers.

'Me too,' Cornelius said quickly. 'To make sure you're safe.'

'I am perfectly safe among the sick and dying,' Tabitha said, dryer than ever.

'But you might be waylaid,' Cornelius said. 'There's safety in numbers.'

Walking across the fields, arms linked, Tamari on one side and Cornelius on the other, Tabitha betrayed no sign of the pain she felt. She understood something now of the jealousy Celia had harboured for Delilah. She glanced up at Cornelius. There had been no one else for her from the moment all those years ago when she had first seen him in the weaving shed at Fairlawns Plantation. And through the years she had never given up the hope that one day he would discover he loved her too. She could see now that it was a false hope. He had discovered love, but it was to be Tamari after all. Perhaps he'd been hers all along, their fate sealed at that first meeting in the slave market in Africa. Cornelius said that where he came from they believed each person chose their own fate.

She would continue loving him, that much she knew, but it had yet to be revealed to her why she had chosen her particular fate: to be everyone's friend but nobody's love, an aunt to all and mother to none.

The walk to Tamari's lodging took twice as long as it had to Tabitha's hospital, though it was a quarter of the distance. Even so, Cornelius lingered.

'I was sincere in what I said,' he told her. 'I would like to learn more about the Christian religion. You could teach me. I am sure you're a very fine Christian.'

'Believe me, I am not. And I can't teach you the scriptures because I can't read.'

'Scriptures?'

'The stories in the Bible.'

'You have them off by heart, I expect.'

'Yes, some . . . in fact, many.'

'That's settled. In return I shall teach you how to read so that you can recognise your favourite stories in the Bible.'

'You're a good man, Cornelius.'

He had the grace to blush. 'Until I return then,' he said, having no more reason to stay. But still he stayed.

'Be safe,' she said, and touched his cheek briefly. She stepped inside, leaving him staring at the door. He'd imagined how it would be if he and Tamari were ever to meet again, but over time the images had faded. Now those half-remembered feelings had returned as if a rainbow had suddenly appeared against a sombre grey sky. As he retraced his steps, thinking of Tamari, Cornelius's mind travelled back. Images of the wedding trains parading round Oyo passed before his eyes, and the music of long-forgotten songs sounded in his ears:

> *I took my calabash and went to Oyo town,*
> *The Prince of Oyo took the calabash from my head.*
> *I said, Sir, why did you do that?*
> *He said it's because I am a slender beauty*
> *I have a neck worthy to wear blue Segi beads*
> *May good luck attend me today.*
> *May good luck attend me today.*

How lovely the young girls of his youth! How beautiful Tamari now.

Delilah and Auntie Sam stopped for a moment to admire the sweep of the bay and the winter sun on the water. A dozen ships of the line, flags fluttering in the breeze, tall masts outlined against the sky, were evidence that, though reduced to a few small enclaves on the mainland, the British were still masters of the sea. White gulls wheeled noisily above them. It was on the landward side that the full defences were. Delilah knew them well; she had worked on them. They all had, except Auntie Sam.

Delilah glanced sideways at her friend, exquisitely turned out as ever. They had not known each other then.

'Shall we move on?' Auntie Sam said. 'I can admire a natural scene only so long. I itch to improve it. For instance, the colour of the water in the bay today is not quite right. I like it greener. And the colour of the clouds grates.'

Delilah gazed up at the sky. 'More pink, perhaps?'

'No, yellow.'

'You prefer artifice?'

'I insist on it. What other way to escape?'

'Was reality so bad?' Delilah asked. Auntie Sam had never confided the story of her life in slavery and she remained silent now. Delilah did not press her.

After a few moments Auntie Sam stopped. 'My master . . . my owner used me as his private midden . . .'

'What? You mean . . .?'

Auntie Sam nodded. 'That was his particular pleasure.'

Delilah's eyes filled with tears. Auntie Sam started forward again.

'So you see, natural and unadorned has been ruined for me.'

They continued up Broad Street, past the poor house, the hospital and the jail clustered at the eastern end of the street, towards the mansions lining both sides near the Exchange building at the western end.

They walked around the side of one of the houses, into the kitchen in the yard, and re-emerged shortly afterwards, accompanied by a beautiful young woman. The three of them turned into King Street, paused to admire the premises where General Clinton had established his head-quarters and then disappeared through the pillared entrance of another fine residence not far away.

'Good day, ladies.' Captain Hawkins and Lieutenant Wyatt bowed, the faintest sarcasm in their voices and the flourish of their actions. Behind them, the quartermaster also bowed. The visitors returned the greeting with curtseys worthy of the highest court in Europe, indicating by their smiles that the sarcasm was not lost on them. They accepted the chairs drawn out for them and, having elegantly arranged their skirts, waited straight-backed and composed, aware of the charming picture they made in their white caps and tight bodices, the light shining into the room, patinating their complexions.

Delilah swiftly priced the furnishings of the airy, high-ceilinged room, covertly examining the wide-striped wallpaper and blue velvet drapes, the French carpet and English furniture. The magnificent footman would not have been cheap either, she thought. He was certainly well trained, proceeding as if it were an everyday occurrence to serve wine in such surroundings to women of his own complexion as if they were gentry. No doubt he had been sequestered with the rest of the contents. She gave him a sly wink as he bent to offer her the silver tray, but he remained serenely unruffled.

She returned her attention to her hosts and their supercilious gallantry. They raised their glasses in a toast. Together with Auntie Sam and Martha, she smilingly responded. How flabbergasted these little turkey cocks would be if they knew the true ages of their guests. Auntie Sam displaying her dimples so prettily, had been practising that same smile before their mothers were born, and even lovely Martha must have seen at least ten summers more than the quartermaster, who, of the three gallants, was longest out of the schoolroom. Delilah smiled especially sweetly at him. He was the one who, after some tough negotiating, had drawn up the papers spread out on the table in front of them. He had more of her measure now and she of his.

'You will be glad to hear that the general has given his permission for an Ethiopian Ball.' Captain Hawkins gathered up the papers. 'And,' he smiled broadly, 'we have examined your proposals and we agree the revised terms.' The ladies inclined their heads. He continued, 'The premises will be supplied by us, as will the horses and carriages to convey the guests to the ball. Is that not so, Mr Quartermaster?'

'Yes, my lord.'

'We will also,' Captain Hawkins said, 'bear the cost of the dinner and the attire of the women. That will be your domain, Mr Quartermaster, in consultation with the ladies. See that they are supplied with whatever silks, ribbons, shoes, stockings, petticoats, et cetera, they require.'

'Yes, my lord.'

'Lieutenant Wyatt and myself will also be responsible for sending the invitations. And that I believe is the end of our obligations.'

'Beverages, my lord?' The quartermaster's quill hovered over the page.

'The selection of those I shall willingly take upon myself.' Lieutenant Wyatt beamed enthusiastically. 'You need none of you trouble yourselves on that score.'

'The decorations, the food, the music all will be supplied by you, ladies. Mr Quartermaster, you will see to it that they are given all the assistance they need.' Captain Hawkins's smile was predatory as he addressed the ladies again. 'There remains only the selection of the . . . ah . . . Ethiopians. Ladies, you know our requirements. I trust that they will be young and beautiful. Indeed, just like yourselves.'

'Indeed,' Delilah said.

Captain Hawkins flicked his fingers for the footman to replenish their glasses. 'To you, ladies, and a British victory.'

'A British victory.'

Delilah's expression became pensive, 'There are those who say that the British no longer have a heart for this war.'

'This ball' – Lieutenant Wyatt slapped his knee – 'will put the lie to that, it will show our enemies our hearts are high. I, for one, believe unreservedly that our American colonies are still recoverable. Mark my words, the spring will see the launch of another campaign.'

'But should the unimaginable happen,' Delilah said, 'and the British are forced to withdraw, what will become of us, I wonder? There are rumours that all former slaves will be returned to their masters.' Her eyes were brilliant suddenly, as if on the verge of tears.

'You can be certain, madam, that, whatever transpires, my country will honour its commitments. And in the unlikely event of a British withdrawal, I give you my word that I will do everything in my power to assist you to safety. An Englishman's word is his bond.'

'Oh, thank you,' Delilah said. 'I shall not forget.' And she gave him a tremulous smile.

Auntie Sam struggled to disguise her amusement, as the true purpose behind this meeting suddenly struck her.

Delilah paid no mind at first when Tabitha told her that Epiphany had set her heart on someone. The girl was sixteen; it was calf love. Though Tabitha insisted it was serious, it was not until she started speaking warmly of the boy that Delilah decided to investigate.

'Brothers and sisters . . .' Reverend George's passion lifted him off his feet; he seemed to hang in the air, his arms thrust out in front of him, fingers pointing at the Sunday-morning crowd, all of whom had trudged the two miles out of Charleston to hear him preach. 'What was it carried you through every day in slavery? What was it, when freedom called, made you throw off your shackles and escape behind British lines?'

Reverend George pulled out a faded red kerchief from his coat pocket and mopped the sweat running down his face, copious as rain, though the January weather was cool.

Without their noticing, Delilah sneaked up behind Tabitha and Epiphany, whose friend Quality stood on one side of her and a young man on the other, his shoulder touching hers.

Reverend George continued, 'It was faith in yourselves brought you through. But now you can have faith in the Lord as well. Put your faith in Him and He will never disappoint you. Never betray you.'

'Hah!' Delilah exclaimed.

'What brings *you* here?' Tabitha turned in surprise.

'I wanted to see the man who has such a hold over my daughter.'

Epiphany and the young man both blushed deeply.

Delilah said, 'Reverend George is mighty persuasive.'

'Reverend George's words do have a shine on them,' Epiphany said, 'as if each one's been specially polished.'

Tabitha hugged her. 'Yes, child; a casket of gems more precious than any jewels. Those of us who have as their adornment the Word of God are the richest people on earth.'

'Beggars more like, scrabbling in the dirt for a few coins tossed down by the rich,' Delilah said. Tabitha had gained too much influence over Epiphany with her new-found Christianity.

'Ma . . .' Epiphany pulled the young man forward. 'This is Caleb.'

Caleb bowed.

Delilah shook his hand. 'I've heard a lot about you. Tabitha tells me your parents were members of Reverend George's original congregation in Georgia.'

'They've both passed away,' Epiphany said.

'The smallpox got them.' Caleb stared at his feet.

'I'm sorry,' Delilah said, and as Reverend George claimed the attention of the women once more she beckoned Caleb aside. She studied him. He was tall and he had a look of Cornelius, but it was a surface likeness. This man was a follower not a leader. 'Are you serious about my daughter?' she asked.

'Yes, ma'am.' Caleb gave her a big smile.

'I can see why she wants you. You're a handsome boy.' Delilah's voice was honey over steel.

'I hope there's more to me than that,' Caleb said, acknowledging the steel.

'So do I,' Delilah said. She jerked her head in Tabitha's direction. 'Auntie tells me you're also a good Christian boy.'

Caleb looked at her as if he were gauging the distance before jumping. After a pause, he said, 'I've been baptised, if that's what you mean.' He shrugged. 'I was a child, mimicking my elders.'

Delilah's smile indicated he had landed safely on the other side. She said, 'It's a mystery to me why so many of our folks are running in that direction.'

At ease now, Caleb grinned. He said, 'They think being Christians makes them equal to white folks, and being *good* Christians makes them *better* than most white folks.'

'What do *you* think?' Delilah asked.

Caleb looked at her, wary again. He said, 'I believe there are more useful lessons we could learn from white folks.'

'You'll do,' Delilah said.

After the service, Tabitha and Delilah walked on ahead.

Epiphany waited until they were out of sight and held out her hand to Caleb. He offered his other hand to Quality, who fell into step beside them.

'So,' Epiphany said, 'what did my mother want?'

'She wanted to know my intentions.' Caleb winked at Quality.

'Well? What are they?' Quality purred menacingly, exactly like Delilah.

All three burst out laughing.

Caleb replied, 'Now we are free, we don't have to decide in a hurry; we have time to take time.'

'Huh!' Epiphany patted the back of her hair, the image of Auntie Sam. 'You just want to wait and see if someone better comes along.'

'No, no!' Caleb threw up his hands, terror personified.

They laughed so hard that for a while they were unable to walk properly, stumbling and tripping over the corn stubble to lean on the trunk of a tree. Epiphany was the first to recover and started to move on.

Caleb restrained her. 'Wait.' She turned towards him. 'I've already decided, Epiphany. I'm yours. When the war is over, wherever you go, I'll go with you.'

'To the end of the earth?'

'To the end of the earth.'

Epiphany started running. 'Lucky for you,' she threw over her shoulder, 'my mother's only thinking of New York.'

Epiphany and Quality leaned dangerously out of the window watching for the carriages. Dressed and ready for the past hour, they were impatient for the evening to begin, aware perhaps that tonight they were as beautiful as they would ever be. Youth and beauty was the only combination in Nature that needed no improving, Auntie Sam had remarked tartly as the girls took it in turns to parade in front of her, but she hadn't been able to resist a little artifice all the same.

A tightening of laces, and a small waist shrank to a hand span. Learn to breathe through your ears. A flick of powder, and a peach-coloured cheek took on the glow of summer. Sneeze and you're finished. A little gloss to enhance the midnight tone of the deepest black complexion. Whatever you do, don't touch. Mindful of Auntie Sam's admonitions, the girls became careful and stilted in their movements, reduced for the moment to exquisite automata in their unaccustomed finery.

'They are here, they are here!' Epiphany shouted as the first carriage swept round the corner, followed by another and another until a line of them had formed in the street below, each one with a liveried driver on the box, two postillions behind and two officers in full regalia on horseback at either side.

'Close that window this instant,' a voice scolded loudly. The window slammed shut, succeeded by the tramp of feet across the floor. 'No, no, no,' the voice shouted again.

Remembering their lessons, Auntie Sam's girls glided softly outside: a bevy of black swans.

Across the city, emerging exquisitely dressed from the kitchens and the slave quarters adjoining the big houses, painted beauties flitted into the darkness to be whisked away by their British beaux. Footmen dashed alongside carrying burning torches to light the way for the carriages rattling in a continuous stream through the crowds towards the magnificent mansion blazing with lights at 99 Meeting Street.

Delilah prowled regally through the rooms on yet another tour of inspection. A look or the slightest gesture from her and one of the many servants stationed discreetly throughout would step forward to adjust a candle leaning crookedly, remove a misplaced dish or straighten the corner of a spotless white cloth. The dining room was laid ready for supper and the surface of the long table was invisible beneath the dishes containing the delicious-looking efforts of Big Mo and her small army of helpers.

Satisfied, Delilah moved on, glancing in at the card room where a game was in progress at every one of the tables. She paused to observe the little turbaned pageboys carefully threading between the tables and spectators with trays of drinks. They appeared to be carrying out their duties competently, she noted, and she passed into the ballroom once more and allowed herself a congratulatory glance in one of the many looking-glasses which stretched from floor to ceiling and made the rooms appear many times larger than they were.

She looked well. Auntie Sam had been right: the blue of Delilah's dress brought out the copper tones in her skin and the white ostrich plumes of her coiffure enhanced the blackness of her hair. She smoothed her bodice. There was no greater aid to good deportment than stays, except perhaps carrying a heavy load on your head. Both involved a high degree of discomfort. Her shoes pinched too. They were Johnson's best handiwork, made when he was in thrall to her so long ago. He would be as disapproving of this occasion as Cornelius. It was lucky, she thought, that they were both far away on one of their interminable missions.

She turned away from the looking-glass and her eyes roved the room, as pleased with its appearance as with her own. The wallpaper was the blue of a perfect day patterned with the gold of high summer, the window drapes echoed the green of spring. She was pleased, too, with the 'Ethiopians'. It was a happy conceit to have them wear masks.

The masks intensified the allure of brilliant black eyes and dazzling smiles. And while little strips of black silk could not hide the women's identities from each other, they easily kept the officers guessing, or so it seemed. Speculating which of their dancing partners were new to them and which were familiar favourites from Auntie Sam's had rekindled the men's excitement. Should it ignite – Delilah glanced across at Carver – fire-fighters had been judiciously posted. Her eyes found Auntie Sam, superb in crimson and white, who gave an almost imperceptible signal. Delilah visibly relaxed.

'Madam . . .' the general was at her side, 'will you honour me with this dance?'

'It is you who honour me.'

'I congratulate you, madam . . .'

'On dancing with you, General?' Delilah smiled up at him.

The general flushed. 'On the management of the ball. I cannot but wonder where you acquired such skills.'

'From my betters, General, where else? Although in law we were *things*, in life we were, as we are now, human beings with eyes to see and ears to hear. It is an ill wind, they say . . .'

Reddening again, the general said dryly, 'Good can come even from the worst evil.'

'Indeed. See, I am dancing with a general. I never thought to do that.' Laughing, Delilah twirled away from him.

'Nor I,' the general said, as the dance brought them together again, 'with a black pearl.'

'Now you mock me. A ruby, perhaps; or a sapphire, yes. Pearls, General, are by their very nature pure white.'

'Madam, I would not dare to mock you. I have seen black pearls with my own eyes. They are much prized in the East.'

'The East?'

'India, a land with almost as many dusky beauties as Charleston.'

'Hm,' Delilah said. She did not know whether to believe him or not.

The music ended and the general led her off the floor. 'You did not expect to learn anything new from me! Life is full of surprises, is it not?'

A sudden crash of drums drowned out all sound, and the general felt for his sword. Reaching up on tiptoe, Delilah spoke into his ear. Seeing him nod and smile, his officers put away their weapons and all eyes followed his to the door as three drummers, naked to the waist, somersaulted into the room and advanced abreast towards the podium, drumming all the while.

They took up their positions in front of the other musicians, feet stamping, arms pumping, all three beating out a different rhythm. Louder and louder the separate strands looped around the room, drawing in the onlookers, entangling each and every one of them, hooking them to the beat and sweeping them along faster and faster until the music reached a mighty crescendo and stopped.

The general mopped his brow. 'I should take these men into battle with me next time.'

'And these too?' Delilah directed his attention to the far door as the beat began again and a young girl, wrapped in vermilion and purple, glided in, bare footed and bare shouldered, hips undulating. A dozen others gyrated behind her, ropes of coloured beads round their necks, wrists and ankles and bright as parakeets in wrappers of emerald, yellow, turquoise, coral, keeping perfect time. The general did not answer and Delilah exchanged an amused glance with Auntie Sam as the music changed pace and the girls began clapping. Delilah and Auntie Sam and the women in the audience took up the rhythm.

'Come, General,' Delilah said gaily. 'Time for *you* to learn something new: one, two, three. One, two, three.'

Obediently, the general did his best to copy her, tapping his foot at the same time. All around them the officers began clapping, one, two, three, and the noise of their boots on the polished boards began to rival the drums.

'Bravo,' Delilah encouraged, simultaneously changing beat. She exchanged another look with Auntie Sam, who, like herself and the other women, was following every twist and turn of the four different rhythms being played by the drummers while their partners continued one, two, three. One, two, three.

The girls stepped forward one by one to dance alone and afterwards in a long line, shoulders shaking, hips swivelling, in unison, winding in sinuous coils down to the ground and up again, to vociferous, whistling applause. Delilah clapped as vehemently as anyone, fondly imagining how Cornelius would have enjoyed this part of the evening. Everything had been designed to accord with his descriptions of festivals in Africa, although she and Auntie Sam had allowed themselves some artistic licence.

Softly, the drum beats started once more and in the hush a tall figure moved smooth as water across the floor and took her place with the other girls. It was Epiphany, clothed in a bolt of crimson silk, crowned and garlanded with coral beads. She burned flame-bright in the centre of the room. The mood changed, the atmosphere became charged, the music hypnotic. Lifting up her arms, Epiphany began to dance, a slender grass waving in the wind, her feet tracing an ancient pattern on the ground. Circling around her, the girls raised their voices in celebration, echoing the drums.

Delilah watched in amazement, this dance, this music, was not what they had rehearsed. It was like nothing she had seen or heard before. She shivered and for a moment felt someone passing over her grave. The music changed, the mood lightened and, as if coming out of a trance, Epiphany danced towards the general and pulled him into the centre. The other girls, following her example, chose partners from the audience.

Delilah pushed her troublesome thoughts away and led Captain Hawkins on to the floor, which was soon crowded with couples moving frenziedly to the beat of the drums as the music caught them up and tangled them in its skeins once more.

'Enough. Enough,' the general shouted, at last removing himself with considerable effort from the arms of the young woman twined round him, tenacious as a vine. He pushed through the press and tapped Delilah's shoulder. 'Madam, call off your hell hounds.'

Reluctantly Delilah disengaged herself from Captain Hawkins.

'Call them off, I say.'

Delilah gave him a measuring look. 'Oh, very well.' She swished away in the direction of the drummers. The music stopped.

'There, General.' Delilah reappeared at his side. 'We're back in America.'

'I thank God for that. Let's have no more drums.'

Captain Hawkins said, 'They have a strange power.'

'The Devil's own.' The general surveyed the room. Captain Hawkins was not alone in his trance-like state.

It was not the Devil, Delilah thought. She saw once more in her mind's eye the image of Epiphany dancing, and remembered what Cornelius had said at her birth. The child was his cousin come back. It had not been Epiphany dancing at all. Delilah searched her memory and found the name: Oluremi. With delayed insight, she realised it was the ancestors who had manifested themselves, come to reclaim the sacred rites which she and Auntie Sam had cynically made use of, profaning Cornelius's precious memories of Africa for the amusement of disrespectful strangers.

The ancestors will not be mocked, Cornelius said. Delilah felt goose-bumps rise on her skin. She lifted her chin and set the ostrich plumes in her hair nodding defiantly. 'Come, General —' she linked her arm through his '— let us go in to supper.'

Dawn was breaking as Delilah trudged home alone, the ostrich feathers forgotten in her hair, bedraggled and drooping. The lights had been extinguished at the mansion on Meeting Street and the carriages long departed. Triumph had turned to ashes. *The ancestors will not be mocked.* The words had become a refrain sounding in her head since the moment she had discovered that Epiphany and Quality were missing. Unable to believe that they had eluded Carver's attention, she and Auntie Sam had searched and re-searched the house and gardens. Discreet enquiries among the officers and rigorous questioning of the servants had yielded nothing.

Carver began scouring the streets: up and down Meeting Street, Church Street and King Street, in and out of every yard and servants' quarters of the mansions commandeered by British officers. Up Broad Street, past the Beef Market, the State House and the Watch House to the workhouse at the very top of Queen Street. Then down Broad Street again to the dockside. He was joined by Delilah and Auntie Sam, but they found no trace of the girls.

Only let Epiphany be safe and well, and Quality too, of course, Delilah prayed. She would have happily given up her life, anything, for that assurance. Giving up her life would certainly be easier than facing

Cornelius on his return from his mission. She pushed open the door to her room. She was not surprised to see the large figure sitting motionless by the fireplace; she had half expected Carver to be there, protective as always. But, then, Carver would have lit the fire, and would not have had that peculiar stillness. She looked again and her heart scraped against her ribs.

'Cornelius. What are you doing here? I thought you were in . . . Virginia?'

'Tabitha told me everything.' Cornelius rose to his feet and Delilah took a step backwards. She did not believe Cornelius would strike her, but looking at his face she retreated another step to stand pressed up against the door. 'There was no shame in it before, Delilah,' he said, 'when it could not be helped. But those days are gone.'

Delilah's grief and terror for Epiphany turned to anger. 'So it was *you*. How could you snatch her away without telling me? I've imagined every terrible thing – even that she was dead. You had no right.' Relief buckled her knees and she slid to the ground, her hooped skirts tented around her in shimmering contrast to the small drab room.

'I had every right to protect my daughter.' Cornelius loomed larger than ever above her, but she had recovered herself and, enraged, sprang to her feet again.

'Your daughter and Quality – I take it you abducted her, too? – were the invited guests of a general, no less,' Delilah said, her voice a whip uncoiling.

Cornelius snorted. 'Guests!'

'Yes, guests. As you said, those days *are* gone. The best way to protect ourselves and earn their respect –'

'– is by continuing to feed our children to them?'

'No. It's by fraternising on equal terms.'

'These people will *never* respect us. I didn't see any black gentlemen at your ball, only footmen and grooms, and no white ladies either. Nor did I see any chaperones.'

'What do you imagine *I* was doing? And Auntie Sam?'

'Playing the harlot.' Cornelius gripped her by the shoulders. 'Delilah, what were you thinking? Your own daughter –'

'It was her I was thinking of! I was trying to ensure that she's not returned to slavery. Who will guarantee us safe passage out of Charleston if the British lose the war? British officers, that's who.'

'That's no justification. There are other ways – except, of course, they don't also provide the opportunity for a quick profit.' Cornelius strode to the door. 'You cannot excuse what you did.'

'I'll be the judge of that. Where is my daughter?'

'Safe with Tabitha.' Cornelius slammed the door behind him.

~

9

HEADS CLOSE TOGETHER, Cornelius and Tamari sat outside her cabin on a bench, placed to catch the last of the evening light. True to his promise, Cornelius was teaching her to read from a copy of the Bible that Lord Fitzalan had been only too happy to present his groom. Within reason, he had assured Cornelius, nothing was too much for the man who had saved the life of his beloved horse. As winter gave way to spring and Cornelius spent most of his free time with Tamari, he realised that his growing love for her resembled the feelings he had harboured for the girls of his youth as distantly as he now resembled the boy he had once been, but he was continuously surprised and dismayed by the openness and trust she displayed towards the world, which seemed childish to him. For her own protection, he felt, she should be helped to grow up. To this end, having finished the evening's lesson, he shut the Bible, moved closer still on the bench and said, 'You wouldn't have lasted for a moment in Oyo. I was taught that the *only* people you may safely trust are those born of the same mother.'

'And when you became a slave?'

'I trusted no one. But then I came to realise that captivity made *all* slaves children of the same mother.'

'The Christian God teaches that *all* of us, of whatever colour, are children of the same mother.'

'That's a step too far. What good can come of calling your enemy brother?'

'Because then he ceases to be your enemy.'

'And if he continues to behave as if he was?'

'You must forgive him.'

'You don't have to be a Christian to do that. At home we have a proverb: "If a strong man ill treats you, smile at him.""

'I mean really forgive.'

'I could not accept a religion that tells you to give your enemy the advantage.'

'Ah, but you don't give enemies the advantage, you gain it. By forgiving them you disarm them, you put yourself beyond reach of their weapons.'

'Have you ever seen a hyena bring down its prey?' Tamari shook her head. 'The hyena rips open its victim's underbelly so that it will be brought down by its hooves becoming entangled in its own entrails. To embrace Christianity, it seems to me, is to present your underbelly to the hyena to tear open. The masters who encouraged their slaves to become Christians were the wise ones.'

'Do you know what frightened me most at first, Cornelius? It was entering the big house. I was afraid it would fall on me and bury me alive under all those stones; then, of course, it was as though it had. But when I started to pray to the Christian God, I discovered that underneath all that rubble I could still breathe. After a while I gave no thought to the stones. It was then I understood that I was being shown the way to overcome slavery, and I was baptised. I no longer wanted to die. I knew that one day I would be free.'

'And our white brothers?'

'They're underneath the rubble too.'

'I don't see any.'

'They're just in a different part and buried deeper.'

Cornelius threw back his head and laughed. 'Every moment of my life,' he said, 'as far back as I can remember, has been a striving to outwit my enemies and to maintain and increase the wealth and status of my house and my own standing within it, exactly as our masters do here. And now that I am no longer a slave, I intend to use my training and the skills I have acquired in America to become a great man once more.'

'Cornelius, I fear for you. Have you learnt nothing?'

'I have learnt much.' Piqued, he drew away from her. 'If you lived as long again it would be too short to tell it all. But how to be a good slave? *That* I have not learnt. And you need not fear for me, I shall have a place of honour among my ancestors when I go to join them in the groves of the next world.' He rammed his hat on his head, punctiliously took his leave and stalked off into the dark, brushing past Quality without seeing her.

'That man,' Tamari said in answer to her daughter's surprised enquiry, 'is stubborn as a mule. If he continues the way he is, he will surely go to hell.'

'Before,' Quality reminded her, 'you said Cornelius was the most reasonable of men and would surely go to heaven now his feet were on the right path.'

'Uncle Cornelius to you. I was mistaken.'

'You really like him, don't you?'

'I do not,' Tamari said.

Cornelius put down his plate of food half-eaten. He had nothing against the food itself. Lord Fitzalan's cook was as accomplished as any in Charleston, but a meal eaten alone lost much of its flavour. Although he had broken completely with Delilah, now that he had quarrelled with Tamari he could not help picturing the evening scene at Auntie Sam's with Big Mo and Carver and one or other of the girls from upstairs gathered round the table, the laughter, the gossip and all the latest news, more reliable than the intelligence reports received at army headquarters.

His loneliness was compounded by his current inactivity. The war appeared to have reached a standstill with neither side able to continue or to end the fighting. There were no more secret missions, no more adventures. Cornelius stared wistfully into the fire. Those long perilous journeys with Johnson across enemy lines had taken him back to his warrior youth; he had felt in charge of his destiny, truly free. He was, he supposed, luckier than most; he had a rich and powerful patron in Lord Fitzalan. But his employment once again as a body servant and waiting man was a painful reminder of his former bondage.

He had hoped that Tamari would approve of his ambition to be a great man and that she would have understood that, by disclosing his plans, he was implying a place in them for her. He had of course wanted to impress, but even to himself his words had had a hollow sound. He had long ago begun to doubt much of the wisdom he had brought from home, but he had no other model for freedom. He felt almost as disoriented now as he had when viewing America for the first time from the auction block. And now, as then, his instinct was to seek the shelter of old familiar trees. He decided to seek out Johnson.

'You're late,' Johnson said.

'Late – are you an overseer now?' Cornelius pushed in beside him. 'Besides, you weren't expecting me.'

'The whole world is expected here tonight. And besides, I *am* a master now, master of my time, and my time is precious. Cornelius, how could you have forgotten? Every Negro in Charleston has his money on Black George's Red Feather to win tonight and thus far has not been disappointed. Red Feather has won all his bouts. If you had been here on time you would be richer already.' Johnson patted his coat pocket. 'But you could still retrieve your situation.'

Cornelius raised his hand and added his voice to the constant shouting and accepting of bets. 'I hope I don't live to regret this.'

'Trust me,' Johnson said. 'You always have before.'

'I never had money before.'

'Freedom has its drawbacks.' Johnson shook his head in mock sorrow.

'Yes,' Cornelius said. He had caught sight of Delilah. Auntie Sam, Big Mo and Carver were with her. He was relieved not to see Epiphany. Delilah's coterie of British officers in their red uniforms made her even more conspicuous than usual in these surroundings. Brady had advertised seven pairs to fight all comers at £10 a battle and, indicative of the times, had set the wagering price low enough to accommodate even those who earned two shillings a day labouring for the British army. A fact reflected in the composition of the crowd now packing the tavern yard.

'I hadn't realised the rift was so serious,' Johnson said, noting how Cornelius and Delilah barely acknowledged each other.

'It's over between us,' Cornelius said.

'What of your daughter?'

'A break with the mother does not necessitate a break with the child.'

'But that might be the result.'

'Not in this instance.' Cornelius was unduly emphatic.

'It has been a long association and . . . a successful one.'

'It was of convenience only, when it suited us both. Lately our minds have grown too far apart to be reconciled. In any case, I'm with Tamari now.'

'I know,' Johnson said. 'And it must seem that love, when it comes, treads boldly, booted and spurred. But I also know that its tread can be so soft, you don't hear it until it's too late and you catch the sound of footsteps walking away.'

Cornelius's reply was lost in a rush of noise as the people behind pressed forward, forcing them to turn their attention to holding their ground in the first row.

Blinded, bloodied and unbeaten, Red Feather stretched his neck in a victory crow and received an answering roar of triumph from his supporters. They continued until they were hoarse, jumping and shouting as Black George, wiry and diminutive, hopped nimbly on to the fighting platform among the dead and dying birds and gathered up his beloved bird, cradling him in his arms.

'Now what do you say? Were you right to trust me?' Johnson turned jubilantly to Cornelius.

'I say that it's unwise to beat them at their own games,' Cornelius replied, a wary eye on the disgruntled officials. Suddenly he understood the reason for Delilah's guard of soldiers. 'We should collect our winnings and run, if it's not already too late.' He glanced towards the entrance. 'Fools that we are, crowing in here while out there they are rubbing their hands in anticipation of the easy pickings they will have tonight.'

'Unless we drink them away first. Mine host, you note, has a grin on him that'd put an alligator to shame. It would be more than foolish, it would be mad to venture out, just the two of us alone. A glass or three first and then we shall see.' Johnson started to push through the throng in the torch-lit yard.

Soon they were seated in a secluded corner inside, winnings safely in their pockets and glasses of hot rum punch in their hands.

Delilah entered with her friends.

'Ah . . .' Johnson glanced up. 'The very person we were speaking of before.'

As if he had not heard him, Cornelius wondered who might know of a position for a seamstress.

'I know you dislike your present occupation, but would seamstress suit you any better?' Johnson asked, laughing.

Cornelius stared at him unsmiling. 'You're drunk,' he said.

'And shall be drunker, by and by.' Johnson called for another rum.

'I'm asking on behalf of Tamari,' Cornelius said in a low voice. Delilah was holding court by the fire. 'Tamari's an excellent knitter and spinner and she can sew a little.'

Johnson peered owlishly. 'That's very good,' he said. 'Except that there's no demand for knitters and spinners, and there's not a Negro woman in Charleston who can't *sew a little*.'

'Is that so?'

'Yes,' Johnson replied, an amused glint in his eye. 'And here's another thing: our best chance of avoiding a fleecing tonight is to attach ourselves to that woman over there, who is not your wife, and who has shown herself more than our equal. If she will let us, that is.'

'No,' Cornelius said.

'Ah, Cornelius . . .' Johnson rose unsteadily to his feet. He shook his head sorrowfully, the glint still in his eye. 'A fool and his money are easily parted. We will have to humble ourselves a little, which is no great hardship when done out of choice.'

Unable to visit Auntie Sam's because he was still avoiding Delilah, Cornelius didn't like to impose himself too often on Johnson, or on Epiphany who was preoccupied with Caleb. He missed Tamari, but could find no common ground with her. Where before he would have been happy with his thoughts and the horses for company, a new restlessness made him discontented with his corner of the stable once his work was done, and he spent most evenings roaming round the town. Lord Fitzalan was billeted in one of the mansions in the White Point district and, as always, walking through Charleston, Cornelius was reminded of home. The wide leafy streets, the houses with their shady verandahs, their pillars and porticos and separate kitchens, the way the public buildings – the State House, the Exchange, St Michael's Church, the Theatre – were clustered in the centre, the fortifications, all were reminiscent of Oyo with its broad boulevards and shaded squares, the Alafin's palace and chiefs' houses with their side verandahs and roof posts, the temples and circuit walls. The hectic, tangled alleys near the gates of Oyo possessed the same flavour of danger and excitement as the mass of narrow streets leading to the wharves that lined the harbour at Charleston.

Shame at his neglect of her in recent months had also kept Cornelius away from Tabitha, but guilt drove him at last to knock at her door. She put him to work in her little hospital, where not infrequently Epiphany and Quality also came to assist. They dressed wounds, spooned soup, spoke words of comfort to the dying or simply kept watch as the spirit left the body to begin its next journey. But Quality and Epiphany also gave him news of Tamari and kept him abreast of the jollities and gossip at Auntie Sam's.

Cornelius wondered why he had not thought to help in the hospital before, and he said so. Quality and Epiphany had returned home and he and Tabitha were alone at the end of another long night.

'Old habits die hard,' Tabitha said. 'It seems nights are no more for

189

sleeping now than they were on the plantation. Remember how we used to travel miles to see friends or family, to help build a cabin, or go to a dance?'

'I remember,' Cornelius said. He dipped bread into a bowl of soup Tabitha had warmed on the fire. 'Sitting here with you feels like the old times.'

'Except,' Tabitha said, 'I don't see much of Johnson these days and you . . . have Tamari.'

'You're the thread though that holds us all together,' Cornelius said. And it was true.

Tabitha said, 'I haven't seen you at church recently.'

She was wondering why he was not spending time with Tamari, Cornelius thought.

He said, 'Church only teaches us how to be good slaves. I have different requirements now.'

'Christianity doesn't teach us to be slaves. Slavery prepared us for Christianity. Look how slavery taught us to be kind to each other. Is that something we should throw away, now we're free? Love your neighbour as yourself, the Bible says. We were halfway there. Don't you remember when Johnson took a flogging in your place? Remember how we stopped to put Cato out of his misery at the risk of all our lives? Christianity simply takes us the rest of the way; helps us to keep in mind the lessons we learned as slaves. If we forget these lessons, the only freedom we'll have is the freedom to die. Cornelius?' Tabitha shook him by the arm. His eyes were staring and his breath laboured. 'Cornelius?' Frightened, she felt his forehead; it was clammy and cold.

Cornelius shook off her hand. 'Someone is calling me,' he said. 'I must go.'

Tabitha tried unsuccessfully to restrain him. He pushed past her and she snatched up her shawl and ran after him, but outside the door she stopped. He was walking swiftly and determinedly down the street and it occurred to her that he might be on his way to Tamari. Love, she thought, was at the root of this crisis, and whether the cause was Tamari or the Holy Spirit, Cornelius had no need of her.

When Cornelius appeared at Tamari's door, she did not reproach him for his absence.

'I am going to be baptised,' Cornelius told her.

'Yes,' she said.

'You're not surprised?'

'I recognised the signs; a fish fights hardest when it's hooked.'

Cornelius leaned against the wall of her cabin. 'I was with Tabitha, telling her how I had no use for the white man's religion, when I was overcome by the grief and terror I felt all those years ago as I stood on the auction block; that emptiness between the death of my old self and whatever I must become. I lay on my bed unable to move until in my mind I heard someone say, "You are ready, Cornelius, when it is the enemy's broom clearing the path ahead." And I understood that I must choose my fate and be reborn a Christian.'

Tamari said, 'You will never be lonely again.' She drew him to sit beside her on the bench.

'How different it would have been,' Cornelius said, 'if we'd met earlier.'

Tamari laughed. 'We did – remember?'

Cornelius traced her mouth with his fingers. 'I don't mean in the slave market. I mean when I went looking for you only to find you'd been sold. We've missed so much. We're old . . .'

'Speak for yourself!' She laid the palm of his hand against her cheek. 'When you were young, you were a spoilt nobleman. I saw you, don't forget, scattering lesser folk beneath the burnished hooves of your fine horse. I would have been your concubine –'

'My wife.'

'Call it what you will, one of many. We would have known each other no more intimately perhaps than a master here knows his favourite slave woman.'

'Only in that one respect, not in any other. No Oyo chief would sell his children or the mother of his children.'

'True, but it's that one respect,' Tamari said, 'which concerns me at present, and I say in that respect slaves are fortunate.'

Cornelius's hand slid possessively from her cheek to the hollow at the base of her neck. 'Have you forgotten how it was to live with the knowledge that at any moment you might be torn away from those you loved?'

'No. But a slave, who can be bought and sold, knows, as no one else does, that the greatest gift is the gift of yourself.'

'I made a vow,' Cornelius said, 'that one day I would return home to Oyo. I intend to keep that vow, although now I have a different purpose.'

'I can guess what it is,' Tamari said. 'But I doubt they will listen to you.'

'Will you come with me?'

'Yes, I will,' Tamari said.

Auntie Sam shook out her lace and removing her turban placed it tenderly on a chair before plumping herself down on the bed beside Delilah. Delilah stretched daintily and yawned, showing pearly teeth, beautiful even when just woken from sleep.

'You should have been there,' Auntie Sam said.

'I take it you mean the baptism? I have had so many accounts of it, I feel as if I was. But you can tell me again, no one has spoken of it so far today. And yes, perhaps,' Delilah conceded grudgingly, 'to see Epiphany. But she had Caleb. And you, and Big Mo, and Carver . . .'

'And Tabitha.'

'And, of course, Tabitha. Who I have to thank for all this Christian fever. It's carrying off more people than the smallpox.' Delilah yawned again. 'All right, tell me all about it.'

'They had a good day for it. Even I could find little wrong with the colours today; the sky was the blue of my favourite satin with creamy white silk puffs of cloud, the trees trailing scarves of tender green and the flowers sparkling and inviting as sugared fruits. You couldn't see the grass underfoot, there were so many people gathered. The riverbank was soon trampled into a morass, my shoes won't be the same again – they were my second-best pair, too. And what a pair Cornelius and Johnson made. Johnson was only there to watch, mind you.'

'Ha.' Delilah punched her pillow.

'As for Epiphany . . .' Auntie Sam continued as if there had been no interruption, 'she outshone the sun, casting a glow on everyone around, including of course her little shadow, Quality, whose mother Tamari *was* present to witness *her* daughter's baptism.'

'Ha.'

'And when Epiphany, who was not expecting to see her father, ran up and threw her arms round him, I don't know which of us cried more! Big Mo, Carver, me or Tabitha. Tabitha is the one we should all thank, of course, for bringing father and daughter together again . . .' Auntie Sam paused.

Delilah examined a fingernail.

Auntie Sam continued, 'The Reverend George is small as a tadpole, but when he preached the sermon his voice rolled over us like a summer storm. "The Christian God will deliver us from bondage, as He did the Israelites from Egypt. He will strike down our enemies and lead us to the Promised Land. All we have to do is follow Him."'

'Ha.'

'The Reverend George took the people who were to be baptised down into the river one by one and we watched the water close over their heads, singing, clapping and shouting, until we were hoarse.'

'Even Cornelius?'

'He was not shouting, but he did look as if he might have seen something.' Auntie Sam gazed out of the window at the sky. 'It must be quite a sight, God in all His glory.'

Delilah sat up. 'The day the Holy Spirit calls *you*, Auntie Sam, is the day I'll sink my teeth into your hat on the chair over there and start chewing.'

'You eat one of your own hats. The Lord Jesus loves a sinner. He likes them best, Tabitha says.'

'Tabitha again. Like the skin on hot milk, she's insult to injury. She has had her eye on my husband all these years; she has stolen my daughter with all her talk of Jesus. Don't tell me she's going to take my friend away from me too!'

'Very good, Delilah,' Auntie Sam dabbed satirically at her eyes. 'Since when was Cornelius your husband? What are you plotting?'

Delilah threw back the covers. 'I have it from Lord Fitzalan himself that the British are preparing to evacuate the city. Once the news gets out, thousands more runaways will rush here in the hope of sailing away with them to freedom. I aim to be among the ones that do.'

'Are you taking anyone along for company?'

'Of course.' Delilah counted on her fingers: 'You, Big Mo, Carver. And Epiphany. And Caleb, now that they are together . . .'

'And Tabitha, for Epiphany's sake.'

'I was coming to her.'

'And?'

'And nothing.'

'All right, where are we all going?'

'New York.' Delilah swung her legs out of bed. 'Auntie Sam, help me to dress. I want to look my best.'

Auntie Sam swept a magnificent curtsey. 'Depend on it, I can turn any sow's ear into a silk purse.'

*

In a remarkably short time, Delilah was sauntering through the gate of Lord Fitzalan's house. She was dressed in a striped skirt that revealed her ankles; a low-cut red jacket accentuated her bosom and small waist and a white kerchief was draped across her shoulders and tucked into the front of her bodice.

'Good day, Cornelius,' she said, slipping into the stable yard, where Cornelius was at work, clad only in his breeches, grooming one of his lordship's horses. He looked up startled at the sound of that familiar voice, insinuating as a cat wreathing itself round your ankles when wanting food. He greeted her warily and his brush continued across the horse's shining flank.

'I've missed you,' Delilah said.

Cornelius laughed out loud.

'It's surprising . . .' Delilah smiled, 'but true.'

'Is that why you've come?'

'Of course not. I have my pride. I am here because of Epiphany, our daughter.' Cornelius did not answer. 'I imagine you've heard the rumours?' Delilah appeared to be examining the ground.

'And the facts. And from the same source,' Cornelius said, referring to another fact, that Lord Fitzalan was Delilah's most recent conquest.

Delilah looked up. 'I would like to know whether it is fact or rumour that you plan to go to London?'

'Of what interest is it to you?'

'I am here because of Epiphany, and I thought you should know that she will be going with *me* . . . to New York.'

'She said she would come with *me*.'

'She has changed her mind.'

'*You* have changed her mind.'

'Epiphany is with Caleb now, and he has no wish to go to London or to Africa. That was your plan, I believe? To go to Africa?'

'I see what you have done,' Cornelius said angrily.

'Epiphany has a good heart, she will not leave me on my own with no one to protect me. I am not as fortunate as the widow Betsey, who may take her pick from any number of *young* men, as well as yourself.'

'You know it was my dream to return one day with Epiphany, to show her the land of her ancestors –'

'I know it was your fantasy. Well, she is a grown woman now and done with dreaming, as you should be. Do you think they're all still waiting for you exactly as you left them? Here in America, Epiphany has the chance of something *real*, a good future for her children. What kind of a life would she have in Africa? She'd most likely be sold back into slavery.' Delilah patted the horse's nose. 'I know how much you love your daughter, I know you will want to spare her . . .' Her voice was full of gentle sadness.

Lord Fitzalan entered the stableyard and stopped abruptly at the sight of Delilah. He looked in perplexity to Cornelius before inclining his head in response to her smiling greeting.

Delilah rose gracefully from her curtsey. 'Well, *husband*, I will leave you to your work.' She nodded to Cornelius. 'Let me open the gate for you, my lord.' She ran to do so and curtsied again as Lord Fitzalan cantered out, before whisking through the gate herself.

Cornelius sank down on to the mounting block and pressed his hands against his face. The image of Tamari rose in his mind's eye. He recalled the words she'd flung at him in the slave market at Ibawe. *They would meet again.* He should be done with dreaming, Delilah said. And so he must. He could not give up Epiphany; he saw the reflection of his mother in her eyes, she was his cousin come back, her destiny was linked to his. To renounce her would be to renounce the fate he'd chosen at the moment of his birth and in which he still believed despite his years in America. With a stick he drew a pattern in the dust as if tracing the shattered pieces of a dream. And he wept for all that he must now forsake.

Delilah took her time returning home, having achieved both her aims. Lord Fitzalan had a high regard for Cornelius if not for herself, and after the discovery that it was Cornelius he was cuckolding, he would be more disposed than ever to smooth their path should any unforeseen difficulties arise in the forthcoming evacuation of the city.

As for Cornelius, she had been reasonably confident from the beginning that he would not be able to give up his daughter, and now she had made quite certain he would come with her to New York. She had won Epiphany by securing Caleb. As well as being handsome, the boy was intelligent and ambitious and he shared her plans for a life in the north.

On turning the last corner, she was surprised to see Carver outside the door, evidently waiting for her.

'Carver, what is it?'

He bent and spoke in her ear.

She pushed past him and raced up the stairs. Through the door of the bedroom she saw at a glance the disarrayed bed, its mattress and coverlets tossed around, the torn curtains, the broken chairs and blood-stained floor. It was true then.

She continued to the next floor and flung open the door at the top of the stairs. The girls inside huddled away from her, fluttering and squawking to the far end of the room.

'Which one of them, Carver? Which one?'

Filling the doorway, he lifted one massive arm and pointed silently. Delilah pounced, wading in among the cowering girls, and emerged with the culprit, who stood before her shaking but defiant. Delilah held her fast by the scruff of her white shift.

'My *curse* on you and yours for ten generations! May you live to see *all* your children buried!'

Released, the girl crumpled to the floor, the noise of her sobbing loud in the silence that had descended on the rest of her companions.

Delilah whirled down the stairs again into the desecrated room below and flung herself on to the mattress, rocking to and fro. 'No. No. No . . .' Carver lowered himself beside her, cradling her in his arms. After a while she asked, 'Big Mo?'

'A gash on her head you could put your fingers into, but she's working in the kitchen all the same. Otherwise she might kill someone. And she came near to it. Two of those brigands will not walk straight again in this life, so the girls said. They saw everything. If only I'd been here. If only I'd been here . . .' Carver stroked Delilah's hair tenderly with his huge hands; his shirt was wet with her tears. 'I went after them, but they were too long gone. I sent one of the girls to fetch Tabitha and another with word to Epiphany while I waited for you.'

'Oh, Auntie Sam . . .' Delilah's voice cracked. 'Think what they will do to her: flay her, burn her, cut out her tongue, put out her eyes – all the old punishments and doubtless some new.' Carver's arms tightened, pressing Delilah's face against his chest, but she continued as if she could not stop, her words shards of glass. 'Imagine it, Carver, being owned again, body and soul, when you have known what it is to be free. I loved her, Carver. I loved her . . .' Carver rocked her tenderly until at last, tearfully, she said, 'We must change our plans.'

IO

ONE HAND REACHING for the handle of the knife he kept under his mattress, Cornelius looked up warily as the door to the stable was pushed open. Lord Fitzalan's two horses, bedded down for the night, whinnied and shifted in their stalls but were easily quieted by the touch of a familiar hand.

'It's only me.' Epiphany closed the door softly behind her and stepped into the circle of the lantern illuminating the corner where Cornelius sat.

'I hope you did not come here alone.' Cornelius hid the knife, put aside the borrowed Bible he had been reading, and patted the place beside him.

Epiphany sank down on to the straw pallet, which served as both couch and bed, and kissed him on the cheek. 'Caleb walked me here and I thought you might walk me home?'

'And if I hadn't been here?'

'We would have walked right back again.'

'You may well laugh.' Cornelius eyed her sternly. 'These are dangerous times to be roving around after dark.'

'I know, I know –'

'I don't believe you do,' Cornelius interrupted in a tone that left no room for playfulness. Epiphany, accustomed to gentleness from him was surprised into silence. 'Our position,' Cornelius said, 'is as precarious as it has ever been. Now that the British have lost the war, we are no more than flotsam on an outgoing tide. Most will be stranded on the shore to be picked over by our American masters, already scavenging for those who might be usefully retrieved and returned to slavery, while a lucky few will be carried out to sea as dependent on the caprices of the British officers as on the vagaries of the ocean. As we aim to be among the latter, the wisest course, my child, is to stay inside after dark.'

Auntie Sam's kidnapping, too painful to mention, was never far from his mind.

'Baba,' Epiphany said, calling him by his pet name, 'I'm a grown woman now and you must know that I would not have risked coming to see you at this hour if I did not think it of the utmost importance.'

Cornelius touched her cheek, disarmed as always by her use of the Oyo word for father. 'So?'

'You must not give up Tamari, not on my account . . .' Astonished, Cornelius drew breath to speak. Epiphany placed a finger against his lips. 'No, hear me out. You have sacrificed quite enough for my sake. You would have tried to escape and go back to Africa years ago if it had not been for me. Auntie Tabitha has told me the whole story. And Uncle Johnson. I can take care of myself now, and besides . . .' Epiphany's colour deepened, 'I have Caleb now and my mother can look to both of us. This is the opportunity you have waited for, Baba. Seize it.'

Cornelius was incapable of replying immediately. *I have Caleb now.* He had barely registered the boy. At length he said, 'What does that mean, you have Caleb now?'

Epiphany said simply, 'We belong together.'

Cornelius nodded. He had not been able, finally, to say the same to Tamari. 'All I know,' he said, 'is that you and I, Epiphany, are destined to travel the same path. You are linked to me as I am to my cousin Oluremi. When you were born, I looked into your eyes and I saw in them my cousin come back.' He grasped Epiphany's hands in both of his. 'We weave a pattern,' he continued softly, 'and we think it is the whole. Then we discover another pattern, and beyond that, perhaps another. And we are only aware, it seems, because sometimes the colours run, bleeding from one into another, as in a dream. It would appear, child, that you who are woven into our pattern, are a colour from another, possibly larger pattern, in which there will also be a little of us. Part of you will always remain with us and part of us will travel with you. For ever.'

'Baba . . .' gently Epiphany removed her hands from his, 'My home is in America, my people are here.'

In Cornelius's mind's eye there flashed an image of a vast, grassed plain, a vault of cobalt overhead and a blazing sun and the generous green of spreading branches muting the scalding heat to consoling warmth against the skin. He saw, within a high-walled compound, a darkened room with red polished walls and a straight-backed figure seated on a stool. He grasped Epiphany's hands again. 'But if the opportunity arises to return one day?'

'How likely is that, Pa? Besides, I can't return to a place I've never been.'

'Promise me?'

'It seems a mockery in the present circumstances . . . Oh, very well.' Withdrawing her hands from her father's, Epiphany jumped to her feet. She smiled and crooked an arm. 'If you're coming to New York on your own account, then you are most welcome. For now, though, will you walk me home?'

'Just one more thing . . .' Cornelius too rose to his feet.

Epiphany sighed. 'What is it?'

'Nothing I have experienced equals the pain of hearing your children confide their dreams if you know that those dreams can never be fulfilled. I fear for your children, I fear the slow whittling away of the spirit which destroys so many and maims all. If there is one thing slavery has taught, it is that we cannot protect our children from their dreams.'

'Pa!' Epiphany shook her head in mock despair. 'Freedom changes all that.' She handed Cornelius his coat and dragged him towards the door.

Cornelius set a brisk pace even though their route from one residential district to another was relatively safe. Their journey passed without mishap and they were soon at the door of a grand house. They moved round the side, across the yard and into the kitchen.

Big Mo greeted them with her usual broad smile and returned to watching her many pots dangling over the fire. Delilah sat nearby warming her feet on the hearth. She had been forced to relinquish Auntie Sam's former establishment, once preparations for the evacuation of Charleston were underway and the protection of the British officers no longer to be relied upon. The profits of the tavern and whorehouse on the quayside were altogether too tempting for the racketeers who had descended on Charleston in anticipation of a resumption of the old order and who in consequence could seize with impunity anything they pleased from a parcel of runaway slaves.

As Big Mo said, Auntie Sam's abduction had cut Delilah off at the knees. Delilah had lain on the bed for days, in a nest composed of Auntie Sam's silks and satins, curled up like a babe. In the end it was Tabitha who'd lured her out of the room, and even then she had refused to surrender the business until it was almost too late. Delilah, Carver and Big Mo barely escaped the bounty hunters themselves. Tabitha would only say that Auntie Sam was the mother Delilah never knew and that the well water had been pure and not poisoned as it was with Celia.

So it was that Captain Hawkins, who had partnered Delilah at the

Ethiopian Ball, and upon whose mercy she deliberately threw herself, acquired in short order, and not entirely of his own volition, a cook and a groom as well as his beautiful laundress and her two assistants. It was surely coincidental that the good captain was a commissary in the transport department.

'What brings you here, Cornelius?' Delilah enquired pleasantly, inviting him to draw near to the fire.

'I thought it wise to accompany Epiphany home.'

'Hardly necessary, I would think, in this part of the city. The bounty hunters and kidnappers concentrate their efforts near the docks and wharves where Negroes now outnumber whites.'

Cornelius stretched his hands to the blaze. 'Where are Tabitha and Carver?'

Delilah shrugged. 'Tabitha is out earning a place in her Christian Heaven and Carver is with her; not that she needs any protection. Brigands are as wary of the smallpox as other people. She does not care that she puts the rest of us in danger.'

Epiphany knelt by Delilah's side. 'Auntie Tabitha does good work, Ma.'

'And as for you –' Delilah put an arm round her shoulders. 'You didn't tell me you intended to visit your father.'

'She came to tell me I should not give up Africa on her account,' Cornelius said.

'Hmm.' Delilah glanced searchingly at Epiphany.

Cornelius smiled at Delilah's evident discomfiture with her daughter's new-found independence. 'She's no longer a child,' he said dryly.

Delilah turned to him. 'And did she succeed?'

'No,' Cornelius said.

Delilah shrugged carelessly. 'Ah well, the same stars shine over America, I dare say.'

'Except in Africa,' said Epiphany, smiling at Cornelius, 'they are nearer at hand.'

Cornelius returned her smile. 'And in Canada, perhaps.'

Delilah and Epiphany eyed him suspiciously.

'I was with the Reverend George and he told me that the British Government intend to show their gratitude to those of us they take with them, both blacks and whites. I don't see how they can do that if we stay in America. In Canada, where the British still govern, there would be no obstacle. There are rumours of grants of land.'

Delilah shrugged dismissively. 'What does the Reverend George know?'

'I checked with Lord Fitzalan, who got it from the general, who got it from the commander in chief himself. Lord Fitzalan is off to Canada and Reverend George's congregation with him.' Cornelius kept his voice even.

Delilah said, 'As you have made a concession to us, I suppose we could make a concession to you.'

Big Mo, whose head had come up at the mention of Canada, broke in suddenly, 'Captain Hawkins has been acting shifty lately.'

Delilah threw up her hands. 'Insurrection all round. Big Mo, hold your tongue.'

'Go on, Big Mo,' Cornelius urged her.

Big Mo glanced from one to the other and then in a rush continued, 'The captain has a mind to keep us as his servants and now he has had our services for free, it stands to reason he will not want to pay for them after. He is aiming to make us slaves again.'

Cornelius folded his arms across his chest. 'Concession, eh?'

Epiphany burst out laughing. 'You're well matched, you two. Neither one of you does anything without a purpose and behind that purpose there is always another.'

The crowds were so thick on the quayside it was all but impossible to make any headway past the shops and stalls selling every kind of goods and the hawkers crying their wares above the bustle and confusion. Cornelius and Johnson stood by the water's edge, caps pulled well down, mingling with the queue of people pushing and jostling for a place in the long-boat tied up alongside. It was already so crowded Cornelius feared it was in danger of capsizing.

Until now, everything had passed off smoothly. Delilah, Epiphany, Tabitha, Big Mo and Carver successfully eluded Captain Hawkins, slipping out of the house in the night and hiding in Tabitha's hospice. Again, by night, they had joined Cornelius, Johnson and Caleb and the rest of Reverend George's congregation on the ship that was to take them all to Canada under the protection of Lord Fitzalan. Once on board they were safe. At first light they had discovered that Delilah was missing.

Cornelius searched the crowds. He could not imagine what could have caused Delilah to jeopardise their plans in this way, and he was beginning to think that something must have happened to her. As if reading his mind, Johnson clapped him reassuringly on the shoulder and disappeared into the throng on yet another foray along the quayside, leaving Cornelius alone beside the fractious but steadily diminishing queue for the long-boat.

He craned for a moment and ducked down again, keeping his knees bent to disguise his height. He willed Delilah to return. Fear crept along his veins. What if she did not? If Tabitha was the thread that held them all together, Delilah held the roof above their heads. It struck him that his feelings for Tamari had been real but as in a mirage, while his merging with Delilah over the years had been seamless and therefore unnoticed. Remembering how he had scoffed when Delilah called him her husband in front of Lord Fitzalan brought to mind something Johnson had once said: Love's tread could be so soft beside you that you didn't hear it until it was too late and you caught the sound of footsteps walking away. Let her be safe, he beseeched silently.

At that moment he caught sight of Delilah pushing frantically through the crowd and he moved to meet her. He gripped her arm. In her hurry, she had lost her head-tie: her hair stood out wildly and she was short of breath, but her expression was triumphant.

'That girl,' she said, 'who betrayed Auntie Sam, she was able to start a grog shop for her pains. It was only a hovel, but it was enough. I burnt it down.'

Cornelius dragged her roughly towards the long-boat, not listening, scolding furiously until he realised that Delilah was afraid and glancing continually over her shoulder.

'Delilah!' a familiar voice rang out and, astounded, Cornelius turned to find himself face to face with Robert Farrer, who appeared maddened by the sight of him.

Cornelius turned away, pulling Delilah with him.

'Stop. Both of you!' – and, when they did not, Robert shouted again – 'Stop, I tell you.'

Wrenching free of Cornelius, Delilah turned. She looked the master in the eye, and spat.

'Seize her,' Robert shouted at his two companions. Delilah laughed and turned to run. Cornelius caught the movement of the pistol and, flinging Delilah out of the way, took the bullet intended for her full in the chest. Without a sound he crumpled to the ground. Delilah screamed and dropped down beside him, calling his name over and over. The crowd advanced menacingly to make a human shield between Robert and his quarry. Arriving back just in time to witness what had happened, Johnson grabbed Delilah and bundled her into the long-boat as it set off across the wind-ruffled waters of the bay towards the ship that would carry them away.

'Where's Cornelius?' Tabitha demanded as Johnson hauled Delilah on to the crowded deck.

'Where's Pa?' Epiphany asked too, registering the shock on both their faces.

Neither answered. Delilah staggered and Big Mo caught her before she fell.

'Johnson?' Tabitha demanded again, her voice rising.

'What's happened?' Epiphany took a step forward, panic on her face.

Johnson moved towards Epiphany. 'Robert Farrer came looking for Delilah and your father took the bullet meant for her.' Johnson wrapped Epiphany in his arms.

'No,' Epiphany wailed, 'no, no.'

'Couldn't you have stopped him?' Caleb asked.

'I was too late. All I could do was get her away before Farrer shot her too.'

'The master wouldn't shoot *her*. Not him.' Tabitha looked accusingly at Delilah. 'He'd want her alive.'

'Except she spat at him and laughed in his face. It seems she pushed him past his limit this time.' Johnson still held Epiphany close but, freeing herself, she stumbled blindly away to join the crowd of people at the rail of the ship. Johnson, Tabitha and Caleb followed. Big Mo and Carver cleared a way for Delilah, and they stood in a line staring towards the shore, where another crowd had gathered. In all their minds was the thought of Cornelius's body abandoned on the quayside to be buried by strangers. Tabitha and Epiphany huddled close together, their tears unstoppable, while Johnson and Caleb did their best to comfort them.

Delilah, refusing the comfort offered by Big Mo and Carver, stood apart, her dress dishevelled, her hair ragged in the wind. She had cried for the loss of Auntie Sam but the loss of Cornelius had carried her beyond tears.

It was a matter of convenience, she'd maintained when she'd decided to keep his child. And though she'd plotted to keep him from the widow Betsey – even now she couldn't use Tamari's name – it was of the African woman Cornelius had been thinking that first night. And no doubt he was thinking of the African woman when he died. Now Delilah realised she would give anything to have been the one he'd had in mind. So it wasn't convenience after all. She remembered how he'd told her once: *It is the thing you imagine cannot happen that undoes you.*

Johnson spoke at last, spoke for them all, desperation in his voice. 'Without Cornelius we are without a compass.'

And never again will the ground feel solid underfoot, Delilah added silently.

As the ship sailed out of the harbour, its wake a trail of blood in the setting sun, Epiphany began her song. Standing in the stern of the ship, her voice rose keening on the wind and a door, long closed, swung open on a treasury hidden in her memory. She spun the verses of her father's oriki into shining loops that spanned the widening distance to the shore. Epiphany sang and sang, weaving line by line, strand by strand, a shroud fit for the body of a fallen warrior.

BOOK THREE

Epiphany, 1789–1818

Big Mo emerged from the house with the baby swaddled in her arms. She stopped in the centre of the yard where the whole family had gathered among the summer fragrance of Tabitha's herbs and lifted the child to the sky, slowly turning to the four corners of the earth: north; west; south; and lastly east, home of the rising sun and Africa.

Traditionally, the naming ceremony, held on the eighth day if the child were a girl, marked the true beginning of life. The birth of her daughter marked the new, perhaps true start of her life, too, Epiphany thought, one hand shading her eyes against the brightness, the other tightly clasping Caleb's. He was the board to which she'd clung amid the wreck of Cornelius's death, when the devastation and darkness within had been mirrored by the bleak misery of those first winter months huddled in makeshift tents in the snow and ice of Nova Scotia. She had given herself up to Caleb entirely through the intervening years, which had taken them south from Halifax to the Loyalist settlement at Shelburne. But now the birth of their daughter had effected such a transformation it seemed to her that she had been sleepwalking all this time, and, like a sleepwalker, she'd been surprised, upon waking, by her surroundings. In the period of grace between the birth and the naming ceremony, Epiphany had spent the days reflecting on what the future might hold for her child. She had been brought up abruptly against the realisation that, despite all their journeying, the terrible risks they'd run, the grief they'd suffered, the privations they'd endured, her daughter could look forward to much the same fate from which Cornelius had fought so hard to save his own daughter.

Big Mo beckoned to Johnson. In keeping with tradition, each of the adults was to be invited to give the child a name and by so doing pledge to care for her as their own.

'You first, Johnson.'

Epiphany felt a surge of affection and gratitude towards Johnson. She knew he blamed Delilah for Cornelius's death, but for his dead friend's sake he had kept faith. It had been he who held the family together when, two months after their arrival in Halifax, government provisions stopped, leaving people dying on the streets from starvation. Caleb had urged a move south where they could earn money building two new Loyalist settlements at Shelburne and Birchtown. Johnson had argued that they should stay in the capital, the better to fight for the land they'd been promised. If Cornelius had been there, things might have been different; as it was, Johnson only had Tabitha's support. Rather than split the family, he had abandoned the principle for which he'd come to Nova Scotia. Epiphany was sure it had been for her sake. She smiled at him as he stepped forward now to name her child.

Johnson beamed at Caleb, who gave him a broad grin back. Caleb's vanity had been piqued that Johnson, twice his age, had produced three children in quick succession before he'd managed to father one.

'I name this child Africa,' Johnson declared, 'in memory of her grandfather Cornelius.'

Tabitha dabbed her eyes, but Delilah remained inscrutable.

'Now you,' Big Mo commanded Elizabeth, and Johnson passed the baby to his wife.

Johnson had been instantly entranced when Epiphany, on learning Elizabeth had no kin, had asked her home for supper one evening after church. How *dainty* she was, Johnson had rhapsodised afterwards. Her skin, he said, was the colour of cinnamon and her eyes like river water after rain! But it was her skill with words that captivated him most. The stories Elizabeth told, handed down from her grandmother's grandmother, conjured worlds of mystery and magic, where spirits could be summoned, where people changed their shapes at will and animals could speak. Johnson heard Cornelius in Elizabeth's tales and when he listened to her it was as if Cornelius was restored to him. Tabitha felt the same. Epiphany reflected that she might have been jealous if Caleb had not assured her he liked his women tall and strong and that Elizabeth's light-coloured eyes could not compare with the absolute black of his wife's fathomless gaze.

Cradling the child in her arms, Elizabeth called out firmly, 'I name her Warrior.'

Delilah rolled her eyes, and Epiphany and Elizabeth exchanged amused glances. On learning that the young woman was a laundress and lady's maid like herself, Delilah had offered to pool resources, but Elizabeth chose to remain independent. Elizabeth had taken the place of Quality in Epiphany's life. But as far as Delilah was concerned, the newcomer could do no right.

'Warrior! I like that.' Caleb raised his fist in the air.

Except that Elizabeth had named her own daughters Peace and Joy. The twins had been born three years ago, when it had still seemed that they might get the farms they'd been promised, might yet become independent. Back then there had been white Loyalists waiting for land too. Now it was only the black Loyalists who remained landless.

'Your turn, Carver,' Big Mo called and Carver stepped forward shyly.

What would they do without Carver, Epiphany wondered as Elizabeth settled the baby in the crook of his arm. He was the only one of the men in regular work, hauling loads for a farmer whose carthorse had expired at the start of the last terrible winter. There'd been plenty of work for them all when they first arrived in the white settlement of Shelburne. Set on a beautiful natural harbour with spruce, pine, birch, maple and red oak growing in abundance, the opportunities for fishing, shipbuilding and trade had seemed infinite at first. But the attractions proved illusory: the harbour froze in winter, the soil was so poor that farmers could never hope to be self-sufficient and the surrounding forests and swamps were all but impenetrable. Business soon stagnated; within five years, three-quarters of the white settlers had fled back to America. As a result, the blacks of Birchtown who had been employed in the construction of the roads, barracks, jails, jetties, wharves and warehouses were jobless. If this winter was as bad as the last, many of them would be sharing the same fate as the farmer's horse.

'Speak up, Carver,' Delilah encouraged.

Carver lifted his head. 'I name this little one Ruth. She'll bring us luck, I'm sure of it.'

At a nod from Big Mo he handed the baby to Tabitha.

Tabitha cleared her throat. 'Her grandfather died a true Christian, so I name this child Mary.' Like Johnson, Tabitha had yet to forgive Delilah.

Without waiting for Big Mo, Delilah took the child from Tabitha.

'Which Mary? There were two, as I recall. One of them a temptress. Don't forget I'm a Christian too, baptised by Reverend George, same as you. And I name this child Sheba. From the Bible!'

Epiphany giggled, quickly disguising it as a cough. It was true Delilah had become a member of Reverend George's congregation, but only when she saw he had influence with the whites. She'd used that influence to good purpose, charming him into procuring them a town lot in Shelburne on which Johnson, Carver and Caleb had been able to erect the little one-room house currently providing a roof for the entire family;

a dozen in all with the new addition. However, now that the rich white ladies had departed, there was scarcely any call for laundresses and lady's maids in the town and it was Reverend George's good opinion of Tabitha that had secured paid positions, not only for her but also for Epiphany and Elizabeth, in the church mission schools in nearby Birchtown.

'Now you, Big Mo,' Delilah ordered, handing her the child.

The naming ceremony was an African tradition and Big Mo had been assigned to officiate because, of all of them, she had steadfastly refused to be baptised a Christian. The ancestors were good enough for her.

'Traveller,' Big Mo announced emphatically. She pointed a large finger. 'And now the parents.'

Epiphany received her daughter tenderly in her arms. 'You first, Caleb.'

'Pearl.' Caleb stroked the baby's cheek. 'She's a pearl.'

Looking directly at Elizabeth, Epiphany said, 'Hope. That's my name for her.'

Epiphany carried the baby into the house to feed her and Johnson followed. After the brightness in the yard it was dark inside; some wild lupins the children had picked glowed candle-like by the hearth, and through the open window shutter they could hear the careless laughter of Johnson's children as they ran about outside.

He spoke softly in order not to disturb the baby. 'Long ago when Cornelius and I were the age that you are now, he made a vow never to give a child of his to slavery. At the time I was in thrall to Delilah and would gladly have had a child with her, but Cornelius was wiser than me. He understood even then that to have a child is to have your heart hang by a thread. Just as a condemned man knows the hour of his death, a slave knows that one day the thread will be broken. Until my son Sam was born, I didn't know the true value of freedom.'

Epiphany nodded. 'Just before we left Charleston, Pa told me that nothing he'd experienced equalled the pain of hearing your children confide their dreams, knowing those dreams can never be fulfilled. If there was one thing slavery taught him, he said, it was that you cannot protect your children from their dreams. And I said, "Pa, freedom changes all that."'

'You were right,' Johnson said. 'When we are truly free, our dreams will be of our choosing.'

Epiphany shook the grit from the bunches of sea-wrack she was collecting for supper. She heard her daughter's laughter, and watched her careening along the beach in oversized boots, bundled against the wind in patched and mended cast-offs: a droll little scarecrow chasing down seagulls. Sheba was two-and-a-half years old. How large the world must seem to her, how limitless the sky and ocean. It was a miracle that she'd survived the smallpox epidemic and the fierce winter following her arrival. The winter just past had been equally severe, bringing famine in its wake and the ghastly sight of bodies lying where they'd fallen on the streets, and many more again when the snow receded.

Their family had been incredibly lucky that they were all still alive. After eight hard years, however, it was obvious that the authorities in Halifax had no intention of honouring the promises made to the black Loyalists. It should have come as no surprise, Epiphany thought; a government made up of white slave-owners was bound to insist that black was a sign of bondage. The truth, and the bitter irony when measured against her hopes in the beginning, was that in Nova Scotia the separation between free black and black slave was but the thinness of a coin.

Her daughter's laughter pealed again as she wheeled back and forth at the water's edge, arms outstretched in imitation of the birds. But like a cloud across the sun, Cornelius's words came to mind. *I fear for your children. I fear the slow whittling away of the spirit which destroys so many and maims all.*

Epiphany sat abruptly on the ground beside her half-filled basket, heedless of the cold damp sand. In her grief and anger after her father died she had been shut off from his spirit and deaf to her inner voice, but the birth of her daughter had reconnected her and unsealed her ears. Not because she saw him in her daughter, as he had seen his cousin Oluremi in her, long ago – far from it; the child resembled her grandmother, and moreover, answered to Sheba, the name Delilah had given her – but because she now understood that Cornelius had viewed the world entirely through her, just as she saw it refracted only through her daughter. His words had a resonance absent before.

Ahead of Sheba, Epiphany caught the glint of Caleb's musket slung over his shoulder. He too was collecting food, but mainly he was there to deter would-be kidnappers looking to make a profit in America or the West Indies. A musket might see off a kidnapper but wouldn't protect them against former owners arriving from America to reclaim their property – now a legal right in Shelburne. She looked out across the harbour where the melting ice gave notice of spring. Robert Farrer or his heir might even now be on the way.

Caleb clapped his hands and Sheba raced towards him, squealing with delight as he swung her high above his head.

The child shouted to her mother. 'Flying! Look! Look!'

Johnson had been wrong when he'd said that, without Cornelius, they were without a compass. As she looked at Sheba, Epiphany realised the compass had been within her all along, its needle pointing in the direction they should go. Slavery was *not* their story; it was the white's, in the country the white man had mapped. Freedom was *their* story, the country that *they* would map. In Nova Scotia they were trapped in no man's land. The time had come to brave the crossfire.

Epiphany jumped to her feet. She had the compass; she would lead the way.

'I could indenture myself,' Carver said.

As always now when the family gathered to eat in the evening, the question of how to put food on the table was uppermost in everybody's mind.

'Very good, Carver,' Delilah replied acidly. 'Let's all indenture ourselves or bind out the children, or better yet, sell ourselves back into slavery . . .'

'No!' Big Mo cried out. 'Better to be a heap of white bones by the roadside than go back to that.'

'It's all right, Big Mo,' soothed Epiphany, putting an arm around her. 'It won't come to that.'

A platter banged on the hearth where Tabitha was doling out potatoes. 'The Almighty has taken care of us this far; we should put our trust in Him.'

'All the same,' Johnson said, 'I'm not sure we could survive another winter. I've been wondering what Cornelius would do . . .'

'We must leave,' Epiphany said. They all stared at her. 'We got away from the plantation, didn't we? Now we must get away from Nova Scotia.'

'Have you "seen" something?' Caleb asked.

'I know we're not fated to die here,' Epiphany said. Whatever strengthened her hand, she thought.

Caleb nodded sagely.

'Boston,' Delilah declared. 'Slavery's been done away with in Massachusetts. I knew we should never have come here; we should have gone to New York instead.' Forgotten now the treachery of Captain Hawkins, the English officer who was to have taken them there.

Epiphany exchanged a dry glance with Johnson.

'I'm for it.' Elizabeth glanced up at the roof space where the children were sleeping. 'For their sake even more than ours.'

Johnson smiled at Elizabeth. 'First we must get to Halifax.'

'Easily said,' Delilah scoffed. She turned to Epiphany. 'Exactly how do you propose we do that, my girl?'

Epiphany laughed, they all did; Delilah and Johnson hated to agree.

With the compass firmly in her hand, Epiphany answered, 'We'll walk.'

In the event, they didn't need to. As Tabitha had foretold, God intervened.

There had been rumours but so fantastic were they, they'd been dismissed out of hand. Only Tabitha gave them any credence. The others were immersed in plans for their departure. They were to be stowaways who would work their passage once 'discovered'. Johnson had struck a bargain with the ship's cook and the pilot of two fishing vessels, shuttling regularly between Shelburne and Halifax. They would leave in the late fall, just before the ice set in.

Their preparations were near completion when Reverend George called a special church meeting in order, it was said, to deliver news of very great import. Epiphany assured herself that she had no expectations, but her heart was a-flutter as she stood pressed against Caleb with Sheba wedged between and Delilah on her other side. Johnson, Elizabeth and their three children, Tabitha, Big Mo and Carver had squeezed in beside them. On this Sunday morning the window shutters and church door had been left wide open to include the people packed into the clearing outside framed by red and gold October leaves.

Reverend George's voice carried effortlessly. 'Brothers and sisters, we have been bitterly disappointed; we have suffered and we have endured. But our trials and tribulations have been for a reason. The Lord has not abandoned us, far from it; His eye is upon us. We have been tested, and we have not been found wanting. "Behold, I have refined thee, but not with silver; I have chosen thee in the furnace of affliction." Yes, God has work for us to do . . .' Reverend George paused and looked around '. . . in Africa!'

Epiphany's heart banged against her ribs.

As if pulling a rabbit from a sack, Reverend George ushered the white man who had been standing behind him to join him at the pulpit. Then he turned to address the congregation once more.

'Brethren, we have the chance to start again, to build a new life, in a new country: Sierra Leone, West Africa. To cast off our shackles and return to the land of our forefathers.'

Reverend George's words sparkled enticingly, paving the way to a dazzling future. He pointed to the stranger, conspicuous as the moon in the night sky. Epiphany was surprised to note that the visitor was no older than Caleb.

'Mr Clarkson,' Reverend George informed them, 'is the representative of the directors of the Sierra Leone Company, in London.'

The white man bowed solemnly as heads craned for a better view.

Reverend George continued: 'You will all have heard how one year ago our brother, Thomas Peters, travelled to London at great risk to himself to lay our grievances before the British Government. It was the directors of the Sierra Leone Company, important men, sympathetic to our cause, who enabled Brother Peters to speak directly to Parliament. Then they used their influence to persuade King George to give those of us black Loyalists who wish to leave Nova Scotia *free passage to Africa*. That is why Mr Clarkson' – Reverend George pointed again – 'stands here before you. He has been charged by the British Government and the Sierra Leone Company to put their offer of resettlement directly before us.'

Mr Clarkson produced a sheet of paper and in a clear voice read out the terms: '*If all those wishing to emigrate can show to the satisfaction of the Company's representatives that they are honest, sober and industrious, they will be transported free to Sierra Leone, where they will receive grants of not less than twenty acres for a man, ten for his wife and five for each child.*'

A lengthy silence followed as calculations were made.

Epiphany was finding it difficult to breathe. Cornelius had made her promise that if ever the opportunity arose to go to Africa she would take it. As well fly to the moon, she'd said. But she *had* given her word.

A voice spoke up. 'We believed in such promises once before, and look what happened. It seems to me that to do so again would be more than foolishness. Why should these white men be different?'

Reverend George held up his hand for quiet. 'The Sierra Leone Company's objects are three-fold.' He marked them off on his fingers: 'To abolish the slave trade, to bring civilisation to Africa, and to introduce the gospel there. The Company believes that to help them achieve these aims there could be no better instrument than a settlement of free black Christians in Sierra Leone.' Reverend George's voice swelled and billowed. 'I believe the directors of the Sierra Leone Company are people we can trust. I believe that what they ask is what God has chosen us to do. He has sent Mr Clarkson to be our Moses and lead us to the Promised Land.'

Mr Clarkson leaned over the pulpit, spots of colour burning in his pale cheeks, and spoke to the crowd with equal passion. 'In Sierra Leone slavery will be *prohibited*. *Everyone*, black and white, will be equal before the law, enjoying the same rights and subject to the same duties. *I give you my oath.*' The silence was absolute as Mr Clarkson paused to let his words sink in. He opened his arms wide. 'My friends, I'm going to Africa with you, and with a glad heart. I shall *not leave* there until each one in my charge is perfectly satisfied.'

'It's the Hand of God,' Tabitha burst out as soon as the door was closed behind them. No one had spoken on the way home. Tabitha threw off her shawl. 'He has reached down, as Reverend George said, and touched each one of us. *We* will be responsible for taking the gospel to the people of Africa. Hallelujah!'

'But we're going to *Boston*,' Caleb's voice climbed in panic. 'We can't change now.'

'Can't we? What do you think, Epiphany?' Johnson asked.

Epiphany rubbed her hand, still sore where Caleb's grip had unconsciously tightened in the church.

'You know as well as I do,' she replied. There was no mistaking where the compass needle was pointing.

'And you, Delilah?'

Delilah put up her hands. 'We were already intending to go to Halifax, and now we can get there safely and for free.'

'Just like that?' Caleb looked from one to the other.

Johnson said, 'Cornelius promised we'd go to Africa, and so we will. We'll walk the wide streets, and linger in the shady courtyards of Oyo just as he said we would.'

'Amen.' Tabitha clapped her hands together.

Epiphany crossed to Caleb and held him close. She smiled reassuringly at Elizabeth and Carver and Big Mo. 'We're going home,' she said. In her mind, she continued: *Our eyes will fill with wonder at the giant porticos, the towering walls and soaring roofs all golden in the sun. In the cool of the night we'll dance to the ancient rhythms of the drums and the sweet scent of camwood will be drifting on the air.*

2

THE BLACK LOYALIST emigrants from Shelburne and Birchtown, six hundred in all, travelled to Halifax by boat in mid November – precisely the time Johnson had first planned.

Once there, Delilah took Caleb aside. 'Johnson and Elizabeth can go to Africa, Tabitha too if she likes, and good luck to them, but the rest of us are going to Boston, which is only a spit away from here.'

Realising that Delilah's aim all along had been simply to secure a free passage to Halifax, Caleb said nothing.

She continued, 'Until now we've been chaff carried on whatever wind was blowing and put down wherever it took us – Charleston, Nova Scotia, Africa. But here we have the chance to *choose*. I say we should stick to our original scheme. In Boston it'll be like Charleston, only better.'

'Or it could be like Nova Scotia all over again.'

'No, not now slavery's been outlawed in Massachusetts. I'm not saying we'll be treated equally, or even well. But it does mean we'll have room to manoeuvre. I've kept something back, acquired for just such an opportunity. It'll give us a start. We can make money and in time we'll be rich.'

'I'd take your word over Mr Clarkson's any day, Ma, and I dearly want to be rich. But Epiphany has her heart set on Africa. I dare not go against her. And what if everything Mr Clarkson says is true? You and I could fulfil our ambitions in Sierra Leone no less than in Boston, and that way we'd all be served.'

'Caleb –' Delilah grasped both his hands '– consider for a moment how completely the intentions of the British Government have been thwarted in Nova Scotia and then tell me what will happen to us in Sierra Leone.'

He removed his hands from her grasp. 'I take your point, but even so . . .'

'Listen! When it comes to it, Epiphany will follow you. Won't you at least try?'

Caleb sighed. In truth he had no wish to go to Africa. He bent his head. 'Let's hear it.'

Delilah whispered in his ear.

Epiphany drew her shawl closer against the biting cold as she hurried, head down, arms wrapped tight across her chest. Even so, she was not oblivious to the mid-winter beauty of the town. Halifax was silvered now with January snow, which lay gleaming on the steep-pitched roofs and piled in sparkling drifts beside the wooden sidewalks. The weight of it bent the leafless branches of ash and poplar trees into a white, latticed canopy, making the leaden sky appear black in contrast, as if bathed in perpetual moonlight. Stamping her feet to keep the blood flowing, she kept within the shelter of the handsome merchants' houses lining the main street.

All things considered, it was remarkable how little friction there had been. Over a thousand people had descended on the town, all needing to be housed and fed and in many instances clothed while waiting for the ships to be made ready for the voyage to Sierra Leone. The whole enterprise was taking longer and costing more than anyone had thought. It seemed all the black people in Nova Scotia wanted to go to Africa. Indeed, they were all desperate for the chance. Only yesterday a group had arrived from St John half dead from exhaustion; they'd missed the boat sent to collect them and had set out on foot, covering three hundred and forty miles in fifteen days. And with only three days to go before boarding people were still arriving.

The past two months, Epiphany realised, had been reminiscent of their time behind British lines. The men were organised in the same companies and under the same leaders as when they first arrived in Nova Scotia, reuniting Johnson with his men; Delilah was in charge of the soup kitchen; Caleb had become Reverend George's right-hand man, and Tabitha was assisting Dr Taylor, the Company physician.

There were significant differences, of course, chief among them the unfailing courtesy and kindness with which they were treated by Mr Clarkson and his ships' captains and officers. It was good too to be able to walk about in safety. The day was drawing in and lanterns were beginning to be lit as she arrived at the harbour, but there would be no respite from the sawing and hammering which all but drowned out the screeching of the gulls, nor from the overpowering smell of burning tar.

The good citizens of Halifax must be torn, Epiphany thought, not unsympathetically, between wishing them gone and wanting their money.

'Where've you been?' Big Mo enquired mildly. She appeared larger than ever, transformed into a looming shadow against the light spilling on to the cobbles from the open double-doors of the enormous warehouse behind.

Epiphany came to stand next to her at the two long trestle tables set out on the road. 'To clear my head. Sheba not with you?'

'She's about the place with her grandmother as usual.'

Epiphany glanced towards the entrance of the warehouse where Caleb was stationed, shepherding people outside to collect their food.

Big Mo waved a ladle at Epiphany. 'You should tell him.'

Epiphany snatched the ladle and stirred one of two huge cauldrons simmering on the fire nearby. She sniffed appreciatively, admiring as always Big Mo's ability to conjure something halfway decent out of beef bones and turnips.

As soon as the queue began to form, Carver materialised, carrying two enormous baskets. His presence imposed immediate order and with each bowl of soup he handed out a wedge of black rye bread.

'What did you say?' Big Mo put her hand to her ear, yelling above the rattle of tin plates and spoons and children's laughter.

'All in good time,' Epiphany shouted back. The fact was she suspected Caleb of keeping something from her. Something he was plotting with Delilah. She'd seen them with their heads together.

The double doors opening on to the harbour had been bolted and guards posted for the night. Heat from the iron stoves at either end of the vast storehouse ensured that it was dry and snug for the three hundred or so who had made their home there for the past several weeks. In their cramped corner, Epiphany and Elizabeth had rolled out the mattresses and settled the children for the night before joining Tabitha and Big Mo in reviewing the contents of the wooden chests they would be taking with them on the voyage. The men were occupied – Johnson with his musket, Carver with his axe and Caleb with his cutlass. They were carefully oiling and re-wrapping their treasures.

Delilah, who'd abstained from the usual evening review of the chests, suddenly announced, 'I have something to tell you.'

Epiphany looked at Caleb, who shrugged in apparent bewilderment.

'We're going to America,' Delilah said, bright and brittle.

So, Epiphany realised, this was what they'd been plotting. She remained silent.

Delilah hurried on. 'There's a ship sailing to Boston tomorrow and the captain's willing to give us passage, which is what we originally planned. I didn't want us to miss this opportunity, so I took it upon myself . . .' No one spoke. 'Someone had to be practical, the rest of you weren't thinking straight. Honestly, if this offer was for anywhere but Africa you wouldn't consider it for a moment. Africa has you bewitched. But all you have to go on are Cornelius's tall tales and some hand-me-down stories from Elizabeth. In all seriousness, do you believe that's reason enough to sail halfway round the world on the say-so of a few white men in England and a boy still wet behind the ears who knows even less about Africa than you do?'

Johnson rose to his feet. 'Thomas Peters has been face to face with the directors of the Sierra Leone Company and looked them in the eye. He's no one's fool, believe me, and he's assured me these are men of their word. They want to end slavery, same as Cornelius. That was his aim from the moment he set foot in America, and if a colony of free blacks in West Africa will help bring that about, then I'm for it. We have a job to do and I for one am prepared to *die* in the attempt.'

Delilah turned to Epiphany. 'There's nothing to stop us going to Africa one day . . . in style. All of us with our heads high, not as we are now, half starved, dependent on white people's charity'

Before Epiphany could answer, Tabitha spoke up: 'Cornelius lived for you, Epiphany. If you reject this opportunity, everything he fought for, everything he suffered will have been in vain.'

Delilah plumped down on her knees in front of Epiphany. 'What purpose would it serve to go to Africa now? You'll feel Cornelius's absence everywhere. Be reminded every waking minute of how it might have been. How could you bear it? How could we bear it? Would it not be better to stay on this side of the world where his presence is so strong and our memories of him so bright? I doubt any of us could be happy knowing he was in a cold grave so far away.'

'That was low, Delilah, even for you,' Johnson growled.

Gently, Epiphany helped Delilah up and made her sit beside her on the wooden chest. Johnson had misjudged Delilah. Epiphany had caught a certain note in her mother's voice that told her she had not been entirely feigning about Cornelius. And she knew that, in her own way, Delilah cared for her no less than her father had. The difference was that her mother thought slavery *was* their story while Cornelius knew otherwise.

At last Epiphany broke her silence. 'When Pa died, Johnson said we were without a compass. It took me a long time to realise that the compass wasn't lost; Pa had passed it on to me with the needle always pointing to freedom. And it's pointing towards Africa, where we'll have not only a compass but a map as well.'

Johnson's face broke into a grin. 'Cornelius is back!'

'No,' Epiphany contradicted him. 'You have *me*. But . . .' turning to Caleb, she patted her stomach, '. . . Big Mo predicts a boy, and who knows . . .'

Caleb looked as shocked as she could have wished before he swept her into his arms. I'm Delilah's daughter too, she thought, before joining in the laughter.

Caleb and Delilah stood looking out to sea. Beyond the mass of boats in the crowded bay a schooner, its lanterns winking in the darkness, was making its way past the lighthouse at the harbour mouth.

Delilah sucked her teeth in frustration. 'All this talk of maps is fanciful nonsense. The simple truth is: in America we *know* where we are, in Africa we'll be travelling blindfold.'

Caleb gave her a sideways look. 'So you *are* coming with us to Sierra Leone?'

Delilah sighed, but there was a predatory glint in her eye. 'We can make money in Africa. And we had best begin straight away.'

Caleb said, 'I saw the good captain, as arranged. He refused to return the down payment but . . .' He mimicked the captain downing a large glass of rum. 'Strange things can happen when a sailor takes a drink.' Caleb made a delicate lifting gesture with his thumb and forefinger. 'Don't get me wrong, Ma, I'm no sneak thief, but at more than double the rate, he was skinning us.'

Delilah threw back her head and laughed. 'I knew from the start you and I could work well together.' She slipped a purse inside the bodice of her dress. 'It seems I can read everyone except my own daughter.'

'Epiphany,' Caleb said, 'has one foot in another world, and it makes her unpredictable.'

'I shan't make the same mistake again.'

'Nor I,' Caleb agreed fervently. 'By the way, it was good of you not to betray me.' He smiled complacently.

'It suits my purpose not to.' Delilah erased his smile.

They strolled along the quayside in the brightness of the harbour lights trying to ascertain which of the vessels crowding the bay were being fitted for the coming journey. In all, fifteen ships had been commissioned to transport them across the ocean.

'You're with Reverend George all day, Caleb, what do you know?' asked Delilah.

'I know people are already divided between Mr Clarkson and Thomas Peters. Many of them believe Brother Peters should be our leader because he was the one who set the whole thing in motion.'

'Whose side is Reverend George on?'

'He's very close to Mr Clarkson.'

'And Johnson?'

'I'd say he inclines towards Brother Peters.'

~

3

AFRICA. GRIPPING THE rail of the ship, Caleb stared at the coast, stretching low and flat on the starboard side, dense vegetation extending down to the water's edge. There was rancour in his gaze. He wiped his face and neck and dabbed at his bare chest with his already damp shirt. The heat and humidity were far worse than he remembered in Georgia or South Carolina. But he barely registered his discomfort or surroundings as he turned back to scan the horizon. Of the fifteen ships that had set sail from Nova Scotia, one was missing.

There was no reason, Caleb told himself, why the *Morning Star* should not make landfall. After the storms that had separated the fleet, she must have enjoyed the same fine weather and mild winds. He wiped his head, clean-shaven against lice, and spread his shirt on the rail. But even the ship's safe arrival would not allay his fears entirely; there was cause to fear that not everyone on board would have survived the voyage. Sixty-five had passed away on one vessel alone, and on the flagship *Lucretia* three elders of Reverend George's congregation had died. It was quite possible, Caleb thought, that his wife and daughter and his unborn son were also dead.

The whole family were to have travelled together aboard the flagship, but after Epiphany's surprise revelation she'd been reassigned to the *Morning Star* where there was special accommodation for pregnant women. To keep her company, Delilah, Tabitha, Big Mo and Sheba had also changed. Caleb would have accompanied them, had not Epiphany urged him to stay where he was with Johnson and Elizabeth. Delilah had persuaded her that, Caleb being his right-hand man, Reverend George's need was greater. Instead Carver was deputed to fetch and carry for Tabitha, who was to be both doctor and midwife on the voyage. Delilah made it clear to Caleb that he had no choice in the matter. Reluctantly he'd agreed.

A burst of laughter distracted him and he glanced behind him. The main deck resembled a fair. People were crowded under colourful awnings fashioned from quilts, jackets and petticoats, their belongings spread out around them as if for sale. In fact, there was a good deal of bartering going on now that they were so near landfall. Wooden chests were hauled up daily from below and their contents brought out for airing. Children dashed about unchecked while men sunned themselves, keeping one eye on the fishing lines trailing over the side. Friends and relations visiting ship to ship added to the carnival atmosphere. Caleb turned back to the rail in the hope that the *Morning Star* had by some chance come into view since he last looked.

He felt a touch on his arm.

It was Elizabeth. Seeing his face she said, 'The others will arrive safely, Caleb, I'm certain of it. I *feel* it.'

Caleb shrugged, unconvinced.

She pointed. 'Look!' A great black-and-white bird plummeted suddenly from its tree-top perch, plunged its feet into the sea and surged upwards again, powerful wings beating, a fish hooked in its talons. 'I wonder what the Africans call it?'

Caleb, attempting to keep desperation at bay, resented her good spirits, begrudged the sparkle in her strange light-coloured eyes. With her hair jauntily tied in a kerchief that had once been red, she still resembled a girl instead of the young matron she now was.

He smiled sarcastically. 'I imagine the Africans call it the same as we do. A fish eagle. Or maybe a tree eagle; it looks very much at home in the branches there.'

'Just like us.' Elizabeth stared after the bird.

'My, we can fly now, can we?'

Johnson joined them at the rail. He too had dispensed with his shirt, revealing a striking diamond pattern of welts all over his back. He slipped an affectionate arm round Elizabeth's waist.

'Come on, Caleb, you know what she meant. I feel the same: as if I was home.'

Caleb stared at the impenetrable screen of mangrove trees and then at Johnson, taking in the older man's confident stance, his broad chest and muscled, blacksmith's arms. He felt callow and timid in comparison.

He thrust out his chin. 'Home is a place whose secrets you know. This looks like a place that guards its secrets well. We can only ever be strangers here in Africa, and it would be foolish to act otherwise.'

Elizabeth replied, placatingly, 'I believe nothing but good can come of our being here. Once the Africans see the advantages Christianity has brought us, black people like themselves, they'll want the same. I can't wait to start telling the gospel stories. Their eyes will be opened and they'll see the *evil* of what they're doing.'

Johnson cradled Elizabeth's hand in his. 'Christianity won't succeed on its own; it's my guess they'll also need to see how they can turn a good profit elsewhere.'

The sight of their hands lovingly intertwined was an unbearably sharp reminder to Caleb of his single state. He said balefully, 'If Mr Clarkson dies, our little adventure will have ended before it's begun.'

It was no secret that Mr Clarkson was in fragile health, no doubt strained by overwork and the burden of his responsibilities.

'He would be a grievous loss to us,' Johnson replied. 'But Thomas Peters is hale and hearty. I believe we'd still win through. However, it won't come to that. And I'm sure that, by this time tomorrow, we'll all be present and accounted for.'

Caleb looked away, ashamed of his ill will, but no less fearful than before.

Drums beating in the African town five miles' distant, a leopard barking suddenly in the forest, cicadas sawing shrilly on the shore – all resounded ominously in Caleb's overwrought mind. Wary of returning to sleep, he rose from his bunk in a state of high agitation. Accustomed, after six weeks, to the lie of the ship, he was able to grope his way out of the sleeping quarters without difficulty.

He found no one stirring above save the two officers of the watch, their pale faces illuminated in the light of the lanterns swinging high on the poop deck. They exchanged brief nods and Caleb moved to the rail of the main deck and leant over it, ears and eyes straining anxiously toward the harbour mouth.

He heard only the creaking of timbers, the gentle slapping of water against the side of the ship and the sighing of ropes in the rigging. He could see nothing beyond the pools of light thrown out by the ships' lanterns, which seemed no more than glow-worms flickering in a darkness so black it belied the imminence of dawn. It was all so different from mornings in Nova Scotia.

The sun came up swiftly, the sky turning from black to orange to pink to broad daylight blue. Caleb clung to his place by the rail, staring toward the sea for a sign of the *Morning Star*, taking little heed of the activity around him as the ship's crew busied themselves with their morning routine. The smell of the vinegar and hot tar used to fumigate the sleeping quarters below mingled with the aroma of cornmeal and molasses, a sure indication that breakfast had begun.

'Eat!' a voice ordered him.

Caleb turned from his contemplation of the ocean to find Johnson beside him, a plate of food in his hands.

Caleb shook his head.

'These have been hard come by.' Johnson thrust the plate at him. 'Spit on them, and you spit on us.'

Caleb took the plate and forced himself to eat. Johnson was right to insist; refusing food was tantamount to blasphemy. People had filled their stomachs with dirt before now to quiet their hunger, and they'd been hungry longer than they'd been Christians.

'And when you're finished, you would do well to attend to your other duties,' Johnson admonished him.

Caleb nodded. Being a man of such resolute character, Johnson could not begin to know the depth of his terror. Without Epiphany and Delilah, he felt as if he had lost all substance, as if he was bleeding away inside like a creature doomed to extinction when deprived of its host.

Johnson pressed him on the shoulder and started towards the kitchen, but the sound of cheering and musket fire brought him running back. The *Morning Star* was sailing into the harbour, red pennant fluttering from her mast, her passengers gathered on deck waving and shouting, the men firing their guns in the air.

'Hallelujah!' Johnson yelled, raising both fists in the air. 'Cornelius's dream may yet come true.'

'Is that all it means to you?' Caleb covered his face with his hands; he was shivering uncontrollably.

Johnson pulled his hands away. 'Make no mistake, I have always considered Epiphany as much my child as Cornelius's. I was a father to her long before I was father to my own children. If she were to perish, a part of me would go with her, as it did with Cornelius.'

Caleb could only nod his head.

Gripping him by the arms to steady him, Johnson continued, 'But death is like the sea reclaiming the land. The people are still there, they're just hidden from our view.'

Caleb twisted out of Johnson's grasp, pushed his way to the front of the throng at rail of the *Lucretia*, and began frantically searching for familiar faces among the cheering crowds on the deck of the *Morning Star*.

It was a measure of the Reverend George's special regard for Caleb that, as soon as he himself knew, he hastened to relay the news that there had been no fatalities on board the *Morning Star* and though three of the women in Tabitha's care had been safely delivered, Epiphany was not one of them. And it was the Reverend George who made sure that Caleb, Johnson and Elizabeth obtained places in the long-boat that carried the three black representatives from the *Morning Star* back to their vessel once their formal visit to Mr Clarkson had been concluded.

The waves rippling past the sides of the boat appeared cool and enticing, and Caleb was tempted to trail his hand in the clear blue water. The sun's rays no longer oppressed but seemed to him bountiful, showering gold everywhere.

'God is good,' Elizabeth said.

Caleb was inclined to agree as he watched a gull swoop low, riding on a current, its outstretched wings motionless, the hooked beak and round eye perfectly outlined.

Epiphany and Sheba, Delilah, Tabitha, Big Mo and Carver were at the rail waiting to greet them. Carver reached out to haul them up the last rungs of the ladder and forced a passage for them through the crowds to a quieter corner, where Caleb swept his daughter into his arms.

'We can hear ourselves speak here,' Carver said, planting his feet firmly, his back a bulwark against the crowd. But for a few short moments they could only stare in silence. It had been in all their minds that they might never be together again.

Released, Sheba resumed running about the deck.

Epiphany covered Caleb's hand with hers as he patted her swollen stomach. 'Imagine if it was Jonah who'd swallowed the whale!' she said to laughter. She had never been so glad to see anyone in her life and, judging by the strength of Caleb's grip on her hand, the feeling was reciprocated. She returned the pressure. 'I have a while yet, apparently.'

Johnson looked sceptically at Tabitha, who told him, 'Auntie Jane says so, and she should know – she's a hundred and three and she's brought more children into this world than I ever will. She reckons Epiphany's will be the first of the crop here in Africa.'

Delilah said, 'Auntie Jane is so certain of it that, even though she had planned to move on to the next world once she'd crumbled a handful of her native earth in her hands, she's now decided to postpone her going until after the birth.'

Elizabeth stroked Epiphany's stomach. 'That's a good omen if ever there was one.'

They fell to hugging again and again, as if the evidence of their eyes were not enough.

'Well?' Delilah demanded in Caleb's ear.

Caleb bent towards her, retaining his grip on Epiphany's hand. 'I've become Reverend George's eyes and ears. Johnson and I are as close as you could wish. This morning he embraced me like a son.'

'Excellent.' Delilah pulled away.

'Are you two plotting again?' Epiphany joked, leaning her elbows on the rail and looking toward the land.

Caleb rolled his eyes in mock offence and leant beside her.

In front of them was Cape Sierra Leone, a chain of mountains jutting out to sea, rising one behind the other, slopes covered in luxurious green vegetation, climbing steeply at first then gradually, up and up, until the highest peaks touched the sky. Cascades of candle-like flowers and flashes of ruby-red earth were bright as lighted flares against the green. Glittering in the light of the tropical sun, it was a landscape that gave the impression of perpetual summer.

'Nothing in the world could better this.' Epiphany sighed with happiness, thinking not only of the view.

Caleb nodded, his eyes on her. 'Did you miss me?'

Epiphany gave him a sideways look. 'I could have managed, but I'm glad I don't have to.'

Caleb grinned. 'Now there's the difference. I could not.'

Epiphany wagged a finger at him. 'Ah, love and need are not the same; one is particular and the other general.'

'They are to me . . .'

'Now *there's* the difference,' Epiphany said, laughing.

Tabitha came to lean beside them. 'How generous is the Hand of God?' She shook her head, marvelling.

'Too much so.' Delilah fanned her neck with her hand. 'He should hold back a little.'

'It looks very different over there –' Epiphany pointed across the harbour, where the ships' masts rose like spires. There was no land to be seen on the opposite shore, only the tops of the trees, as if a giant forest were growing out of the sea.

'That's called the Bullom shore,' Big Mo said. 'It means low-lying land.' The others turned to her in astonishment. She smiled deprecatingly. 'I learned that this morning when I traded the pineapple and oranges Epiphany and Sheba ate for their breakfast.'

Lean and elegant African canoes, piled precariously with fruits and vegetables whose unfamiliar scents wafted upwards, skimmed across the water like dragonflies, vying for passage among the tall ships, narrowly avoiding collision with each other and the long-boats busy ferrying passengers and more recognisable goods from one vessel to another.

Delilah asked what Big Mo had traded in return for the fruit.

Big Mo shrugged. 'I pressed them to take a button in exchange; the fact is they wanted nothing in return.'

Delilah, eyes narrowed on the hectic activity below, said, 'They'll want something tomorrow, Big Mo, wait and see. Africans are no different from anyone else.'

Caleb said, 'I don't see any evidence of that. Facial scars are one thing – Cornelius had those – but these people are scarified all over, their bodies pinked and pricked like so much quiltwork.' He put a handkerchief to his nose as a canoe laden with bloody carcasses of unidentifiable small creatures was swiftly waved on by the crew.

Delilah said, 'They can shout, all right. They put us to shame, with their –'

Epiphany interrupted, pointing. 'What on earth . . .?'

'Yams,' Big Mo supplied helpfully. 'And cassava—'

'No, no. Over there.'

A long-boat from one of the vessels already at anchor when they had arrived in the harbour was bearing down fast on the *Lucretia*. The seven white men on board wore cockades and epaulettes, and they jostled among themselves, pecking at each other like angry bantams, tangling oversized swords in their eagerness to be first, all but capsizing their boat as it crossed the harbour. Their quarrelsome transit brought the passengers of every ship of the Halifax fleet up on deck.

It was only as Epiphany looked again at the thick forest marching down to the water's edge that she recalled the promises made to them of how the land would be cleared and a jetty built for their arrival. Slowly she realised nothing at all had been done. There were no houses, nor any supplies of wood for building houses. It appeared that those responsible for the initial preparations had done nothing. They had remained on their ships without lifting a finger.

From across the water she heard Mr Clarkson order a thirteen-gun salute for his visitors as he welcomed them, still barging and bickering, aboard his flagship. The gunpowder left the smell of sulphur hanging in the air.

∾

4

A LARGE CROWD milled in the early-morning sunlight, impatient to proceed with the service of thanksgiving to mark their first Sabbath in Sierra Leone. Every available long-boat and cutter had been dragooned into use, plying from ship to shore since daybreak, transferring the entire population from their transports to the beach. It had been a long wait for the early arrivals, made bearable only by a cool breeze blowing off the ocean. Aside from the Nova Scotians, who numbered more than a thousand, there were over one hundred Company officials and employees, as well as the captains and crews of the two dozen ships in the harbour. All had laboriously to be rowed ashore.

Epiphany and Auntie Jane were among the last to arrive. Both had insisted on coming ashore, despite attempts to dissuade them. Auntie

Jane, frail as a leaf, was lifted out in a trice, but it took the combined efforts of Caleb, Johnson and Carver to transfer Epiphany from the long-boat to dry land. As Caleb pretended to stagger under her weight, Epiphany cuffed him over the head.

'Stop that,' she said, unhitching and smoothing down her long skirts.

Standing on the soil of Africa at last, she was tempted to copy Auntie Jane, who had gone down on her knees to kiss the earth, scooping up handfuls of warm sand and letting it pour through her fingers in a silver stream, but she resisted the impulse, thinking dryly of the comical figure she would cut with her huge belly if she tried to do the same. Instead she contented herself with burrowing her feet deeply in the sand. As a space opened around Auntie Jane, it was clear that the old woman was praying, her words winging upwards like captive birds suddenly released. Epiphany recognised the words. She was speaking in the Oyo tongue.

Helping Auntie Jane to her feet, Tabitha said with a hint of criticism, 'I thought you were a Christian, Auntie Jane?'

'And so I am.' The old woman straightened her faded head-tie and tucked a spidery hand securely in the crook of Epiphany's arm. '*That* was just in case.'

'Cornelius is here,' Epiphany said.

'And he's not alone,' Big Mo added.

'The ancestors must be with him,' said Johnson.

Auntie Jane raised a sightless face towards the sky. 'They've been waiting a long time for this.'

'And the Heavenly Host,' Tabitha put in.

'As if this beach wasn't crowded enough already,' Delilah said.

The Anglican chaplain sent out by the Sierra Leone Company headed the procession from the beach. He was carrying a large black Bible, his white surplice belling in the breeze. Immediately behind him walked Mr Clarkson, newly appointed superintendent, soberly dressed in his naval lieutenant's uniform. There followed the seven members of the governing council; fractious even now, much frogged and tasselled in gaudy green and gold. They were accompanied by their wives; muslin shawls afloat, lacy parasols aloft to protect wan complexions. Next came the higher Company officials with their spouses gamely aping their betters, and walking beside them, the ships' captains, sporting dress uniforms. Behind them marched the lower Company servants and ordinary seamen, queues neatly tied. Bringing up the rear came the settlers, barefoot like the sailors, their red army coats and cast-off attire colourfully patched and mended. Divided into their separate congregations – Baptists, Methodists, Huntingdonians – they lined up behind their preachers, who strode ahead of them, each carrying a Bible.

The long procession climbed the winding path from the palm-fringed beach to the lap of the wooded hill nearest the shore on which stood a canvas house large enough to accommodate them all. Brought from England, the capacious white edifice was church, council chamber, officers' mess and meeting house. Significantly, as it was almost exclusively for Company employees' use, erecting it was the total effort that the officials sent ahead to prepare for the arrival of the settlers had seen fit to make.

Epiphany felt her child kick and placed both hands protectively on her stomach. She looked beyond the ranks of the settlers, past the whites at the front, to the small group of Africans peering through the open door flaps. They were not at all as she had imagined from Cornelius's descriptions; she had expected flowing robes and elaborate headdresses. Instead, the women and girls were bare-breasted – to show off the raised filigree patterns etched on their bodies, she supposed – while the children ran naked save for bead necklaces and waistbands. Apart from the constant refrain of drums in the night, there was probably an equal disparity between the African town five miles away in the forest and the great walled city of Oyo. Other expectations had been similarly confounded, and these gave cause for real disquiet.

Contrary to what Mr Clarkson had told them in Nova Scotia, the settlers were not to rule themselves after all. The directors of the Sierra Leone Company, having changed their minds in the interim, had appointed seven councillors and various other company officials to govern them instead. The councillors sat in a row, fidgeting on their narrow bench, red-faced and sweating in tight uniforms. It was not a sight to inspire confidence. Mr Clarkson looked conspicuously pale and still beside them.

Brother Peters and his followers, Johnson among them, advocated ridding the colony of whites by driving them all into ocean forthwith. Reverend George, however, said they should all continue to put their faith in Mr Clarkson. The Reverend had half the settlers on his side, including Delilah and Caleb. Epiphany glanced at the rows of devout faces. Christian, English-speaking and free they might be, but their nearest neighbours were African slave traders and European slave factories. Like it or not, the black settlers would stand little chance if the Sierra Leone Company withdrew protection.

Caleb caught her eye and grinned. 'Who would have believed it? We've made it back to Africa, safe and sound!'

Her spirits lifted and she gave him a broad grin in return.

'Sing!' he commanded. 'Today is ours.'

A thousand triumphant voices threatened to lift the canvas house from its moorings. Epiphany's voice soared with the rest.

The day of Jubilee is come;
Return ye ransomed sinners home.

At first the settlers lived on board their ships, the men rowing ashore before daybreak to begin clearing the land. The sound of their axes resounded through the forest as they felled the trees and hacked their way through the razor-edged grass and brush that stood at more than twice their height, until at sundown they emerged and rowed back to their ships. Caleb complained that the searing heat made the work a thousand times harder than when they'd had to clear the land in Nova Scotia. Laughing, Big Mo reminded him that in Nova Scotia he had said the work was a thousand times more difficult than in South Carolina on account of the freezing cold. Big Mo, as usual, was labouring alongside the men.

The transformation from virgin forest into the beginnings of a settlement was swift. Eight large tents fashioned from sails and ships' spars clustered behind the rectangular canvas house. A wide swathe was cut on the slope leading up to the mount, now named Thornton Hill in honour of the chairman of the Sierra Leone Company. And flying in the breeze on the top of the hill was the Company flag, featuring a sailing ship, an English merchant with his parcels, and an African leaning on a huge ivory tusk. Mr Clarkson had brought a plan on the American model for the new capital, Freetown. There were to be three broad boulevards running parallel to the ocean, with nine streets – each named after a Company director – crossing them at right angles and running inland towards the mountains.

Epiphany had been adamant that her child must be born on African soil, even if quitting the ship meant giving birth inside a crowded tent or out in the open. Happily, it had not come to that. With a sigh of satisfaction, she leaned back on her seat in the shade provided by the overhanging roof of the hastily built hut she shared with Caleb, Delilah, Tabitha and Big Mo.

'I like my new house,' she declared, running a hand along the wall behind her. 'No,' she corrected herself. 'I *love* it.'

'It will do for now.' Delilah slumped down on another wooden chest that doubled as a bench. 'One day, though, we'll build a proper house.'

'This *is* a proper house,' Tabitha said, coming to sit beside Epiphany. 'A proper African house.'

'How would you know?' Delilah scrutinised the bold geometric patterning on the mat at the entrance, rolled up at present to let in the breeze.

Tabitha patted the mud-and-plaster wall proprietorially.

'Johnson used the African model to build his hut and ours. It stands to reason, they know what works best here.'

Delilah sniffed. 'And I suppose in America you'd have preferred to live in an Indian tepee? *I* am going to build a beautiful house, right here, on Water Street, facing the sea. Made of wood at first, but eventually out of stone – just like the ones in Charleston.'

Tabitha waved a finger at Delilah. 'You're running ahead of yourself,' she said. 'There's no guarantee, once the land has been properly surveyed and we draw lots, that ours will be on this same spot.'

'I'm an optimist,' Delilah said firmly.

'Is that what you call it?' Epiphany looked sideways at her.

'Lucky is as lucky does.' Delilah smiled enigmatically.

She had lost no time in setting up as laundress to the ships' captains and officers and, on their recommendations, to the Company's higher officials, whose wives declared it nothing short of miraculous that in this God-forsaken corner of the world they were able to secure the services of such an accomplished lady's maid. They paid accordingly, of course, but even more than they knew. Their careless talk and their husbands' habits of leaving confidential correspondence in pockets ensured that Delilah knew as much about the government's business in the settlement as anyone – excepting perhaps Mr Clarkson.

Sheba joined them noisily, and threw herself down at the feet of the women.

'We're all living in a rainbow!' she announced.

Laughing, the adults agreed as they sat facing the gold-and-silver dazzle of the sunlight on the ocean, where a large number of ships rode at anchor, whole communities still living on board. High above was an azure sky and beneath their feet red earth. Birds darted continuously among opulent blossoms, which shone like cascading gems against the differing shades of green vegetation pressing in on all sides.

Noting the larger than usual contingent of African girls clustered at a little distance, Sheba whispered loudly, 'Why they got no clothes on?'

Epiphany reached down and clapped a hand over her daughter's mouth, reprimanding her for her rudeness, before remembering that their audience spoke no English. Each day hundreds of Africans travelled to Freetown from their villages along the coast to trade fruit and vegetables and country lore in exchange for biscuit, dried beef, soap and spirits. Their noisy, friendly presence formed a permanent and exotic background to all settler activities. The modesty of the young girls was preserved by a narrow strip of cloth looped over a belt of beads circling slender hips.

'One or two are quite fetching, despite the filed teeth!' Delilah said. 'Auntie Sam would have liked them for her –'

'Delilah!' Tabitha's face flamed.

Delilah held up her hands, 'Don't worry, Tabitha, I've quite different designs on them.'

Suppressing a smile, Epiphany said firmly, 'I imagine, Sheba, that they don't wear clothes because of the heat.' Sheba immediately began shedding hers. Epiphany glared at her. 'No.'

'Why not?' Sheba stepped out of her petticoat.

'Because, because . . . it's not Christian,' Tabitha said, recovering her equilibrium.

'They not Christian?' Sheba demanded.

'They are . . . Africans.'

'Me too. Me too!' Sheba cried, skipping and twirling, stark naked now. 'I'm African. I'm African.'

'You are *not*,' Delilah snapped. Sheba stopped her twirling and, arms folded across her chest, looked beadily at her grandmother.

'You're the same as us: Nova Scotian.'

Epiphany opened her mouth to contradict her mother, but closed it again without speaking. Because of Cornelius, she had thought of herself as African all these years. Now, she was not sure what to think.

Tabitha swooped, catching Sheba by surprise, held her imprisoned on her lap, and pulled her shift over her head. 'First and foremost we're Christians. And soon' – Tabitha jerked her head in the direction of their audience, who were staring wide-eyed – 'they will be too.'

233

Delilah broke into laughter. Epiphany averted her eyes to avoid doing the same but failed, and soon they were all laughing. A sharp pain in the small of her back made Epiphany grimace, which increased the merriment among the others who imagined she was laughing. Before she could correct them, Elizabeth's daughters burst in, evidently distraught, extinguishing the laughter. Epiphany sat them down, smoothing their plaits while they caught their breath and Tabitha fetched a drink of water.

'Samuel's sick,' the elder one, Joy, blurted.

'Sick, how?' Tabitha asked gently.

'With the fever,' Peace, the younger twin, answered.

Epiphany and Tabitha exchanged involuntary glances and Delilah's arms tightened reflexively around Sheba, nestled at her side. A mysterious fever, which had broken out among the settlers still living on board their ships, had become an epidemic ashore, claiming an alarming number of lives.

'Has the doctor been sent for?' Epiphany asked, knowing it was probably a vain hope. Of the three Company physicians, only one remained, one having died of drink and the other already returned to England. But if anyone could persuade the doctor to come, Johnson would. He would pluck the moon right out of the sky for that son of his, she thought.

Joy nodded her head vigorously in confirmation. 'Ma sent us to find Pa first, and he's gone out looking for the doctor, and she said when we'd done that to come and ask Auntie Tabitha to attend Samuel meanwhile.'

Tabitha had already gone inside to collect the things she would need, but at a slight sound from Epiphany she hesitated.

Epiphany waved her on. 'Go quickly, Tabitha. It's not what you think. The baby won't arrive today. I'm sure of it.'

Epiphany lay on a pallet on the floor, sweat streaming. Delilah knelt beside her. The child was clearly disinclined to wait upon Tabitha. It was time to fetch Auntie Jane.

'This is what comes of tempting fate, my girl.' Delilah rubbed her back, straightened the quilt and moved the candle so that its light would not shine in her eyes.

'It was the laughter that lured him,' Epiphany said.

Delilah sank down abruptly on a wooden chest just inside the door.

'Before you . . .' she said, and fell silent. She took a deep breath. 'Before you, I had just one babe who was born dead. I know now it was because I was too young when my . . . Miss Celia's father, first . . . my body wasn't ready to carry a child. At the time, though, I reckoned it was because he knew what was in store for him. And that's why he died. But now your boy . . .' Delilah rose quickly and the door flap dropped behind her as she left to fetch Auntie Jane.

Epiphany lay on her pallet. The well of her mother's soul was deeper than most, that much she knew, but she was astonished to find reflected there the same glimmering stars of hope she herself nurtured; she had imagined them extinguished long ago in Delilah. As she fell to studying the candle shadows, she pondered the paradoxical world her child was about to enter: a tiny haven of freedom for blacks under the protection of the country which profited the most from trafficking them. As Cornelius used to say: in each thing is its opposite. She settled down to wait, her body racked by painful contractions but her mind at ease. Whatever else might befall him, hope, she thought would now be a part of her child's inheritance.

'Who is it?' Auntie Jane woke the instant Delilah touched her on the shoulder.

'It's me, Auntie. Epiphany's time has come.' Delilah helped the old woman dress and was handed a little bundle that had been prepared in advance. She must be used to this, Delilah thought; children always seemed to arrive in the night.

Auntie Jane took her arm and they started down the hill.

The night chorus sounded louder than ever. The cicadas were besting countless other nameless insects, but their noise was as nothing to the hooting of the owls and the screeches of the parrots.

'What do you remember of Africa, Auntie Jane?' Delilah asked.

She calculated that to reach the same age she would have to live as long again and then some. It would be a miracle if Auntie Jane remembered anything. The old woman stopped, her face turning this way and that. The sound of the surf travelled upwards, there was smoke from the fires, the tang of salt and citrus, the heady scent of night-flowering blooms.

'My home was not here. It was a big city with courtyards open to the sky and surrounded by high walls,' Auntie Jane said. 'It was far, far from the sea, where the air is dryer and there are fewer trees. I was happy. I remember the smells. The faint odour of rain on the wind, the smell of violet root and wild honey; of camwood on my mother's skin – those are the ones that sweeten the memory, but even they cannot erase the foulness of the slave ship. That will accompany me to the next world.'

Delilah remembered that Cornelius had told her how the smell of the slave ship had eaten into his soul. How it had marked him as surely any branding. How it became a coat he could never shed.

'How old were you, Auntie, when they snatched you?'

'Eight summers by my reckoning now, perhaps ten.'

Delilah was humbled into silence. She marvelled at the strength of will that had enabled Auntie Jane to see Africa again. She had survived kidnapping, the Middle Passage, decades of slavery, a hazardous escape, a civil war and nine years of freezing winters in Nova Scotia, all to make a second journey across the Atlantic to reach home at the age of a hundred and three.

Big Mo's smile of relief lit up the darkness as Delilah led Auntie Jane into the hut. The midwife pressed her hands to Epiphany's belly. She settled to her work and soon had Delilah raiding Tabitha's medicine chest for the things she would need.

'It's a shame Tabitha won't be here for the birth,' Delilah said, searching amongst the store of herbs.

'May God forgive you,' Epiphany said, laughing despite herself at the satisfaction in Delilah's voice.

'Oh, He'll forgive me,' Delilah said. 'But will she forgive *you*?' Another contraction prevented Epiphany from answering.

'A child chooses its own time,' Auntie Jane said. 'Sister Tabitha is a wise woman, she knows that.'

'Knowing is one thing, Auntie, forgiving is another,' Delilah said, unabashed.

'Tabitha isn't like you, Ma.'

'Thank God,' Delilah said.

'Oh, we do,' Epiphany said sweetly, and caught her breath as pain swept over her.

'It's time,' Auntie Jane said.

The delivery was quick and easy, and the infant – a boy, as predicted by Big Mo – began exercising his lungs as soon as the womb fluid was removed from his mouth. He became quiet immediately he was laid on his mother's breast, gazing at her with eyes that she knew well.

Auntie Jane appeared to be listening intently, 'He will be a warrior,' she said.

Epiphany nodded. 'Will you give him a name, Auntie?'

'What's the smell, Auntie?' Delilah asked from the doorway, where she kept one eye on Sheba, asleep outside, 'Is it the herbs?'

Auntie Jane's nostrils flared. 'No,' she said. '. . . it's the scent of camwood. I would recognise it anywhere, even though . . . How strange . . .' She lifted her face and turned towards the door, tears spilling from her sightless eyes.

'Auntie, choose a name,' Epiphany urged her once more.

'After all the trouble we've been through for both their sakes, they should be called the same,' Delilah said. 'Give the boy his grandfather's name. Call him Cornelius.'

'That's not our way,' Auntie Jane said.

'*Our* way?'

'Call him Abiola,' Auntie Jane said, turning to face Epiphany.

Behind her, Delilah gasped.

'Why that name, Auntie?' Epiphany asked. She could guess the reason, but she wanted it confirmed.

'It is the destiny he has chosen,' Auntie Jane said.

'Abiola . . .' Big Mo, entering with a bowl carried carefully in two hands, tested the name on her tongue. 'What does it mean?'

'It means,' said Delilah briskly as she removed the child from his mother's grasp and motioned Big Mo forward with the infusion, 'that Cornelius is meddling still.'

Delilah's cheeks were wet, Epiphany noted, as she stared hard into the baby's dark eyes before handing him once more to Auntie Jane. The old woman immediately began massaging his body and limbs with oil and at the same time deftly checking with her fingers to ensure that all was as it should be.

'Abiola means "born in honour",' Auntie Jane said. 'It signifies that this child has reclaimed his birthright, which was stolen from him.'

'Abiola. Freedom Child.' Big Mo stroked the baby's cheek with a tenderness equal to her strength. 'This one,' she said, 'has been here before.'

Auntie Jane returned Abiola clean and sweet-smelling to his mother's arms. Epiphany looked down at her son and, as he gazed gravely back at her, she was conscious of something hovering just beyond the margins of her memory, fragments of meaning which, as she tried to retrieve them, dissolved like a reflection in a pool when the surface is disturbed. She had an image then of a straight-backed figure seated on a stool, of a darkened room and polished red walls. Words formed in her mind: *We weave a pattern and we think it is the whole. Then we discover another pattern and beyond that, perhaps another. And we are only aware, it seems, because sometimes the colours run, bleeding from one into the other, as in a dream.*

Epiphany looked up to find Auntie Jane's blind eyes fixed on her.

The old woman rested her hands for a moment on Abiola's head.

'God speed, Auntie,' Epiphany said.

The midwife patted her goodbye and turned towards the door. 'I can go now,' she said.

Epiphany knew it was not the journey back to her tent she had in mind.

Delilah walked Auntie Jane up the hill and settled her comfortably in her bed as the new day was breaking.

'You're quite sure you're going up there, Auntie?' Delilah pointed her chin towards the entrance of the tent at the pink and yellow sky.

'I am quite sure, my daughter. I will be waiting for you in heaven.'

'You'll be waiting a long time.'

'Eternity is a long time,' Auntie Jane replied.

Delilah smiled. 'Even so . . .'

Auntie Jane reached out and her fingers traced the contours of Delilah's still beautiful face.

∾

5

EPIPHANY WAS AWAKE in an instant, heart racing, groping in the darkness for her son only to discover him safe at her side, sleeping soundly. But the presentiment that had propelled her from deep sleep did not diminish. Instead it gathered strength and, terrified now for the safety of her daughter and her mother, she strained, eyes wide open, to hear above the pounding of her heart. She heard nothing except the even tenor of her family breathing. Her heart slowed. But the feeling persisted that some disaster was near. Gradually she became aware that the African night had lost the use of its thousand tongues.

She pulled on a shift and slipped soundlessly outside. Candlelight spilled from many of the huts and glowed dimly inside the tents on the hillside. Lookouts paced the boundaries of the settlement, restless silhouettes against the light of the night fires. Out in the bay, illuminated in the ships' lanterns, the third watch were taking their turn on deck. The crickets, ordinarily strident until dawn, were eerily silent; no dog barked; no lizard scurried about in the undergrowth; no moth fluttered past; no rat skulked along the paths rummaging for food. Not a breath of wind rustled the leaves and even the waves spent themselves noiselessly on the sand.

Epiphany stood looking towards the ocean where all was black with no division between sky and sea. Then a rumble of distant thunder made her turn and look inland towards the mountains where sulphurous clouds were piled one upon the other. It seemed to her that the Angel of Death was poised in mid-flight between Heaven and Earth, his face turned towards her. Fear overcame her and she fled back inside the hut.

'Tabitha, is that you?' asked Delilah, accustomed to Tabitha's comings and goings in the night. The fever epidemic continued to spread and Tabitha's main employment now was tending to the sick, just as she had in Charleston.

'No, it's me.' Epiphany kept her voice low so that the children would not wake.

Delilah reached across and lit the candle on top of the chest at her elbow, revealing the absence not only of Tabitha but also of Caleb, who was out hunting most nights with Big Mo, Johnson and Carver, the council having decreed that the settlers be put on half-rations. A measure which could have been avoided, Delilah thought as she cupped a hand round the candle flame, if that parcel of incompetents had even the smallest grasp of how to conduct their business. Epiphany's expression drove the thought from her mind.

'You look demented,' Delilah told her. 'Where's the boy?'

Epiphany pointed to the baby, asleep on the pallet she and Caleb shared. She stepped carefully across the beds crowding the floor of the hut and lay down beside Abiola. She was shivering.

Concerned now, Delilah tucked a shawl round her shoulders. 'What's the matter?'

'I have seen . . .' Epiphany buried her head in her hands. 'Something frightful is about to happen.'

Delilah made a face. 'Something terrible happens here every day.'

'I have seen the Angel of Death.'

Delilah was not as unaffected by Epiphany's foreboding as she appeared. There was no denying Epiphany had second sight; even as a child she had possessed it. Furthermore on this occasion Delilah had a firm idea of what the disaster might be, which was why she had arranged a private meeting with Caleb on the pretext of fetching water from the spring.

She set off carrying two empty gourds just as the notes of the great bell signalling the end of the day's work died away. Ordinarily it was the women and children who gathered at the watering place at the cool of day break and again in the brief dusk when the worst of the heat was over, but now with so many sick the men too were obliged to take their turn. Caleb's presence would pass without comment.

Instead of walking down Water Street, Delilah chose the path along the beach even though the smell of rotting food and supplies, tainting the air of the whole settlement, was strongest there. It was nothing short of scandalous, the number of times supplies were ordered ashore and then left to rot. She could not resist the temptation however to revisit the old and discover the new. If there was a want of method in Sierra Leone, there was mismanagement in London too – whole shipments of watering cans, chamber pots and looking-glasses had been sent out when axes and hoes were in short supply. But useful or not, any cargo was immediately pilfered by the settlers or visiting Africans. Delilah covered her nose and mouth with a cloth. Even food consignments, so badly packed as to be worthless, often had something to be salvaged. Insect-infested sacks of flour, leaking casks of molasses, damp tea-leaves and weevilled biscuits could be repackaged and traded with the Africans, visiting ships' crews or even with careless company wives. If you were sharp enough.

On this occasion, though, there was nothing to be salvaged. The stink of rancid butter and spoiled pickled tripe making her retch, Delilah did not linger. She continued on her way more preoccupied than ever with thoughts of impending disaster.

Hundreds were ill, most were without proper shelter, and now famine was becoming a real prospect. The settlers were beginning to blame the waste and mismanagement not on incompetence on the part of the government, but on spitefulness and discrimination. In Nova Scotia they had shown their dissatisfaction at such treatment by leaving the country, but in Sierra Leone there was no such option.

Caleb came hurrying to meet her. She gave him the empty water gourds and led him away from the entrance of the clearing to the far side where a stream of clear water gushed down the mountainside, tumbling noisily over green-covered rocks into a large pool several feet below. Here, although in full view of the crowd, they could talk without arousing suspicion or being overheard. She sat on the grass and Caleb sat too, placing the water gourds between them.

Delilah said, 'Epiphany has had one of her visions. She says something terrible is about to happen.'

'What did she see, exactly?'

'The Angel of Death with his face turned towards us.'

Caleb made the sign of the cross. 'Us who?'

'All of us . . . in the settlement. She has seen the death of Sierra Leone.'

'My God, we're to be wiped out by the fever?'

'No. By following Thomas Peters. We'll be destroyed if we do that.'

Caleb wiped the sweat from his face, his hand shaking.

'Ah,' he said, 'you've heard about the meeting. You have it all wrong, Ma. Brother Peters doesn't want to take Mr Clarkson's place. He just wants to be his deputy. Reverend George and Johnson have both told me that it was agreed by the settler captains to make Brother Peters our representative to the council. He's to be the speaker general. You can rest easy on that one, Ma, but it still leaves –'

Delilah interrupted: 'Brother Peters may *say* he only wants to deputise for Mr Clarkson, but I don't believe him. If I was in Brother Peters' place I would want to be superintendent. And, no matter what he says, so does he.'

'Ma, our leaders can't all be mistaken.'

'The Company directors in London changed their opinion of him. They got to know of his ambitions. I learned that from those loose-tongued gossips whose linen I launder in private and they wash in public.'

'That's nothing to go by; those kind of men expect deference and when they don't receive it they read rebellion.'

Delilah looked away. 'Maybe,' she said.

'So you'll wait and see?' Caleb rose to his feet and moved towards the pool to begin filling the water gourds.

Delilah nodded. She would act without him.

Elizabeth's son was sick with the fever again and she came looking for Epiphany in the night. Tabitha was tending the child, she said, and Johnson was there too, but she wanted Epiphany with her. One glance at her friend's face in the light of the candle and Epiphany was out of the door carrying a sleeping Abiola in a sling over her shoulder. Caleb, on guard outside, wanted to accompany them, but Epiphany insisted he stay at his post. Just a few nights ago a baboon had been caught abducting a sleeping girl.

The two women found Tabitha applying an infusion-soaked cloth to the boy's burning forehead. Johnson knelt at the foot of the pallet, eyes fixed on his son's face; he did not look up. It was hot and very close inside with the mat rolled down over the entrance.

'The fever began again this evening,' Elizabeth said. She tucked the piled quilts tighter, for though the sweat was running, the child was shivering uncontrollably.

Epiphany laid a sleeping Abiola on the floor in the corner and removed the cloth from Tabitha's hands, noting how tired she was. 'You go and get some rest, Auntie. I can do this.' She dipped the cloth in the bowl, wrung it out and applied it to the boy's face as Tabitha had done. The child moaned, tossing his head from side to side on the pillow. His eyes, open but unseeing, appeared huge.

'There is a childbirth I should attend, but . . .' Tabitha glanced at Elizabeth, who managed a smile.

'Others need you too,' she said. 'But Epiphany's right: you should rest.'

Tabitha agreed to leave on condition that she would call in later. At the sound of the door flap closing, Johnson muttered as if to himself, 'I thought the fever was over and my boy quite recovered.'

'He'll recover again,' Epiphany said.

'Will he live? Have you *seen* it?' demanded Johnson.

'Our son's a fighter,' Elizabeth said when Epiphany made no reply. 'He drove off the last attack and he'll beat this one too. We mustn't give up hope . . .' Elizabeth repeated the words again and again.

Epiphany's chest constricted, her tongue locked by anxiety and guilt. She blamed herself. If it had not been for her they would never have come to Africa. Delilah had named Nova Scotia the graveyard of their dreams, but now that Epiphany had seen the Angel of Death she wondered if Sierra Leone would prove the same.

Over the days that followed, Epiphany took up permanent residence in Elizabeth and Johnson's hut. Though he tried many times, Johnson was unable to repeat his success in persuading the doctor to attend his son; so many were sick now and the whites had priority, he was told. Violent bouts of fever left the child unconscious for days at a time and any moment, it seemed, might be his last. Keeping watch with Johnson, both of them powerless to ease the boy's suffering, Epiphany was unable to keep her feelings of guilt to herself.

Johnson smiled crookedly. 'I would have come to Africa, Epiphany, with or without you. If you must blame anyone, blame your father. It's difficult to believe now, but I thought him quaint and exotic at first because he was African. Until one day, to show him up, I'm sorry to say I asked him what surprised him most about America. Do you know what he answered?'

Epiphany shook her head.

'I can hear his voice now. What surprised him most, he said, was the discovery that, in America, to be a slave was never to be a man; the colour of your face determined your place for ever. My amazement could not be measured. What I had taken for granted, he dismissed as fantastical. As I grew to know Cornelius, I can honestly say that was what I envied most about him, above all his other attributes. That was what I wanted to achieve, first for myself and then even more for my son . . .'

A piteous wail from the child brought Johnson to his feet. 'I'm going to find that doctor, and fetch him back here by whatever means.' He smacked his fist into the palm of his hand.

Walking into the room at that moment, Caleb said, 'The Company doctor is dining ashore tonight. He'll be with the officers in the canvas house . . .'

Johnson clapped Caleb on the shoulder. 'I'll get him straight away.'

'You go too, Caleb,' Epiphany urged, pouring water from the cool jar.

Johnson and Caleb passed Elizabeth and Tabitha at the door.

Elizabeth replaced Epiphany at the bedside. 'That doctor will never come.'

Tabitha measured some drops into the water. 'White people are dying too.'

Cold comfort, Epiphany thought, but she bit back the words. Of all the roads through life, Aunt Tabitha only ever saw one.

Epiphany retrieved Abiola, who had begun to stir, and retreated outside to feed him. Carver, musket across his lap, made room for her on the wooden chest near the fire. Stars stippled a rain-washed sky and the air was filled with the sounds of night and the distant echo of drums. The sick boy's twin sisters were bedded down at their feet, the two neatly braided heads close together, faces gilded in the glow of the fire. Epiphany's sense of foreboding intensified, she shifted her son from one breast to the other, silently praying, prepared to trade all hope of Salvation if only the children might be spared.

It was still dark when Caleb arrived. At the rapid approach of footsteps, Carver leapt up, gun at the ready, but when he realised who it was and that Caleb was alone, he demanded, 'Where's Johnson?'

Caleb was panting, the firelight revealed one eye badly swollen and his shirt torn. 'Johnson,' he began loudly, threw a quick glance in the direction of the hut and lowered his voice. 'Johnson's in jail. There was nearly a riot. He's been locked up for threatening the doctor.'

Epiphany was waiting with Elizabeth and her daughters outside the jailhouse as the prisoners emerged into the drenching rain. At Epiphany's request, Reverend George had approached Mr Clarkson to secure Johnson's release, but the other councillors had rejected the appeal despite being informed of his son's desperate condition. Now though, with half the population in the grip of the fever, it was patently foolish to have able-bodied men sitting idle. All prisoners were being released.

Johnson appeared at first so shrunken and insubstantial Epiphany fancied it was his ghost walking towards her, but then she realised it was his inner self that she had glimpsed.

He almost passed by without realising and only looked up when Elizabeth put out her hand.

She faced him squarely as his daughters clung to him. 'Our boy is gone.' She put her arms round her husband. 'Peacefully, in his sleep.'

Epiphany watched through tears; Elizabeth's composure was heartbreaking. Not a word of blame had she uttered these past weeks, there had been no recriminations and no railing against her fate. Delilah, who had been there at the end, put it down to bad luck, pure and simple. Delilah saw chance, where Epiphany saw a pattern. The child had died for a reason that had yet to be revealed.

'Reverend George gave your son a true Christian burial,' Elizabeth said. 'And we've marked his grave with stones.'

Johnson said flatly, 'His is not the only life that's finished –'

'No!' Elizabeth cried. 'Don't say that, we still have our lives and our daughters.'

Johnson disengaged himself and went to stare at the rain-veiled ships anchored in the harbour. Epiphany and Elizabeth followed him. 'First Cornelius and now my son,' he muttered.

Elizabeth slipped an arm through his. 'Come home.'

'I will,' he said. 'But not just now. If I come face to face with the doctor, I shall surely kill him – or any other white man, for that matter. And I dare say they don't deserve to die any more than my Samuel did. You'll hear from me by and by, I promise.'

Johnson bent to kiss both his daughters, then, straightening, he embraced Epiphany. Finally he held Elizabeth for a long time. Releasing her, he said, 'I have to see what will come to me.'

Epiphany thought his rage dangerously cold. The Angel of Death might have passed on, but they were still in his shadow.

6

LONG BEFORE SUNRISE small knots of settlers had been making their way towards the square of levelled ground midway up Thornton Hill. The trickle soon swelled into a steady stream. It was a painful struggle for many, overcome from time to time with bouts of trembling, clearly in the grip of the fever. Equally evident was their determination to witness an historic occasion.

Daybreak brought with it a cloudless blue sky and a fresh wind blowing from inland, carrying the sweet, green, forest smell of the rainy season in place of the white salt tang of the sea. The crowd had an expectant air as people toiled up the hill, the men wearing their Sunday shirts and breeches, the women in their best petticoats, heads tied with their brightest kerchiefs. They might have been going to church except, Epiphany thought, that their cheerfulness was not, as on a Sunday, of people certain of salvation; it was more the defiant gaiety of confessed sinners. All her family were there: Caleb, on one side; Elizabeth on the other; Delilah, Tabitha, Big Mo and Carver. No one had seen Johnson since his release from jail but, as Elizabeth said, he was almost certainly in the forest somewhere, licking his wounds.

Epiphany studiously avoided catching anyone's eye. The truth was she felt ashamed, having been at first so vocal against attending. Why, she'd asked, could Mr Clarkson not have found some other way of proving his good faith? She'd declared categorically that, no matter how they reasoned, the event would only diminish them all. She had discovered, however, that deep down the thought of the tables being turned filled her with a secret vengeful pleasure, which had given rise to an irresistible urge to be present even though she knew it was wrong.

Everyone in the colony – settlers, Company officials, ships' captains and crews – had been summoned to witness the spectacle. As soon as they were all assembled, a drum roll claimed the crowd's attention. A small procession entered the square; at its head the superintendent, Mr Clarkson, accompanied by the councillors, attired as ever in their green-and-gold uniforms. They were followed by three prisoners under guard and the public flogger in a fine buff coat and breeches issued by the Company. A black tricorn hat was pulled low over his face.

The three white Company sailors were to receive ninety-seven, sixty-seven and forty-six lashes respectively for disobeying an order to take their ship's cutter upriver to collect roof thatch for the settlers' huts. The public flogger being a settler, it was clear to everyone that the sailors were being made an example of, and the severity of their sentences was to serve as proof that justice was even-handed in Sierra Leone.

The militiamen presented arms and a cacophony of startled birds erupted from the branches of the surrounding trees.

'It's not right,' said Tabitha, who resolutely refused to manoeuvre for a better view.

Standing on tiptoe, Delilah said, '*My* heart is rejoicing at the prospect of seeing a white man flogged by a black one. Although I can't decide which I'll enjoy the more, the sight of *them* screaming' – she pointed her chin towards the prisoners in the centre of the square – 'or of *them* squirming with the shame and humiliation of it all' – her chin tilted towards the white spectators. 'I never thought to see this day as long as I lived. *This* was worth travelling halfway across the world for.'

Elizabeth shook her head sadly. '*This* just shows we've sunk to their level.'

'I could go lower.' Delilah's eyes glittered with relish. 'I only wish it was Carver who was giving the lashes.'

'Me too,' Caleb said, glancing at Epiphany, who could not meet his eye.

Carver shifted uncomfortably but he did not disagree.

'Vengeance belongs to the Lord,' Tabitha said. 'We should remember that.'

'Yes, yes, you're a saint, Tabitha, but we can't all be.' Delilah made an adjustment to her elaborate head-tie. 'Besides, if you think it's so wrong, why are you here?'

'I have a duty to bear witness.'

Mr Clarkson finished his address, bringing all talk to a halt. They had not heard a word he said. At a signal from him two soldiers marched the first prisoner to the middle of the square and tied him to the whipping post. The crowd strained for a better view and in the square the silence stretched tight as the flogger, having doffed his coat and hat, measured the distance. He swung his arm and the whip uncoiled. It left a runnel of blood that showed startlingly red against the prisoner's pallid flesh.

Epiphany glanced instinctively at Caleb and flinched at the expression on his face. She had seen that ugly gloating countless times on white faces in Virginia and, recalling how faithfully white children had reflected that ugliness, she took some comfort from having remained adamant that her daughter should not be present. The prisoner sagged against the whipping post, his features horribly contorted, biting on the bullet between his teeth, as an identical stripe was drawn below the first. The whip struck again, viciously, and again, until there were six slanting weals marking the skin from shoulder to hip. Powerful and deliberate, the flogger moved now to stand on the opposite side of his victim, passing in front of him in order to look into his face and assess his condition. Satisfied, he positioned himself carefully and once more raised the whip over his left shoulder then brought it down with his whole strength until another six stripes crossed the first set diagonally from left to right. The flogger's hair dripped, his shirt, sweat-soaked and transparent, clung to him, revealing the flesh on his back, which was neatly divided in a raised diamond pattern like the crust on a pie. Epiphany gave a loud cry. If, before, there had seemed something oddly familiar, there was, now, no mistaking the flogger's identity. It was Johnson, methodically reproducing the bold latticework that had been the specialty of the overseer on the Fairlawns Plantation.

Swaying on her feet, Elizabeth would have fallen had Carver not caught her. Simultaneously the prisoner broke, the bullet fell from his mouth and he screamed. Johnson's shoulders drooped and his arm fell to his side, the whip dangling on the ground.

Rigid with remorse herself, Epiphany felt she knew Johnson's mind exactly and that, if he could read hers, his would be eased. She willed him to look up and when he did she locked eyes with him. *I know we have failed to measure up to Cornelius, but I also know that now is the moment to look the leopard in the eye, accept the truth of what this says about us, and walk away free to become the people we know we can be.*

'Ma! Ma!' a voice called out and Epiphany, who had until that moment been oblivious to the commotion round her, turned sharply and saw her daughter Sheba and Elizabeth's twins pushing through the crowd. Appalled, she immediately began shepherding them away, with Elizabeth and Tabitha following close behind her.

'Let them stay,' Delilah said. 'The fun's not nearly over yet.'

Aside from Abiola, asleep in the hut, Epiphany was alone. She glanced warily at an overcast sky; the squat clouds promised yet more rain but not, she concluded, until the evening. Resignedly she turned over the garments spread out to air on an improvised clotheshorse. In the ubiquitous dampness, cloth rotted, leather became mouldy and iron rusty if they were not carefully tended. She stirred the contents of the large black pot simmering on the fire and resumed her seat, her mind occupied by recent events.

After the flogging, the evening service at Reverend George's house had been packed and the atmosphere almost as charged as it had been on Thornton Hill. It was soon common knowledge that Brother Johnson, elder of the Baptist congregation, had wielded the whip. By evening there could not have been a single settler in ignorance of the substitution. The Methodist and the Huntingdonian churches had also been filled to overflowing, despite the desertion of considerable numbers to the Baptists. Many had come just to touch Johnson's hand and thereby share the power they now felt was invested in him. They knew full well that, though he might have been prompted by the death of his son, his action had been in retribution for the beatings they had all suffered. And he had come away unscathed. But it had been equally evident to Epiphany that, like her, many had come in search of absolution.

Reverend George had not disappointed. Before making way for Brother Johnson, he reminded his flock of the joy in Heaven at the one sinner who repented. Johnson had stepped forward, head bowed, and humbly begged God's pardon for taking it upon himself to avenge the death of his son. He then asked forgiveness for failing to set an example as an elder of the church and a leader of the community. Reverend

George declared that every one of them had failed to live up to their own standards, but if God could forgive, so should they.

Forgive, but not forget, Epiphany thought. She placed more wood on the fire and sat down for a moment, watching the steam spiralling up from the cooking pot towards the sloping thatch. Deep in thought, she was unaware of Johnson's presence until she heard him say her name.

Startled, she said, 'I was just thinking of you.' She made room on the chest.

'And I of you.' Johnson sat down beside her.

It was odd how your eyes and mind play tricks, Epiphany thought. Johnson had seemed ten feet tall on Thornton Hill on the day of the flogging, yet in church afterwards he had appeared small and vulnerable. Now, sitting next to her, he was his normal size again.

She said, 'Our days of righteousness are gone.'

Johnson nodded, his eyes on the ground. 'Some would say freedom has made white men of us all.'

'Not me.' Epiphany was emphatic. 'And you neither. We've looked the leopard in the eye . . .

Johnson glanced up. 'I know, and I'm beholden to you.'

Epiphany took his hands in both of hers. 'We know that though we've slipped and fallen we don't have to wallow in the mire.'

Johnson squeezed her hands. 'I used to imagine that Cornelius and I were walking the same path and that, once he was gone, I would continue on it alone. But since my boy passed on, I've realised that we each have our own path. Cornelius's and mine were just running side by side.'

Epiphany nodded; she needed no convincing that the child had been taken for a reason.

'Do you remember, back in Nova Scotia, you said that freedom was the country we would map?' Johnson asked.

Epiphany nodded.

'We began well: by coming here to Sierra Leone to set a Christian example to the Africans we marked the ending of slavery. But now we're in danger of letting others chart the rest.'

Epiphany nodded again; she could guess where this was leading. Deliberately or not, there was no denying that the settlers had been lured to Africa under false pretences; now their English benefactors had them in their power, they saw no need to honour their pledges.

Johnson continued: 'Once the slave trade is ended, a new pattern will be set in Africa. And as sure as night follows day, that pattern will be determined according to how we blacks have gone on here in Sierra Leone.'

Epiphany recalled the words of the old African woman, who, on seeing the cannons unloaded on to the beach, had declared that the strangers had come to take her land from her. Mr Clarkson had denied it, of course, and Epiphany believed him, but then she had also believed his promise of a share in the government.

She said, 'The councillors have shown they can picture our kind as free, but I doubt they can picture us as equal.'

'We have to make them; otherwise they'll continue to sue in honour and act in dishonour. And they will discover the lie of the land before us. We have to act right away.'

'What do you propose?'

'The settler captains have voted to make Thomas Peters our representative to the council, and in due course, Mr Clarkson's deputy.'

Thank God, Epiphany thought, cool heads had prevailed over those who wanted rid of the government entirely.

'I do believe that partnership is the way forward,' she replied. 'What do you want from me?'

'Speak to Caleb, he's close to Reverend George and he has influence with the younger men.'

Almost as soon as Johnson had departed, Tabitha and Elizabeth arrived with Elizabeth's twin daughters for the midday meal. The girls had spent the morning assisting Tabitha on her rounds. Observing the children closely Epiphany noted with sadness that their faces had lost that open look of untouched sand; a wind-blown smoothness as of tracks covered over had taken its place.

Delilah arrived soon afterwards with Sheba. They had been working in the storehouse. Essential courtesies aside, Epiphany had not spoken to her mother since the day of the flogging and neither had Elizabeth. Delilah continued to maintain that Johnson's action was cause for celebration, not hypocritical breast-beating. She had not denied responsibility for the children's presence in the square, nor was she in the least repentant. And, unforgivably, Epiphany thought, her defiance had extended to contradicting Elizabeth in front of her daughters.

As Delilah sank gracefully on to a wooden chest, her smile conveying that she knew she must be forgiven eventually, Epiphany and Elizabeth busied themselves serving the food, ladling it into shallow gourds for the girls to pass round. Tabitha attempted to lighten the atmosphere by recounting the events of her morning round, but being a catalogue of the sick and dying it had quite the opposite effect. Epiphany jumped up. She had decided, she said, to take Abiola for an airing along the beach and, resisting the clamour of the three girls to accompany her, she promised to return in good time to assist in Tabitha's newly planted garden.

'If you see Caleb on your walk,' Delilah called after her, 'tell him I'd like to speak to him.'

Epiphany nodded without looking back.

Caleb climbed down from the roof of the hut he was thatching. 'Nothing wrong, I hope?' He dandled Abiola in the air.

Epiphany shook her head. She was surprised to find Caleb alone.

Johnson, Carver and Big Mo had moved on to the next hut, where they were to eat their midday meal. He would be joining them shortly, he told her.

Epiphany admired his handiwork. Johnson had taught him well, she thought, but did not say, as she might once have done. Instead she said, 'I've a message from Delilah. She wants you to meet her when you've finished for the day. I wonder what she wants?'

'You should have asked her.' Caleb grinned and pointed out a passing butterfly to Abiola.

'I'm not speaking to her, as well you know.' Epiphany smiled despite herself. Serious again, she said, 'It pains me to say it, but . . . at times my mother doesn't seem to know right from wrong.'

'That's harsh.' Caleb cradled Abiola in his arms.

'I should have known you'd take her part.'

Caleb did not answer.

'Are we all to take orders from my mother now? In future, should I tell our children to go to her?'

'It wasn't Delilah; it was me. I decided the children should be there.'

Epiphany stared, wordless. She snatched Abiola from Caleb's arms.

'I wanted them to learn that the white man is not invincible,' Caleb said.

Epiphany shook her head incredulously. 'You sound exactly like Delilah.'

Caleb bristled. 'I do not.'

'A Christian upbringing will teach the children the same lesson.'

'You truly believe that?'

251

'Yes, I do. And I thought you did too.'

Caleb walked a few paces and turned. 'Telling is one thing, Epiphany, showing is another. Seeing a black man wield the whip on the back of a white man is worth any number of sermons in church.'

Epiphany rocked Abiola back and forth. 'I'm disappointed in you, Caleb; I imagined you to be more ambitious for your children than becoming mere slave masters and overseers. I thought you wanted them to be free.'

'You're deliberately misunderstanding me.'

'I think not.'

Caleb glanced up at the drifting clouds. 'The chains that bind the mind are not easily broken.'

'I agree. Nothing binds us more securely to the past than failing to learn from it. Caleb, we have to forgive, or at least, not to take revenge, not to exercise power simply because we can.'

'I prefer to forgive from a position of strength.'

'That kind of strength is a house built on sand, and about as dependable as your word. Have you forgotten what Cornelius said? We are *all* children of the same mother.'

Epiphany turned to leave.

Caleb barred the way and brought his face close to hers. 'I changed my mind. And I would do the same again. I am not answerable either to your father or to you. Do you hear me?' He was shouting.

Abiola, crushed between them in his sling, started to cry.

'I hear you.'

Epiphany pushed past Caleb. She remembered a crystal glass that had broken on her very first day up at the big house at Fairlawns and the realisation that, even though she held all the pieces in her hand, the glass could never be restored. Such was her shock at Caleb's betrayal that she quite forgot her promise to Johnson.

Caleb, his work over for the day, cast a weather eye as he descended the steep incline from Water Street to keep his appointment with Delilah at the landing place. It was all but deserted and he watched the last stragglers, anxious to reach home before dark, hastily loading up. He could not but admire the way the Africans sent their long canoes skimming between the tall ships into the wide mouth of the river beyond the harbour and out to sea. He waited patiently until a canoe left the anchored ships and drew up beside him. The single oarsman secured the

252

boat while Caleb scrambled to help the only passenger lift out two large baskets full of dirty linen and haul them up the sand.

Having dismissed her boatman, Delilah set off across the beach, dragging a laundry basket behind her. She said, 'I've made my move against Thomas Peters.'

'But you said you'd wait,' Caleb said, following with the other basket.

'Did I?' Delilah shrugged. 'I changed my mind.'

'What have you done?'

'You'll have to wait and see.'

'Ma,' Caleb said exasperatedly, 'we can't work together unless you take me fully into your confidence.'

'Before I can do that, I must be sure of you, Caleb. You have to choose.'

'I *have* chosen,' Caleb said.

Delilah was late, arriving at the meeting just as Mr Clarkson was about to depart. Caleb, who had been looking out for her, was unaware of her presence until she was right beside him. He glanced at her warily; when she wanted, Delilah could make herself noticed in a host of a thousand, but if she wanted not to be seen you could miss her in a crowd of one.

'So?' Delilah asked.

Caleb seemed not to have heard.

She nudged him and asked again: 'Well? What happened at the meeting?'

'I think you know.'

'Know what?' Delilah appeared mystified.

'How could she know? She wasn't here.' Big Mo shook her head reproachfully at Caleb and turned to Delilah. 'Mr Clarkson got it into his head that Brother Peters here' – Big Mo jerked a thumb in Brother Peters' direction – 'planned to usurp his place as superintendent. He had it on good authority, he said, and, if it should be proved, one or other of them would hang from that very tree you see before you.'

'My God!' Delilah patted her chest as if to calm her heart. 'What did Brother Peters say?'

'Not a word,' Big Mo said.

'The settler captains spoke for him,' Caleb said. He looked meaningfully at Delilah. 'And they were all agreed that Mr Clarkson's informants had got it wrong. And –'

'The informants were *your* people,' someone shouted, pointing at Reverend George.

'Shut your mouth.' One of Reverend George's followers squared up to him.

'I'd bet my life on it.'

'You'll not live long then.' Reverend George's man shoved him in the chest and they sprang at each other.

Supporters on both sides joined in. Johnson and Carver immediately intervened, leaping in to stop the fighting. And Big Mo, seeing two men brought down amidst accusations that they were the informants, rushed to their aid.

Caleb had caught the glance Delilah gave the two suspects.

'Ma!' he said. 'You promised to take me into your confidence.'

'In future I will.' Delilah looked him straight in the eye.

After a pause, Caleb nodded.

As Caleb ran to join the fight, jumping on the back of one of Johnson's assailants and grappling him to the ground, Delilah stayed on the sidelines, a dainty contrast to the mud-covered combatants.

'Whose side are you on, Caleb?' Johnson lifted a red-smeared face.

'Same as you, Johnson.' Caleb twisted his victim's arm, making him yell.

'Which side would that be?'

Which indeed? Caleb thought, aware of Carver watching him closely.

Carver banged two heads together and, as their owners fell unconscious into the mud, he said, 'Seems Brother Peters should watch his back.'

'Seems he's not the only one,' Caleb said.

Brother Peters sickened and died shortly thereafter, of a broken heart it was said, following a conviction for theft. He had been accused by a fellow war veteran. It was said the war veteran had been set up. And that Mr Clarkson was entirely blameless. But it was a fact that Mr Clarkson had a clear run from then on.

7

TWO YEARS ON, life was sweet. Delilah had been wont to compare her situation in Sierra Leone with what it might have been in Massachusetts. If only she had been in Boston, she used to tell herself, she would have repeated the success of Charleston. But she knew differently now, and the proof was weighing down her purse.

As she threw open the last of the shutters in the storehouse where she worked, pale dawn light slanted in on all sides. She leaned her elbows on the windowsill and looked out over the waterfront, jingling the coins in her pocket. She could never have secured such a loan in Nova Scotia, which took its cue from its slave-owning neighbours. The interest was crippling, of course, but even so, if your hands were free there was always the potential to use them to untie your feet.

The shouts of the porters and store men on the wharf below mingled with the sound of praying from the church next door. Inaugurating public prayers, morning and evening, signalled by the great bell, had been one of Mr Clarkson's successor's first acts and each of the governors who followed – there had been three in as many years – had continued the practice. The prayers were to remind people that Sierra Leone was supposed to be a religious colony, but all it had achieved, Delilah thought, was to provide an excuse for workers turning up late. She had not been one of those who had been grief-stricken when Mr Clarkson left for England, but compared to the two who had come after him he seemed an angel in disguise.

The settlers had sent a couple of representatives to London to put their grievances before the directors and had received short shrift. But, as Delilah said at the time, what did they expect from people who had appointed a former officer of a penal colony and a one-time overseer of a West Indian sugar plantation to govern a free black settlement?

As well as hot heads like Johnson, moderates such as Reverend George had also signed the petition the delegates took with them to England. With all opinions represented, the Company had been persuaded to agree to one small concession, abandoning its monopoly of the retail trade.

A smile spread across Delilah's face. She was one of the few settlers to be allowed credit and a licence to set up shop. The profits she had made had funded the building of a house on the farm Caleb had won in the first country lottery, as well as a modest expansion of the other enterprises in which the entire family was engaged. They were chameleons all. After she had finished in the storehouse, Delilah – lady's maid, laundress and caterer – now turned shopkeeper in her own small store. Big Mo, after her work as a day labourer, assisted with the heavy laundering and cooking, as well as running their market stall. After teaching in school, Elizabeth became laundress and lady's maid, while Epiphany and Tabitha, who also taught in school, grew the vegetables in both town and country for the Company officers' tables and the market stall. The children were not spared. After lessons they went looking for specimens; the Company's botanist paid a halfpenny for butterflies and sixpence for large bats.

With this loan, Delilah thought, she would build a boat in which she could trade a hundred miles or more along the coast. She could bring in rice, cattle, camwood, ivory, even gold, and provide her family with the independence their farm was to have secured. Whoever had said that the settlers could live off the land in Sierra Leone had got their facts wrong. Even if they had received their full allotment, they could never have become self-sufficient for the soil was mostly poor. As it was, settlers had been obliged to make do with farms a fifth of the size promised. Local chiefs had demanded not only that they be paid twice but also that the original grant of land be reduced to a strip a mere two by six miles deep along the coast. With Freetown surrounded on all sides by Africans, Mr Clarkson had had no option but to agree, in order to keep their neighbours sweet. Personally, Delilah favoured trading over farming; she found the jingle of coins as pretty as any birdsong.

She had been entrusted, since the institution of public prayers, with the responsibility of opening and closing up the stores. The storekeeper handed her the key at the church door before the service in the morning and she gave it back to him after the service in the evening. This way, she conceded dryly, he killed two birds with one stone; he not only showed off his piety, but, as everyone knew she had the key, he also placed a limit on her unofficial borrowings from the shelves.

She was about to turn away from the storehouse window through which, absorbed in thought, she had been looking but not seeing, when she became aware that the sound of prayers no longer emanated from the church next door and the noise rising from below had altered in tenor. Glancing down and seeing a large crowd gathered on the waterfront, she hastened out, locking the door behind her; since her pocket was already full of coins, she slipped the large iron key, cold against her skin, safely inside her bodice.

In the midst of the throng on the beach Epiphany felt a flicker of apprehension. Such was the climate under the present governor, even the slightest incident could end in uproar. The last time everyone had been gathered together like this, barely two months past, a riot had ensued. It had been the worst yet. Threats were made against the governor's life and the colony had been brought to the brink of rebellion. Instinctively she looked across at Johnson, standing at a distance with Elizabeth. He must have sensed her apprehension for he gave a reassuring smile.

Delilah caught the smile as she squeezed between Epiphany and Caleb. She glowered at Johnson. Since the death of Thomas Peters the rift between the two of them had deepened, and things had come to a head during the recent uprising. Methodists to a man, the insurgents had tried to persuade a local chief to enter the fray on their behalf; had Johnson not dissuaded the chief, the governor's troops would certainly have been overthrown. Convinced, however, that Johnson's purpose had been quite the contrary, Delilah was only prevented from denouncing him by Epiphany's threat publicly to declare herself a rebel – a move that would have destroyed the family's credibility with Reverend George's Baptists, who had taken the government's side. By dissuading the chief, Johnson had left Epiphany in no doubt of his commitment to partnership.

'Has the governor declared a holiday?' Delilah enquired sarcastically.

'Look –' Caleb pointed out to sea.

A fleet of ships was moving into the harbour. Epiphany glanced over her shoulder towards the governor's residence and caught sight of the governor on his verandah with some of his colleagues, watching the arrival of this strange fleet. It must be a friendly invasion, she thought. Relieved, she turned back.

And, as if in confirmation, Caleb said, 'They're flying British colours.'

The crowd cheered and Abiola, perched on his father's shoulders, clapped his hands excitedly, at which his sister Sheba clamoured to be lifted up too.

'My God!' It was Big Mo speaking. 'Do you see what I see?'

They all strained forward as she pointed. 'There's a man on that frigate aiming a cannon at the governor's house!'

'He can't be,' Caleb said. 'Those are British ships, they're even rigged the British way. In any case, how would they know which is the governor's house?'

Epiphany rolled her eyes. 'Perhaps because his house has the Sierra Leone Company flag flying from it?'

Delilah laughed and linked arms with Epiphany. 'Big Mo,' she said, 'your eyes are deceiving you.'

A shot whistled overhead. Caleb and Carver whisked the children from their shoulders and Epiphany swivelled in consternation to see the governor and his party speedily withdraw inside the house. Moments later, the Sierra Leone flag was lowered and a white cloth draped over the verandah. She swung round to face the sea again in expectation that the flag of truce would be honoured. Instead there was a spurt of flame followed by an explosion. Someone screamed and blood from the bodies of a woman and child, dismembered in the blast, spattered the sand. Shells bursting all around them, people ran shrieking in panic and trampling one another in the scramble to escape as the wounded cried for help.

In the ensuing turmoil, Carver somehow shepherded the family safely home where the men grabbed their guns and rushed out again to report with the rest of the militia to the governor's house.

The children huddled close, shocked into silence.

Epiphany closed the door, lessening the noise of the firing only slightly. Very dryly she said, 'Reckon they aren't British after all.'

Delilah laughed distractedly.

Big Mo gave a grim smile. 'Whoever they are, they don't fight fair.'

Tabitha said, shock in her voice, 'They ignored the white flag, firing on innocent women and children . . .'

Epiphany said, 'We should leave town and go to the farm as quickly as possible. But first I must fetch Elizabeth, I'm not leaving without her.'

'Nor I,' Tabitha said.

Delilah asked, 'Have you *seen* something Epiphany?'

'No, Ma,' Epiphany replied impatiently, her hand on the door latch.

'All right, all right.' Delilah threw up her hands. 'Fetch Elizabeth. You can go on with the children. Big Mo and I will follow.'

Epiphany hid a smile. Her mother was not about to leave her worldly goods behind until it became an absolute necessity.

*

Epiphany, Tabitha, Elizabeth and the children set off for the farm, laden with as much as they could carry from Delilah's shop: flour, tea, oatmeal, sugar, barley, molasses – all imported goods, which, as Delilah pointed out, should the present crisis be prolonged, could be used for barter. They joined a host of women and children and old folk fleeing the town in desperate disorder with whatever belongings they could muster.

'I propose,' Delilah said, once she and Big Mo were alone, 'that we wait to see how the wind blows. I've rum and glassware in the shop, bought on credit. I can't afford to be robbed.'

'My lone musket will be no protection against looters. We'd lose our lives as well as the rum and then our loved ones would be burdened with funeral expenses besides their debts. Better we flee now.'

'No. We'd have our men to help us. Let's at least wait for them.'

While Big Mo was busy packing some stores, Delilah slipped outside, past Tabitha's neat rows of vegetables to the kitchen, which stood separate from the little house. The noise of the continuing bombardment was deafening and the smoke-thick air infused with the smell of saltpetre made her throat close as she bent to lift two of the hearthstones. She swiftly removed the stash of money that not even Caleb knew existed, and as quickly restored the stones before returning inside.

'You're right,' she told Big Mo. 'Let's go.'

As Delilah and Big Mo made their way out of Freetown the crackling of wooden buildings in flames was an ominous counterpoint to the bursts of cannon-fire. They made slow progress and it was well into the afternoon by the time they arrived at the farm. Big Mo wondered aloud whether Delilah was perhaps not quite herself. Delilah, who, besides being hung about with great jars of rum, had large amounts of coin hidden about her person, put a hand to her forehead. 'This trouble weighs heavier on me than you can know.'

Caleb, Carver and Johnson arrived with the darkness the following day.

Epiphany said, 'Johnson, this is your house and Elizabeth's for as long as you need.'

'I've already told him,' Caleb muttered, aggrieved.

She said, 'Come, sit Caleb,' and drew him down beside her. She loved him no less than before, but now she saw his weaknesses more clearly. Sitting at the long wooden table in the soft lamplight, Johnson recounted

259

the story. The invaders were a French squadron, piloted into the harbour by two American slave ship captains. The French commander, his fleet already increased by a number of British prizes, needed little encouragement to ransack the colony, which he considered to be English and fair game, the two countries being at war. From the moment they landed the sailors rampaged through the town, pillaging everything they could lay their hands on – even the clothes from people's backs. What they could not steal they smashed. The settlers should have put up a fight instead of surrendering, Johnson said. True, the colony's few defences were ultimately no match for a hundred and thirty twelve-pound cannons and fifteen hundred men. But if the French, more a disorderly rabble than a formidable fighting force, had met with resistance at the outset they might well have been driven off.

Delilah said scornfully, 'It's just because you like a fight, Johnson –'

She was interrupted by the sound of voices outside, where Big Mo stood guard.

'I bet it's those Frenchmen.' Caleb leapt from his seat and reached for his gun.

'I'm surprised they'd travel out this far.' Johnson kept his voice low. The men started for the door.

'Stop,' Epiphany commanded in a loud whisper. They whirled round. 'Best you hide. Let them think we're just a parcel of women. *Then* come out and surprise them.'

'Good girl!' Delilah rose to her feet and, a finger to her lips, waved the children towards the back room then beckoned the men to follow them. 'I'll go.'

Epiphany, Tabitha and Elizabeth moved to sit close together and Delilah marched to the door, pulling her bodice down to expose her shoulders as she did so.

Outside she found Big Mo. The huge young woman was standing with a gun pointed at four Company officials blinking up at her in the light of the lantern. They looked, Delilah thought, as if they might die of fright – whether at the sight of Big Mo and her musket or because of what had happened in Freetown, it was difficult to know. One of them was Delilah's storekeeper.

Turning aside the muzzle of Big Mo's gun, Delilah hitched her bodice back into place and welcomed the visitors warmly. 'Can't you see it's my storekeeper and his wife?' she hissed at Big Mo, as she drew them across the yard and into the house.

The visitors started violently when Johnson, Caleb and Carver emerged from the back room, muskets in hand. Epiphany felt genuinely sorry for them. With the settler riot still fresh in their minds, you couldn't blame them for thinking they might have jumped out of the pan only to land in the fire.

Revived by a cup of rum and water, the storekeeper found his voice. 'We, the Europeans, are bearing the brunt of the terror. We've been stripped and beaten and driven from our homes by these Frenchies. Damn Jacobins, every one of them.' He drained a second cup.

Equally indignant, his wife tearfully took up the tale. 'We had to run for our lives with nothing but the clothes we stand up in. Imagine! While you blacks have been largely spared.'

The storekeeper shrugged. 'It's understandable, I suppose. Boney has a quarrel only with the *English*, after all. I heard the governor say the exact same thing to the French commander. It's him you have to thank.'

Tabitha said stiffly, 'We are all Christian subjects of His Majesty King George.'

Epiphany, her compassion spent, caught her husband's ironic glance.

'"Out of the abundance of the heart the mouth speaketh,"' she said, slyly. 'St Matthew, chapter twelve, verse thirty-four.'

The colour came and went in the storekeeper's wife's pale cheeks.

Delilah stifled a chuckle.

Epiphany smiled to herself; even her mother knew how that particular verse began. 'O generation of vipers, how can ye, being evil, speak good things?' It was one of Reverend George's favourites. Her spirits lifted. If the French had no quarrel with the black settlers, their worldly goods might yet be saved.

Delilah waited until Carver had relinquished the nightwatch to Caleb and was sleeping soundly on the other side of the curtain put up for the benefit of the storekeeper's wife. She crept from her bed and, silent as the moonlight, padded outside. Caleb turned, alerted by the click of the latch.

'We have work to do,' Delilah whispered.

Caleb raised an eyebrow.

'A burial,' Delilah said.

'How much?'

Delilah grinned. 'All that was in the strong box and then some.'

'Where from?'

'A loan I secured. There's a spade out the back. Now, give me the gun.'

Caleb worked fast. He dug a hole and, returning silently, held out his hand for the strong box.

'Oh, no, you don't,' said Delilah. 'Here, you stand guard and look the other way. It's my money and I'll stash it myself.'

She came back smiling. 'I kept some back for show. No one would believe I'd ever leave Freetown without my money.'

'You can't expect me to help you if you keep me in the dark,' Caleb said roughly. 'So tell me, will you? How much did you borrow?'

'Twenty guineas.'

Caleb whistled.

'Let's keep it between ourselves.' Delilah patted his arm. She still had her other secret, the money she had rescued from under the kitchen floor.

Each day the men journeyed from the farm into Freetown, deserted now save for settlers like themselves bent on salvaging what they could. At the farm, Delilah fretted. She worried about her property, and especially the goods she had secured on credit. Every evening when the men returned, the stories they recounted were worse than the day before.

With nothing to restrain them, the invaders ran amok. All the shops were looted, every house broken into and plundered, and all the coin stolen. Having driven out the people, they killed the livestock, shooting pigs, poultry, dogs, cats, as they went. Furniture, books, papers, the new printing press, the library, telescopes and barometers were deliberately smashed. They broke every single bottle in the apothecary's shop and uprooted the botanical garden. Then they razed the buildings, beginning with the governor's house. They burnt the church, the school, the two hospitals, the storehouses, the government officers' homes. Every one of the Company buildings and eight of its ships were utterly destroyed.

The storekeeper looked meaningfully at Johnson. 'This is what revolution brings,' he said.

'Tyranny,' Johnson replied, 'produces the same result.'

On the following evening the men reported that the French were preparing to leave and should be gone the next day.

'Well, Praise be to God that the settler homes still stand,' the storekeeper said.

He was a good man, Tabitha declared, and shook his hand.

Even so, Johnson warned, as the French Commander had failed to control his men, it would be tempting fate for the women to venture into town.

'A fate worse than death.' The storekeeper's wife shuddered.

Delilah looked at her witheringly. 'Plenty here could tell you otherwise.'

Carver arrived unexpectedly at the farm in the middle of the afternoon. Delilah was playing at hoops with her grandchildren on the small bamboo-fringed clearing at the side of the house.

'The French have gone.' Carver mopped his face; his shirt was soaked.

'Good riddance. But why are you here now? What is it that couldn't wait until this evening?' She sent the little ones to fetch water.

'The French fired some settler houses last night. By mistake, they say –'

'No!' Delilah clutched his arm. 'No!'

'Yes.' Carver held her tightly. 'Ten altogether; including both of ours.'

They left the farm at first light, umbrellas fending off the morning downpour. The wet season being almost at an end, the rain was not prolonged, and when the showers died away the umbrellas gave equal protection from the sun. A mass of white clouds fluttering against the newly rinsed blue appeared to Delilah like rows of fresh linen hung out to dry. Humming birds darted among the flowers, parrots swooped and chattered in the trees. There seemed little amiss until the first taint of putrefaction caught her; by the time they approached the outskirts of Freetown, it reached long fingers down her throat making her gag. Decomposing animals lay on the road and littered the gardens on either side. More were sprawled among the weeds and unharvested fruit and vegetables. Covering her nose and mouth she looked about her. The wooden houses, their doors and window shutters hanging open, stared empty-eyed and dishevelled, as if aghast at the brutal violation of their town. All that was left of the governor's house were the foundations. Amid the charred ruins of her own house the red laterite columns stuck out from the ground like headstones in a graveyard.

When Carver had brought her the awful news, she'd heard the words clearly enough but she had not believed them, indeed could not, until she had seen for herself. Epiphany and Big Mo were huddled together, both of them in tears. Delilah glanced across at them impatiently. When Tabitha had been told she had simply observed that nobody had died, electing to remain behind with the children and the storekeeper and his wife. The white couple categorically refused to leave the farm until the governor was once again in residence in the capital. Only then would they consider it safe to return.

In agreement with Tabitha for once, Delilah said, '*This* is not something to sob about. When Auntie Sam was snatched, *that* was a crying matter. When Cornelius was shot and killed, that was a crying matter. What we have here isn't to do with the heart, it concerns the head; something to think about.'

'Our tears are for you, Ma,' Epiphany said, '*not* for the house.'

Big Mo blew her nose. 'Actually it's a *back* matter. And backs is what we'll need for the rebuilding. What do you think, Caleb?'

Caleb angrily stirred the ashes with the toe of his boot. 'I think things come in threes: Elizabeth and Johnson's house, completely destroyed. Our house, gone. I ask myself, what's next?'

Epiphany said, 'Cornelius used to say that in each thing is its opposite. I see in these ashes a beautiful mansion, bigger and better than was here before. And why . . .?' She gave Caleb a sideways look. 'Because we already have the means. *You* should know that.'

On their daily visits to Freetown during the French occupation, the men had been able to salvage a great deal of lumber and ironmongery, spiriting it away under cover of darkness and secreting it in the forest. Some of the property they had rescued they intended to return, including the frame of the old hospital, but most of it they considered theirs to keep.

'So?'

Epiphany said, 'Better to dream of the things we could gain than of what we might lose.'

They turned to leave and Delilah linked her arm through Caleb's. 'Cornelius,' she said, under her breath, 'tended to overstate the case.'

Black men cleaned up the town just as they had cleared the land on arrival, working under the same captains and with equal despatch, while the women, no less industrious, restored order to their homes. Within a few days Freetown was returned to an appearance of normality, the gardens had been tidied and smoke once again wafted up from the outside kitchens. But many of the houses had an uninterrupted view of the harbour now that the Company buildings were gone; the blackened remains served as a reminder that the 'normality' was a semblance only. Habitable once more, the town saw the return of the governor and Company officials and their installation in the best of the remaining houses.

Before departing, the French commander had deposited on the beach over one hundred British prisoners of war who had somehow to be accommodated and fed. All the food the settlers had managed to 'save' was shared and augmented with the produce of farms. Nobody starved.

'The storekeeper wants his money back. *And* the interest in full . . .'

'So it *was* him,' said Caleb. 'I guessed he was the one who lent you the money, Ma, when I saw how certain he seemed of his welcome at the farm.'

'Of course I told him the French had got it, stolen along with all the rest of the coin in the colony.'

'What did he say to that?'

'He said I must bear the loss, it was my money by then, not his.'

'We'll have to stump up the interest, of course.'

'Quite.'

'I take it the first instalment's due?'

'I told him I'd pay when the second instalment's due. Then he'll get the first and second instalments together.'

'What sweetener did you give him?'

'I offered him an extra instalment. Five payments instead of four. By the end of the year.'

'And what did you finally settle on?'

'Six.'

'Ma, you have the money. You buried it yourself. You could pay him back today. What's in your mind?'

'Coin.'

Caleb stared.

'The paper money that the Company is obliged to issue is worthless. We have coin. We can trade . . . Instead of crawling, we'll fly.'

~

8

EPIPHANY STOOD IN the open doorway of the farmhouse and watched the messenger boy, his bare feet raising a long red frill of dust, until he entered the trees and disappeared from sight, travelling in the direction of Freetown. She lifted her face to the morning breeze. She fancied she could detect a faint smell of the sea mingling with the scent of lemon, lime and pineapple and coffee brewing in the kitchen outside. She stepped across the yard to the hearth and poured herself a large mug of coffee, set the pot back on the fire and went to sit on the bench at the side of the house; in front of her the rich green of Tabitha's little physic garden was separated from the fields by a thick canebrake.

Half-risen above the horizon, the sun lent gold to the drab-feathered bulbuls, perched on a nearby pepperbush, noisily scolding a snake as it sneaked through the grass. A flock of starlings, glossy coats shot with iridescent purple, chattered in the branches of the tall trees at the far end of the house. Placing her mug of coffee on the bench, Epiphany retrieved the unopened note from inside her bodice and broke the seal.

Inside nothing was written, but the white vellum streaked with red was imbued with the scent of camwood.

Closing her eyes against the sun, Epiphany leant her back on the wall of the house so that she was completely in the shade under the eaves. Camwood used to be Delilah's codeword for Cornelius on the plantation and now, by extension, Delilah was clearly using it to refer to Abiola. Old habits die hard. The message was unmistakable: the moment Epiphany had been dreading had finally arrived – but why in code? She could only guess that once again trouble was stirring in Freetown and for the same old reason. Whatever guise the trouble might take, the root cause was always the continuing pressure for a share in the government. After eight years, Sierra Leone was still a long way from the society of equals promised by Mr Clarkson. But there had been gains and, despite the slow progress, she remained hopeful that an accommodation could be reached.

The sound of children's voices and the smell of biscuits cooking, a sure sign that Tabitha, having returned from her morning round of the fields, was overseeing the preparation of breakfast, roused Epiphany from her reverie. She replaced Delilah's note inside her bodice and what it said she must do she put to the back of her mind. Reluctantly she rose from her place on the bench to face what promised to be a difficult day. Try as she might, she was unable to concentrate fully as she took the children through their lessons, guiltily aware that she was merely marking the hours until it was time for Tabitha to ring the bell signalling the end of classes.

Epiphany gathered up the few precious slates on which her older pupils had been practising their letters, abstractedly wiping the surfaces with a cloth and filling the air with motes of white chalk dust. One by one she stored the slates in a wooden chest beneath the open window and then sat at the table staring vacantly, fingers tapping on the scrubbed table running the length of the room. *We choose the fate which accompanies us into this world and once we have chosen we cannot escape it.* Waking and sleeping, these words had become a constant refrain in her mind. It was Cornelius speaking to her; ensuring she took the next step along the path towards the fulfilment of the destiny that had brought her to Africa. And the next step was to set her son's feet on that same path.

Squeals of joy erupted outside. Glad of the distraction, Epiphany rose from the table and looked out of the door to see the children rushing to meet a visitor. Big Mo in full sail, making her stately way towards the house, bountifully laden. Balanced on her head she had a huge straw basket, piled with provisions from town. Great cloth-wrapped bundles were strapped in front and behind, while half a dozen weighty-looking parcels dangled on string handles from her hands. Three small girls laboured cheerfully in her wake, each dwarfed by the loads on her head. They called out greetings to the noisy flotilla of children rushing to accompany them the last few yards, all laughing and talking at once.

Epiphany felt a flicker of apprehension. Was this unscheduled visit a laying up of provisions against the possibility of another rebellion? These days, Epiphany relied on others for news from Freetown, having lived for the past six years exclusively at the farm. Following the French attack there had been a dispute over goods salvaged from the invaders during the occupation – the settlers and the governor both laying claim to them. In the face of the people's obstinacy, the governor had decreed that those who refused to return the property and sign a new oath of loyalty would be barred from Company employment and their children from free education. Epiphany had suggested opening an alternative school at the farm. Her hunch had paid off handsomely. She, Epiphany and Tabitha ran one school in the country, while Elizabeth was soon presiding over a second in Freetown.

Epiphany joined the children in welcoming Big Mo.

Big Mo's face split in a grin. 'I've come to help.'

Epiphany recalled how when she was twelve years old, digging trenches in Charleston, Big Mo had come to her rescue; how after

Cornelius's murder she had woken in Big Mo's arms. If Delilah was the roof, and Tabitha the walls, Big Mo was the solid earth beneath. Epiphany hugged her; she felt lighter already. But before she could reply, Tabitha appeared and began marshalling the unloading of the provisions. Freed of her parcels, Big Mo sat on the bench in the shade and called the children to take their reward. Epiphany brought out a crock of beer. She waited until the last of the sugared cakes and candied fruits had been distributed, and the contents of the crock drained, before saying: 'How did you know to come now? Did you know Delilah had sent me a message?'

Big Mo shook her head. 'At times like these, the right hand doesn't know what the left is doing.'

'So how *did* you know?'

Big Mo wiped the beer froth from her mouth with the back of her hand and tapped the side of her nose with her forefinger.

Epiphany nodded, but she was none the wiser.

Big Mo's head snapped back and her laugh boomed out. A flock of parrots rose screeching from the trees on the far side of the garden. 'I knew you'd leave it till the last moment to tell the boy, that's all.' She threw up her hands. 'There was no magic involved.'

Epiphany smiled, but she was only half convinced. She glanced in the direction of Abiola, sitting with the other children in the shelter of the canebrake, licking sugared crumbs from his fingers one by one. Sensing her eyes on him, he looked up from his game and she waved.

Soon he would recognise her smile for the Judas kiss it really was.

'Magic,' Epiphany said, 'is what we need now.' *Freedom has its own sacrifices*, Cornelius used to say; how well she understood that now.

She took Big Mo's hand in both of hers. 'I'm glad you came.'

Big Mo touched Epiphany's cheek. 'Caleb should be here.'

Epiphany nodded. Like Delilah, he took no interest in the school other than the balancing of its accounts, and rarely travelled out to the farm. Elizabeth and Johnson, by contrast, were frequent visitors and Carver made the journey to the country almost as often as Big Mo, transporting fresh fruit and vegetables to Freetown. All the same, Epiphany had hoped that Caleb might have made the effort on this occasion.

'It's strange, isn't it,' she said, 'how the idea of freedom united us all, but the reality drives us apart. It's as if, in slavery, our true natures were hidden even from ourselves.'

Big Mo tilted Epiphany's chin and looked into her eyes. 'Epiphany, we're being put through the fire. You have to melt the iron first before you can shape it, and to shape it you have to hammer it. But once it's done, it's well-nigh indestructible. Now call your son.'

Epiphany had known from the moment he was born that she was the one who must hold the light steady for Abiola as her father's cousin, Oluremi, had done before her. Now she insisted on allowing him a few more hours' carefree play, and it was not until she had begun to cook dinner that she called him. Abiola, who was helping to put the hens to bed, ran up obediently but was clearly impatient to return to his friends.

'Hey!' One of the girls helping Epiphany in the kitchen caught Abiola by the shoulders and removed the chicken feathers lodged in his hair.

Big Mo set aside the bowl of boiled groundnuts she was shelling.

'Stand up straight,' she commanded.

Smiling, Abiola stood straight as a palm tree. This was a game they often played. Big Mo looked sternly into his eyes; his smile wavered and vanished. There was a charged silence. The boy appeared younger suddenly than his eight years and the woman graven and monumental. It seemed to Epiphany that unseen presences had been summoned to the yard.

'What are you, Abiola?'

'A lion.'

'And what is a lion?'

'Brave.'

'What does a lion know?'

'His strength surpasses all others.'

'And what does that make him?'

'A chief.'

'What must a chief do?'

'Prove himself.'

'Are you ready, Abiola?'

'Yes,' Abiola replied firmly, and through her tears Epiphany saw he understood that on this occasion it was no game.

'You're going away, Abiola.'

'Where am I going?' Abiola asked.

'To England,' Epiphany interrupted, unable to help herself.

Abiola did not flinch but she caught the terror in his eyes. Epiphany knew that this betrayal would not be forgiven, even when the reason was understood.

After a long pause, during which all those present, both seen and unseen, awaited his answer, Abiola replied, 'I'll write to you.'

Epiphany hugged him; she could feel his heart thudding. He would prevail, she thought. Bravery, as Cornelius said, was not to be without fear, but to overcome fear. 'A lion can come to no harm in England,' she whispered.

Two years before, awake but dreaming, Epiphany had 'seen' the ocean spread out before her and on the far horizon a ship bound for England with a very young Abiola on board. She had journeyed to Freetown the next day to talk to Caleb and Delilah.

Caleb had said smugly, 'Perhaps the boy does have a special destiny. African kings have been sending their children to England for generations. This could be a sign.'

Delilah replied tartly, 'African kings have rather more resources than we do, but I take your point, Caleb. I see no reason why we shouldn't give fate a hand; between us we should be able to manage it. But I'll only agree if Sheba goes too.'

'Ma,' Caleb protested, 'Epiphany didn't see Sheba on the ship.'

'I couldn't bear to lose the two of them,' Epiphany said.

Delilah shrugged. 'That's the condition.'

Epiphany had given way. Both her schools were flourishing, but even so she could not afford to send Abiola to England without Delilah's help. And in truth Sheba was more her grandmother's child than hers. It could be said Delilah was only fighting for her own.

Now that the time had come, Epiphany could not stop crying. She and Abiola had travelled into town accompanied by Big Mo and Tabitha to spend the last week with all the family before the children sailed. Epiphany wept silently throughout, her tears falling in a constant stream, like some Egyptian plague, Delilah said.

'I understand,' Elizabeth said. 'I felt just the same when I lost my boy.'

Caleb circled his son and daughter protectively in his arms. 'Except that these two are coming back.'

Johnson put his arm round Epiphany. 'Remember,' he said, 'the eye of the leopard.'

Delilah ensured that Abiola and Sheba were thoroughly familiar with the various family enterprises and aware of the sacrifices being made on their behalf. Young as they were, they could not fail to note the contrast between the two houses on Water Street, rented out to company officials, and the cramped dwelling that they called home. She pointed out the vacant lots on which two more houses would soon rise, let them sample the ale in her tavern and handed out treats from her shop. Together they visited the market to see Big Mo, the building site where their father and Johnson were hard at work, and the docks to watch Carver and his team unloading a cargo vessel. They inspected the family's trading ship and accompanied their grandmother on her laundry round. Settler ventures were nothing compared to what the Europeans could achieve, Delilah told the children, and that was why they were going to England, so that they could gain the same advantages as the whites.

'I want to be an English lady,' Sheba declared.

'I thought you despised them, Delilah?' Tabitha said.

'I don't despise what they *know*,' Delilah replied.

Abiola and Sheba sailed for England in the care of the storekeeper and his wife, who, since taking refuge at the farm during the French attack, had formed a close attachment to Delilah. They would deliver the children safely to the school established in London by the directors of the Sierra Leone Company. And Epiphany took further comfort from the knowledge that there were several children from settler families among the pupils already.

She watched the ship out of sight and carried on watching even then, willing them a safe passage, her heart in splinters.

As she turned away, Tabitha said to her, 'You're free now to do the work that led you to Africa,' which was no comfort.

On her morning round about the town, Delilah found her way blocked by a considerable crowd, but by making judicious use of her elbows she was soon at the front, vying for a closer view of the bill pinned to a window shutter. She crammed a pair of gold-rimmed spectacles on her nose, quickly scanned the notice and forced an equally ruthless passage back through the throng. She resolved to send a message forthwith to the farm. For safety's sake, Epiphany must close the country school and transfer the children to Freetown immediately. But first, Delilah pocketed her spectacles, and went in search of Caleb.

A few cabbage heads were set to ruin everything. The previous governor had drawn up a constitution for the colony composed of two chambers, which would have satisfied even the most disaffected amongst them. But the elected men had immediately seized upon the reforms as an opportunity to abolish the hated land tax that, from the very beginning, had been seen as a betrayal of the promises made to the settlers when they left Nova Scotia. Delilah sucked her teeth in exasperation. Being the one issue calculated to provoke a united opposition to the government, the tax had never been enforced. If the representatives had left well alone, the constitution would have been put into effect and the settlers would have got, by consent, the very reforms they were now demanding by force.

Delilah started towards the harbour, Caleb was almost certain to be there; the waterfront was the best place for news. She found him near the entrance to their tavern at the lower end of Water Street. The smell of stale beer and wine was sour after the fresh sea breezes, but they would be safe from inquisitive ears.

Caleb whispered excitedly, 'The governor's called for all the whites and those settlers who are loyal to the Company to go up to Thornton Hill to be armed.'

'I'm not surprised. Four of our captains, Methodists to a man, have taken it upon themselves to declare a change of government. They've posted a bill, which says that from now on we are to be ruled by a governor and council of our own choosing. I suspected this would happen.'

'Pointless to ask how you knew, Ma?'

'I know in the way I know everything I know . . .' Delilah ran a finger along the wooden counter. It was dust free. Big Mo's African girls were doing their job well. She looked up. 'How many?'

'Settlers? Thirty perhaps.'

'You must volunteer, Caleb, and so must Carver.'

'We agreed long ago that we would always remain neutral.'

'That was before I knew Johnson had signed the notice.'

'What!'

'Hush. I've just seen his name. We must be seen to be completely separate from him. If you'd been at the meeting last night you'd know that our new governor made an important announcement. A Royal Charter is on the way from London with a force of fifty soldiers to back it up; it might arrive at any moment. A more experienced man than our twenty-three-year-old governor would have known to keep the information to himself. I'm sure that's what prompted the rebels to make their move, because it'll not be the Sierra Leone Company they'll have to

answer to, but the King of England. And the charge will be high treason.'
She drew a hand across her throat.

Caleb fingered his own. 'I'm not prepared to risk my life, Ma, for either
one. So why volunteer?'

'Listen to me. We may be free, but there are times – and this is one –
when it pays to think like a slave.'

Caleb choked.

Delilah smacked him on the back. 'Hear me out. A slave has to think
of every single consequence of any action he takes. If the rebels win, it will
be Christians to the lions for everyone. The African traders and the slave
factories must be licking their lips. But for those of us who threw in our
lot with the whites, it'll be like it was in Charleston all over again. The
Sierra Leone Company will feel obliged in all conscience to take us with
them back to England, where your two children are. But it won't be the
same as in Nova Scotia; slavery is against the law in England.'

Caleb's coughing doubled him up and Delilah was obliged to smack
him on the back again.

At last he said, 'You don't believe Abiola has a special destiny at all.'

Delilah continued as if Caleb had not spoken. 'If the governor wins,
the fact that we fought on his side will be as good as money in the bank.'

Seeing Caleb's mind working she said, 'There's every reason to believe
that this conflict will be resolved by negotiation, the same as always. So
by volunteering you risk nothing, but we have much to gain.'

'And if you're wrong?'

'Pray.'

How blue the sky, how sparkling the ocean, how fresh and sweet the air
and how precious his life to him, Caleb thought, as Delilah waved him
off. Acutely conscious of her eyes upon him, he held his back straight and
injected purpose into his stride. Once he was out of sight, his shoulders
slumped and his pace slackened; only his prayers remained purposeful.
He prayed there would be no fighting. He thought of doubling back to
the harbour by another route to find Carver and walk up the hill with
him, but decided against it. If in the end there was no conflict, the fewer
who knew he had volunteered on the government's side, the better.
Carver was unmistakable, people would remember seeing the two of
them together. For the same reason, having taken an indirect route home
in order to pick up a change of clothes, Caleb deliberately left his gun
behind; walking the streets with a firearm at this juncture would draw too

273

much attention, and he would be issued with a government weapon in any case.

The town seemed unnaturally quiet; most folk were staying home, awaiting events. He could feel the tension in the air. No one knew how the situation would develop – apart from Delilah, that was; as usual, she had everything planned. And in all probability she would be proved right. If not, Caleb thought sardonically, he could only hope that Epiphany's belief in a special destiny proved to be true. He could be sure then of coming out of this present ordeal alive and it wouldn't matter which side won.

As soon as he passed through the gates of the fort, Carver loomed towards him. 'You took your time, Caleb. I expected you long before this.'

'I'm here now. Besides, nothing's going to happen.'

'You think not? The governor's decided to make a stand.'

Johnson turned restlessly, unable to sleep, listening to the rain pounding against the makeshift shelter protecting him from the storm. A few more weeks and the rainy season would be over. Having grown accustomed to the comforts of a bedstead, he had slept little these several nights. He smiled wryly in the darkness; the ground seemed harder than he remembered. He was getting old, and would be glad to be home. He missed his wife's warmth beside him and the sound of his daughters' breathing. Closing his eyes, he tried once more to doze, but to no avail. Expecting this to be his last night in the forest, he resigned himself to wakefulness. In the beginning he had refused to join the rebellion because the leaders were the same men who, in his opinion, had provoked the previous governor to abandon plans for a new constitution and thereby had lost the settlers their best chance of self-government. But when the governor, acting with all the rashness of youth, had forced a con-frontation Johnson had put his name to the notice; and when armed constables had rushed his house, there was nothing for it but to escape.

He adjusted his position. Through his coat he could feel the damp rising from the ground. He had learned later that two of his fellow signatories had been seized and one had been slightly wounded; he was lucky to have escaped. Incensed that the constables had fired on an unarmed crowd, most of the young men of the town had joined the rebels. They had demanded the release of the prisoners and taken up a position at Buckles Bridge on the main road leading out of the capital.

274

With numbers so finely balanced between the government troops and the rebel forces, the stand-off had continued for some days, with neither side willing to risk defeat.

The governor's latest suggestion, through intermediaries, was that the next naval captain to anchor in the harbour should be asked to arbitrate. The conflict would be resolved, as usual, by negotiation. He would be home next day, and by nightfall he would be teasing Elizabeth about her unnecessary anxieties.

The sound of gunshots and shouting propelled him instantly from his reveries. He grabbed his musket and shot and crept out carefully into the dawn light, imagining a dispute amongst his own men, the bulk of them young and inexperienced, carrying firearms for the first time, nerves stretched by the waiting. Almost immediately, he realised that the heart of the disturbance was at the bridge where guards had been posted. He made for the river, cutting straight through the encampment, which was in uproar now as the rebel force hurriedly armed themselves and raced after their leaders. The headlong dash was stemmed abruptly at the riverbank by a barrage of covering fire from the far side as a phalanx of Redcoats advanced across the bridge. The rebels milled about for a few moments in confusion. Two young men dashed forward and were instantly cut down, their bodies sprawled across the bridge. Seeing how greatly they were outnumbered, Johnson yelled at his men to take cover and dived for the ground, but not before he took a bullet in the leg.

After a short exchange of fire the rebels turned in disarray and ran for the trees, the British soldiers in pursuit. Johnson slithered in the opposite direction. Hidden by the long grass at the river's edge, he tied a kerchief round his leg and slid unobserved into the water and under the bridge. Feet planted on the riverbed, he anchored himself firmly against the bank, up to his neck but able to breathe in the narrow space between the water swirling round his chin and the wooden planks just inches above his head. There he waited hour upon hour until it was dark, then floated several hundred yards downstream until the current washed him ashore. Hauling himself out of the water, he continued on his belly through the under-growth, making for an old hunting hide where at last he was able to rest.

He awoke to shouts and gunfire and men crashing through the bushes, making the ground shake. In his feverish state he heard the sound of galloping hooves and the baying of hounds drawing closer and closer. He froze, attempting the hunter's trick of remaining utterly still that Cornelius had tried to teach him. Cornelius would have been able to judge the size of the troop and, to within an inch, how near they were. Johnson feared they were nearly upon him and that at any moment he would be discovered. But to his surprise the noise of trampling feet and shouting faded. An eerie silence fell. He breathed more freely. It had been close and he was afraid of the dogs . . . He eased himself into a sitting position. No doubt there was a bounty on his head. He would have to flee. But first he wanted to get word to Elizabeth that he had survived and was heading for the interior.

A branch creaked. Again Johnson froze, cursing himself for a fool. It was the oldest trick: to appear to leave. The silence should have alerted him. How he wished he had Cornelius's skills. There was a faint rustle of movement at the entrance to the hide. He strained his ears; he could see nothing in the blackness. His injured leg would prevent escape and he lost his weapons in the waters of the river. He braced himself: a cornered rat could still be dangerous.

'We guessed you must be wounded,' Carver said, striking a light, revealing Caleb at his side. 'Because Elizabeth had had no word.'

Johnson fought to cover his astonishment and relief but did not quite succeed. 'It's only a flesh wound,' he said.

'And festering.'

The air smelt rank, overlaying the odour of dank leaves, and in the tinder glow Johnson's skin was grey. Setting down the light, Carver immediately turned surgeon, cutting the cloth from Johnson's injured leg. Caleb proffered rum while heating a knife in the flame. Carver unwound his belt, gave the thick leather to Johnson to bite on, and cauterised the wound.

'How much is the bounty?' Johnson asked when he was able to find his voice.

'Not enough to risk falling foul of the Maroons. Straight out of the jungles of Jamaica, they're up to all the tricks,' Caleb said.

'So that's who they were.' Johnson winced as Carver dressed his wound. 'They have a reputation.'

'Justly earned,' Carver said.

'Yes, but why are they here?'

'The Company agreed to them coming, in return for the Royal Charter. Their arrival at this particular time though was entirely fortuitous,' Caleb said.

'No need to ask who for,' Johnson said. 'I see you're both wearing government uniforms, despite agreeing to stay neutral.'

'We're wearing the uniforms,' Caleb said, 'so if anyone sees us, they'll think we're taking you in.'

'And are you taking me in?'

'We're wearing the uniforms,' Carver said, 'because we fought on the government side.'

Caleb shrugged. 'That too.'

'You haven't answered my question.'

'Nor you mine.'

'I agreed to remain neutral in order to put Delilah off the scent. *I* haven't forgotten how she betrayed Thomas Peters, even if others have.'

'We're here to save *your* skin,' Carver said.

They chose the wide track leading from Freetown and walked boldly along, Caleb in front, keeping to the centre of the road. Their pace was necessarily slow for Johnson's leg could barely support him and as his wrists had been roped together he had to lean heavily on Carver's arm.

'Halt.'

'Trust me,' Caleb whispered.

'What have you there?' It was the British lieutenant who had led the successful attack at the bridge. Johnson thanked God. Having arrived in the colony only the night before, the officer could have no idea of the connection between the three of them.

Caleb saluted smartly. 'A prisoner, sir.'

Carver jerked roughly on the rope securing Johnson's wrists. Playing his part, Johnson lifted his chin defiantly.

'His name?'

'John Waters, sir,' Caleb answered without hesitation.

'You may hand him over.'

'If you please, sir,' said Caleb, sly and ingratiating, 'we thought to take him in ourselves.'

'And thought to take the bounty too, no doubt.' The lieutenant looked him up and down, then Carver and Johnson too. At last he smiled and dismissed them. He gave his troop the order to march on and when casually he glanced behind him, he saw Caleb and Carver still saluting.

Once the troop was out of sight Caleb drew himself up triumphantly. 'You see?'

Yes, Johnson thought, as Carver loosened the ropes binding his wrists and they set off again, suddenly he did see. Caleb was quick and clever and as slippery as water: the person he was depended where he was and who he was with. Johnson remembered how close they had become on the ship bringing them from Halifax, but he now realised that what had pleased him so in Caleb was the reflection of himself. Delilah was reflected there now. He glanced up at Carver, whose arm was easily supporting him. Carver was fixed like the earth, which must be turned to discover its true character. He recalled the dumb brute with the strength of ten, hauling the long-boats overland in Charleston. Carver, he realised, had simply been lying fallow until Delilah took up her hoe. The yield belonged to her. At a stroke, Johnson understood that these two would not have come to save him unless Delilah had sanctioned it. Delilah was no friend of his, so why would she come to his rescue?

Caleb pointed to the side of the road and, following his example, Johnson and Carver sank into the thick undergrowth, working their way along the ground, doubling back in the direction they had come towards a hiding place in the mountains.

Carver placed a log on the flames and sent sparks flying and shadows leaping up the walls. He had discovered the cave by chance on one of his hunting forays. Approached by a narrow ledge high in the hills, the entrance was hidden behind a waterfall, which spilled noisily down the mountain into the river far below. It was an ideal hiding place for Johnson until he was fully recovered and could make his own way upriver to the interior, beyond the reach of the Sierra Leone government. Caleb and Johnson huddled close to the fire on which some bush meat roasted. Both their faces showed the strain of recent days.

Caleb stabbed the soft surface of the cave floor repeatedly with the point of his knife. If it had been left to him, Johnson would have had to take whatever came. He burst out furiously, 'You rebels never had a chance of winning, Johnson. You must know that. You jeopardised all of us – *all* the settlers – and for what?'

Johnson stared into the flames. 'For what comes after. The rebellion was not about overthrowing the government: it was an attempt to gain an equal share in it. It was important not just for us settlers but for the Africans too.'

Carver broke in: 'What's important, surely, is to bring an end to the slave trade. Isn't that why we came?' He turned the meat on the fire.

Johnson answered, 'How *we* behave now will determine how the Africans are treated in the future –'

'More to the point,' Caleb interrupted him, 'how we behave now will determine *our* future. For God's sake, we're *not* Africans. Between the time our people first climbed off the boats in America and now, we have become another breed *entirely*.'

Johnson smiled pityingly at Caleb. 'Cornelius used to say that in order to defeat the enemy you must learn to think like him. However much white people differentiate between themselves, they make common cause when it comes to black people. All black people. Any black people. When those soldiers arrived, they immediately took the Company's side. Why? Not because they're English; we're English. It was because they're *white*. The Sierra Leone Company claim that, by setting the example of Christianity, we'll advance the cause of black people everywhere. I say that we must make the whites take us into *equal* partnership. Epiphany understands; on the map of freedom, *equality* is very clearly marked.'

Caleb shook his head despairingly. 'Epiphany has her head in the clouds. What do you intend to do now?'

'My task is to warn the Africans. To warn them to start thinking like the enemy.'

Johnson was a deluded old fool, Caleb thought. But Carver said calmly, 'In a day or two you can make your escape. Let's eat.'

'I'm not leaving until I've spoken to Elizabeth.'

'No!' Caleb exclaimed. 'That would endanger us all.'

'I mean to see her,' Johnson said. 'With or without your help.'

A lamp still burned in the room above Delilah's shop but in accordance with the curfew a cloth was draped across the window to ensure that no light escaped through the chinks in the shutters. Elizabeth had agreed to a meeting with Johnson and, as it might be their last for some considerable time, she was anxious to look her best. Epiphany had persuaded Delilah to open her coffers, hence the gold earrings glinting in Elizabeth's ears, the scarlet satin petticoat and brand-new blue beaver hat secured on top of her elaborate coiffure by a dazzling white kerchief.

'How do I look?' Elizabeth twirled tentatively in her borrowed finery.

'As befits a good Christian woman.' Tabitha nodded approvingly.

Elizabeth's face fell.

'You look just like the girl Johnson first knew,' Epiphany told her, and it was true. Elizabeth's face appeared girlish in the lamplight.

'A turkey's a turkey, no matter how you dress it up,' Delilah said, but not so Elizabeth could hear.

'What do you think, Delilah?' Elizabeth asked.

279

'You know what I think.' Delilah stepped forward to give a last tweak to the petticoat. 'You should tell him to go to Hell. The man has sacrificed you and your children for no good reason.'

'He's risking his life, just to see me.' Elizabeth put a hand up to her hair.

'And other lives too.' Delilah slapped her hand away and adjusted the kerchief herself.

'She *is* still his wife,' Tabitha said. 'It's her *duty* to go to him.'

'Duty, my life. She owes him nothing after the way he's behaved.'

'I owe it to him to hear what he has to say.' Shocked and angry at Johnson's break of faith, Elizabeth had been determined at first not to meet him. But as Epiphany said, no one had anticipated such a desperate turn of events.

Delilah pulled at the gathers on Elizabeth's bodice. 'Johnson's no use to you now. Even if he escapes a hanging, he can't come back. And you're surely not going to follow him into the jungle?'

Elizabeth did not reply.

'Love is a precious thing for its own sake, Ma,' Epiphany said.

'One of the many we can't afford.' Delilah altered the angle of the hat.

Epiphany hugged Elizabeth and knocked it awry. 'Take no notice of my mother,' she said, laughing.

Delilah straightened the hat again. 'Where are you meeting him?' As Elizabeth whispered in her ear, Caleb slipped silently into the room, making them all jump. He gave a low whistle of appreciation.

'Ready?' he asked.

Elizabeth nodded.

Epiphany and Tabitha wished her good luck.

Elizabeth took a deep breath. 'I'll surely need it.'

She knew what Johnson would ask, and she had all but made up her mind.

She kept close to Caleb's side as they moved swiftly through the unsettlingly dark and deserted streets of Freetown before striking inland. Twice they were challenged, but Caleb's militia uniform, allied to his smooth tongue, slid them easily past the guards.

It was fine for Johnson, Elizabeth thought, going off to live among the Africans. He was a good age and according to Big Mo they would respect that. He had much to offer, not least his knowledge of white people, and, when this trouble had blown over, his connections within the colony.

However kind the lamplight earlier, she was past her first youth and past childbearing. What could she expect? From what she had heard, Africans were no better than white people when it came to lording it over their women. And then there were her daughters to consider; old enough to know their own minds, they had made their decision.

Caleb broke into her thoughts. 'This is where I must leave you, Elizabeth.' They had reached the farmland bordering the far outskirts of town. 'You'll be safer without my uniform at this point, but I'll be here to escort you back.' He melted into the darkness.

Elizabeth was too preoccupied to be afraid. At this hour, bounty hunters were unlikely to venture so far from the centre. As Johnson's wife, she would be in no danger were she to encounter any rebels foraging for food. She was familiar with the road from frequent visits to the farm and in the starlight she could easily make out the narrow track she must take, branching off between fields planted with cotton and vines.

Arriving at the house hidden among the fruit trees, she scratched softly at the door.

Johnson opened it. He and Elizabeth looked at each other as they might have gazed on a much-loved landscape: familiar, but lately unvisited. Elizabeth thought she had forgotten the wealth of meaning that could be conveyed without words. Johnson, she saw, was able to read the depth of anger in her eyes and in his she read contrition. And desire.

'You're magnificent, Elizabeth,' Johnson said. He took a step towards her and her anger fell from her like a discarded robe.

Later, stepping carefully between the colourful islands of her finery strewn over the floor, she poured a cup of water from the jar in the corner. She took a sip and passed the cup to Johnson. He turned it round and drank from the same place she had.

'I'll send for you.' He pulled her down to sit on the bed. 'It'll not be long, I promise.'

'Will you now?' There was a faint but unmistakable edge to her voice.

'Of course.' Johnson held her away from him, and looked into her face. His brow creased. 'And the girls. I'm to be appointed a chief at Mugbaraka, ten days away, up river. As soon as I'm settled, I'll send a party to escort you all. Believe me, you'll be like a queen. Returning home, Elizabeth. To Africa!'

'My, and I imagined I was already there.'

'Sierra Leone isn't Africa. It's a white man's ship moored at the coast.

And among its precious cargo it carries a plague that might, one day, destroy this entire land.'

'You may well be right, Johnson, but the present is my concern. What advantage would I gain in removing myself from under the heel of the one, only to lay myself down under the other? Now, if you'd said, "Come with me, Elizabeth, because I cannot live without you . . ."'

'Love is not at issue, Elizabeth. Freedom is.'

'All I know is that I am freer here than I've ever been. I am free to live, work and worship where and how I please.'

A low whistle from outside the window interrupted them.

'I have to go,' Johnson said.

This day had been looming, Elizabeth thought, ever since the death of their son. The string had unravelled then, and now was about to be cut. He was completing the journey begun the moment he met Cornelius those many years ago. She recalled how she had lured Johnson with the stories of Africa that her grandmother got from her grandmother. How could she hold him now? Like the kindling of love, she thought, separation was the work of an instant.

'When I send for you, will you come?'

Her silence spoke for her.

∿

9

CARVER SAT AFT in the long black canoe, his vast bulk helping to counter-balance the rowers in front – paddles, dipping and lifting in unison, scarcely disturbing the calm surface of the water. As the canoe slipped smoothly upriver he marvelled as always at the immensity of the trees which provided a shady canopy overhead. Sunlight shimmered through the close-latticed branches dusting the surrounding green with gold.

Carver felt like shouting and singing: he had such good news. He suppressed the urge, however, conscious that his African rowers would have considered such behaviour inappropriate in one of his position. On his first visit, Delilah, not one to miss an opportunity, had pressed him to take with him some trade goods. Sales had proved so successful that on this occasion no less than sixteen oars were required. Carver eased his cramped knees, swollen with arthritis, and wished, as usual, that he had taken a second craft instead of squeezing in with the cargo, but the habits of a lifetime of hardship and thrift were not easily broken.

He was on his way to visit Epiphany and Tabitha. On the recommendation of Reverend George they had accepted an invitation from a chief in the Port Loko region, thirty miles north of Freetown, to establish a school in his town. Of the whole family, Epiphany and Tabitha were the only ones who had kept to the purpose that had drawn them to Africa. He closed his eyes and pictured once again the packed church meeting in Nova Scotia. The Lord's eye was upon them, Reverend George had said. The Almighty had chosen them. They had been tested and not been found wanting. Carver opened his eyes. The Lord would find them wanting now, he thought, wanting in everything on account of wanting everything.

It had been seven years since Johnson had quit the colony and left the family divided and for ever changed. Elizabeth had renounced teaching in favour of going into business on her own account. She said it was because she feared that, without Johnson's contribution, she and her daughters would become a burden. Carver was pretty sure the reason was that she mistrusted Delilah and was afraid of being too much in her power. He would have given his life for Delilah but, being clear sighted where she was concerned, he could not quarrel with Elizabeth's decision, and he was genuinely pleased by her subsequent success as a trader.

The rowers shipped their paddles and jumped into the shallow water. They edged the heavily loaded canoe towards the shore. Each time Carver returned, it seemed that the landing place had shifted, and as always, once through the screen of the mangroves standing sentinel in the water, he immediately lost his bearings. Almost imperceptible, and just wide enough to take single-file traffic, the pathways wound round and round so that you would have thought yourself miles from any human habitation. Only within yards of the town did the sound of voices betray its existence, and even then there was no visible sign until you stood at the narrow entrance gate of the outer palisade.

Cries of welcome greeted Carver as soon as he stepped through the gate of the inner palisade and people came running from all sides to shake his hand. He gripped the outstretched hands in turn and his fixed expression turned to one of genuine joy at the sight of Epiphany and

Tabitha hurrying towards him. In response to the enquiry in their eyes as they accompanied him to greet the chief in the Palaver house, he told them that all was well in Freetown and that he carried letters from England. He also whispered that he had some other news.

The formalities attendant upon the arrival of an important guest were lengthy. Carver's visits over the years had been a catalyst in the transformation of the town. People came to trade from all the surrounding area, and the hugely increased wealth and standing of the ruler had doubled the number of inhabitants. Carver laid his gifts before the chief. He had brought rum, brandy, imported tobacco, and a rich velvet coat that particularly pleased his host. Impatient to relay his news, Carver did his best to make the audience as short as possible but, even so, as everything had to be relayed through the chief's speaker, the proceedings took up the entire morning. It was past midday before he was free to retire.

Epiphany and Tabitha shared a house in the centre of the village distinguished from its neighbours by bunches of herbs hung up to dry under the eaves. The moment they were inside, Carver handed Epiphany and Tabitha the letters he had brought, but before they could open them the words burst from him: 'The slave trade's been abolished! The British have banned it at last!' He took a deep breath, enunciating carefully to begin with and then in a rush. ' "His Majesty's Government has made it against the law for British merchants to engage in the buying of Africans for transportation to America or the West Indies." '

Epiphany and Tabitha sank on to the seat behind them. They stared at Carver, who could not stop grinning.

After a while Epiphany recovered her voice. 'I can't believe it.'

'As true as I stand here in the year of Our Lord eighteen hundred and seven!'

Epiphany pulled Tabitha up and danced her round the room; their long swirling skirts created a draught that made the fire flare up, sending sparks flying. Carver, one eye on the tinder-dry roof thatch above, warned them to be careful, but they took no notice, merrily spinning, laughing like girls, until, short of breath, they collapsed on to the mat-strewn couch, flushed and jubilant.

Tabitha flung out her arms. 'God is good.'

According to the governor, Carver said, Sierra Leone had played a vital role in turning Parliament against the slave trade.

'If only Cornelius could have seen this day.' Epiphany dried her face with a corner of her petticoat.

There was a long pause.

'Mind you,' Carver said, 'no sooner are you rid of one problem than another takes its place.'

A British naval squadron now patrolled the coast of West Africa with a mandate to attack foreign ships suspected of carrying slaves and to release their captured cargos in Freetown.

Carver leant forward. 'Instead of us going to them, the Africans are coming to us. A pitiful sight they are too: hundreds of broken souls arriving almost daily. There's plenty of scope to do God's work in Freetown, quite as well as here.'

Epiphany gathered up the letters Carver had brought with him, poignant reminders of how much she had sacrificed. She cradled the folded sheets of paper in her lap, one finger tracing the neatly penned letters which spelled her name in black below the red wax seal. Although the school had been an unqualified success, it was an undeniable fact that in all the time Epiphany and Tabitha had spent with the people up country they had not made a single convert to Christianity. Experience had taught the Africans that white men were clever but not good, so it stood to reason that they were convinced by the education but not the religion.

Up country, the unchanging rhythms of life had fostered the illusion of time standing still. To Epiphany, looking about her in the dawn light as the canoe sailed up the wide river mouth to Freetown, the scene seemed little changed at first. The shining curve of the bay, and the appearance of the town spread like a coloured kerchief at the foot of the mountains, matched the picture held in her memory. But the resemblance was momentary. After a while, she sat hand in hand with Tabitha in such bewilderment that Carver laughed to look at them. African canoes crouched low in the water, side by side with larger settler craft, dwarfed in turn by European merchant vessels of every description and the British warships of the West Africa squadron. Their boat could hardly find a way through, so crowded was the harbour. Carver, his voice carrying effort-lessly above the hubbub, was able to tell them about almost all the vessels in the harbour – the names of the captains and senior officers, their ports of origin, their ultimate destinations, and this extended even to the provenance of the African canoes (some from as far as two hundred miles away) that appeared to fill every last patch of water. Freetown itself shone in the sunlight, its brightly painted houses fortified behind a line of blockhouses with a battery of eight cannon commanding the bay.

As their boat came alongside, Carver disclosed that the wharf, one of a dozen lining the harbour, belonged to the family and that the men rushing to unload the cargo were in their employ. Over the years on his visits up country, Carver had described the family's growing prosperity but until now Epiphany had not grasped how successful Delilah and Caleb had become. Aside from the wharf, the list of their possessions now included a fleet of three vessels trading along the coast and two of the most valuable properties on Water Street.

'I don't care for any of it,' Tabitha said. She had to shout to make herself heard. 'Peace and quiet at the farm is all I want.'

Carver grinned contentedly. 'It'll be just like the old days.'

Not quite, Epiphany thought.

During the period that Epiphany and Tabitha had been away, responsibility for the colony had been transferred to the Crown, and the Union Jack now flew above the governor's residence. African families rescued from the slave ships by the British naval squadron were settled on land outside Freetown on condition the children attended school. It was a neat arrangement, allowing the parents to become self-sufficient while at the same time making sure their children received a Christian education. Reverend George, who had arranged for Epiphany and Tabitha to take up the African chief's invitation in the first place, now helped them re-establish their school on their return. In no time at all the voices of twenty children could be heard reciting their afternoon lessons under the mango trees at the farm. The parents were as eager to learn as the children, and like the Nova Scotians when they first arrived, took their turn with the slates in the midday break or in the evening after work had finished in the fields.

Sitting opposite Caleb in the tiny room behind Delilah's shop, Epiphany reflected that settling back into the family had been relatively simple too. She should not have been surprised, she thought wryly, because clearly it was all the same to them whether she was at the farm or up country. She glanced covertly at her husband. Since her return from the interior there had been little opportunity for any private talk.

Caleb smiled at her and Epiphany surprised herself by smiling back. The thin grey light entering through the single unglazed window directly above was not unkind, but even so she thought Caleb appeared younger, if anything, than when she had left on her mission. He was very sleek, every inch the prosperous merchant in a blue linen coat, his fob watch on

286

a silver chain. He seemed to be enjoying a second youth, for in spite of his fine clothes he put her in mind of the boy she had first set eyes on all those years ago in Charleston – although the confidence he exuded now was that of a man basking in his success. He was certainly attractive; it was no wonder that his name had been linked with a string of women while she had been absent. Neither Big Mo nor Carver had denied it.

Caleb said, 'You've not changed, Epiphany. Still as lovely as the day I first saw you.'

Epiphany laughed. He had been shocked, she knew, by her work-worn appearance on the night of her arrival. She was willing to concede though that being out of the forest had worked as miraculous a transformation as rain on parched earth.

'You too,' she said.

Her eyes roamed the room. The table was the same, hand-crafted by Johnson and occupying much of the floor. The old aromas still clung and although it had been sometime since this small space had served as Delilah's storehouse it was easy to conjure up the days when Carver and Big Mo had shared the floor every night with sacks of flour, biscuit, salt beef, coffee, casks of rum and molasses.

Caleb leant back in his chair. 'We've come a long way,' he said, reading her mind. 'I admit I didn't think so at the time, but we made the right decision in coming to Africa.'

A certain quality in his voice reminded Epiphany of another time and another place. She found herself looking into the face of the master in the counting house of Fairlawns Plantation. It was only for an instant, but it left her shaken and perplexed.

Caleb leant across the table. 'Didn't you hear what I said?' His smile was a little sheepish now. 'I admitted I was wrong and you were right. Sierra Leone has proved to be the making of us.'

'What has it made of us, Caleb?'

'It has made us rich.'

'There are things we've lost,' Epiphany said.

'Like what?'

'Things you can't see or touch . . .'

Caleb laughed and shook his head. 'All those years up country have made you wood-wild. But I'll tell you one thing: soon our holdings won't touch Elizabeth's.'

'Carver said she's doing well,' Epiphany said. In fact, she knew just how well from Elizabeth herself. They'd quickly resumed their former closeness, easily bridging the gap of the intervening years and, unlike Caleb, Elizabeth and her daughters were frequent visitors to the farm.

Caleb snorted. 'She's doing better than that. The moment she decided to go into business, she sought out Johnson, bold as you please, and she's been able to penetrate deeper inland than any other trader in the colony.'

'Surely that's a good thing. Isn't that why we came to Sierra Leone? To persuade the Africans that there are more profitable ways of making money than trading in their fellow humans?' Epiphany giggled. 'Perhaps Elizabeth will succeed where Tabitha and I failed.'

'It's not funny. She's persuaded Johnson to favour her above us. He's big in his own right now. He's quite a sight, apparently, in his ceremonial cloth, surrounded by his warriors and I don't know how many wives. His knowledge of the white man has given him tremendous influence among the other chiefs, and where he leads they tend to follow. Elizabeth's acquired a host of trading concessions' – Caleb reeled them off on his fingers – 'muskets, gunpowder, European manufactured iron goods, silks, satins, velvets, rum, brandy, wine, rice, kola nuts. And where she's not the only licensed merchant, she can undercut the rest of us because she can deal directly at source.' Caleb shook his head, sucking his teeth in disgust.

'I'm sure you and Delilah have something up your sleeve.'

Caleb glanced away. He fidgeted with his watch chain, and did not answer immediately.

'Well, don't you?' Epiphany asked; she was enjoying teasing him.

Caleb explained earnestly. 'We mean to bypass the interior trade entirely and with our new boat we have the means to do it. There are two commodities in short supply in Freetown: beef and hides. And now that we're a Crown Colony, demand will be greater than ever. There are the new officials to be housed and fed, the officers and men of the naval squadron. Last, and of course least, there are the captives being released here; they too will have to be fed and clothed. By the time anyone else thinks to do the same we will, as they say, have cornered the market.'

'My, my.'

She was laughing at him, Caleb realised.

'All right; all right.' Smiling, he rose to his feet. 'Shall we go?'

Caleb hoped to find a suitable apprentice among the liberated Africans released from a captured slave ship, and Epiphany had asked to accompany him. She squeezed round the table and moved the two steps to the door. The light shining in through the window was no longer grey and the morning breeze blowing in off the sea sent cool wafts into the room.

Caleb closed the window shutter, locked the door and, pocketing the key, sauntered down the steps leading from the verandah into the garden. He had quite regained his composure, Epiphany noted, and his swagger. The problem with Caleb, Epiphany thought, was that he had so many good qualities but again as many bad. She linked an arm through his; he squeezed her hand.

The two of them set off down the road, Epiphany's skirts swishing round her ankles. There was a jauntiness in her step and it was evident even to an undiscerning eye that she had taken pains with her appearance. A new beaver hat was prettily angled on her elaborately braided hair while a pair of coral earrings drew attention to the swan length of her neck. Tabitha had commented that you could be forgiven for thinking it was the Sabbath, seeing her turned out in her finery.

Caleb glanced appreciatively at her. 'There are days and there are days . . .' he said.

'And what kind of a day is this one?' Epiphany asked, her skirt brushing against him. It seemed they could not stop smiling.

'Promising,' Caleb said.

When they arrived at the King's Yard, Caleb held open the gate with a flourish and, laughing at him over her shoulder, Epiphany passed through. Instantly she recoiled as if struck. Caleb was obliged to take her by the elbow and propel her away from the entrance as others pressed behind them. He offered his handkerchief as she slumped against the wall.

'I should have warned you the smell can overpower.' Caleb inhaled gingerly. 'We're in luck today, these last were detained in the harbour for only a short time.'

Epiphany heard not a single word as she gazed round the yard. The sun beat down and inside the high walls there was no protection from the heat save at the far end, where the white superintendent and his clerk sat writing at a long trestle table beneath a crisp white awning. Freetown settlers strolled near the walls, in groups, in pairs, singly, exhibiting varying degrees of affluence in their dress, but all of them smart and clean, the women twirling parasols aloft. Handkerchiefs pressed to their noses, they eyed with cold calculation the mass of humanity penned in the centre.

Filthy, emaciated, sick, dying, their nakedness barely concealed by the country cloths they had been issued, the recaptured Africans stood, sat or lay mute on the ground. Epiphany, her breath coming fast, searched their faces. She heard Cornelius's voice again describing how the planters had come on board the slave ship to view the merchandise, their wives in silks and satins as merry and gay as if on a picnic.

Caleb touched her arm. 'I don't like to leave you, but I've seen a fellow over there who'd suit my purpose and if I delay someone else will take him. Although' – Caleb glanced anxiously over his shoulder – 'I'm surprised he hasn't been enlisted. Usually the army creams off the strongest before we take our pick.' He turned back to Epiphany, 'I'd better examine him first. Stay here.'

Seeing someone else approaching his quarry, Caleb hesitated no longer. He plunged into the centre of the courtyard and, moving swiftly, succeeded in pre-empting his rival by laying his hand on the object of his choice.

Feeling dislocated, as if on the cusp between two worlds, Epiphany ignored Caleb's injunction to remain where she was and followed him like a sleepwalker through the crowd; she was behind him as he made his swoop.

'Stand up,' Caleb commanded, gesturing with his hands.

Warily, the young man obeyed. He was as tall as Caleb, who now peered closely into his eyes as if to discover signs of his character there.

Epiphany recognised the horizontal markings on the man's cheeks and her breath caught in her throat. Caleb turned, surprised to find her at his shoulder. Seeing the accusation in her face, he shrugged. 'If I'm to pay good money, I want to be sure.'

'Since when did you have to pay for an apprentice?'

'Since the governor hit on it as a way to raise the prize money. Two years ago it was a hundred dollars, but now there's so many of them it's only twenty – a big improvement.'

Epiphany sensed that the young man understood their conversation and, noticing him looking to his left, she followed his glance and saw a woman lying on the ground watched over by a man and a girl.

'Your family?' she asked. The young man nodded.

'I'm interested in him, not his hangers-on,' Caleb said irritably. 'The mother's clearly sick and the other two don't look too healthy. They're packing them in tighter, now that the trade's been banned. The returns are so high the slavers can afford to lose half.' Caleb returned to his scrutiny of the young man. 'I see it now. He must have feigned sickness to avoid being enlisted into the army.' Caleb eyed him speculatively. 'Smart – perhaps too smart.'

'Caleb!'

'What?'

'They mustn't be separated.'

'Who?' Caleb looked at her blankly, still busy with his calculations.

'The family –' Epiphany gestured towards them.

'It's unavoidable. I want only one. Even if I was in the market for more, it would not be these.'

'Is your memory so short?'

'On the contrary, I've forgotten nothing. And I learned my lessons well. Save your pity for those who complete the journey.' Caleb looked round the yard, his face flushed. 'Fate has favoured every one of these. Wretched they may be, but slaves they are not.'

'You're right, Caleb. They can choose to work for me, not you. And whatever you're prepared to pay, I shall go higher.'

'The price is already too high,' said Caleb. 'You take the sickly ones; I'll have the young man.'

Husband and wife glared at each other, their new-found tenderness exposed for what it was, nostalgia merely, a shallow pool formed after rain, swiftly evaporating in the heat of the sun.

Caleb took a step back. 'Mark my words,' he said, 'you'll regret this.'

'Where are you from?'

'We were taken as captives from a city called Oyo. First they took us to –'

'– Apomu, in Ife territory,' Epiphany broke in. 'From there to Ijebu Ode. Next, to Oworu, on the coast, then you followed the Lagos River to Badagri.'

'How do you know this?'

'It's a long story,' Epiphany said. 'One day I'll tell you it, in exchange for yours.'

Glancing at the young man's sister who stood by his side, Epiphany felt a shiver of recognition as if they had met before. She immediately dismissed the presentiment as fanciful. It was impossible.

Facing each other once more across the table in the office, Epiphany and Caleb finished the quarrel begun in the King's Yard.

'I've come to pay my debt,' Epiphany said, sitting very straight.

'You needn't have troubled.' Caleb tipped his chair back and slipped his thumbs in his waistcoat pockets, looking at her from under his lids. 'As I told you, I'm happy to lend you the money.'

'I know you covet the boy.'

Caleb shook his head. 'You can take as long as you like.'

'No. I want to pay.'

Caleb laughed. 'You don't trust me? Your own husband?'

Epiphany's response was to reach into her purse and place a coin on the table.

Caleb's lips thinned; he said nothing.

Epiphany continued laying the silver pieces on the table one by one in a single line. 'There,' she said. 'Paid in full.'

A deep flush spread across Caleb's face. He brought his chair upright, its front legs jarring loudly on the floor, and scooped up the money. 'Bills would have sufficed.' He made a show of counting the coins. 'Will that be all?' He dropped them jingling into the pocket of his jacket.

'No,' Epiphany said.

Caleb met her gaze and held it, his flush deepening.

Her eyes scoured his, searching for the man she thought she knew. Not the boy whom she had loved and married in Nova Scotia, but the Caleb who had passed her father's scrutiny; who, instead of dismissing her belief in her family's destiny, had taken it on trust and followed her to Africa, accepting without question the sacrifices that belief had entailed. She realised now that the impression of Robert Farrer's face she had seen in Caleb's before the expedition to the King's Yard had been a premonition. Feeling that she, too, was contaminated she blurted, 'You're loathsome.'

Caleb responded with cold fury: 'Putting up the money for that African family was an act of Christian charity. I –'

Epiphany interrupted him. 'Cornelius said you should *think* like the enemy, not *become* him. You told me you hadn't forgotten, Caleb, but you have.' In a cracked whisper she began to recite: ' "We were kept chained below, laid head to head in long rows, like so many sacks of grain, layered one above the other, on wooden planks, with precious little light and without the means to relieve ourselves decently. The living lay side by side with the dead, shackled to each other at wrist and ankle, two by two in the fouled spaces between the planks. The healthy, steeped in the secretions of the sick and dying, could only bear impotent witness to their last agonies, while the stench, feeding on itself, overpowered strong and weak alike, a living, poisonous presence, ingested with every breath. A people who valued life above all called for death to come and take them –" '

292

'Stop!' Caleb shouted.

They sat mute.

After a few weeks in Tabitha's care, Epiphany's African family no longer bore any resemblance to the sickly, dispirited group first encountered in the King's Yard. Having discovered they were from Oyo, Epiphany was inordinately curious to know their history, but she had been forced to curb her impatience. Although he was fluent in Arabic and trading pidgin, the son, Olu, possessed only a smattering of English. His parents, Lola and Dotun, and sister Tosin had not a word of the language between them. Anxious to repay Epiphany's faith in them, all four had applied themselves assiduously, studying in the classroom by day and, when lessons were done, stooping over the rows of seedlings, diligently weeding, helping to return the farm, so long neglected, to its former state. After only a few months it was a pleasure each evening to wander the winding paths among the fruit trees and well-tended fields. In the same length of time, Olu had learnt enough English to satisfy Epiphany's curiosity.

One Sunday evening after church, as moths fluttered about the lantern on the table in the yard, Olu translated as Dotun began recounting the story of his family's enslavement and subsequent liberation in Freetown. Barely able to contain her excitement, Epiphany exchanged glances with Tabitha who like herself was leaning forward in anticipation.

'I was born far from here in a city called Oyo, many leagues from the sea, whose king, the Alafin of Oyo, lord of the world and the representative of the god Shango on earth, rules a vast empire. My father's house is a noble one, headed by the Lord Asipa, ranked seventh of the king's chief ministers . . .'

Epiphany's heart fluttered; the stately phrases and the familiar but half-forgotten music of the Oyo language brought Cornelius vividly to mind.

Dotun continued, gazing into the darkness beyond the circle of the lantern. 'There have been times in the history of Oyo when the political and the military were so closely connected as to be the same, when the Chief Minister, the Bashorun, had become more powerful than the Alafin himself. One such was the Bashorun Gaha. At the height of his power as kingmaker, the Lord Gaha ruled all Oyo. His sons, each as vicious and blood thirsty as his sire, were scattered the length of the empire, and it was to them and not to the Alafin that the tributes were paid. People lived in dread of their wanton cruelty. But with age Lord Gaha's power declined –'

'What happened to him?' Epiphany interrupted.

'The Lord Gaha held sway in Oyo before ever I walked the earth. But I know the story.' Dotun took a gulp of ale thoughtfully poured by Tabitha and continued: 'In Oyo, they say if you have the heart of a cruel man, take note of Gaha's fate. The Alafin, in alliance with the chiefs and army generals, rose up against him. After his palace had been fired and the remains built into a pyre in the main courtyard, Lord Gaha was brought out in chains and made to prostrate himself before the Alafin under a burning sun. Even children dared to approach him, yanking the stalk-like growths on the old man's forehead and howling with laughter at hearing the all-powerful Bashorun offering to become His Majesty's poultry keeper. But Lord Gaha's pleas were in vain. After many hours of untold indignities, he was lifted to the top of the waiting pyre, doused with oil, and set alight. His entire household was put to the sword; all his relatives were hunted down and massacred; his supporters, high and low executed. It was thought every single one of his children had been killed, even those still in the womb. The Lord Gaha's enemies, it appeared, had triumphed utterly . . .'

There was a long silence.

Tabitha broke it at last. 'And you?' she asked.

'It transpired,' Dotun said, 'that one of Lord Gaha's infant sons had escaped. He survived to manhood in the Bariba country. A great warrior, he returned to Oyo at the head of an immense army to avenge his father's death. The Lord Asipa had been foremost among Lord Gaha's enemies, for he blamed the Bashorun for the death of his only daughter. Foremost among the victims of Lord Gaha's vengeful son were the sons and daughters of the house of the Asipa. Those of us who were not slain were sold into captivity. That I stand here today together with Lola, a junior wife of mine, and these two children of the same mother, is the work of fate alone. Perhaps now the cycle is broken and it is to the Christian God that we should give thanks.'

'It's Him, all right,' Tabitha said. 'The Lord be praised.'

Dotun was not to know, Epiphany realised, that the beloved daughter the Asipa had lost was none other than her father's cousin and pathfinder, Oluremi. She glanced involuntarily at Dotun's daughter, Tosin: the young girl sat straight-backed as always. Her face, with its high cheek-bones, was unreadable in the lamplight. For an instant their eyes met.

Epiphany caught a hint of camwood in the air and the image of a darkened room, red polished walls and a straight-backed figure seated on a stool. *It is not yet over*, she thought.

Having tacitly banished Caleb from the farm, Epiphany was left to balance the books, a task to which she readily admitted she was less than equal. Upon discovering, however, that Olu was far in advance of anything either she or Tabitha could teach him in mathematics, she happily surrendered the accounting to him. Olu, it transpired, had received his training as a warrior at the court of a prince of Oyo considered the greatest soldier of his day. And it was there at Ilorin that he had studied arithmetic and Arabic under the Fulah merchants attracted to the town. With the farm ever more productive, Olu also began helping Big Mo transport the produce to market, returning each time with a few trade goods, which he bartered for the surplus produced by the liberated Africans settled on land nearby. With Olu acting as middleman between their neighbours and Big Mo, it wasn't long before porters were required to transport the goods to and from Freetown.

Delilah descended on her daughter.

'Caleb sent you,' Epiphany said, unsurprised.

'He picked the boy first. His instinct was correct. The boy's clever, and I bet he's ambitious. What are his prospects if he remains with you? Apprentice him to Caleb —'

'He'd refuse.'

'You'd be within your rights to insist.'

Epiphany bristled.

'Put it to him. He must realise he's wasted here.'

Tosin appeared with refreshments. Delilah looked her up and down. The young girl bore the scrutiny with her habitual self-containment, waiting politely, eyes lowered, until she was dismissed.

The moment she was gone, Delilah asked, 'Is that the sister?' Epiphany nodded. 'Handsome. How old is she?'

'Twelve or thirteen. She seems older than her years, I suppose because of what she's suffered.'

'Hmm. Why doesn't she look you in the eye? What's she hiding?'

'That's just the Oyo way. It's considered improper.'

'Even so . . . This one is deep. I sense iron underneath. She reminds me of someone, but I can't immediately think who.' Delilah rose to leave and, as she shook out her skirts of striped blue-and-white silk, the sun caught the glint of gold rings on the toes of her bare feet. 'To return to the brother' – she adjusted her hat, patted Epiphany's arm – 'I'm sure you'll do what's best for him.'

Olu was woken by a roaring wind so strong that the house seemed to rock on its foundations. Lightning turned the darkness into light and thunder burst about his ears. In Oyo he would have said that Shango was visiting his wrath upon the town, but he was not in Oyo. Rubbing sleep from his eyes, he raised himself on one elbow and peered across the room; the sound of snoring from the iron bedstead where Caleb slept continued undiminished. His new boss, Olu concluded, must have drunk more than his usual complement of liquor before retiring. He settled down again on his pallet and was soon asleep. But it was not long before he was woken once more by rain pounding on the corrugated-tin roof and pouring into the room, drenching him where he lay in the corner.

Hurriedly quitting his bed, Olu's first concern was for the belongings stored on the ledge between the wall and roof where the water was gushing in. Moving quietly, for he could hear that Caleb still slept soundly, he lit the lamp, drew up a stool to stand on, reached up and removed the items stored there. He staunched the leak as best he could with a wad of cloth and, in the light of the lamp, looked to see what damage had been done to the things he had rescued. He realised, intrigued, that one of the ledgers – a small volume protected by an oilcloth cover – was unfamiliar to him.

In three years, Olu had risen from raw apprentice to chief clerk and bookkeeper, managing the accounts of all the individual arms of the business. Arguably he knew as much as Caleb and Delilah, not only of the daily transactions, but also of the overall state of affairs. He could tell you to the nearest halfpenny just how healthy Big Mo's market stall and catering concern were; the profits accruing from the shop, the tavern, the laundering, how well Caleb managed the properties and the trading fleet, how tightly Carver ran the dock and wharf, and finally how the school and farm were prospering under Epiphany and Tabitha. He wondered why this particular ledger had been kept secret.

He glanced over his shoulder. Caleb had still not stirred. For a moment Olu struggled with his conscience, but his curiosity overcame him and, keeping his back to the bed, he scanned the pages. The entries, dating from the present, stretched back nearly twenty years. Hearing movement behind him, Olu quickly put down the book and pretended to be examining another of the packages.

Caleb's voice demanded irritably, 'What's happened? What are you doing kneeling on the floor there?'

'There was a storm and a leak in the roof. I rescued these few things. I was afraid the rain would ruin them.' He held them out, unable to still his trembling.

'Give them here,' Caleb ordered roughly, fully awake now that he recognised the oilcloth cover. Recovering himself, he added, 'You did well. Thank you.'

Olu bowed, respectfully, aware that Caleb was trying to fathom whether or not he had looked inside.

Delilah closed the ledger, her fingers smoothing the book's oilcloth cover. Until now, its existence had been known solely to Caleb and herself.

'I can't be sure that Olu hasn't discovered our secret.'

'What possessed you? You should have removed the book when he started sleeping in the same room.'

'I thought it was better up there than here in the office where he has licence to pry. He's a principled young man, and I knew I could depend on him not to put his nose where he shouldn't.'

'Well, you were wrong.'

'We don't know that for certain. In any case,' Caleb continued quickly, 'it's time we brought this business to a close. We *have* to find a way.' He sucked his teeth. 'It's ironical, isn't it? When we could we wouldn't, and now we would we can't.'

Delilah nodded thoughtfully. 'True, the goad is no longer in our hands.'

'The man's greed beggars belief. Will he never be satisfied?'

Delilah gave him a wry look. 'Who knows? Each trip he promises it's the last.'

'I should be going, not you. The stakes are higher than ever before. As well enter a lion's den unarmed . . .'

'But I *am* armed.' Delilah removed her head-tie; her beautiful face was as smooth as ever, but her hair shone silver in the lamplight. 'A woman with my number of years goes unnoticed unless she wills it otherwise.' She heaved a deep sigh; she did not want to travel. And she was afraid. But she had never been a woman to shirk danger, and she intended, yet again, to journey to the Northern Rivers territory, outside the jurisdiction of the Sierra Leone government. 'But you're right. I'll tell him it must end. I shall see to it.'

Caleb smiled, relieved. 'I'm glad that's settled. Take very good care, though.' He wagged a finger at her. 'He who sups with the devil should have a long spoon. Let's hope ours is long enough.'

It was late in the evening and Olu was still at the office, having returned to work after supper, when the door was quietly pushed open. Looking up and seeing that his visitor was Delilah, he rose and greeted her with a bow. Her visit was not unexpected. Since the night he'd discovered the secret ledger, he had been expecting her to seek him out. Delilah inclined her head and, gesturing to him to sit, took the chair facing him. She pushed aside the candle, cleared a space among the jumble of papers, placed both elbows on the table and leaned towards him with her chin cupped in her hands. Her lips curved in a conspiratorial smile. 'What do you intend to do, dear boy?'

Olu leaned away from the pull of her eyes, his chair scraping noisily on the floor. There was evidently no doubt in her mind that he had read the ledger. His hands were suddenly clammy and he had to clasp them tightly under the table.

'I shall do my duty.' His voice squeaked. Delilah continued to smile. Gruffly, he repeated, 'I shall do my duty.'

'You haven't forgiven Caleb, have you, for the King's Yard?'

'No . . . I . . . I mean, that's not true.'

'You haven't forgotten, though.'

Olu did not answer. He had not forgotten.

Delilah looked at him calculatingly. 'And for Epiphany's sake?' Her tone was cajoling.

Olu looked away, sweat beading his smooth-shaven head and trickling down his back.

Delilah sat up with a snap. She was without her head-tie. The candlelight lent her hair an ethereal whiteness and deepened the hollows of her dark, transfixing eyes. 'Betray my secret, and I will curse you.'

Recalling the words of the Alafin Aolé of Oyo, Olu's spirit quailed. Rejected by his people, the king had shot three arrows into the air: one to the north, one to the south and one to the west. *To all the points I shot my arrows will ye be carried as slaves. My curse will carry you to the sea and beyond the seas; slaves will rule over you, and you their masters will become slaves.*

'I shall curse you,' Delilah repeated, 'and your children and your children's children and all the ones that come after them.'

Olu understood the power that words could hold.

'Well?' Delilah demanded.

He made no reply, for he also understood the value of silence.

Carver surveyed his audience – with the exception of Delilah, who was away on business, the entire family were gathered together – a broad grin on his face. He was revelling in the attention. Epiphany smiled at his evident relish in the story he was about to tell. It was not the first time, and it certainly would not be the last.

He began. 'The English captain, lick-smart in his scarlet uniform, was so careful towards the lady as she descended the gangplank, a lace parasol in her dainty white-gloved hand shielding her face from view, that I assumed them newly wed.' Carver chuckled. 'Soon she was seated on the wharf, surrounded by enough luggage to fill an entire warehouse. My suspicions were confirmed; a bride, I thought, for sure. But then she changed the angle of her parasol . . .' Carver paused. 'Her face was black as mine, only a thousand, thousand times more beautiful.' He shook his head, still amazed. 'There she sat, quite composed, her white finery pretty as new milk, while all the world stared and the captain busied himself to no purpose.

'I walked across. "It seems there's no one here to meet you, miss. I expect I can be of help if you tell me who you are."

' "I'm the Queen of Sheba," she replied, a glint in her eye. "And you, sir?"

' "I'm the King of England," I replied.

' "Then we shall get on very well," she came back, cool as you like, the minx.'

'The clue was there, Uncle!' cried Sheba to shouts of laughter.

Epiphany wiped her eyes. Sheba had arrived very much earlier than expected for the wedding of Elizabeth's daughter, Joy, having decided not to wait for her brother, who still had business to attend to. Admittedly, Sheba had been ten years old when she left for England, and had been away as long again, but even so Epiphany could not imagine how Carver could have failed to recognise her. To see Sheba was to see Delilah in *her* day, a looking-glass image so exact it had made Epiphany gasp. And the likeness did not end there. Carver had confided privately that Sheba had blithely abandoned the English captain, so solicitous of her. She had swept away at the head of her train of porters without so much as a backward glance, while he hovered on the quayside, gazing after her like a dog that had just lost its master. And, clearly, in the breasts of the younger women present, Sheba provoked admiration and envy in equal measure, as much for her sprigged gown and beaded reticule as for her beauty. There would be no shortage of patrons for the ladies' emporium she was planning to open.

Sheba entertained them throughout the feast specially prepared to celebrate her homecoming, making them laugh and cry with stories of England. She had the storyteller's gift, Elizabeth said, which was high praise from one so possessed of it herself, and she'd even managed to make Tabitha laugh. Looking down the length of the white tablecloth, Epiphany wondered if her face was as flushed as Caleb's from the combination of pride and ale. The rift between them was as wide as ever, but they had agreed to tolerate one another on occasions such as this. All except the sweetmeats had been cleared, pewter tankards gleamed in the lamplight, and the glow of candles was reflected in the panes of the glass-fronted cabinet, gracing the corner of the room as if aware of the status it conferred. Tosin and Olu, having helped to clear away the dishes, stood uncertainly by the door; Epiphany beckoned them over to the table and they squeezed into their places on the bench again.

'You haven't told us,' Epiphany said to Sheba, 'why you didn't wait for your brother.'

'I didn't want to miss out on the preparations. In my experience, as with a ball, preparing for the wedding is nearly always more enjoyable than the event itself.'

'That won't be the case with my marriage, I hope,' Joy laughed.

'It depends. He's rich, I assume?'   ·

'That's no recommendation; beauty of the soul is what matters.' Tabitha was indignant.

'Joy's made a good choice. He's a fine young man.' Epiphany looked sideways at Tabitha. 'And not so rich he won't fit through the narrow gate.'

'As yet,' Caleb said to laughter. Joy's betrothed was the eldest son of one of Freetown's most eminent settler families.

'He's rich, but he *does* make my heart beat faster,' Joy said. 'Was there no one in England who made yours do the same?' she added, stepping boldly where others might have hesitated.

Epiphany and Elizabeth exchanged a dry smile. For all Sheba's airs and acquired graces, to Elizabeth's daughters she was still their little sister.

'Plenty,' Sheba replied. 'But I have a strictly debit-and-credit approach, and rich men are two a penny in England.'

'So why didn't you find a husband over there?'

'There wasn't enough sugar in my coffee.'

There was a sharp intake of breath. The older guests appeared stricken. The young ones exchanged baffled glances.

'Not enough *milk*, surely?' Caleb attempted lightness.

'True, but if it's sweetened by a whole sugar plantation, they're happy to drink it black.' Sheba's smile was corrosive. The young ones laughed loudly now they saw the joke.

Oh God! What have we done? Epiphany asked herself. She was reminded of Auntie Sam, who bore deep wounds that had left no outward mark, and were all the crueller for that.

'So you didn't find a husband! What about Abiola?' It was Peace now gaily putting the question. 'We know the men are rich. Are the girls correspondingly beautiful?'

'An Englishwoman's beauty is in her garden,' Sheba said. 'And her garden is indeed beautiful.'

'That is so tender,' Olu said, clearly astonishing himself by speaking aloud.

Sheba smiled at him.

Epiphany knew *that* smile; it was Delilah's, a shrewd investment merely, calculated, as was the remark. Not tender at all.

Joy jumped up. 'Here in Freetown, *we* are our gardens. And at my wedding I want mine to shimmer and shine. I want to be clothed in a radiance of silver and gold. But short of pulling down the moon and stars . . .'

'I've seen such a cloth.' It was Olu again. They all stared at him.

Elizabeth named a European merchant.

Olu nodded.

Elizabeth clicked her tongue. 'I know him. Believe me, that cloth is destined for the inland trade. He won't part with it except for ivory or gold.'

Joy slumped back in her seat.

Caleb turned on Olu. 'You got her hopes up for nothing. I'll thank you to keep your mouth shut.'

Showing admirable restraint, Olu obeyed. His sister Tosin, though, gave Caleb a glance from under her lids that silenced him. The girl had power, there was no denying it.

Sheba leant across the table. 'I'm sure Olu could convince the merchant.'

Olu nodded.

Olu would move heaven and earth, Epiphany thought. Sheba's investment was already yielding interest.

Big Mo spoke softly in her ear. 'That boy is purblind and the girl is heart-injured.' Epiphany could not disguise her surprise, the more so when Big Mo continued, 'Just because I broke no hearts doesn't mean that nobody broke mine. Sheba will wreak havoc, and not just with him.'

Was Sheba like this, Epiphany wondered bleakly, because of what she was – or because of what had happened to her in England? And what of Abiola?

10

ABIOLA THRUST GLOVED hands deep into his pockets and hunched his shoulders inside his coat. His hat was pulled down and his collar up against the harsh weather at the start of the New Year. He was on his way from his lodgings in Clapham to Bramwell's Bank in the heart of the City of London where, for the past two years, he had been employed as a ledger clerk. The position had been procured for him by one of the sponsors of his former school. Looking up as a few white flakes swirled down from an ominous sky, he smiled at the recollection of his eight-year-old self, waking for the first time to find the world around him blanketed in snow. Convinced that it must be the snow that turned people white, he had refused to venture out until his sister Sheba, capering about with a great powdery dab on the end of her nose, had chased away his fears.

For the most part he had enjoyed his years at the school, which had been established by the directors of the Sierra Leone Company the year before he joined. As all the pupils were from Africa, life had not seemed quite as strange as it might have done. His sister's accusation that their education was designed to turn them into accomplished servants was, in his opinion, harsh; but then he was fortunate in having an exceptional head for numbers coupled with a knack, discovered early, for turning a quick penny or two.

Today, instead of walking down the side of the tall red-brick house to the tradesman's entrance, Abiola ran up the three wide white steps leading to the front door. Without betraying that they had ever set eyes on each other before, a footman admitted him and proffered a silver tray for his card. He relinquished his hat and coat with a dry smile, receiving a slight nod of acknowledgement in return. While the footman went to present his card, Abiola crossed the flagged hall to warm himself before the fire and leaned against the stone mantel, gazing into the flames.

When he had first joined Bramwell's Bank, confident of his ability and as yet protected from the reality of the outside world, he had pictured this moment, but he had imagined himself a partner, not a client. This would in all likelihood be the first and last time he would enter these premises through the front or any other door, for in a matter of days he would return to Africa.

Throughout his time in England, Africa had been the music playing constantly in the background. At first it had drowned out all other sounds, such had been his longing for home, but as he grew older the sound had gradually faded until only by straining his ears could he hear it at all. In those around him, however, the opposite had occurred: people, who, when he was a child, had seemed barely to hear the music became by degrees deafened by it. Africa, ignored in him as a child, now defined him as a man. He threw another log on the fire. He had been lucky to encounter two notable exceptions to that rule. The first was no less a person than the owner of the bank, Mr Bramwell. The second, Mr Bramwell's chief ledger clerk, Mr Burgess, into whose care the old man had confided his new protégé with the words: 'Money sees neither class nor colour. Is that not so, Jack?'

Abiola was subsequently to discover that, for Jack Burgess, the son of Mr Bramwell's coachman, a position at the bank represented an astounding piece of good fortune.

Burgess inducted and nursed Abiola in his early months at the bank and taught him the many subtleties necessary for survival.

'Tell me . . .' Burgess had asked over a convivial supper in the Cock and Feather, a favourite haunt near the docks, 'what, in your opinion, marks out an English gentleman?'

'Everyone knows that,' Abiola had replied. 'His speech, his dress, his impeccable manners . . .'

'No, no, no. It's none of those. It is what he *abhors*. Take you and me. In a man of my complexion, the lack of suitable address and polish denotes a member of the servant class, which your gentleman abhors. In one of your colour, it is the abundance of refinement that he abhors' – Burgess adopted a dandified accent – 'for he sees in it only a grotesque mimicry.' Abiola burst out laughing. 'You may laugh,' Burgess admonished, no longer able to keep a straight face, 'but ridiculous and paradoxical though it seems, there is truth in what I say. And most abhorrent of all to our gentlemen friends at the bank is that we *aspire*; our very presence there shows that. If you do not want to be abhorred, Abiola my boy, you must be yourself: an African prince, a good Negro, either will do.'

'Can I alternate?' Abiola could barely speak for laughing. 'And what about you, Jack?'

'Honest Jack, clever Jack, but not Jack is as good as his master.'

Even now the recollection made Abiola smile. After that evening, shafts that had previously wounded fell harmlessly about him. Indeed, on many occasions it was all he could do not to laugh out loud.

A bell rang from above. The footman reappeared and, recalled to the present, Abiola followed him to the first floor. At the top of the stairs he caught sight of Burgess, who had just left Mr Bramwell's presence. His friend silently indicated that, when his own audience in the library was over, Abiola should meet him next door. Abiola remembered how his knees had trembled climbing the stairs from the clerks' room to the library when he and Burgess had been summoned to explain the large number of guilders deposited with the bank in their name. Soon after he started at Bramwell's, Abiola had devised a way profitably to combine his mentor's knowledge of Europe and his own knowledge of Africa. Thanks to his contacts within the African community in London, Abiola knew where to procure at source valuable raw materials such as ivory, gold and hardwood. The chief ledger clerk, in his turn, had access to the representatives of the merchant houses of Europe, whose business it was to trade these commodities into Amsterdam, Bruges, Cologne, Hamburg and all the Hanseatic ports. With only a modest capital sum, carefully husbanded from Abiola's allowance from Freetown, they had embarked on their first venture – the purchase of a small consignment of ivory. As soon as the ivory reached Bristol, its landed-worth had increased fourfold;

by clever auctioning they had been able to increase the differential yet further. Within a short period they had begun a series of even more lucrative deals, contracting sales to Europe. Mr Bramwell had listened attentively to their story and then congratulated them, remarking that their returns were higher than the bank's. Why Burgess should have been summoned on this occasion, however, Abiola could not imagine. He felt nervous on his friend's behalf.

Seated at his desk, Mr Bramwell invited Abiola to take the identical wing chair opposite. Having been assured that everything was in readiness for Abiola's departure to Africa, he said, 'Well, young man, you will be missed. Your work at the bank has been excellent. My good friend, your sponsor, was convinced you had promise and I am grateful to him for the recommendation. His faith, like my own, has been amply repaid.'

'Thank you, sir.'

'I envy you.'

Abiola registered the height of the ceiling and the width of the polished oak floorboards, the bookcases filled with leather-bound volumes, their spines lettered in gold, the turkey carpet in front of a blazing fire, the marble chimneypiece and the lavish silk at the windows, outside which snow was steadily falling. He looked at Mr Bramwell across the gleaming expanse of desk arrayed with freshly sharpened quills, silver inkstands and paper in orderly piles. 'Why envy me?' he asked in frank disbelief.

The old man smiled over the rim of his half-spectacles. 'You remind me, Abiola, of myself at your age. But you have such broad horizons, whole new worlds – Europe, of course, but also Africa and America.' He picked up the book lying in front of him on the desk. 'This slim volume was written by one Olauda Equiano, a former slave kidnapped from West Africa, a man possessed of considerable intelligence and sound common sense.' Mr Bramwell opened the book at the leather marker and proceeded to read aloud with the aid of a large magnifying glass held close to the page. ' "Supposing the Africans, collectively and individually, to expend Five Pounds a Head in Raiment and Furniture yearly, the Cloathing etc. of a Continent Ten Thousand Miles in Circumference, and immensely rich in Productions of every denomination would make an interesting Return indeed for our Manufactories . . ." '

Mr Bramwell closed the book and put it to one side. 'Those words were written some twenty years ago. Their author was a prescient man, he grasped the simple fact, glaringly evident now, that there is more profit to be gained from trading with the Africans than trading in them. It is an

305

argument guaranteed to persuade even those who remain untroubled by the morality of Christians merchandising their fellow beings.' He looked at Abiola. 'You grasp my meaning?'

Abiola nodded, but in truth he was not sure what it signified for him.

Mr Bramwell continued: 'Your intention, I understand, is to join your family business in Sierra Leone. I would like you to know that lines of credit can easily be made available.'

Abiola could only nod again. He did not trust himself to speak, so great was his surprise and elation at the offer being made to him.

Steepling his fingers, Mr Bramwell gazed intently down at them. 'Each generation forges its own enterprises,' he said, 'and in new worlds there will be novel ways of doing business. There will be ventures in which it would be inappropriate for the bank to involve itself *directly*, but from which, through a third party . . .' he smiled, 'it could still profit.'

'Indeed, yes,' Abiola said.

'And there will be occasions when the bank might usefully provide a hedge against unforeseen disasters.'

'Quite.'

'Although you're leaving us, Abiola, you are not losing us. We are ever your friends and partners. Remember that.'

Mr Bramwell rose from his chair and held out his hand. Abiola leapt up, took the proffered hand, and pumped it up and down. The old man accompanied his visitor to the door. As he reached out to open it, he said, 'I am not an overly religious man, but there is one precept to which I hold: cast your bread upon the waters, Abiola. Cast it wide.'

Abiola hurried straight to the adjoining room. As he closed the door behind him, his eyes flitted randomly over the exhibits lining the walls of the little cabinet of curiosities. He had glimpsed them once before and been unimpressed. A giant fossil and a fly caught in amber were covetable, perhaps, but a hen's tooth, a saint's fingernail? The two-headed rat merely made him queasy. He stood for a moment, affectionately contemplating the man with his back to him, intent on inspecting a glass case opposite, before tapping him lightly. Seeing who it was, Burgess clasped him by the shoulder and then held him at arm's length. Bursting with elation himself, Abiola wondered at his friend's obvious excitement. His cheeks had become a lustrous pink, his blue eyes sparkled and his thick dark hair stood on end.

Burgess drew himself up. 'Good news, my friend. I, too, will soon be landing on Africa's gilded shore.'

'What . . . ? Why . . . ? How is it possible?' Even as he put the questions, Abiola knew the answer. 'Mr Bramwell,' he said.

Burgess nodded and then shook his head as if unable to believe his luck. 'It's an extraordinary opportunity, nothing short of miraculous. I'm to set myself up as an independent agent in the Northern Rivers. You and I can continue our partnership on a scale we couldn't dream of in England –'

'And,' Abiola broke in, 'he's taken me into partnership, in all but name.'

Burgess gripped Abiola's hand. 'I owe this good fortune to you.'

'Let's have no talk of owing,' Abiola said. 'Just make sure' – he adopted an air of mock severity – 'that you don't succumb to the temptations of slave trafficking. The trade is still rife in the Northern Rivers.'

Serious at once, Burgess assured him earnestly, 'I could never do that! I considered it an abomination before, and now, since knowing you, doubly so.'

Abiola laughed. 'Good man!' Becoming serious in his turn, he continued, 'This adventure might cost you your life. We risk much, Mr Bramwell risks little.'

'In England we have a saying: "Cut your coat according to your cloth." I'm the son of a coachman –'

'And I'm the child of slaves.' Abiola grinned. 'And in Africa, *we* have a saying: "No condition is permanent."'

Merchantmen and men-o'-war rode at anchor on the sparkling waters of the bay. Easily recognisable were the American and French slavers captured by British naval patrols. Built for speed, the raking masts of the slaving ships betrayed their business. The flags of Holland, Spain and Portugal fluttered in the morning breeze. Having officially renounced the slave trade, commissioners from each of those countries now sat at a special court in Freetown to adjudicate intercepted slave ships.

Settler craft, pilot boats, and canoes of every description plied ceaselessly back and forth, ferrying goods and passengers. Freetown harbour deserved its reputation as the busiest on the coast. Abiola surveyed the hectic flow of activity from the bow of his hired pilot boat. As the helmsman zigzagged expertly through the traffic, the noise was beyond measuring.

He had arrived the previous evening, but had elected to spend the night on board the ship that had brought him from England. Prolonging the transition, postponing the moment. He had quit the boat early, ready for a new day, a new world, a new life.

The throngs on the dockside were thickest and most vociferous at the landing place where a flight of twelve steps led up from the beach to Water Street. Passengers were received here, goods were landed and searched, and custom duties decided. Soldiers, sailors and merchants' clerks rubbed shoulders with the dockworkers, pilots, petty traders and washerwomen who stood by, waiting to board any new vessel arriving in the harbour.

At a little distance, in front of a breakwater of loosely piled stones, a crowd had gathered. Abiola sauntered across. His height afforded him a glimpse of the entertainment and, edging forward, he decided to stay and watch. A red squirrel, bushy tail flagged up behind, was perched on the shoulder of a sailor fresh off a boat from England. The solemn eyed little creature, attached to a silver chain, was arousing quite as much interest as its owner, who was barefoot and dressed only in a pair of loose canvas breeches reaching to the knee. The man's fair skin was burnt a deep brown and his hair, bleached almost white, hung in a lank pigtail. In front of him a rough plank lay across a pair of upturned barrels. Seemingly completely absorbed in what he was doing and unaware of the tight circle of spectators, he made a great business of brushing invisible specks of sand from the surface of his makeshift table. From his pocket he withdrew three playing cards, and only then did he appear to notice the crowd. He gave a start.

'Bless me,' he exclaimed, addressing the squirrel, which gazed at him attentively. 'They all look sharp as ginger, which is not what I had a mind to expect.' His tone was aggrieved. 'I'm in a dither now whether to proceed or not, lest I lose my trousers as well as my shirt.' A burst of laughter greeted his words, and when he made as if to put the cards in his pocket again, the crowd objected loudly, urging him to stay. Abiola felt a pang of nostalgia. Squirrels were a familiar sight on the common at Clapham and he had witnessed countless shows like this in the port of London.

The sailor bowed low, cards held loosely in his hands. He looked round the ring of expectant faces. 'Like a reed in the wind, I bend to your wishes. But I take it very hard to discover that you Negroes may be as smart as the rest of us!'

His wonderment elicited another burst of laughter from the crowd. As the men pressed nearer, Abiola gained the front.

'That's it, come closer, close as you like.' The sailor placed three cards one by one face down in a row on the table. Being slightly bent in the middle, they did not lie flat. He picked up the two on the outside by slipping his thumbs underneath each card and spreading his fingers over the back, then flipped both hands over to show two red cards – the eight and nine of hearts – cradled face up in his palms. His eyes swept the crowd. Keeping his left palm facing up, he placed his right hand face down over the middle card, picked it up with his thumb underneath as before and turned it to show the queen of spades.

'Watch closely.' The squirrel jumped from his perch on his master's shoulder to the makeshift table. 'Good boy,' the sailor said. He flipped his right hand over again, and dropped the card back in the middle as before. Quickly turning over his left hand, he placed that card on the right and dropped the card he still held in his right hand on the left so that once again the three cards were face down in a row.

The sailor rubbed his palms together and spat on them. The squirrel jumped back on to his shoulder 'Now, let's see if you can find the lady.' Slowly he switched the position of the cards, sliding them over the surface of the table. Once. Twice. 'Who can tell me where the lady is?'

'I can,' someone called from the crowd.

The sailor looked the speaker up and down, head on one side. 'Why not put a little money on it?'

The bet placed, the sailor's hand hovered and swooped. He turned over the selected card. It was the queen of spades. There was a roar from the crowd.

Dipping his hand in his pocket to pay the debt, the sailor shook his head despairingly. 'These people,' he addressed the squirrel, 'look set to clean me out.' The squirrel flicked its fiery tail.

Amid laughter, a second wager was proposed and the crowd pressed closer still. With a fatalistic shrug, the sailor placed the three playing cards in a row on the table and proceeded exactly as before. Once again, to the huge delight of the crowd, he lost. He swore long and eloquently, and it was only after much loud persuasion that he consented to continue.

Fools would be as easily parted from their money here as elsewhere, Abiola concluded, and he was backing away when his attention was suddenly seized. The girl was tall and slender. She stood very straight, head held high, her eyes downcast. In the midst of the restless throng her absolute stillness appeared uncanny. All else faded away and for a long moment Abiola was aware only of her. He saw her glance up at the young man beside her, and felt he would give everything he had in the world if she would only look at *him*. He stared and stared, willing her to acknowledge his presence. He knew his conduct was unseemly, but he could not help himself. Her eyes remained resolutely downcast.

A voice called out a wager and, barely knowing what he was doing, Abiola staked a sum large enough to catch everyone's attention. The sailor's exaggerated nervousness as he prepared to shuffle the cards served to heighten the tension. He took his time.

'Which one is it then?' he asked at last.

Abiola pointed. Slowly, reluctantly, the sailor reached out and turned the card face up. It was the queen of spades. The sailor groaned and threw out his arms. The squirrel hopped on to his head. The crowd laughed and cheered.

'I suppose you want to go again?' the sailor enquired glumly.

A voice called out, wagering twice Abiola's previous stake, and Abiola promptly doubled it. He shot a glance at the girl. She did not look up. The same voice now trebled the stake. Abiola raised it by half. The sailor flexed his arms and the squirrel jumped from his master's head to his shoulder and on to the table once more. The crowd fell silent. The sailor aligned the three cards precisely in a row, picked them up and displayed the faces as before – the eight of hearts, the nine of hearts and the queen of spades. The silence tightened.

'Now keep your eyes on the cards!' Turning his wrists sharply, the sailor dropped each one face down on the table – one in the centre, one to the left, one to the right. 'Keep watching!' Slowly he switched them round, once, twice, three times. He clasped his hands behind his back.

'Find the lady!'

Abiola pointed to a card.

'Are you sure?' the sailor asked him.

Abiola nodded.

'Quite certain? You don't want to change your mind?'

Abiola shook his head emphatically, and the crowd began to chant.

The sailor held up the card: it was *not* the queen of spades. There was a collective gasp from the crowd. The sailor scooped the squirrel into his arms, stroked its ruddy coat and spoke loudly in its tufted ear. 'Our friend should try his luck once more, shouldn't he? He struck lucky before and he could again.'

Abiola, his face burning, made a hasty exit, the crowd parting in sympathetic silence. He removed his high hat, its grip suddenly vice-like around his forehead, and mopped his brow with an already damp handkerchief. His fine lawn shirt clung to his body and his leather shoes had begun to pinch. Sweltering in his faultlessly tailored black woollen coat, tight-fitting buff breeches and white stockings, he wandered disconsolately along the teeming dockside, incredulous at what he had just done. All because of a girl! She was certainly striking and she had undeniable presence, but to be carried out of himself like that, by a stranger he would never meet again . . . And were he to do so, what then? Beneath those high cheekbones he had spotted tribal marks. She was likely from some up-country tribe with no English. The whole episode now seemed like an aberration he simply could not account for.

Looking up, he saw Foster's Wharf written in large letters and he thanked God that nobody who knew him had witnessed his humiliation.

He replaced his hat, straightened his coat and adjusted his necktie. Seeing a tall figure leaning against a mooring post on the all but deserted wharf, he hailed him. The young man approached and Abiola was surprised and disconcerted to discover that it was none other than the person who had been standing beside the girl in the crowd. Mortified, he noted the same facial marks, revealed on closer inspection to be four horizontal lines, half an inch long, on either cheek. He dabbed at the sweat on his upper lip, eyeing with no little rancour the young man's light linen jacket and breeches and bare feet. Removing his hat, he nodded to him, receiving a small bow in return.

Pre-emptively Abiola said, 'An old man I know told me only to bet on a certainty. I shouldn't have neglected his advice.'

'In my experience, old people are not always right – but they're usually wise.'

'That same old man would say young people are not always wrong but they're usually rash. I knew there was a trick. I've seen countless such and I thought I could beat it, but . . .' Abiola shrugged. 'Unless you're in the know . . .'

'You could have beaten it.'

'Of course *you* would have.'

The young man winced at the sarcasm. 'I was trained to observe. As a hunter and as a warrior your life might depend on catching the smallest movement. The trick here was to condition us to believe that because the black card was underneath, it was always dropped on to the table first. In

311

fact, by sleight of hand, the cards could be switched and the red card dropped instead. You noticed how the cards were bent in the middle and the way the sailor slipped his thumb underneath?'

'Of course,' Abiola said.

The young man smiled. 'The question then,' he continued, 'was when would the switch be done? I'd noticed the signals passing between the sailor and his partner, who, as it happens, was standing near you in the crowd. When he doubled the stake, and you doubled it again, I knew the sailor would throw the red. It was easy after that to "follow the lady" because she was the second card to drop on to the table.'

Abiola was impressed but said merely, 'Most instructive. *You* could've bet on a certainty. Why didn't you?'

'It's a foolish antelope that risks being taken by a leopard for the sake of food that's far away when there's food nearby. If I'd neglected my work and not won, I'd have lost the esteem of my boss.'

Abiola put on his hat. 'Thank you for your time. But I must get on, I have business to attend to at this wharf. My ship, the *Lucy* – see her there in the river with a red pennant? – will be unloading here later. So I must find –'

'Of course! You're Mr Abiola. I was sent to meet you, in case you decided not to wait for your ship to be piloted in. I'm your father's clerk. My name is Olu.' He gave a broad grin.

Abiola, his smile circumspect, shook the outstretched hand. His father's clerk had watched him make a fool of himself and witnessed him throwing his money away. He had considerable ground to make up. And then there was the matter of the girl. The 'trained observer' could not have failed to notice the attention he had paid to his companion earlier. What was she to him? Too bad, he thought, if she should be his sweetheart.

Having been so long away, Abiola remembered little about Freetown. Even within the family he had difficulty finding his bearings. His memories of home were preserved in the recollections of others as a fly is caught in amber, real but unreachable. The period following his arrival was necessarily busy and he was grateful for the opportunity to immerse himself in familiar practicalities. The cargo of the *Lucy*, which included a considerable quantity of merchandise for the ladies' emporium that Sheba intended to establish, had to be unloaded and inventoried prior to warehousing. Values had also to be assessed for those items destined for trade in the interior and the Northern Rivers. The daylight hours being insufficient for all that needed to be accomplished, lamps burned far into the night at the warehouse and in the office. Abiola, with Olu at his side, worked on long after Caleb and Carver had retired. There was an unspoken rivalry between them, deadly serious on Abiola's part until he discovered that the girl he had seen in the crowd, who was rarely out of his thoughts, was not Olu's intended, as he had feared, but his sister, Tosin. However late Abiola stayed, Olu remained to lock up behind him and no matter how early in the day he arrived, he found Olu already installed.

Once the unloading was completed Abiola was eager to assume his place in the family business.

He was still pondering how he might broach the subject when his father said, 'Abiola, you should begin your new life in the same way you ended your old one.'

'I should?' In vain Abiola cast his mind back. He shook his head. 'Remind me.'

Caleb replied, 'Your grandmother Delilah walked you round our various little enterprises to show you on the one hand that you could hold up your head with pride in England, and on the other to let you understand the effort involved in keeping you there. Do the same now and you'll see not only how successful we've become but how best to repay that effort. And this time Olu can be your guide.'

Neat, Abiola thought, with new respect. He was being tested.

He said carefully: 'If I didn't know, I'd swear your apprentice slept in the office.'

Caleb smiled. 'Olu's industriousness is ingrained.'

Abiola discovered the truth of this for himself in the following days as he accompanied Olu on his rounds or painstakingly pored over the books in the office. On Sundays Olu visited his parents, Dotun and Lola, and sister, Tosin, at the farm. After church in the morning he helped his father with any heavy work that needed to be done before running an eye over the accounts with Epiphany. And when evening service was over he walked the five miles back to Freetown laden with goods for market on Monday morning. Abiola, as soon as he learned of these visits, insisted on accompanying him. He could not persuade Olu to make the journey on horseback, so he joined him on foot. Allegedly, it was to see his mother and Tabitha, but no one was deceived for, although Abiola and Tosin barely acknowledged each other, there was no mistaking the electricity between them.

'So?' Caleb asked, finding Abiola alone for once in the office. 'Now that you've had the opportunity to find your way about, what do you think of our operations here in Freetown?'

Abiola took in the contrast between the magnificence of Mr Bramwell's library and this small cramped room with its unglazed window and tamped earth floor. Considering the lack of credit available to them and the European competition, which laboured under no such restrictions, the family had been remarkably successful.

'I'm impressed,' he said.

Caleb thrust his thumbs into the pockets of his canary yellow waistcoat. 'Your grandmother will be happy to hear that.' It was only a matter of days now until Joy's wedding, and Delilah, away on a trip to the Northern Rivers, was expected home at any moment.

'I'm surprised Grandma still travels on business, especially to the Rio Pongas.'

'You think she's too old? You'd better keep *that* to yourself.'

'I think it's too dangerous. I understand it's a free-for-all up there, what with the French gunboats, the British naval squadron and the illegal slave runners. I could go in her stead. It's no place for a woman, however doughty she might be.'

'Your grandmother thrives on danger; craves it, I sometimes think. But I agree with you, and the timing's right. She could be persuaded.'

That wouldn't be difficult, Abiola thought, once she knew the whole story. He said, 'I could take Olu with me. You were right about him. He deserves an increase in salary.'

Caleb gave Abiola a sharp look. 'Apprentices don't get paid.'

'I know, but he should be made an exception.'

'Take up the matter with your mother. She's the one who bought him.'

'*Bought* him?'

'His apprenticeship.'

'Smacks of slavery to me.'

'You know nothing about it,' Caleb snapped. 'In any case, his entire family is apprenticed to Epiphany: father, mother, sister . . . And speaking of the sister . . .' Caleb cleared his throat. 'I never knew my father; Delilah was the nearest to a father I ever had, and I'm sure she would agree with me when I say that I see no advantage in a penniless, rescued African girl. A bride should bring something more than her personal attributes.'

*

314

The church, built to seat a thousand, was full, and there were still more people outside peering in through the windows and crowded round the doorway. Settler and Maroon families were represented, and there was a large turnout of government officials and naval officers, as colourful as any of the wedding guests in their dress uniforms. They sat bolt upright, white gloves and cockaded hats resting on their laps, boots creaking and swords clanking whenever they shifted on the over-crowded benches.

The organ struck up, announcing the arrival of the bridal party, and the congregation rose to its collective feet and turned towards the entrance. Elizabeth clutched Epiphany's hand, tears starting at the sight of her daughter on Caleb's arm, framed in the arch of the double doors. Epiphany handed her a handkerchief. Epiphany had insisted on the wedding being a joint affair, pre-empting any objections by reminding Caleb and Delilah that, just as Johnson had been father to her before his own children were born, so she had been mother to his. And with only a little prompting, Caleb had offered to give the bride away in the absence of her father. 'In remembrance of past kindnesses,' he told Elizabeth. Now Joy lit up the interior of the church like a sunburst, Epiphany thought, watching her glide down the aisle to stand in front of an altar decked in green branches and sweet-scented flowers. Her gold lace veil matched the gold tissue of her skirt, the silver buckles on her shoes complementing the silver in her bodice. Coral ornaments at her neck and wrists enhanced the darkness of her skin.

Sheba, her dress and bonnet the height of fashion in London, no doubt, was seated next to Delilah, who was dressed in her favourite blue. Abiola sat between Carver and Olu, who both appeared enviably cool in their plain-cut Freetown linen. He was as fashionably dressed as his sister but, unlike her, seemed somewhat absurd in this setting. Watching as he eased a finger inside his elaborately high neck cloth, Epiphany strongly suspected that his tight-fitting jacket, striped waistcoat and nankeen breeches had only succeeded in making him ridiculous in the eyes of the person he'd hoped to impress.

Abiola caught her eye and quickly bowed his head in response to the chaplain's invitation to unite in prayer. As she too bent to pray, Epiphany was haunted by the memories of the child he had once been, and Sheba . . . Her daughter's resemblance to Delilah, in whose doting admiration she was once more enfolded, was evidently more than skin deep. It remained to be seen, however, whether Abiola's uncanny resemblance to

315

his grandfather also extended beyond the physical. If not, then perhaps she'd been wrong to send him to England.

'That went off well,' Delilah said, as the bride and groom made their way back down the aisle. The conspicuous European presence was a tribute to her, and the colony chaplain had officiated at her behest.

'I wish Reverend George could have married them,' Elizabeth said, unashamedly crying. Epiphany hugged her; she too was in tears. Reverend George, who had died the year before, had conducted their marriages in Nova Scotia.

'Solomon in all his glory couldn't hold a candle to your daughter today.' Carver shook out his handkerchief and handed it to Elizabeth.

'The Good Lord didn't mean it quite that way.' Tabitha rapped him on the arm with her fan.

'Freedom's a great leveller,' Carver retorted. 'There's not one of us as pure as we used to be.'

The Parade Ground had been commandeered for the wedding feast. The hectic activity put Epiphany in mind of their time in the American War, with Big Mo and Delilah as the generals, ordering their troops to the front line to mind the giant cauldrons, gather firewood, procure more stores from the hawkers and vendors waiting in the certain knowledge that, however much food had been cooked, more would be needed to feed the multitudes. The festivities continued all day, and the guests danced long into the evening until finally the night was ceded to the young.

Hundreds of torches burned in the clearing, so bright that they eclipsed the stars. In the still night air a horn sang, a row of fiddles took up the refrain, and the dancers, packed tightly together and keeping time with the beat of the drum, made the ground tremble beneath their feet.

Abiola moved slowly round the edge. He had discarded his finery in favour of a linen shirt and breeches and now walked barefoot like the majority. As he completed half the circle, he heard Olu call his name.

'Aren't you dancing?' Abiola asked him.

'I'm a poor dancer and I don't enjoy it.'

'Ah.' Abiola searched among the dancers.

'My sister, on the other hand, is known for her dancing. She sings too. Look, there she is, with her partner.'

Tosin danced flame-bright, her red wrapper turned to crimson silk, her head-tie a garland of coral in the light of the torches. Her arms were lifted to the sky and her feet traced an ancient pattern on the ground. Abiola watched, transfixed by the aura of otherness about her.

Olu said, 'I'm thirsty and I expect my sister will be too when this dance is ended. Allow me to fetch a drink for you.'

'No, no. I'll go, you stay . . . wait here,' Abiola volunteered. Tosin, he calculated, was bound to return to her brother's side.

In search of fresh coconut he made his way briskly to the stalls heaped with fruit where the market women were frying fish and roasting bush meat over smoking braziers. He re-emerged with Sheba and her English captain in tow to find Tosin, as expected, standing beside her brother. Sheba was *not* barefoot, her little slippers and white froth of a gown daintily complementing the captain's scarlet uniform. They made a handsome couple and, though carrying a coconut each, appeared not in the least incongruous.

The captain tipped his head back and drank the milk of the coconut. Clapping him on the shoulder, Abiola saluted his obvious enjoyment of the true life of Freetown.

Sheba said gaily, 'This is nothing. The man is so eager to enter into the spirit of the occasion, it was all I could do to move him past the dram shops on the way here.'

'I couldn't be better suited: a balmy night, the greenwood tree, music to soothe the savage breast – my savage breast, that is . . .' The Captain blushed bright red.

Abiola and Sheba fell against each other, laughing. Olu and Tosin looked at them, mystified.

'Time to dance,' Sheba declared. 'Tosin, you can dance with my captain and I'll dance with your brother.' She dragged a protesting Olu by the hand. 'You, Abiola, can look after yourself.'

Abiola stared bitterly after the captain. In a very short time Sheba and Olu returned.

'He can't dance,' Sheba announced indignantly. 'So come on, brother, do your duty. Follow me.'

Abiola glanced at Olu, who shrugged. Sheba skipped away to join the dancers.

'The captain dances better than Olu,' she informed Abiola when he caught up with her.

'He did try to warn you.'

'I thought he was shy, not hopeless.' Sheba leaned towards him as the dance steps brought them together.

'You're very cruel to Olu.'

'I can afford to be, for a good while yet; and not just to Olu. When the time comes, I shall be kindness itself.' She swayed away.

Abiola laughed despite himself. Only he knew what prejudice Sheba had endured in England. She never talked about the cold and the loneliness, or the humiliations she had suffered. But he had seen how she had forced herself to grow a thick skin. A sharp tongue had become her favoured weapon, mockery and laughter her defences.

He said. 'Olu has eyes only for you.'

'The captain too.'

'Which will you have?'

Sheba's smile flared. 'Neither, I imagine. I have learned to my cost, dear brother, that you can't choose where your heart will settle, but you can decide not to follow where it leads. Oh, and remind me to tell you something about your friend Olu . . .' She snaked away and was soon lost in the throng. Abiola's attention immediately reverted to Tosin. Craning his neck, he peered into the crowd.

'I'm here,' a voice said behind him. He swung round. For the first time she raised her eyes to his.

'I've been looking at *you* ever since that first time on the quay.'

'I know you have, but have you been seeing me?'

Abiola had wanted her to look at him. Now, he wanted her good opinion, craved her deep and rigorous approval, without which he felt his life would have no meaning.

Tosin said, 'We are the same, you and I. We're cut from the same cloth, have the same threads in our making. In Oyo, where I come from, they say we choose at the moment of our birth the fate that will accompany us in the world, and once we have chosen we cannot escape it. Our fates, yours and mine, are intertwined. How and why I do not know –'

Abiola interrupted, 'That's one story, but here's another: it could be love.'

'Love is a story like any other.'

'Except I know how this one will end.'

Tosin lowered her eyes. 'All I know is that it's begun.'

Abiola held out his hand and, as they entered the dance, he asked, 'Tell me, what pleases you in a man?'

Over her shoulder, Tosin replied, 'The things that displease tell you more.'

Abiola laughed. 'You're right: liking *does* change but disliking does not. Well?'

'In general or in particular?'

They circled each other back to back.

'In particular.'

'I could never like a braggart, who throws his money around and –'

'That's unjust!'

They came face to face.

'And then makes excuses.'

Abiola made a grab for her. 'Shall I tell you what *displeases* me?'

'No.' Laughing, she ducked under his arm, her backward glances drawing him behind her as surely as a scarf looped round his neck.

Abiola chased after her. 'Believe me, I'll get even with you for this.'

Tosin danced away from him. 'And then makes promises he cannot keep.'

Abiola followed her giddily. Africa, it seemed, was full of promises.

It was not until a few days later that Abiola remembered to ask Sheba what she had to tell him about Olu. Brother and sister were inspecting the location of Sheba's emporium: two rooms on the ground floor of a newly refurbished property on the corner of Rawdon Street and Cross Street. The worst of the afternoon heat had subsided and it was pleasantly cool as they stepped outside into the yard, shaded by a huge banana tree. In answer to Abiola's question, Sheba recounted how Joy had come by her incomparable wedding dress.

'Olu,' Sheba said, 'happened to know an English merchant in possession of the cloth. He also knew of an up-country chief who had sent his gold and ivory to the coast, where he had no contacts. Olu brought the merchant and the representative of the chief together. Thus was the merchant spared the expense and dangers of a trip into the interior, and the chief's representative, who had journeyed to the coast laden with all that gold and ivory, was able to achieve a successful sale.'

'And Olu's reward,' Abiola said, critically examining the cerulean blue paint on the outside of the house, 'was that Joy had her cloth of gold.'

Sheba, dressed in white as usual, twirled her parasol. 'I'm surprised Father didn't tell you. Now we can be the middlemen for all sorts of deals. Besides solving the immediate problem of the wedding dress, Olu has shown us the way forward.'

~

II

ANXIOUS TO MAKE a start with Burgess, Abiola requested a meeting with Caleb and Delilah as soon as the wedding celebrations were over. Arriving at the office at first light, he found them both waiting for him.

Caleb eyed Abiola's breeches as he squeezed through the door of the crowded little room. 'It's true what they say, there's always someone in a worse position than yourself. At least I can sit down.' Caleb's girth had increased with the years but he was dapper as ever in an embroidered waistcoat and starched and frilled cravat.

Mindful of Mr Bramwell's adage that prosperous is as prosperous does, Abiola had dressed with care. He suspected that his father, natty, but by London standards somewhat outmoded, was envious of his dark blue coat, cut very short at the front with a high standing collar and facings, which matched the grey-and-white stripes of his waistcoat. His breeches, intended to show the calves to advantage, were indeed fashionably tight at the knee.

Delilah's smile was gently mocking. 'We can't allow the boy to stand, Caleb. We're big chiefs, you and I, his head must on no account be higher than ours.' And as Abiola lowered himself gingerly into the one vacant chair at the table, she said, 'We know what *we* can do for you, Abiola. The question is, what can *you* do for us?'

At nearly seventy, Delilah was still formidable. She was straight and slender and her skin unlined. With her white hair out of sight and her teeth discreetly hidden behind her smile, she could pass for a woman more than twenty years younger. Her eyes revealed that her mind had lost none of its sharpness.

Subjected to that beady scrutiny, Abiola was thankful he had heeded one of Mr Bramwell's firmest injunctions: never talk to your clients before first listening carefully to them.

He drew a deep breath and, in answer to Delilah's question, replied, 'Accompanying Olu on his rounds and having scrutinised the books, I have learned in these past few weeks as much about business as I absorbed during the whole of my two years at Bramwell's Bank.'

Let your competitors feel that *you* are learning from *them*, Mr Bramwell had advised – and how right he was, Abiola thought, observing the undisguised satisfaction of his father and grandmother. He continued, 'There is potential, it seems to me, in two areas. One is in construction: I understand the new governor is about to embark on an ambitious building programme and he has announced that all public works are to be put out to contract. By securing just one of those contracts we could treble our profits in Freetown. I also envisage expansion of trade in the Northern Rivers, the gains from which would be immeasurable. But such expansion would, of course, require investment on a grand scale. And in answer to your question, Grandma, that brings me to my contribution to the business . . .'

'Go on.'

'Money,' Abiola said.

Delilah leant forward, Caleb too, both fully engaged now.

'In all but name, I've been taken into partnership with Bramwell's Bank. Mr Bramwell will not only make lines of credit available, he has given me his assurance that I will have a hedge against unforeseen disaster, and, where appropriate, I can act as a proxy.'

His father and grandmother digested this in silence. Caleb was clearly dumbfounded, and even Delilah was unable to conceal her astonishment.

'Furthermore,' Abiola continued, 'my friend and mentor, Jack Burgess, has been appointed Mr Bramwell's agent and representative in the Northern Rivers. A decision prompted, apparently, by the modest successes we achieved on our own account, coupled with my returning to Sierra Leone at this time. And in light of that, I believe I would be best employed in the Rio Pongas.'

Delilah said: 'Europeans go to the Rio Pongas for one reason and one reason only: *slaves.*'

'Exactly.' Abiola leaned across the table. 'Only, now that most of their countries have outlawed the trade, the day will inevitably come when slaving will be superseded, as it has been here in Sierra Leone. But, as we have also seen, the European merchants with their unlimited credit have taken over the most valuable areas of trade. Even with the money now available to me, the best I can do in Freetown is compete. But in the Rio Pongas I can make a killing. The Europeans are not yet alive to the opportunities that exist up there. Between Mr Bramwell and my friend Jack Burgess, I am most advantageously placed. Surely it makes sense to release Grandma to help oversee the expansion in Freetown? Lucrative contracts would certainly come our way.' Abiola sat back, confident he had won his case.

'It makes sound sense.' Caleb cracked his fingers.

'No,' Delilah said.

'No?' It was Abiola's turn to be confounded.

'It would be better for you to start in Freetown. The family name will secure you all the contacts you need. Up in the Rio Pongas it's the person, not the name. And everyone knows me. I've been trading there for twenty years; not on the scale you're contemplating, but profitably all the same, and steady. Let me prepare the ground, introduce this Burgess to a whole network of people and . . .'

'Let's go together, I could learn as we go along.'

'Patience, Abiola. Your Mr Bramwell must have told you that the more patient you are, the more money you'll make.'

'Father?' Abiola appealed to Caleb.

'The boy's right,' said Caleb.

'No,' Delilah said firmly. 'And that's my final word.'

'But why?' Abiola demanded, baffled.

Delilah folded her lips.

She was not to be swayed, Abiola saw. He pushed his chair back with a clatter, made a perfunctory excuse and strode out of the door.

Caleb turned to Delilah. 'I don't understand, why not let the boy take over the Northern Rivers?'

Delilah did not reply.

Caleb shot her a suspicious glance. 'You promised.'

'I know.' Delilah drummed her fingers on the table. 'It wasn't possible.'

'But what Abiola has just told us about the money changes everything.'

'It certainly means we could continue to cut the ground from under Elizabeth.'

'Delilah!'

'Yes, yes. I understand the position just as well as you. Abiola should go, and soon, if he's not to jeopardise his position with the bank. But I'll have to make one last trip . . .' Caleb eyed her sceptically. 'I *will* finish it this time,' Delilah said. 'Once and for all.'

'So what shall we tell Abiola?'

'Tell him I've changed my mind. Tell him yes.'

Urging his horse forward, Abiola gave himself up to the moment, speeding dangerously along the road leading out of Freetown towards his mother's farm and the mountains beyond. As he emerged from behind the screen of trees at some distance from the house a gaggle of children was already running to meet him, for the drumming of the horse's hooves on the baked earth could be felt a mile away.

He immediately slowed his pace and, amid loud cheers from the children, brought the horse to a stop in front of the house, rearing it back on its hind legs, hooves pawing the air. The noise drew Epiphany into the yard. She was carrying a jar of ale and a cup. After watering his horse Abiola left it leisurely cropping grass under the watchful eyes of the children and went to sit on the bench with his mother. Epiphany handed him the cup, which he drained, gratefully rinsing the dust from his parched throat.

Smiling, she poured him another. 'No one could accuse you of neglecting your old mother.'

Nursing the ale in his lap, Abiola leaned back against the wooden shingles, grinning a little sheepishly. Filial duty, as she well knew, was not the reason he was so frequently to be found at the farm.

Epiphany laid a palm tentatively against his cheek. 'When you were away in England, I used to try to imagine you there, the games you played, the life you led, what you felt . . . Now here you are, but still it's as if a whole ocean lies between us.'

For his part, Abiola remembered the fierce attachments he had once felt rather as an amputee might remember a long-lost limb. After an awkward pause, he said, 'I know that in every stranger there's either a friend or an enemy in waiting. But –'

'That could be your grandfather talking.'

'If I had a shilling for every time someone mentions how like Grandpa Cornelius I am, I would be a rich man by now.' Abiola's voice was harsher than he'd intended and he took Epiphany's hand in his. 'I'm your son, Ma, and always will be. So you can be sure that in this stranger a friend waits.'

'Your grandmother doesn't think so,' Epiphany chided gently. 'She thinks you want rid of her.'

'I want no such thing. I want to make a start, that's all.'

'Perhaps she's not ready to be put out to pasture just yet. Give her time.'

'I don't have time if I'm to make the best of the opportunity I've been given.'

'Oh, Abiola! Sheba's the same, you're both –'

323

'What?' Abiola snatched his hand back, his chin thrust forward. 'We were children when you sent us to England all those years ago. You can't claim to know us now.'

Epiphany said firmly, 'Abiola, I believe that you and I and Grandfather Cornelius are each a link in a chain of destiny that took him out of Oyo and across the ocean to America, brought me back to Africa and carried you to England.'

'Grandpa's fate was not unique.' Abiola's voice rose angrily. 'And others besides you returned to Africa – nearly everyone in Sierra Leone, in fact. Fewer have travelled to England, but, even so, many more than just me. I don't believe in any special destiny, and I certainly don't think it was worth sacrificing your husband and children for.'

'At the moment of our birth,' Epiphany replied doggedly, 'we choose the fate that accompanies us into the world, and once chosen, we cannot escape it. You had to go to England so that you could return armed for the task ahead.'

'I came back to Africa, Ma, because it was made very clear to me that I had best pursue my ambitions at home. My destiny is to build on and expand the gains we have made, to beat the Europeans at their own game.'

'No. That is *not* what you're here to do. Whether you believe it or not, *your* destiny is to carry on the work that we began: to put an end to slavery. You are here to find the way. When the time comes, you'll hear the voices of the ancestors and you'll follow where they lead.'

'Will Sheba hear them too? What purpose did it serve sending her to England?'

'It was to serve your grandmother's ambition –'

'In the same way that my going served yours? Sheba's ambition was to marry the man she loved. Did you know that? No, I thought not. He bowed to the wishes of his family and abandoned her for one of his own kind. That last betrayal broke her.'

Epiphany flinched. 'I know that Sheba's spirit is a crooked thing . . .'

Abiola folded his arms across his chest.

At last Epiphany said, 'My mother is a law unto herself. I can't help you there, but I hazard you already have a plan to get round the problem.'

'You're beginning to know me.'

'I knew your grandfather . . .'

Abiola smiled dryly. 'Grandpa Cornelius wasn't all nobility and goodness then?'

'A coin must be stamped on both sides to have value.'

Restless, Abiola rose to his feet. 'Let's take a walk.'

They strolled about the farm, Epiphany pointing out the plots of cassava and yams, pumpkins, corn, beans, but Abiola's mind was plainly elsewhere.

'You have something to tell me,' Epiphany stated rather than asked.

'I intend to marry Tosin,' Abiola blurted.

Epiphany did not answer immediately. Then she said: 'Have you told Sheba?'

'Good God, no. She'd no more approve than Father and Grandma. Only, instead of saying we're too young or it's too soon, she'd say straight out that it ought to be someone with a hefty dowry, a Freetown property or two.'

Epiphany squinted up at him, a hand shading her face. 'What would you reply to a person who doesn't care about a dowry but still thinks you're too young and it's too soon?'

'Tosin's been through the fire; she's already the woman she's going to be. I've had no such tempering. There's no brand etched on my breast. But it appears she can see the man I'm going to be. I can't see him yet, but I do know that by being with her I'll be a better man than I otherwise might.'

'You mean she'll curb your Grandma Delilah tendencies?'

'Quite.'

Epiphany said emphatically, 'Marrying Tosin is the best thing you could do for your children. It's true she's been tempered, but in *her* the wellspring still runs clear, full of sweet water. Slavery has salted ours and many generations will have to pass, I fear, before the spring runs clear again.'

The sound of children's voices drew Abiola to the dappled shade among the orange trees, where Tosin was taking a class through their lessons. Soon after coming to the farm, she had declared that she wanted to be a teacher one day. Delighted, and realising that she was every bit as clever her brother, Epiphany had nurtured her ambition, and to that end had arranged for her to attend the school established by a scholarly English gentleman in Freetown. Tosin was particularly skilful in helping with new arrivals from the King's Yard. Having been on a slave vessel bound for the Americas herself, she was intimately acquainted with the ordeal each of them had undergone. She it was who calmed their night terrors, coaxed them to eat, to speak, and finally to play and laugh again.

As Abiola watched, the children formed a circle, clapping and singing, taking it in turns to be in the middle. It occurred to Abiola that it was at moments such as this that Tosin was truly herself. Since Joy's wedding they had been virtually inseparable. Most days when her work was done, Tosin would walk into town and Abiola would ride back to the farm with her sitting in front of him on the saddle. While his horse paced gently in the moonlight they exchanged stories until in his mind's eye he could conjure the steep vaulted roofs of Oyo, thatched with bere grass and turned to gold in the sunlight; the shaded courtyards and market squares within a triple circuit of walls three times the height of the tallest warrior. And no doubt she could as easily picture London's city walls, studded with towers and turrets, the bridges over the river and the tall red-roofed houses and palaces built of stone.

Tosin had not spoken about her family's capture until pressed. It took time before she felt able to tell him how she had been herded to the coast in chains, afraid every day for her life, and for those of her mother and father and brother. She told him of the infants who did not survive the branding, of the mothers who died from the shock and grief of witnessing the iron searing their children's flesh. She recalled how they'd been driven on to the ship and confined in the darkness of the hold, naked, the pain of their branding still fresh, overwhelmed by the heat and smell, manacled to each other and to the narrow decks made slippery by mucous and blood. She recounted how, in order to protect her daughter from rape, her mother had smeared her with excrement. Wrenched from home and friends and loved ones, they were terrorised into submission by the absolute violence of those who were transporting them into bondage.

Her words had left him shaken, humbled, scraped to the bone. He should not pity her, she said; pity should be reserved for the dead. As his love for her deepened, he was more and more in awe of the strength, which had enabled her to survive with her spirit intact.

The bell rang, signalling the end of lessons for the day, and Abiola called out to Tosin as the children dashed to the house in search of supper. Gathering up the few slates she beckoned him to follow and led the way through the orange grove to the bank of a small stream where they could sit hidden from view. She set the slates in a pile and trailed her feet in the water.

Abiola sat beside her. 'My mother believes that the best thing I could do is marry you. In you, she says, the spring runs sweet and clear.'

Tosin smiled. 'I'll be a river, a constant flow, a source of sustenance and comfort, wind ruffled and still by turns, cool in the heat of the day and tranquil under the stars.'

'And me?'

Tosin laughed. 'A strong swimmer is what you should be.'

Abiola said, 'I'll never leave you Tosin. I prom—'

Tosin put a hand over his mouth. She began to sing:

> *'I took my calabash and went to Oyo town*
> *The prince of Oyo took the calabash from my head.*
> *I said, Sir, why did you do that?*
> *He said it's because I am a slender beauty*
> *I have a neck worthy to wear blue Segi beads*
> *May good luck attend me today . . .'*

'That was beautiful. What does it mean?'

She smiled. It was a song that a young girl sang on the eve of her wedding.

'It means yes,' Tosin said.

Olu was bent over a ledger, working by the little light lancing through the window. Abiola burst in and Olu, as usual, took no notice of his remonstration that for the sake of a candle it was not worth the risk to his eyesight. His quill continued undisturbed down the page, meticulously entering long columns of figures neatly inked in black. Abiola jolted the table. Olu eyed him reproachfully and returned to his figures. Abiola stood undecided.

Olu looked up.

'I've an important matter to discuss with you.'

Olu laid down his quill and folded his hands.

'But not here.' Abiola edged away from the table.

Unhurriedly Olu put away the pen, shook sand on the ink to blot it, blew the sand from the page and stowed the ledger carefully in a drawer. He removed his coat from the back of his chair, closed the window shutter and locked the door behind them.

Abiola set a brisk pace to the top of Thornton Hill where they spread their coats on the ground against the morning dew. Backs against the

327

walls of the fort, they sat in companionable silence enjoying the cool breeze after their climb, listening to the doves calling softly in the governor's garden behind them and the harsh cries of the sea gulls overhead. From their vantage point, they could look down on the whole of the town. Brightly painted houses and riotously blooming gardens stretched right round the bay and high up the slopes of the surrounding hills. It was still possible to trace the original grid of three broad avenues facing the ocean intersected at right angles by nine narrower streets. But since the Nova Scotians first took their axes to the forest, Freetown had changed much. Its population had more than trebled, with the original settlers now outnumbered by Maroons and the Africans released from the slave ships. The number of officials had burgeoned too, once it became a Crown Colony, but Freetown's public buildings and government accommodation had fallen into such a state of disrepair that the entire colonial establishment from the governor down was obliged to rent both offices and houses from the settlers. To remedy this, a new building programme had been inaugurated and tenders invited.

Abiola said, 'There's money to be made.'

'If you have money already.'

'I *have*: my bank in London is prepared to extend me as much credit as I need. Both of us have the brains and *you* have the contacts. My father is too set in his ways to take proper advantage of the new opportunities in Freetown, so I propose that you become a partner in the business.'

'Your father and grandmother will oppose it.'

'Then we'll start up independently, the two of us, *equal* partners.'

Olu looked at him doubtfully and Abiola continued, 'Old Mr Bramwell taught me that, in business, trust is paramount.'

Olu nodded.

'This is our opportunity. The time is ripe to make a fortune in the Northern Rivers, and we can use the profits to finance expansion here in Freetown. But we must act immediately because, once the new lines of business are established up there, the Europeans will sweep us aside and we will be forced to look for opportunities elsewhere. By then we will have made our money and have the whole of Africa to choose from.'

Olu nodded again.

'My friend, Jack Burgess, knew Europe, while I, through my contacts, was familiar with Africa. That's why we were successful and why Mr Bramwell has set us up in business. Here, I know Europe and you know Africa. What do you think?'

'I think someone told you the story of how Joy got the material for her wedding dress.'

'True. But it was merely confirmation of what I already suspected. What do you say?'

Olu held out his hand and Abiola grasped it in both of his.

'I'm glad you agreed, Olu, because I have something else to tell you. Your sister has consented to marry me. I swear, though, that's not why I asked you to be my partner.'

'Now your father will be doubly angry.'

'In the one he has only himself to blame. As to the other, he has no proper cause. My mother's more than happy. She thinks I'm doing the right thing.' Abiola gave Olu a playful punch on the shoulder, 'I hoped that you might think so too . . .'

He broke off. Olu had not returned his smile.

'Surely you're *not* of the same mind as my father?' Abiola stared, incredulous.

Olu said, 'A wife who brings no dowry –'

'You, of all people,' Abiola interrupted grimly.

'A business partner who brings no money?' Olu smiled his slow smile. 'You're either very rich or very reckless, my friend.'

Abiola beat his brow in mock fury, roundly cursing himself for a fool.

Standing on the deck of his hired sloop, sailing rapidly towards the Rio Pongas and the Northern Rivers, Abiola, a bridegroom of only four months, smiled to himself as he recalled the occasion which had signalled the start of a new and supremely happy period in his life. Abiola and Tosin had been married in the Baptist church, where, according to Epiphany and Tabitha, the spirit of Reverend George still presided. The day had been crowned by a gift from Delilah. A house, no less. And she had presented the key not to Abiola but to his bride, whose only flaw, she said, had now been corrected. His grandmother had plainly enjoyed Caleb's discomfiture; he had been as surprised as anyone by the gift and not best pleased.

Admittedly, the house was very small, being one of the first settler dwellings and in the least fashionable part of town. But, as Delilah said, the best kind of capital was the kind that accrued. Then she had surprised them all again by toasting Epiphany, whose stubborn determination had ensured the family's safe return to Africa. After that Epiphany had raised her glass to the memory of Grandfather Cornelius, who would no doubt be rejoicing that, having come home, they were now putting down roots.

His mother was right, Abiola reflected: the child that he and Tosin were now expecting could never be described as Nova Scotian. In marked contrast to Joy's nuptials, there had been but one European at the wedding. Sheba's handsome captain had made it clear he would not be at all averse to resigning his commission, becoming a merchant and tying the knot himself in the not too distant future. Sheba had told him he should hold fast to his uniform; traders were two a penny in Freetown – a remark that had brought a shy smile to Olu's face. The captain could look out for himself, Abiola thought, but he felt sorry for Olu, who had declined to come up on deck to admire the moon in favour of working on below.

They had planned to make the journey to the interior immediately after the wedding. But Elizabeth, who had only just returned from a business trip inland, had spared them the journey. On learning of their partnership and Abiola's credit arrangement with the bank, she had brought her goods straight to them. She also sent them an African client whose consignments of ivory and gold were well beyond her financial reach. Keeping in mind Mr Bramwell's advice that you should never humiliate with the power of your money, Abiola gave her a generous commission in return. Mr Bramwell, Olu remarked, was a most unusual man. And a successful one, Abiola replied. Abiola was generous, too, to his grandmother, supplying her with goods for the journey she had suddenly decided upon. Delilah had claimed that she was heading south in search of new markets, but Abiola wondered whether perhaps Caleb was nearer the truth when he said that, having ceded the Northern Rivers, she still craved adventure.

Abiola's thoughts turned to Jack Burgess. In this languorous heat beneath a sky cleared of stars by the splendour of the moonlight, London seemed a world and a lifetime away. Jack's letters since his arrival in Africa had been cheerful enough, but Abiola knew only too well how unbearable the longing for home could be in a strange and foreign land. And this was dangerous territory, where, on the shark-infested waters along the coast and for many miles inland, African war canoes and French and British naval squadrons played catch-as-catch-can in the fight against slave-running. Until he had seen his friend face to face, his mind could not be at ease.

*

A full moon hung low above the mangroves and coconut palms, enhancing the mood of sylvan calm. In the two-storeyed house by the waterside, close shuttered against the night, tranquillity prevailed. Polished mahogany, gilt and crystal gave back the soft shine of many candles. Delilah was holding court, the only woman in the company of five men, playing guest of honour at the foot of the long table. Dressed in her favourite blue, her hair out of sight beneath a silk turban, and the light from the tall candelabra lending gold to her still smooth skin, she appeared not only beautiful but also youthful enough to merit attention.

As Delilah and her companions, three American and two English gentlemen elegantly attired in evening dress, raised their glasses in a toast, there was a triumphant as well as a festive atmosphere. Delilah smiled without showing any gaps or rotted teeth. Throughout the evening she had held her own on subjects as diverse as the price of commodities, the war with the French and Napoleon's retreat from Moscow, the state of politics in Sierra Leone, and European ambitions in Africa. She was reminded of another occasion half a century before in the richly appointed dining room of the Fairlawns Plantation when the slave Cornelius had performed for a group of French visitors. Cornelius, she thought dryly, would not have been amused at her antics tonight. In truth, though, she was tired and would not be sorry when the evening – or indeed this, her last visit to the Rio Pongas – was over. The following day would see the conclusion of the remainder of her business and the next day her return to Freetown, from whence, she promised herself, she would never stir again.

One of the Americans raised his glass once more but set it down abruptly as a huge explosion rocked the house. A servant, eyes large with fright, came running into the room and knelt to whisper in his master's ear. There was the sound of another, smaller explosion, followed by gunfire. The American spoke rapidly to his servant who hurried from the room. The guests needed no bidding to help extinguish the candles and run outside. They stood on the jetty in front of the house momentarily immobilised by the sight of flames leaping through the walls of the small warehouse on the opposite bank of the river. Black smoke, turned to a grey mist in the moonlight, rose high in the air. A day or two earlier, Delilah thought, and the warehouse would have been fully stocked, the open-sided slave pen next to it crammed with chained captives. Between them, she and her companions had in the past two days despatched over five hundred slaves to the Americas.

331

She peered into the distance. The shelling must have come from a ship lying out of sight behind a lip of land, providing covering fire for its long-boats, whose occupants were even now exchanging shots with the warehouse guards.

'Quickly, quickly!'

Delilah clambered into the first of two waiting canoes. The rowers immediately unshipped their paddles and in a moment they were speeding upriver. One of the long-boats gave chase. Delilah looked back, her pulse racing with excitement rather than fear. There was no real danger of capture; the canoes had the advantage of being much lighter and soon they would be in sight of safety. A bullet flew past her ear and she turned to the front again, keeping her head down as the canoes streaked through the water, banked tightly round a sharp bend that led into a narrow creek, then drew up by the shore. The passengers scrambled out, running up the slope towards the wooden palisade at the top. Their jubilation at seeing their pursuers overshoot the bend was cut short as a second long-boat entered the creek and began firing. Delilah made a dash for the fort. Just a step from the gate, a bullet ripped into her shoulder. A cry of pain escaped her as she tripped and fell. Her companions ran back and carried her to safety.

The naval squadron's single cannon was no match for the six guarding the fort, and the long-boats were soon driven off. They would be back, though, now that they knew of the stronghold. And next time they would come better prepared.

Scouts sent by the local king had been keeping pace on the north bank for the last few miles so that, by the time Abiola's ship dropped anchor mid-river, a small crowd had gathered at the landing stage. The village, a cluster of round, thatched houses, stood on the crest of a wooded slope above.

'Look –' Olu pointed. A hundred yards to the left of the landing place was a long rectangular house with adjoining store, set back from the river behind an orderly garden planted with rows of young fruit trees.

Abiola laughed. 'That little estate must belong to Jack Burgess. It has the same neatness as the entries in his ledgers.' He waved at the one white face in the crowd, but there was no response until they were halfway to the landing. Recognising his friend at last, Burgess pushed his way to the front, smiling and waving frantically.

Abiola and Burgess hugged and slapped each other on the back for a long while. Afterwards they both coughed and blew their noses, eyes suspiciously bright. Abiola introduced Olu and the ship's captain. Burgess dabbed at his eyes. First, he said, they must visit the king. They climbed the hill in the company of a great crowd and, having presented His Majesty with a present of French brandy, they regaled the assembly through interpreters with news of the outside world. The king, through his speaker, gave his visitors a graphic account of the raid just two nights earlier on a European slave factory in another branch of the river. The British naval squadron had been defeated on this occasion, but they would doubtless return, the king said, which could be very disruptive to trade in the area.

The daylight hours passed swiftly, occupied with the unloading of the sloop. Once her cargo had been checked and itemiscd, Burgess made his appraisal of the quality of the goods to be exported and those intended for the African trade. A special selection was prepared for the king and his chiefs to take their pick, and runners were despatched to the local rulers.

It was not until the lamps were lit in Burgess's house that they had the opportunity to catch up on each other's news. The last few months, Burgess assured Abiola, had been the most eventful and exciting of his life. Abiola searched his friend's face closely and, satisfied that he was sincere, he sat back, his mind eased.

'I could not but notice,' Burgess said to Olu, 'that you appeared uncommonly interested in the king's story. If I may be of any assistance, you have only to ask.' He glanced at Olu's facial marks. 'Although I understand that the captives had been transported and the baracoons emptied by the time of the attack.'

Burgess, Abiola realised, imagined that Olu might have a friend or relative among the victims.

Olu said, 'I am from Oyo.'

'Ah.' Burgess nodded sagely.

Abiola hid a smile. For all Burgess knew, Oyo might as well have been on the moon.

Burgess cleared his throat. 'As chance would have it, I discovered through a local chief the whereabouts of the slave factory and I was able to relay the information to the commander of the naval squadron. In the scheme of things, I grant you, it's no great step, but in however small a measure I'm proud to have contributed to the ending of this evil traffic.'

'Good man!' Abiola clapped his friend on the arm. 'Renegade

American slave runners and the Portuguese are the main culprits nowadays, I believe.'

'The prohibition is disregarded on all sides, apparently,' Burgess replied. 'But oddly, rumour has it that one of those surprised at the factory was a trader from Sierra Leone. I doubt there's any truth in it, though.'

Olu downed his tot of brandy in one gulp, earning a startled look from Abiola, who nonetheless yawned and declared himself ready for sleep. Burgess offered Olu another nightcap and, when it was accepted, happily offered to join him. Shaking his head in mock disapproval, Abiola departed.

When the door had closed behind Abiola, Olu asked whether it would be possible to discover if there was any truth in the rumour.

'It shouldn't be difficult.' Burgess looked at him curiously.

Olu, his expression guileless, said, 'Perhaps, if we knew his identity, he could be brought to justice . . .'

'Ah,' Burgess said. 'I'll send a messenger first thing in the morning.'

The messenger returned after nightfall. The trader from Sierra Leone was a woman, and she was injured unto death.

Olu took Abiola aside. Wild-eyed, he tried to speak but failed, labouring to catch his breath, his hands shaking, his skin grey.

He drew breath once more. 'Abiola, I scarcely dare say this, but I have reason to believe that the slave trader from Sierra Leone wounded in the raid may be none other than your grandmother Delilah.'

Burgess's rowers spirited the three young men away as the morning mist was lifting, just one more canoe unnoticed among the horde of small boats swarming round the tall ship anchored in the middle of the river. At the fort, the visitors were courteously received. Olu volunteered to wait with Burgess, but Abiola insisted he accompany him.

An English gentleman escorted them upstairs. Outside the room he paused, his hand on the latch, and quietly informed them, 'Madam Delilah was injured and the wound, though trivial, has become infected – but she should recover.' Opening the door, he gently made known the presence of the two young men and then retreated.

Propped against the pillows, Delilah appeared very slight in the large bed, her face a small dark triangle amid a profusion of snowy coverlets and white-painted walls.

Olu remained by the door as Abiola approached the bed. Although he trod softly, a board creaked underfoot. The gaze that met his was razor-edged.

'How unexpected,' his grandmother remarked, dry as ever.

Abiola took an involuntary step backwards. 'You . . . you said you were going south.'

Delilah shrugged. 'You followed me . . .'

'I had no intention to deceive.'

'No?'

'No! It's thanks to Aunt Elizabeth that we're here. She also sent us a client.'

'Hah! Elizabeth.' The venom made Abiola recoil. 'How fitting. I'd have finished with this business long ago if it hadn't been for her and Johnson cutting me off at the knees from the inland trade. And now because of her . . .' Delilah lay back against her pillows to catch her breath. 'There's a certain neatness to it.'

'Does my father know you're hurt?'

'He knows my business, but not about this last transaction. I actually came here to cover my traces, but I was offered a deal too good to let pass . . .'

Abiola's anger erupted. 'It's disgusting! Greed, pure and simple.'

Delilah ignored his outburst. 'Let's keep this between ourselves, shall we? Aside from your father, only Olu knows. No one else even suspects.'

Abiola whirled furiously on Olu. 'How *long* have you known?'

'Don't blame *him*,' Delilah said before Olu could reply. 'He stumbled on the secret by accident and afterwards confronted me. That took courage. But I knew how to handle him. I knew he'd be afraid of an old witch like me with powers from the new world as well as the old. I hexed him. And he's still afraid.' Delilah glanced past Abiola. 'Aren't you, Olu?'

He did not deny it.

Delilah laughed unpleasantly. 'You see,' she addressed Abiola, 'our secret is safe.'

'Not with me, it's not.'

'Do you want your mother to know?' Delilah enquired, silencing him. Sinking back on the bed, she continued: 'It's finished now. You have my word.' She waved Abiola towards the door.

'How can I be sure?' he demanded.

'Dear boy, in this life nothing is sure.'

*

Runners had spread word of the arrival of a merchant ship laden with goods, drawing traders from all the surrounding countryside. Abiola and Olu set themselves up in Burgess's palisaded garden, their trading post a table and two chairs. During the day all three immersed themselves in work, and in the evening they studiously avoided the matter uppermost in their minds. Abiola was only too aware that his friends were waiting for him to speak first. Though the initial shock had receded and there appeared no immediate threat to his grandmother's life, he was so overwhelmed by feelings of anger and shame that for several days he was incapable of broaching the subject. Finally, when the table had been cleared after a fine dinner of baked fish, pickled pork and raisin cakes to which they had done scant justice, Abiola at last addressed the topic.

Staring down at his hands he said, 'Forgive me for not speaking until now, but having discovered that the foundations upon which my life has been built are rotten, it grieves me more than I can say that, through no fault of your own, you too will both be besmirched by this corruption.'

'I'm not blameless,' Olu replied, anguished. 'I could have spoken out and perhaps saved –'

Abiola interrupted him. 'You were promised it would be ended. Don't reproach yourself.'

Burgess shook his head dejectedly. 'If I could take back the part I played . . .'

'Nor you. You both acted rightly. And now' – Abiola drained his glass of brandy – 'I'm ashamed to ask this of you, but ask I must: wrong as it is, I need you now to bury this secret for my mother's sake. I'll see to it that my father and grandmother are relieved of their authority, and reparation made.'

'No one will hear of it from me.' Burgess downed his tot.

Olu followed suit. 'Nor me.'

The three of them shook hands and Burgess refilled their glasses.

Olu said, 'We'll need to concoct a story.'

Abiola's anger flared again. Already they were compromised.

Two days later Abiola and Olu were once more ferried to the slavers' hidden stronghold to be greeted as courteously as ever.

'The poison has spread,' their host informed them, leading the way to the room.

Once again Olu remained by the door as Abiola tiptoed to the bed.

Delilah gave a small start and stared at him intently. Her eyes glowed, but it was with a fevered brightness.

'Ah, Cornelius. I thought you'd come.'

'It's me, Grandma. Abiola.'

'I know it's you. You're here to judge me, aren't you?'

'Grandma, I'm not Cornelius.'

Abiola glanced over his shoulder at Olu, who shrugged and spread out his hands.

'You want to know why I took up slave dealing, don't you?'

'Yes,' Abiola said. He did want to know. He knew his father well enough to understand that it must have been his grandmother's decision.

'I was weary of having to rise above the circumstances one more time. I was tired of being exceptional because that's what a slave has to be if he's to conquer hunger, pride, anger; if he's to live with constant fear and exhaustion; if he's to suffer the beatings, maiming, rape, and bite his tongue while every bone in his body is screaming and his spirit is crying out for revenge. You know how it was, Cornelius, whether we were in the big house or in the fields. We had to rise above the circumstances, each and every day, just to survive till the next day and then start all over again. I was tired, Cornelius. Tired to death.'

Abiola shook his head.

'Do you deny it?' Delilah leaned forward.

Again, Abiola could only shake his head.

'So . . .' Delilah sank back against the pillows. 'I gave in to a moment of weakness. You had one, too. Remember, Cornelius? Epiphany was your weakness. For her sake you gave up the fight. Well, if it wasn't for my slave-dealing, your spoiled girl wouldn't have had her mission up country or her precious school . . . her children wouldn't have been wealthy and secure in Sierra Leone, or sent to England for their education . . .'

'But our lives have been paid for in blood.'

'Everyone's lives are paid for in blood. The difference is, when you're a slave or poor, it's your own blood. But if your position is high enough, it's not you who suffers when you fail to rise above the circumstances. General Washington, Mr Jefferson – they could have risen above their circumstances and freed us, but they didn't. The directors of the Sierra Leone Company, they could have kept their word and let us rule ourselves, but they didn't. European governments, African chiefs, slave traders – it's a long list. I'm not proud of what I've done. Who knows, if it hadn't been for the French attack back in '94, I might not even have been tempted. And I would have stopped long before now if it had not been for the threat of exposure these past ten years by the very man in whose house we now are. A former councillor of Sierra Leone, no less! But I tell you, if it happened again, I'd still do the same.'

Feeling a rush of tenderness towards his grandmother, Abiola edged very gently on to the bed beside her so that she could rest her head on his shoulder. Olu tiptoed from the room, leaving them alone. Abiola stroked the soft white hair away from Delilah's burning forehead.

Slavery as the source of all evil had been instilled in him from his earliest years, yet until now it had been an abstract notion. The subject was never discussed; family stories always began with the escape to Charleston to join the British. Understandable, Abiola thought now. Who would wish their children to dwell on their degradation? His mind was filled with conflicting thoughts and irreconcilable images. He was ashamed of having rushed to judgement, of concluding it was greed that had driven Delilah. Cradling his grandmother, he was divided between pity and revulsion; shifting between the realisation that he had no idea of the reality of slavery and the conviction that there could be no justification for what she had done. And, try as he might, he could not relate the august figures of his mother, father, grandmother, Tabitha, Johnson, Elizabeth, Carver and Big Mo with the images Delilah had depicted.

During the days that followed, Delilah was in a delirium for much of the time, drifting in and out of consciousness. In her ramblings, she revisited many of the events of her past. Abiola remained hopeful until the moment when she gave up the struggle and turned her face to the wall. By that time, the Fairlawns Plantation was as familiar to him as Freetown.

Delilah was buried in a shaded corner of Burgess's neat orchard. He was happy to have her company, he said. At the graveside, Abiola read a psalm from the Bible and Olu sang a warrior chant from Oyo. It was important to remember, Olu said, that the day you were captured was not the day you were born. Your birthplace – even if it was only a name you bequeathed to your children – would tell them that once they had had a home in the scheme of things and could have it again. Oyo, Hausa, Temne, Susu, Ashanti, Ibo, Ga . . . It was Delilah's misfortune, Olu said, that America, Nova Scotia and Sierra Leone were the only names she knew. These places told her only that she was a slave.

The trader from Futa Jallon, the high country, which was home to the Fula people, masters of the interior trade, received Abiola and Olu with ceremony. Once Burgess, having effected the introductions, had departed, their host invited them to sit opposite him on a mat of the finest quality, liberally scattered with tooled leather cushions. He was courteous, too, to the Susu interpreter, indicating a place near the entrance where the young man might easily follow the conversation without being intrusive. Having placed a bowl of kola nuts on a low stool in the centre of the floor, the trader arranged the folds of his blue embroidered gown gracefully around him and leant back against a cushion with the air of one whose patience in the course of a long life had been amply rewarded. Politely, he waited to learn from his guests' own lips the purpose of their visit.

It was said that this trader could name every waterway and market along the mighty Senegal and Niger rivers, the trade route through which flowed all the wealth of West Africa. He possessed an unrivalled knowledge of the intricate forms of credit, pricing and currency used throughout the region, and understood the fluctuations of supply and demand. His compounds at Labé and Tembo were filled with cinnamon, rice, beeswax, Indian corn, salt, dye and, most valuable of all, the hides for which the Futa Jallon was justly famed.

The trader knew that those hides were much sought after by the Yankee traders from Massachusetts. He knew that the French and English came in search of Senegal gum and forest timber. He could tell you that the Americans offered rum and tobacco; the French, spirits and Flemish textiles; while the British excelled in providing all kinds of ironmongery – iron bars, cutlasses, rifles and gunpowder. He was aware that the Spanish and the Portuguese and the Americans were always interested in slaves. He was one of their biggest suppliers.

'Father,' Olu said, addressing the old man in the customary way, 'we travelled here from Freetown to seek out new partnerships in preparation for the time when the Europeans no longer trade in slaves. In Sierra Leone, that time has already come . . .' He paused for the interpreter.

The trader listened intently and, when the interpreter had finished, he observed, 'Elsewhere, my son, that day will be long in coming. The inland chiefs now trade the captives north-west in order to evade the British, and the American and European dealers turn even more handsome profits than before. The value of a slave has tripled in the Americas since the British outlawed the trade.'

Abiola leant forward. 'Father, it seems to me inevitable that the inland chiefs will come to realise the advantage of profits which accrue from legitimate trade, increasing steadily year on year, over the violence and uncertainty of slaving. And those who stand to profit most will be those who facilitate the transition.'

The trader remained silent for a considerable time after the interpreter had spoken.

At last he said, 'I hear you.'

Abiola sat back. They understood each other.

Now Olu spoke, and the interpreter translated: 'Father, we also travel in the footsteps of another trader from Sierra Leone, as her agents. I believe you met with her.'

The trader's face remained impassive, but he allowed the warmth of remembered acquaintance to colour his voice. The interpreter relayed the words: 'Ah, Madam Delilah! A lady of deserved renown. She will be missed and long remembered. I had the honour of receiving her in this very house. She drove a hard bargain, very hard. But we were able to reach agreement.' The trader straightened a fold of his robe. 'I have a record of the exact tally and I am ready to discharge my debt.'

Me too, Abiola thought.

Abiola broke the news of Delilah's death to Caleb first. He gave him the true story, quietly, across the table in the small cluttered office behind the shop on Rawdon Street. Caleb listened without interruption and, after Abiola had finished speaking, continued to sit with his hands clasped in front of him, head bowed, tears glistening on his cheeks in the light of the candle. Abiola offered him his handkerchief and, wiser now than when he last faced his father across this table, he experienced the same rush of tenderness he had felt for his grandmother as she lay dying. It occurred to him, watching Caleb visibly shrink, that here no less than in the Rio Pongas he was witnessing a death: the death of that part of his father which had owed its life to Delilah.

'I know what the loss of my grandmother means to you,' Abiola said.

'I believe you do,' Caleb replied.

Caleb, Abiola realised, was not yet ready to confront his guilt. He said,

'Your secret is safe, Father, I've made sure of that. But in return you must relinquish the business to me. That's my price.'

Epiphany held a separate wake at the farm. Aside from herself and Tabitha, only Big Mo and Carver were present. The four of them sat round the long table, tears falling unchecked, as they recounted their stories of Delilah.

Tabitha's memories reached back to the day the beautiful fifteen-year-old had arrived at Fairlawns Plantation, as part of the dowry of the master's new bride. She spoke first and the others took up the tale in turn until Delilah had been reshaped and made a part of their lives again.

When they had each spoken their fill, Epiphany said, 'Delilah's kept Cornelius waiting a long time.'

'And Auntie Sam,' Tabitha added.

'That was Delilah's power.' Big Mo's grief rocked her back and forth. 'She saw into Auntie Sam' – Big Mo put her hand on Carver's – 'just like she saw into Carver and me. She could see that inside we were dainty. She brought our insides out.'

~

12

IN FREETOWN ALL work had stopped. It was Fair and Race Week, the high point of the social calendar. Now in its third year, the Fair, inaugurated by the present governor, and growing ever larger and grander, was indicative not only of his style but also of the transformation that had taken place in Sierra Leone. Already home to the Vice Admiralty Court, Freetown had become the naval victualling depot and army headquarters for the West African coast. Besides the new public buildings, houses had gone up on every street to accommodate the influx of Europeans. As a result, shopkeepers could charge inflated prices for imported food, and rents were steeper than in London. For the first time since the colony was founded, whites and blacks mixed socially.

For the week of the Fair, Africans from neighbouring territories and people living in the countryside all converged on the capital. At noon on the first day the mayor and aldermen rode in procession through the town, bugles blowing on every street corner proclaiming the start of the festivities. There were wrestling contests on the quayside and pony races through the streets. Ships' crews raced their long boats in the bay, workmen raced canoes in the river, and the gentry raced horses at the racecourse. Luncheons, dinners and balls were hosted daily inside the canvas tents billowing in the ocean breeze like clouds pegged to the ground down the length of Water Street. Morning and evening the Freetown beauties, bedecked in coral and gold, paraded beside the harbour, revelling in the attention they received.

Abiola had taken the opportunity of working undisturbed through the morning, for once the public holiday was over he would be away from town on an extended visit to the Rio Pongas, accompanied by his wife and their three-year-old daughter, Precious. Tosin had long wanted to visit Delilah's grave, but, heavily pregnant at the time, she had been unable to join the pilgrimage Epiphany, Tabitha, Carver and Big Mo had made. Now, however, in the early stages of a second pregnancy and with the journey to the Northern Rivers rendered far less hazardous by the defeat of the French, the time seemed right.

Pausing in his work, Abiola glanced round the room. The small high window remained unglazed. The office no longer served as a store, but with the recent addition of a desk for a new apprentice, space was as scarce as before, and as ever the atmosphere was steeped in the mingled aromas of coffee, molasses and tea seeping in from the shop next door. Delilah's death had edged all their lives with the dark of mourning and, although on the surface things seemed much the same, everything had changed. He now sat in Caleb's place; Sheba and Olu were his partners. He was grateful for the way that the older generation had stepped back. Epiphany needless to say had quoted Cornelius: 'When the wind blows,' she said, 'you must bend with it, let it work for you.'

Abiola locked up the office and set off on foot through the crowded streets to join his family gathered for the traditional picnic on the opening day of the horse racing. He was apprehensive, for Sheba had asked to speak to him privately. Recently she had begun to question the generous donations Abiola had been making to aid the resettlement and care of Africans released into the King's Yard. Had Sheba somehow stumbled upon the truth of what Delilah had been up to?

Threading carefully through the throngs of picnickers and their children running to and fro, Abiola made his way to where his family had

342

gathered. Tosin beckoned him to sit beside her and he promptly complied, wrapping his arms round her and smiling into her eyes, prompting Sheba to throw up her hands in mock distaste. Precious erupted loudly into their midst, jumping on to her grandfather's knee. Caleb consulted his pocket watch, adjusted the gold chain, and declared it nearly time to move on to the racetrack. Epiphany held out her arms to the child, but Precious shook her head and leant back against Caleb's yellow waistcoat. Abiola exchanged an amused glance with Tosin. Epiphany was irked by her granddaughter's preference for her grandfather, especially as she was convinced that Precious was the reincarnation of Cornelius's cousin Oluremi. Abiola wondered wryly which of the ancestors would be reborn in his second child. There was no denying that Precious had united Caleb and Epiphany as surely as Delilah had divided them. Caleb had taken to spending days at a time at the farm, travelling with Tosin from Freetown most mornings to look after his granddaughter while her mother, grandmother and aunt taught in the school.

Big Mo clapped her hands. 'Now, everybody, its time to study the form before we make our bets.' Big Mo had the names of all the horses and details of their previous outings written on a piece of paper. There were fourteen runners in the Grand Horse Race, the main event of the day. As Big Mo expounded on each one, Sheba regaled her audience with a scurrilous anecdote about each of the European owners.

Calling time again, Caleb put Precious gently from his lap and set off with her to the racetrack. A long ribbon dangled between them, Epiphany having taken the precaution of attaching them together at the wrist. The others followed in a more leisurely fashion, mindful of the pickpockets working the turf and careful to avoid the hawkers weaving through the crowd with their trays of coconuts, oranges, mangoes and guavas.

Sheba, polished-perfect, linked arms with Abiola. He threw a concerned glance over his shoulder at Tosin, walking between Tabitha and Carver.

'Fret not; you'll be reunited with your beloved soon enough.' Sheba smiled disarmingly.

Abiola returned her smile guardedly. Sheba's smiles were nearly always aimed.

'Olu has asked me to be his wife.' Sheba directed a brief smile over her shoulder at Olu, walking with Big Mo and Epiphany. 'I told him I needed time to reflect, but I intend to accept.'

Hugely relieved that the subject was not to be Delilah, but also genuinely surprised, Abiola said dryly, 'Your feelings have undergone a radical change, I take it?'

'No.'

'I see.'

Sheba laughed. 'No you don't, you have no idea.'

Abiola put up his hands. 'Enlighten me.'

'It's a business decision.'

Abiola stopped abruptly.

Sheba dragged him forward again. 'Listen, I like being a big fish and I intend to continue being one, but recent developments have made it clear to me that it won't happen here in Sierra Leone. First the Europeans usurped the government, now they're squeezing us out everywhere else. With several ships a week now arriving from Europe, more and more of them are settling here, and they're going into farming as well as trade. They're opening hotels, setting themselves up as bakers and pastry cooks, hairdressers, tailors and even watch-makers.' Keeping her arm linked through Abiola's, Sheba adjusted first one white glove and then the other. 'Eventually the Europeans will take over the rest of Africa, just as they're doing here, only the people who'll be paving the way this time will not be the Nova Scotians but the freed African slaves, returning to the places they came from. Instead of hanging on the coat-tails of the Europeans in this country, *we* can act first, and establish ourselves somewhere else before either the Africans or the Europeans make *their* move. With Olu, I can carry on being a big fish.'

He had always imagined that Sheba would be in agreement with Caleb's frequently expressed view that the best course was to ally themselves with the Europeans. But he realised he had underestimated her. She had read the signs aright. He was concerned, though, for Olu.

Reading his mind, Sheba said, 'I'll be kind to him.'

'Kindness is a poor substitute for love.'

'Olu has enough for both of us. And besides, if his principal aim was happiness, he wouldn't be marrying me. I believe what he truly desires is success, and that I can guarantee him.'

'Tosin will be pleased.'

'As I was when she married *my* brother?'

Abiola laughed. 'You approve now.'

Sheba's eyes narrowed. 'Ah, but she is a *good* person.

*

Idling up the coast, the boat made frequent stops to take on water and fresh food, and at many of the little ports Abiola, with his wife and little daughter, rowed ashore to barter enjoyably in the markets. Consequently the voyage to the Northern Rivers lasted twice as long as usual and it was more than a week after leaving Freetown that their schooner finally arrived in the Rio Pongas and anchored in the middle of the river opposite Burgess's landing place.

Burgess and Tosin took to one another on the instant and were soon like old friends. First there was the obligatory visit to present gifts to the king in his village up the hill where Tosin – and especially Precious, dressed in a white frock and pink satin sash – caused a stir among the royal women. Then, in Burgess's compound, the four of them stood vigil beside Delilah's grave in the corner of the orchard. Afterwards Tosin remained there for a time on her own. She returned each morning to pour a libation.

Abiola and Burgess had necessarily to attend to the unloading of the cargo, but Tosin and Precious were not short of amusement. Caught up in a round of activities staged expressly for them, they were up and down the hill all day long. The village women were so eager for gossip and an exchange of stories, songs and dances, the visitors had barely a moment to themselves. But the evenings were long and leisurely, and it delighted Abiola as they sat over supper and talked late into the night that deeper acquaintance served only to increase Tosin's and Burgess's liking for each other.

Beneath a blue-black sky awash with stars, the drums began a seductive invitation to the dance. Abiola and Burgess sat watching side by side. A line of women danced towards them and away again. Abiola thought of his wife and wished she were with him, but Precious had developed a slight fever and Tosin had elected to remain with the child.

'Have you never been tempted to take a wife?' Abiola asked in Burgess's ear, his tongue loosened after the long evening's entertainment.

'My dream,' said Burgess, 'is one day to have a wife to love and a child to dote on.'

Abiola grinned. Burgess and Precious had formed a strong attachment.

'But not here?' Abiola said.

'No, not here,' Burgess replied. 'As we both know, some wines don't travel.' He stared wistfully into his glass.

'So?' Abiola's tone was bracing.

'My mother's people came from Sussex. She took me there once when I was just a boy, and the countryside made a great impression on me. Were you ever in Sussex?'

Abiola shook his head.

'It's all farmland with rolling hills, wooded valleys and sheep everywhere you look. And in the far distance you can see the sea. Another four or five years should do it.'

Abiola clasped his shoulder. 'You'll have your dream one day, I'm sure of it. Once upon a time, remember, it was Africa you dreamt of, and here you are.'

'I'm a patient man,' Burgess said, wagging his finger for emphasis.

'And you'll be a rich man.'

'I suppose I will.'

'And could have been richer still. You're a remarkable man, Jack.' Abiola patted him fondly on the cheek.

'No more so than you.' Burgess raised his glass in a toast.

Abiola raised his in return. 'Not true, my friend. I've not strayed *one* step from the path allotted me by fate. But you, you have risen above the circumstances . . .'

Burgess stared at him owlishly.

Abiola stabbed a finger in the air. 'You could have gone into slaving,' he said, enunciating very carefully and slowly. 'But you didn't: you rose above it.'

'That's as maybe, but whatever the case,' Burgess said, his words somewhat slurred, 'neither of us would be here if it wasn't for Bramwell's Bank.'

They raised their glasses. 'Mr Bramwell!'

At that same moment a servant ran into the compound, breathless.

'Fire! Fire!' he yelled. The music stopped abruptly and the dancers made way as he threw himself on the ground in front of the king. 'The white man's storehouse is on fire.'

Abiola brought his face close to Burgess's. 'Isn't that one of my men?'

Burgess peered at the messenger. 'He's not one of mine.'

They exchanged uncomprehending glances.

Meanwhile, the king's speaker gestured urgently to the men at the entrance to run and look down the hill. They returned immediately with confirmation of the blaze.

'Come! *Come!*'

Abiola was instantly sobered by the sight of Burgess's warehouse engulfed in flames. The two friends careered down the hill. A great company streamed out of the village behind them. Tongues of fire from the blazing roof thatch leapt into the sky and the smell of burning timber filled the air. The lurid glare revealed a troop of men ferrying water from the river to the compound, labouring desperately to prevent the fire from jumping the short distance separating house from store. Frantically calling out for his wife and child, Abiola plunged into the noise and chaos. He dashed hither and thither, looking about wildly for Tosin and Precious. When he could not see them, he sped into the house, only to find it deserted.

'Where are the women?' he yelled, trying to make himself heard above the roar and crackle of the flames.

'I can't see them,' Burgess shouted back, crashing through the smoke and ash. 'Nor any of my men.'

The captain of Abiola's ship hurried up to them.

Abiola pointed towards the house. 'The women – where are they?'

'They must have been taken.'

'Taken? Where?'

'Impossible!' Burgess cried. 'I had guards posted –'

Burgess broke off at the screams coming from behind the house. Abiola raced off to investigate and, as he pushed his way through to the front of the crowd, the village women set up a wail. Among the overturned hearths, broken pots and scattered belongings strewn about the courtyard lay the bodies of about twenty men, their throats cut.

Burgess stood, breathless, stunned into silence.

Abiola rounded on the captain. 'What in God's name happened here?'

'We saw nothing, no sign, until the storehouse was fired. I ordered the crew ashore immediately, but by then the attackers were gone. It was a raid. They must have moored their canoes round the bend in the river and travelled the last mile overland. We would have spotted them otherwise, anchored as we were in the middle of the river. Once they'd ambushed the guards, they fired the warehouse, seized the women and escaped in another fleet of canoes which had presumably been lying in wait upstream.'

'But *why*?' Abiola dropped to his knees, staring up at Burgess. His friend could only shake his head helplessly.

The king whispered to his speaker, who stepped forward: 'Three years ago the fort and . . . certain . . . warehouses were destroyed. It has long been rumoured at which door certain white merchants lay the blame for this and who they hold responsible for the decline in their . . . particular trade.'

Burgess found his voice at last. He addressed the king. 'We have no time to lose.'

The king himself replied: 'My rowers are at your disposal. Come.'

Abiola gripped Burgess's arm 'You know where they've gone?'

The speaker answered, 'The king's scouts will lead you there.'

Abiola forced his thoughts outward. The thick greenery curtaining the river on either side was a uniform black in the darkness. At night more than ever there was an awareness of unseen eyes. As the canoes moved inland, the torches carried fore and aft burnt more steadily as the air became thicker and more humid and the banks climbed higher and higher, blocking the last of the breeze from the sea.

Burgess said, 'We *will* fetch them back, Abiola, I'm sure of it, especially as the king is helping us. The traders were looking to drive me out of business, that's the reason they fired the warehouse. I don't believe, though, that they ordered the kidnapping of the women and children. I'm almost certain that was an opportunist strike by the people they hired to carry out the crime.'

Abiola put his arm round him. 'I was thinking much the same,' he said. 'I feel easier.' And it was true.

A sharp bend sent them rocking from side to side down a narrow neck of water and into a wide basin reflecting a starlit sky. Lights glimmered in the distance but the buildings outlined on the far shore were in darkness.

Moving quickly, yet cautiously, they entered the slave pens. Empty. But their torches, held aloft, revealed signs of recent habitation. Abiola took a step forward: it seemed to him that the spirits of the captives still lingered.

Through his speaker, the king said, 'For some weeks now a ship has been expected at Falangia. It seems it has arrived. If you go now, you may be in time.'

A fresh team of rowers brought Abiola and Burgess to Falangia just as dawn was breaking. The rowers shipped their paddles, backs gleaming, sweat streaming. Abiola pointed to the tall-masted sailing ship in the river mouth some distance from the shore.

'Look how low she is in the water! She's fully loaded. We're too late!'

'No!' Burgess gripped his elbow. 'We're in time, she's still at anchor. Calm yourself.'

The little port was already bustling with activity, canoes tied up along the shore and market stalls laid out. Alongside the jetty Burgess, looking about him, saw a ship's long-boat conspicuous amongst the swarming canoes. He ordered the rowers to pull up at its side and, as Abiola made to jump aboard, kept a restraining hand on his arm.

'Abiola, you'd best stay here. That's an American vessel . . .'

'So?'

Burgess coloured. 'I fear her captain might not accord a black man the . . . respect he deserves.'

Abiola stood back to let Burgess ashore first. 'You're right. We don't want to put temptation in his way. My hide is worth more than yours.'

Unable to look away, Abiola watched the long-boat until it reached the ship. Only when his friend climbed the ladder and disappeared from sight did he turn away to mingle with the crowds, his eyes searching every face. His expensive European clothes aroused intense curiosity, and, though he accepted the attention with grace, tears stung his eyes at the irony of his situation. He moved in and out of the crowds like an automaton, his mind circling continuously round the fact that he did not know whether his wife and child were still alive or whether or not they were aboard the American slaver.

Never had he felt so powerless, nor so wretched – made worse by the sight and sound of life continuing around him as usual, the bustling crowds seemingly impervious to the fate of the wretches imprisoned just off shore. To Abiola, it seemed as if their fear and despair were carried inland on the breeze. But he sensed also, on that same breeze, the poison of indifference, as deadly as any snake venom. He imagined how it might feel to be plucked suddenly from your life – on your way home after a day's work, in the middle of an evening meal, or as you slept peacefully in your bed. How it would be to disappear without trace, never to see, or to be seen again by those you loved and who loved you. To be snatched from the daily certainties of your life and transported to a world where chaos, confusion and terror reigned. It took him a while before he realised someone was tapping him on the shoulder. Shaking his head, as if to clear it, he looked up to find Burgess in front of him.

'Your wife and child are not among the captives on board the slaver. But that's good; it points to their being held to ransom.'

349

Assuming, Abiola thought, that they were still alive; although in the abyss, any reassurance, however slight, was a foothold.

'You're sure?' he asked.

Burgess nodded emphatically. 'Quite sure. It was not difficult to ascertain. The women and children are loaded first and kept separately. Even so, the captain insisted I inspect all the decks. He's proud of the conditions aboard his ship. He prefers to carry less cargo and to land it safely. Insurance against those that perish is hard to come by these days, apparently.'

He fell silent.

'You can tell me,' Abiola said.

Burgess shook his head. 'I cannot.' He looked haunted.

'Tell me.'

Burgess began to describe what he had witnessed on board the ship. His face acquired a greenish tinge. 'I doubt,' he added, 'whether one half of them will be alive at the finish.' Turning aside, he walked a few paces and vomited into the reeds at the edge of the water.

Silently, Abiola offered his handkerchief. He knew, as Burgess could not, that the journey's end was merely the beginning. Worse awaited them.

Burgess mopped his face and folded the handkerchief tidily away.

'We should return,' he said. 'The king might have news.'

The king had no news, though he had placed eyes and ears in every village. He had also enlisted the aid of the merchant from Futa Jallon: along the trade paths, not one leaf could fall without the old man's knowledge. If, as they all now suspected, the women were being held to ransom, it was only a matter of time before a demand was received.

Abiola and Burgess scoured the countryside, returning each night in the hope that Tosin and Precious had been brought back. In Freetown, meanwhile, Caleb stationed spies at the dockside. He placed informants among the traders and market women and let it be known among the laundresses, housekeepers and maids that there was a substantial reward for any information leading to the return of the mother and child. Veering between hope and despair, the family waited, lives in abeyance. At last the king received word from the trader from Futa Jallon. They waited no more.

The raiders had sent the women and children north, to the River Nunez, beyond the king's territory, where another slave ship had been

350

anchored. All those who had been seized from Burgess's compound had been shipped to the Americas.

Tosin and Precious were lost to them for ever.

Abiola slammed down the ledger. 'I knew this day would come.' He flipped open the cover, rifled through the pages. 'Look, there! It's all written down. Our prosperity was bought with blood . . . One day, the reckoning had to be paid. Now it has been.' He snapped the book shut and sent it sliding across the polished surface to rest in front of Caleb. Epiphany and Tabitha, silent witnesses, sat at the table, motionless.

Epiphany sat in her favourite place at the farm. Overhead, a flock of white egrets were flying home to roost. Behind her the palm trees rustled in the evening breeze. In front of her the void.

Abiola had taken to his room. She respected his need to be alone, but nevertheless every day after school was over she made the five-mile journey into Freetown, accompanied by Elizabeth, who had taken up residence at the farm. Each day, Epiphany kept a short vigil outside Abiola's door before visiting Lola and Dotun, who were understandably reluctant to leave their one remaining child. Epiphany felt suspended between the living and the dead.

Abiola had said that the reckoning had been paid, but he was wrong. The kidnapping of Tosin and Precious had enslaved them all, as surely as if they too had been shipped to the Americas. The true mark of slavery, the irreducible sadness that only freedom could disperse, was the pain within. It would be with them always. The guest of honour, as now; the uninvited guest at all their future feasts and celebrations, an ever-present witness to all the events of their lives. The reckoning would never be paid, not in all their lifetimes.

Dusk had fallen and soon it would be dark, but Epiphany lingered outside, reluctant to face Tabitha, who was certain to deliver another homily on the subject of Caleb. After the first shock and disbelief at the revelation that Caleb and Delilah had been dealing in slaves all these years, Epiphany had declared that she never wanted to see her husband again, and she had kept her word. But Tabitha insisted that Caleb deserved Christian forgiveness instead of condemnation. He blamed himself for what had happened. But Epiphany could not forgive, even while conceding that her anger was partly driven by her own guilt at abandoning Caleb to Delilah. Their actions had made a mockery of

Epiphany's belief in the family's God-given task. They had travelled thousands of miles yet had covered no distance, it seemed. She recalled her father's words from long ago: *It is the thing you imagine cannot happen that undoes you.*

Sheba opened the door and at first did not recognise the slight figure in the street. She stood four-square in the doorway, peering at him, a lamp held high in her hand.

'Mr Burgess?' Surprised, she moved out of the way, beckoning him forward. They had last met in London. 'My brother is not receiving visitors at present . . .'

'He will see *me*.' Burgess stepped inside, blinking in the lamplight, his bow hampered by the large bundle in his arms.

Sheba glanced at the bundle, openly curious. 'Can I ask what you want with us at this hour that wouldn't wait until the morning?'

Burgess's cheeks reddened. 'If you would tell your brother I'm here, I'd be much obliged.'

'Very well.' Sheba swept from the room, reappearing shortly afterwards with Abiola. Burgess stood awkwardly near the door where she had left him.

'I'm glad to see you, my friend.' Abiola's attempt at cheerfulness resulted in a ghostly grin. 'What brings you to Freetown?'

If Burgess was shocked by Abiola's altered appearance, he gave no sign. Stepping forward, he said gently, 'Sit down, Abiola. Please.'

Exchanging a glance with Sheba, Abiola sank heavily on to a chair. Sheba stood protectively at his side.

Burgess placed the bundle he carried on Abiola's knee.

Abiola recoiled.

Gently drawing back the cloth, Burgess unveiled a peacefully sleeping Precious.

Abiola automatically cradled his daughter, rocking her back and forth, back and forth, quite unable to speak. The only sound in the room was Sheba's sharp intake of breath.

The child's eyelids fluttered open. She smiled drowsily at her father then, looking at Burgess, she said, 'I've been very good, haven't I?'

Burgess nodded.

Her eyelids drooped and she was asleep once more. Abiola's arms tightened round her. He was still incapable of speech.

'How can this be?' Sheba asked in a whisper.

Burgess began to answer.

'No, wait –' Sheba held up her hand. She waved him towards a chair, hurried out of the room and as speedily returned, shepherding ahead of her Lola and Dotun, sleep-dishevelled and confused. Burgess jumped to his feet and bowed to the old people.

Sheba waved him down again, placed a finger to her lips, and on tiptoe led Lola and Dotun to stand in front of Abiola. She lifted a corner of the cloth on his lap.

Sheba drew up the wooden settle and Lola and Dotun sat in unison as if their knees had suddenly given way.

'You can begin now, Mr Burgess,' Sheba said.

When Burgess did not speak, Abiola looked up and correctly guessed the cause of his hesitation.

'You're wondering why Olu isn't here. By day, he haunts the dockside and the King's Yard in the hope that the ship carrying his sister may yet be intercepted and its cargo set free. At night, he works, often burning a candle in the office until dawn. He thinks, in this way, to cheat his demons. Not so, Sheba?'

Sheba nodded sorrowfully.

Burgess cleared his throat, and began.

'On his way home to the high country a rumour reached the ears of a certain Fula merchant, well known to Abiola and myself, that the people of a village on the northern bank of the River Nunez were harbouring an "English" child, whose appearance in their midst coincided with the raid upon my compound in the Rio Pongas. At once, the trader travelled to the village in order to verify the truth of the story. Finding that the child answered to the name and description he'd been given, he negotiated a ransom and brought her safely to me.'

'Why was the child spared?' Again it was Sheba who asked.

'Because of the strength of her mother's will . . .' Burgess paused. 'The trader was told that Madam Tosin, having narrowly failed to persuade her captors to look to the ransom they stood to gain for the return of their captives, continued to bargain for her child. To a slave captain, a three-year-old infant, which almost certainly would not survive the crossing, is of little worth. Madam Tosin made it clear that, unless the child was spared, they would have to kill the mother and thereby lose their profit. In this way she traded her life for her daughter's.' Burgess unfolded his handkerchief and held it pressed to his face.

'God forgive me,' Sheba said. 'I didn't rate her as I should.'

Tosin's kidnap had left Abiola withering at the root. But while listening to Burgess he had heard his mother's words again: *in each thing is its opposite.* And he understood then that, in Precious, Tosin had thrown him a lifeline. *Love is in the doing, proved over time,* she had said.

Abiola looked at Sheba. 'Nor I,' he said.

At first light the next day a clerk carried the news to the farm, and then accompanied Epiphany and Tabitha back to the house in Freetown. Tabitha immediately set about examining the child, who appeared outwardly none the worse for her adventure. Epiphany hugged her close, marvelling at the change in her in just a short space and remarking on how poignant a reminder she was of her mother.

Abiola quoted her own words back at her. *In each thing is its opposite.*

'They're not my words,' Epiphany replied. 'They're Cornelius's. And, if I remember rightly, they were said to him by his teacher . . .'

'. . . The famous hunter of Oyo.' Dotun took the words from her mouth. Tenderly, he cupped Precious's small round head. 'This child is both our strength and our weakness.'

The family gathered at the farm. The long table had been carried outside and another added so that everyone could be accommodated. Epiphany glanced down its length to Caleb, seated at the opposite end. Precious had succeeded where Tabitha had failed in persuading her to overturn her decision never to see him again. The restoration of Precious represented a rebirth. Now, in a traditional ceremony, Precious was to be given a new name as a symbol of that rebirth.

Epiphany caught Burgess's eye. He gave her a modest smile in response to hers. Sitting between Abiola and Sheba, he was trying to make himself as inconspicuous as possible.

Lola dipped her finger into the first of the seven bowls laid out on the table and touched it to her granddaughter's lips: pepper, so that she would be resolute; water for purity; salt for wisdom; oil for health; honey for happiness; palm wine for prosperity; and finally a taste of kola nut for good fortune. Lola walked Precious past each of the people at the table, then around the house and finally across the little clearing in front, as if she were indeed being newly introduced to her surroundings, as Oyo custom demanded.

Returning with Precious to the head of the table, Lola said, 'The name

I've chosen is Oluremi; it means God consoled me.'

Epiphany straightened, suddenly on the alert.

'Why that name?' Tabitha asked, head up as if sniffing the air.

'Because it fits the circumstances,' Lola said.

Epiphany and Tabitha exchanged glances, an unspoken question in their eyes.

'Nothing could be truer,' Caleb said, lifting Precious onto his lap.

The child smiled winningly at her grandmother and Epiphany was conscious of something hovering just beyond the margins of her memory, which, as she tried to retrieve it, dissolved like a reflection in a pool when the surface is disturbed.

Sheba jumped up. She lifted her glass. 'A toast –'

'Wait!' Knocking on the table with his fist for silence, Abiola rose to his feet. 'I have something to say to you all.'

They gave him their full attention.

Abiola continued: 'I imagined that my life was ended, but in truth it has just begun –'

'And not only yours!' Sheba put her hand on Olu's.

Abiola inclined his head and smiled at Olu.

Sheba waved him on.

Abiola became serious again. 'I do not believe, as my mother does, that I am my grandfather come back, but I do know now what drove him. It was for the same reason that our family came to Africa – mother, father, uncles, aunts – all of you risked everything so that the children could be free. Grandpa Cornelius swore he would give no child of his to slavery, and I've vowed to do the same. That's why I am going to America to redeem my wife and –'

'That was different!' Caleb banged on the table and, handing Precious to Epiphany, he struggled to his feet. 'You must abandon this idea of yours immediately. It's not only dangerous, it's insane. We were not on some doomed quest; we were returning home, to *our* people – *your* people. Your duty is *here*, not in America.'

Epiphany and Tabitha exchanged ironic smiles.

Tabitha said, 'We came to Africa on a mission – some of us, at any rate – to put an end to the slave trade. We now know the fight is far from ended.'

'The trade,' Abiola said, 'will not finish until slavery itself is ended. Where there's demand, there'll always be supply.'

He walked round the table and took Precious in his arms. Looking at his mother, he said, 'No matter how great the distance, no matter how many years pass, I know from my own experience the link will never be broken.' To his daughter's evident delight, he threw her up in the air and caught her. 'And I know my mother will guard you well.'

'Again,' Precious commanded, laughing, making them all laugh.

'How will you find Tosin in the whole of America?' Carver persisted.

'The return of this child has given me the courage to believe that I will.' Abiola held Precious tight. 'I'll find Tosin. I made her a promise I intend to keep. When the time comes, I shall feel her heart close to mine.'

Epiphany had a swift vision of a darkened room and polished red walls, a straight-backed figure seated on a stool. The figure turned slowly towards her, illuminated by a sudden shaft of light.

'I am certain of it.' Epiphany said.

Tabitha stared at her in surprise, but Epiphany merely smiled. She saw the way clear once more. Her faith had been restored. The past was not erased, just hidden from view, like the dark side of the new moon, to be revealed again when the disc was full. Abiola was following his destiny, just as Cornelius had followed his.

Words formed in her mind: *We weave our pattern and we think it is the whole. Then we discover another pattern and beyond that, perhaps another. And we are only aware, it seems, because sometimes the colours run, bleeding from one into another, as in a dream.* Epiphany looked from Abiola to his daughter. *Some, who are woven into our pattern, are colours from another, possibly larger pattern, in which there will be a little of us. For part of us will travel with them, just as part of them will remain with us, for ever.*

There was no mistaking the scent of camwood in the air.

Author's Acknowledgements

I am deeply grateful for the unstinting help and encouragement given to me by my publisher Penelope Hoare and my agent Vivien Green. Thanks, too, to Anne O'Brien who edited the manuscript in its closing stages. I am indebted to Peter Morton-Williams, Karin Barber and Christopher Fyfe for so generously giving me the benefit of their scholarship. Finally I must thank family and friends, in Nigeria, the USA, France and the UK for their constant support throughout the long writing of this book, particularly Adam Welfare, Moti Feingold, Martin Bedford and David Landau.

Yoruba Poetry by Ulli Beier, Bayreuth African Studies 62. Compiled and edited by Ulli Beier, with Timi Laoyel, Bakare Gbadamosi, Duro Ladipo and Ademola Onibonokuta. (Bayreuth University, 2002)

I quote verbatim from *Oracle Verses*, section 19. The English rendition from Yoruba is by the Timi of Ede, Timi Laoye and Ulli Beier.

From the same book I also quoted from *Animals & Plants*, section 44, *Leopard*. The English rendition from Yoruba is by Bakare Gbadamosi and Ulli Beier.

I also quoted verbatim verses from the Rara Iyawo or Bride's Chant from the book *I Could Speak Until Tomorrow* (oriki, women and the past in a Yoruba town) by Karin Barber. Published for the International African Institute, London. (Edinburgh University Press, 1992)

During my research the books I relied most heavily upon were:
Journal Of A Second Expedition To The Interior Of Africa by Captain Clapperton to which is added the *Journal of Richard Lander*, 1829. (J. Murray, 1829)
The History of the Yorubas by the Rev Samuel Johnson. (C.M.S. Nigeria Bookshops, 1921)

The Black Loyalists (the search for a promised land in Nova Scotia and Sierra Leone 1783–1870) by James W. St. G. Walker. (University of Toronto Press, 1992)
The Loyal Blacks by Ellen Gibson Wilson. (Capricorn Books, 1976)
A History of Sierra Leone by Christopher Fyfe. (Oxford University Press, 1962)

Every effort has been made by the publishers to trace the holders of copyrights. Any inadvertent omissions of acknowledgement or permission can be rectified in future editions.